GAYLE

THE
DARK RIVER
SECRET

The Dark River Secret
Copyright © 2018 by Gayle Siebert

No part of this publication may be reproduced, distributed, or transmitted in any form or by any means, including photocopying, recording, or other electronic or mechanical methods, without the prior written permission of the author, except in the case of brief quotations embodied in critical reviews and certain other non-commercial uses permitted by copyright law.

tellwell

Tellwell Talent
www.tellwell.ca

ISBN
978-1-77370-831-7 (Hardcover)
978-1-77370-830-0 (Paperback)
978-1-77370-832-4 (eBook)

Also by Gayle Siebert:
The Pillerton Secret

To Lorna, for all your help and encouragement.

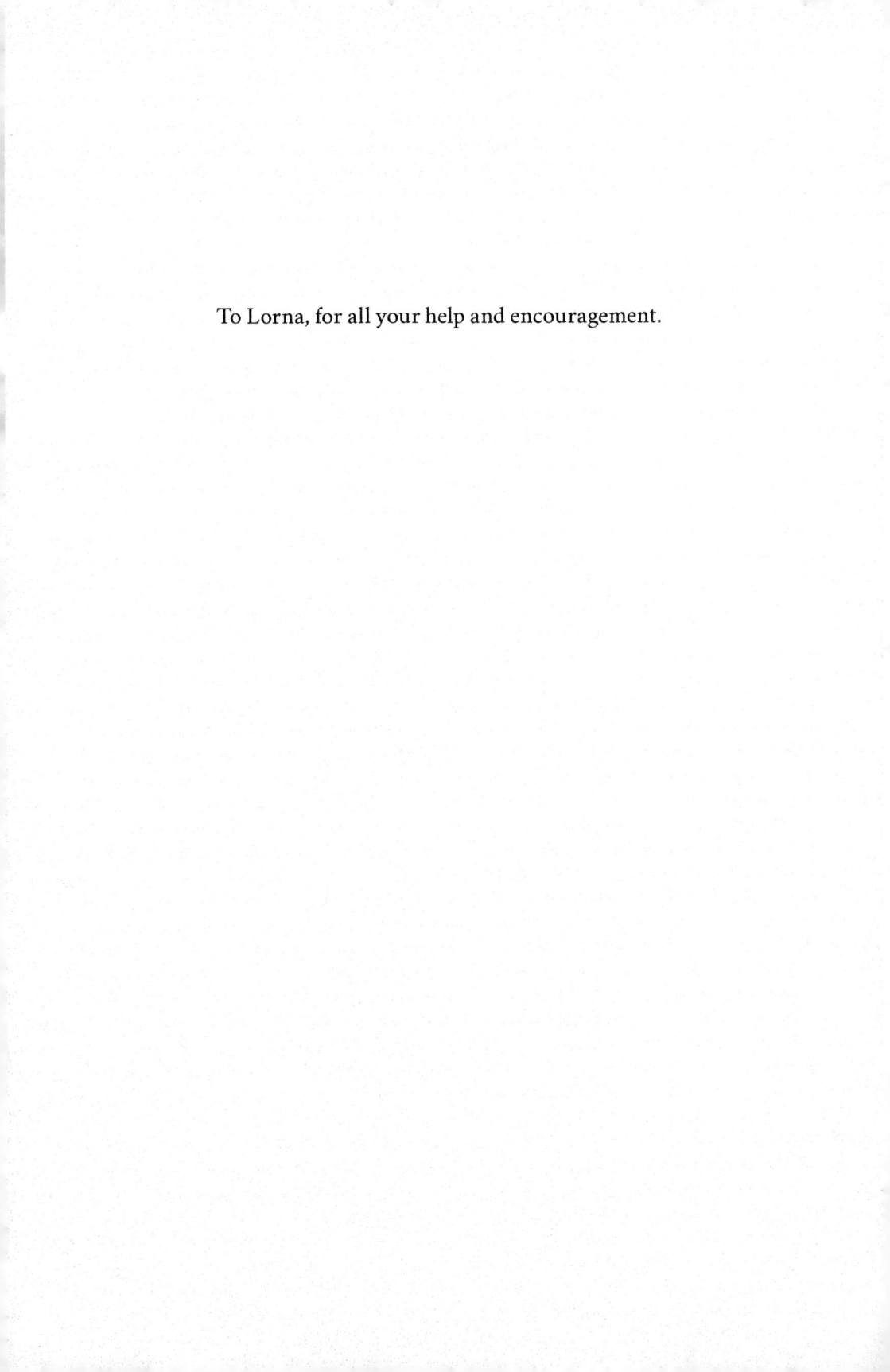

TABLE OF CONTENTS

The Spider and the Fly.........................1
One 3
Two 5
Three 9
Four 13
Five 17
Six 23
Seven 29
Eight 39
Nine.. 45
Ten 59
Eleven 71
Twelve 75
Thirteen 85
Fourteen 91
Fifteen 107
Sixteen 113
Seventeen 117
Eighteen 123
Nineteen 131
Twenty 137
Twenty-one 143
Twenty-two 157
Twenty-three 163

Twenty-four *171*
Twenty-five. *175*
Twenty-six *185*
Twenty-seven *191*
Twenty-eight. *197*
Twenty-nine *201*
Thirty *215*
Thirty-one *221*
Thirty-two *229*
Thirty-three *239*
Thirty-four. *247*
Thirty-five *255*
Thirty-six *267*
Thirty-seven. *273*
Thirty-eight *277*

THE SPIDER AND THE FLY

"Will you walk into my parlour?" said the Spider to the Fly,
"Tis the prettiest little parlour that ever you did spy:
The way into my parlour is up a winding stair,
And I've many curious things to show when you are there."
"Oh no, no," said the little Fly, "to ask me is in vain,
For who goes up your winding stair can never come down again."

-from "The Spider and the Fly" by Mary Howit

ONE

He stands perfectly still, concealed in the dense thicket at the edge of the small clearing, watching the cabin. He left his old Jeep some distance away and stealthily made his way on foot through the forest to where he now stands. There's no sound other than birdsong, and no sign anyone has been snooping around. There never is, but it pays to be vigilant. Get sloppy and get caught!

Satisfied, he steps out of the bushes and crosses the open area, his footfalls in the carpet of duff as silent as fog, then hops up onto the porch with a thump. He leans his .22 up against the wall with a clatter and drops a small dead animal on the porch floor, then roots in his jeans for a key. He fusses with the padlock, cursing under his breath. Maybe it's time to get rid of the padlock and install a deadbolt. Something less awkward. Something that can be unlocked one-handed. After some jiggling, the lock springs; he frees the hasp from it, and the hinges squawk as he pulls the door open.

Although it's mid-day, the interior of the cabin is gloomy. The shade in the forest is so deep only thin yellow-grey light squeezes in through gaps in the rag covering the only window, but now, more daylight floods through the doorway and backlights him. His shadow falls across the mattress on the floor.

The girl huddling in the corner flinches. She gathers a dirty quilt around her naked body, rattling the chain on her wrist, and sobs.

TWO

The parking lot door opens, and sunlight pours in. There's a man in a cowboy hat silhouetted in the doorway, backlit, so all Astrid can make out, aside from the hat, is that he's tall and well built. He takes a few steps and scans the room before choosing the table nearest the end of the bar. He slides onto the bench, back to the wall, and takes his hat off, placing it upside down on the table while he massages his head as if to banish a headache. His face is illuminated by the dim pot light overhead.

Watching from behind the bar, Astrid is struck by the thought he looks nice. Not flashy like the lawyers from the law offices across the street, or grubby like the millworkers and construction crews; just a nice, clean-cut, handsome man. A little careworn, maybe. A little melancholy. Then he resettles his hat.

Sharon goes to his table to take his order, blocking her view. Astrid sighs and goes back to stuffing the pages describing today's specials into menus. If the printer hadn't jammed, she would have had this done half an hour ago.

When she next looks up, Sharon has moved. The man in the cowboy hat looks her way. Their eyes meet. She smiles. After a heartbeat, the webs at the corners of his eyes deepen and he smiles back.

"Two screws 'n' a Chivas straight up." Sharon says, interrupting the moment. "Where've you been, Astrid? I made my last drink order myself." She steps up to the server's station and slides her tray onto the bar, dirty glasses clattering as she upends them on the dish rack. Then she chuckles as she looks at Astrid. "What've you been doing? Your nose is black!"

Wheeling, Astrid checks her look in the mirror behind the bottles. Then bending over the sink, she wets a paper towel, and scrubs her nose. Cheeks burning, she straightens and turns to look at the man again. He's still smiling, tilting his head slightly, and rather than feeling embarrassed, she's drawn to him. For a moment, she thinks he's going to say something, or come and sit at the bar. But one of the regulars slides onto the bench beside him, and he turns to face her. Astrid's shoulders slump.

"Hey, how about my drinks?" Sharon scolds. Then she notices what Astrid's looking at, and clucks. "Oh, for Pete's sake! Now you're moonin' over that guy at nine." She shakes her head, tossing her blue-streaked curls. "When're you gonna learn, Astrid? He may be wearin' a cowboy hat but that doesn't mean he's not a jerk like all the rest of the guys in here, even the ones in the expensive suits. Present company excepted." She elbows the man hunched over the bar next to the servers' station, nursing his Rusty Nail. "Right Ken? Probably broke like the rest, too! Jerks! All of them! Right?"

"Right! Right! Whatever you say!" Ken straightens, slipping his tie out of its knot, pulling it free and stuffing it into a pocket. He grins at Astrid. "She would know, she's tried enough of 'em." He swirls the brown liquid in his glass, sloshing some onto the bar. Astrid takes the bar cloth to mop up the puddle.

"Hssst!" Sharon glares at him. "Watch it, or I'll cut you off!"

"You're not the only one who can make me a drink."

"If I cut you off, Astrid won't serve you either."

"Oh no?"

"No. Why would she?"

"'Cause she has the hots for me."

"Oh yeah, of course I do, don't we all?" Astrid hands him a swizzle stick, giving him a pointed look. "You couldn't have told me about my black nose?"

He barks a laugh. "Wanted to see how long it would take you to notice!"

Sharon frowns at Ken, then turns back to Astrid. "What did you have on your nose, anyway? Where'd it come from?"

"That crappy old printer had two major paper jams. Of course, I got toner on everything. Didn't think to check my nose, though." She closes the last menu, straightens the pile, and gets the glasses for Sharon's drink order.

"So Astrid," Ken says, "How about we go over to the Queens after your shift? I hear they have a good band this week. Could pick up a pizza and go back to my place for a nightcap after."

"I wish you wouldn't keep asking me, Ken," Astrid replies. She scoops ice into the two tall glasses, pours vodka and orange juice into them, and Chivas into the stubby one, and stands them on Sharon's tray.

"Aww fer cryin' out loud, Astrid! You still lookin' fer Prince Charming? I'd of thought you'd of learned!" Sharon snorts. She's at the monitor entering her orders, her black acrylic nails clicking on the screen. Then she adds orange slices and straws to the screwdrivers, and says, "Lookit him," she nods at table nine. "Droolin' over Jennifer. As usual she's leanin' in like everything he says is so-o-o interesting. Course she's really only leanin' over like that to give him a view of her fun jugs."

"He looks melancholy."

"*Melancholy?* Oh. My. Gawd! Not another one! No offence, Astrid," Sharon continues, "but if she's his type, you think you have a chance? You know Jennifer—perfect clothes, perfect make-up, lookin' purdy 'n' talkin' durdy? You, Miss I-don't-like-lipstick-and-wouldn't-say-shit-if-I-had-a- mouthful-of-it? Always getting ketchup or red wine or clam chowder on your shirt and today, a new one, toner on your nose? Besides, you think he's lookin' for everlasting love?" She bats her eyes, then turns to Ken. "Bah! Lookit that face! She won't listen. She really believes Prince Charming is out there somewhere, no doubt riding a white horse and wearing a cowboy hat." She lifts her tray, turns and moves off, dropping the Chivas in front of the guy in the cowboy hat who's looking down Jennifer's blouse.

"Well, I don't wear lipstick, but I *do* say shit," Astrid says, more to herself than to Ken. She starts taking wine glasses from the dishwasher, wiping them with a clean dishtowel, and sliding them into overhead slots. A slurping noise from Ken's straw draws her attention.

Astrid removes his empty glass. "Coffee?"

"Naww! Hit me again!" Wobbling slightly on his stool, he leans closer. Moist beads of perspiration stand on his forehead. He says, "I can get a cowboy hat and look sad, if that's what turns you on."

She hasn't heard him, though. She's watching the man in the cowboy hat as he tosses back his drink, gets to his feet and walks out the door, leaving Jennifer frowning.

She draws a deep breath, looks around the room, and thinks, *I need a change.*

THREE

Her old Honda Civic, loaded to the roof with everything she owns in the world, is starting to run hot. The mechanic told her there's nothing wrong with it a thousand dollars worth of parts and labour wouldn't fix. A thousand dollars she doesn't have. So, she adds oil every time she puts gas in, lets it cool down for an hour or so, then starts off again. Around town, it's not a big deal, but it's a nuisance on a long trip like this. But the gas gauge is nearing empty anyway, and she's tired and hungry, so she pulls into the Chevron station. There are a couple of service bays attached to the convenience store, so she asks the woman behind the glass to get one of the shop guys to top up the oil and check the antifreeze while he's at it.

"It'll be about half an hour."

"That's okay. I was ready for a break anyway." She checks the selection of pre-made sandwiches and other offerings in the display case. Finding nothing appealing, she goes back to the cashier and asks, "Is that place across the road any good?"

"Dot's? Sure. Cheap and fast."

"I guess I'll go over there and have lunch while I'm waiting. You can phone me if you need me for anything." She leaves her phone number and keys and makes her way across the highway to the diner. Inside, she heads for the ladies' room first, then comes back, slides into a booth next to the window, and pulls out her phone. In a moment, the server comes with a mug in one hand and a carafe of coffee in the other.

"Coffee?" she asks, setting a mug in front of Astrid as if it's a rhetorical question.

"Mmmm, yes please!"

"Lunch special today is a Turkey BLT on your choice of white, sourdough or multigrain. Comes with a cup of Bisque of Tomato soup and coleslaw for $4.95," the server tells her as she fills her mug. "You can substitute fries for the soup if you want. Would you like a menu?"

"No, I'll have the special on multigrain, with fries, please. And water, when you get a chance?"

"You bet."

"By the way, what's the WIFI password?"

"Goodpies, all one word."

"Thanks."

The server nods and scurries away. Astrid checks in on her Facebook page, then opens her email. There's a message from the latest company she applied for an office job with. Despite knowing if they wanted an interview they'd phone rather than email, she feels a surge of hope. But it's another rejection. Of course, it's not a firm 'no' because they're keeping her resumé on file in case of any future openings. Right. She didn't want the lousy file clerk job anyway. But if they'd requested an interview, she'd have turned around and headed right back to Nanaimo.

When the server returns with her lunch, Astrid says, "I noticed the help wanted sign in the window. You're hiring?"

"We are. You interested?"

"I am."

"Have you got any experience?"

"Well, I've worked as a server and bartender for over ten years. Just in pubs, though. Never worked in a restaurant."

"When can you start?"

* * *

She notices him when he comes in: movie-star handsome, his neat western shirt tucked into well-fitting jeans (no drop crotch here!), tooled belt with big silver buckle, narrow hips and wide shoulders. He slides into a booth where three other men in stained ballcaps with Hazen Sawmills emblazoned across the crowns are already digging into their burgers and beers. He looks around and sees her with the coffee carafe, and calls out, "Hey, beautiful! Hustle yer little sugar shaker over here, wouldja?"

She gets a clean mug from the rack behind the counter and comes to his booth. At her approach, he gets to his feet and when she puts down the mug, he takes her hand. She finds herself staring deep into intense brown eyes. "Ain't often we get such a gorgeous new waitress in this dump!" he says in a husky voice. "I'm Hank. Who might you be?"

Her cheeks grow warm; she stammers, but manages to tell him her name.

"Well, Aster, you know what I wanna know?"

She shakes her head.

"I wanna know where you been all my life." He squeezes her fingers and brings them to his lips.

"I … er … Nanaimo?"

She knows her face must be glowing. She pulls her hand out of his and scurries back behind the counter.

"Hey, beautiful, what's yer name? Ester? You fergot my coffee," he calls after her, waving his empty mug. Then he huddles with his friends; she thinks she hears him say something about blondes, and they all laugh.

The other server comes behind the counter with her carafe empty. "Don't let him get to you," she says quietly. "This is a mill town, and his family owns the mill. He thinks the sun shines out of his asshole." She studies Astrid's face, then holds out the empty carafe and says, "Here. Trade me. Make a fresh pot while I go take care of him."

"Thanks, Franny," Astrid's grateful for the diversionary task, embarrassed she'd forgotten to pour Hank's coffee or take his order, and at her over-the-top reaction. She's no virgin schoolgirl! Will he think she's a total ditz?

She realizes she's blushing again. She feels the sweat glands in her armpits prickle and she wipes sweat off her forehead on her sleeve. What an intense physical reaction! How did he do it? Those eyes! She takes a deep breath, makes a mental promise to be ready next time, and congratulates herself on making the move up from Vancouver Island. Imagine! Only in town a few days and she's already found a hot boyfriend prospect. And one with a good job, too!

"Order up!" the cook calls out as he slides a couple of lunch specials onto the pass through with a clatter. She closes the Bunn and hits the "on" switch, then checks the bill to see what table the orders belong to. It's the booth right behind Hank! She takes a deep breath, pats her French braid, picks up the plates and heads out, ready for anything he might say.

But he doesn't look at her; he's focusing his attention on the man across the table from him, who's saying, "Hey, Boss, you know Jake Binder ain't coming back to work for a while?"

"No. How come?"

"He's in jail."

"Jail? What the hell did he do now?"

"Beat up his wife. Put 'er in the hospital."

They all murmur sounds of concern. Hank says: "But that was weeks ago. He ain't still in jail?"

"Yeah, he done it again. This time they're keepin' him in."

"That ain't right!"

"Well, he wasn't supposed to go around there. Not within half a kilometer or somethin'. And they say he beat her up pretty bad."

They're all quiet for a heartbeat. Then Hank says, "Well, she does have a big yap on her. You'd think by now she'd've learned to learn keep it shut."

They all nod and murmur agreement.

Her heart sinks. Has she moved a thousand kilometers to trade arrogant, insincere jerks in expensive suits for guys like these, still misogynistic but not as well dressed? She doesn't need another one of those in her life!

Maybe they're everywhere. Or maybe she just hasn't gone far enough. Her stopover in Dark River may not be long, after all.

FOUR

Another day, another dollar, Astrid thinks. Carafe in hand, she makes the rounds of the few customers still in the diner, topping up mugs as requested, then goes back behind the counter. As she lifts her arm and reaches to put the carafe back on the warmer, she gets a whiff of b.o. *Damn, that really is me,* she thinks. *I'll have to wash this shirt again tonight.* She has a second shirt, but it was so wrinkled from being wrung out by hand and dried over the shower rod it had to be ironed before she could wear it. It nearly started on fire when she left the iron sitting on it to go and pull the burning toast out of the toaster. As it is, there's a partly melted, crinkled, iron-shaped scorch mark on the front, so it's ruined. She doesn't want to tell the boss. She can't afford to have it deducted from her pay. Fifty bucks for a cheap, polyester-blend, made-in-China shirt! And ten dollars on top, to pay to have her name embroidered on it. As if that's necessary! But, you want the job, you pay for your shirts, embroidery and all.

She sighs, rubs her neck, and leans back against the stainless-steel counter below the kitchen pass-through.

"Runnin' outta steam, Astrid?" Hank, the only customer still at the counter, asks.

"It's been a long day," she replies. "Landlord's dog barked half the night. Finally got to sleep and then the neighbour started up his truck—it's a big noisy diesel, you know? — at five. His driveway's right outside my bedroom window. I thought, why fight it? I just got up."

"Same old complaint."

"Yeah, I know, Hank. I'm always crying about it. I need to do something instead of just whining. Thing is, it's a nice suite for the money, and they've already told me my hours'll be cut when the tourist season ends and your mill shuts down. Hardly get any hours as it is. Last one hired, first one fired, I get it. I guess it was a mistake moving up here."

"Why did you?"

"Seemed like the right thing at the time. I was in a rut. Expected a change of scenery to work magic." She shrugs and sighs.

"Dunno why anyone would move up way up here for a change of scenery. Other than guys thinkin' to make big money as fallers, maybe. Ain't you got trees on Vancouver Island?"

"Yeah, of course. You know what I mean! Anyway, getting up early I got to the laundromat when no one else was there. It's nice watching a decent TV, with the sound on, not like the ones in here. Although there's nothing much on but the news. You hear there's a girl missing?"

"Yeah. Ladies at the feed store were talkin' about it. They're all in a flap, thinkin' it's that serial killer startin' up again."

"I heard that too, but he'd have to be, like, a hundred years old by now, wouldn't he?"

"Well, they had a police sketch of some old bastard who tried to grab a woman a couple months ago, remember?"

"Hmm. Didn't hear about that. Must've been before I moved up here." She scans the tables, hoping everyone's getting ready to go. It would be nice to close on time for once. The man in the back corner is holding up his mug, beckoning. She thinks, *another refill! How does he sleep with all the coffee he drinks this late in the day?* He's so creepy it's hard to be pleasant. But he never does anything, really. Maybe he's just shy. "I'll be right back," she tells Hank, picks up the carafe and a plate of creamers and goes to the man in the corner booth.

As usual, as she comes toward him, his hand dives into his lap and his arm begins to twitch; he says nothing, just stares at her. She sucks in a breath, forces a smile and as she tops up his mug and slides the creamers onto the table, asks, "Will there be anything else tonight?" His close-set eyes squint out from beneath heavy dark brows, reminding her of a beetle. He shakes his head. She was hoping he'd be finished, and has his bill ready. She puts it on the table in front of him, and with another smile, says, "Whenever you're ready. No rush."

She escapes back behind the counter, and blows out the breath she didn't know she was holding. *There is really something wrong with that guy*, she thinks. She quietly asks Hank, "That guy in the corner—you know him, don't you?"

Hank swivels in his stool and watches for a moment. "Yeah, of course, that's Fletch. Why?"

"He started coming in here about a week ago. He gives me the creeps!" Astrid whispers. "Never says anything, other than to grunt 'coffee' or 'apple pie'. Well, he does always say please. But he sits in that corner for hours, looking at his phone, drinking coffee. And every time I look around, he's staring at me. I swear he must put six creamers in every cup, and he doesn't want me to clear away the empty ones. He makes pyramids with them, like he's six years old. And why does he always have his hand in his crotch?"

"Aww, that? That ain't nuthin'."

She shudders. "Well, he gives me the heebie-jeebies."

"You scared? You ain't here alone, closin' up, are you?"

"No, Al or Suki always stays. If there's anyone still hanging around at closing, Al walks me out, or Suki and I go out together."

"Maybe you should report him to the cops," he suggests, his tone conspiratorial.

"And say what? That he stares at me?" She heaves a big sigh then chuckles. "I guess I'm being stupid."

"Well, you don't have to worry. He's just shy. Or anti-social you might say. Keeps to himself. Fletchers have a few acres next to our place. His ol' man 'n' ol' lady, they're gone, so it's just him now. Didn't finish high school." He drains his coffee and continues in his normal speaking voice, "A course I wouldn't of neither if I didn't have a mother who was on the school board. She couldn't do nuthin' fer Johnny Fletcher, though. He's dumber'n a bag a hammers."

"Hank!" Astrid hisses, "He'll hear you!" She looks over Hank's shoulder at Fletch, who is watching them and has narrowed his eyes even further.

"So? He knows I'm just kiddin'." He swivels his stool, looks at Fletch and says with a chuckle, "You know I don't mean nuthin', ain't that right, Fletch?"

Fletch lifts his chin in acknowledgement, his expression unchanged.

"Anyway," Hank swivels back around to face Astrid, "as I was sayin', he lives close to us. He's harmless, a sucker fer cats, always takin' on strays. Must have a hundred of 'em by now. He works fer us." He picks up his bill. "Speaking of work, I gotta shove off. Critters'll be lookin' for their night feed and I got it in the truck." He gets off his stool and roots in his hip pocket for his wallet. "You know, they're organizing search teams to look for that missing girl tomorrow. I'm goin'. You wanna come?"

"Oh! Yes."

"Assembly's in the Plaza parking lot at eight. I'll swing by and pick you up."

"No, it's okay, it's not even a block. I'll walk."

"If I didn't know better, I'd swear you don't want me to know where you live. I might be pissed, thinkin' yer worried I'm gonna bother you, or bust in 'n' rape you." He fixes her with his intense brown eyes. "You know I could find you if I wanted to. Dark River ain't that big. Neighbour with a diesel truck in a driveway right next to the house, within a block of the Plaza..." His expression softens; he smiles and winks, then slaps a couple of twenties down on top of his bill and says, "Add Fletch's in there, 'n' keep the change. See you tomorrow," before going to the door, and out.

Astrid watches his departing back, wondering why she's reluctant to let him know where she lives. He's not so bad, just insensitive, like the spoiled rich kid he is. Maybe they got off on the wrong foot. Maybe she should give him another chance.

The diner's last customers leave and only Fletch is left, hulking over his mug, demolishing and rebuilding his pyramid. As Astrid's ringing off the till, he looks up as if he's just realized everyone else has gone.

"Hank took care of your bill," she calls to him, hoping he'll take the hint.

He nods, slides out of the booth and heads for the door without giving her more than a sidelong glance. Once he's out, she scurries around the counter and turns the deadbolt, then goes back into the kitchen where Al's shutting everything down, tidying up, putting things away. He looks up and asks, "Walk you to your car, Astrid?"

FIVE

Denver Danielson slides onto a stool at the bar, orders a beer with a Chivas chaser, and scans the gloomy room. There are few empty tables, and the pub is filled with the noise of many people well into their cups, mostly ignoring the big TV's at both ends of the room.

The bartender drops a coaster in front of him, sets the glass of beer on it and the shot glass of Chivas next to it. "Wanna run a tab?" she asks.

"No, I just have time for one." He pulls a wad from his pocket and hands her a bill. "Have one yourself."

"Thanks," she says, then leans an elbow on the bar across from him. "You know, we don't get many guys in cowboy hats comin' in here. New in town?"

"Just visiting."

"Where're you from?"

"Merritt."

"Oh! Merritt! I went to the music festival there a few years ago."

When he pulls out his phone and focuses his attention on it, she straightens, wipes the already spotless bar in front of him for a few moments, then starts to move away.

He looks up and says, "Sorry. I'm waitin' on a message." He shoots his whiskey, then takes a swig of his beer. "You have a good time? At the festival?"

"Par-tayed for three days solid! One day must've been a hundred of us in the river. It was unbelievably hot. We just went in clothes and all."

"Yeah, you people from the Wet Coast can't take the kind of heat we get up in the Interior."

"Once it was dark, it got even hotter. *So* hot some of us had to take our clothes off," she leans forward and winks. "You actually a cowboy? I mean, the real thing?"

"We-l-l," he drawls, "I'm fourth generation on the ranch. I suppose I'm the real thing."

"Oh. Nice! So, what brings you to town?"

"Quarter Horse show."

"Oh! I like horses. I rode one once," she says, holding out her hand. "My name's Sharon."

"Pleased to meet you, Sharon," he says, giving her hand a quick shake. "I'm Denver."

"Denver? Like in Colorado?"

"Yeah. Parents seemed to like American cities. Named my brother Dallas. My sister, Abilene."

His phone buzzes and he answers it. Saying, "Bad signal. Be right back," he gets up and walks to the doorway, talking into his phone. When he returns he doesn't sit, but swigs the rest of his beer and turns to leave. Then he stops and says, "By the way, where's the tall blonde that was here last year?"

"Astrid?" Sharon takes his empty glass away, picks up the coaster and wipes the bar. "Said she needed a change of scenery and moved to the mainland. Way up north, Prince George I think she said."

"Prince George?"

"Maybe Smithers. Terrace maybe. Somewhere up there. Don't remember," she says, smile replaced with a frown that makes the furrow in her brow deepen and the corners of her mouth curve down. She turns her back on him, picks up a tray and strides away.

He stands for a heartbeat, wondering at the abrupt freeze. Did he insult her by asking about, what was the name, Astrid? *Women*, he thinks. He shrugs and leaves.

It's nearly dark but traffic is still heavy. It takes longer than he expected to get to the theatre. As he approaches, he sees Trisha standing next to the curb, hands on her hips. He can almost hear her toe-tapping. The truck barely stops before she wrenches the passenger door open, hurls her oversized purse onto the floor and climbs in, slamming the door behind her.

"You took your sweet time! I've been waiting half an hour."

"Really? Couldn't've been that long."

"Well, it was! Start with my text, which you ignored, it's half an hour!" her voice rises.

"Okay! Sorry. I came as soon as you called."

"If you came when I texted, I wouldn't've had to call, and I wouldn't've been waiting half an hour!"

"Well, I didn't see your text. Then I hit some traffic snarls."

"Yeah, well, it's always something," she sniffs. "You could've just come to the movie with me."

"Why in hell would I go to a movie? If the show was over, wouldn't we just head back to the mainland?"

"Oh, I know, anything you got to do's more important than spending time with me. And now we won't make the 9:30 ferry, so that means waiting for the 11:30. Be lucky if we're home by breakfast!"

"We'll get a room, maybe in Tsawassen."

"Get a room at two a.m.? What's the point? Might as well drive right through."

"Okay, let's get a room here then, like we originally planned."

"Stay in Nanaimo and be all day getting home tomorrow? Might as well at least get back to the mainland." She blows out a sharp breath. "You should've come when I texted you."

"Like I told you, I didn't see your text. And you didn't have to go to a movie. You could've waited at the show grounds."

"I would have stayed at the show despite how frickin' boring it is, if you hadn't insisted you had to be there to the end! You could leave early. They know you have to catch a ferry."

"They actually pay me to judge every class, you know. And there's no way of knowin' how late the show's gonna run."

"You could've made a deal when they hired you, that you had to leave in time to get the ferry whether everything's done or not!"

"They wouldn't've hired me if I insisted on that, for chrissakes! I'm not the only one who has to get back to the mainland, you know! They try to schedule classes so the show ends in time for everyone who has to catch a ferry, but sometimes it doesn't work out. Delays happen. Those people paid good money to get to the show; it's important to them. You don't really think I can say 'I gotta catch a ferry so I'm leavin' now, you all figure out who the winner is' and then bugger off?" He takes a deep breath and blows it out through pursed lips. "I don't know what planet you live on, Trisha."

"Well, you didn't have to go to the pub to wait."

"I was parched, and it was one beer! It was a long day! I should wait in the truck?"

"Would it kill you to wait for me for a change? I'm *always* waitin' on you."

"Whaddya call hangin' around until you call?"

"Pretty nice waiting in the pub with a cold beer. Wasn't you standing out on the sidewalk!"

Denver thinks, *yup, once again I've been drawn into one of her circular arguments. How many times have I promised myself I won't let her do it again? And yet somehow, I always do.* He turns up the volume on the stereo.

"Goddamn Dwight Yokum again! You know I can't stand this crappy old CD." She turns it off and they ride along in silence for a few minutes.

"You could ask if I liked the movie."

"Did you like the movie?"

"No. It was crap. I knew it would be. Wouldn't've gone if it wasn't for having nothing to do while you're having a good time with your horse friends. Oh, why do I bother? As if you give a shit."

He sighs. In truth, he doesn't give a shit, and it's been a long time since he did. He thinks, *maybe it's time I acknowledged it.* But it's been a long day. His headache, a dull throbbing in the hot sun of the afternoon, now feels like something inside his skull is pounding to get out. This isn't the time.

He turns the stereo back on.

Trisha pushes the eject button and pulls the CD out of its slot. She powers her window down and Frisbees the CD out onto the sidewalk, startling a group of pedestrians. "There! End of *that* shitty thing." She sniffs and glares at him. "Nothing to say?"

Eyes narrowing, he frowns but looks straight ahead. He shakes his head slowly, but doesn't answer.

"Just gonna ignore me? As usual?" She lifts her purse onto her lap, roots through it, and pulls out an emery board. "This is a lousy excuse for a weekend getaway," she snarls as she begins attacking already perfectly-manicured nails with a vengeance, "a couple of dinners with a bunch of horse people who can't talk about anything but horses! This pedigree, that pedigree, this one's an own son of who gives a fuck."

"Didn't you go to the mall?"

"Sure. That took two hours and was no better than shopping in Merritt. Why would I want to shop here when we could shop in Vancouver?"

"We still can…"

"Forget it. I already missed one dance class for this miserable trip and I don't want to miss tomorrow's."

"It was your idea to come with me, remember?"

"Oh, I suppose I spoiled it for you? Who would you be sleeping with if I wasn't with you? That flat-chested old redhead you kept smiling at, maybe?"

"Jesus, Trisha! Now I can't smile at anyone?"

"You were ogling her, don't deny it!"

"I wouldn't call it ogling, but I'm married, not dead! And we know each other from…"

"So, you and her get it on when I'm not around?"

"Jesus, Trisha, like I said and like I told you before…"

"Know what?" she cuts him off again, "next show, you go alone. That should make you happy, eh?"

He's pulled into a right turn bay and is watching out his side window for a break in traffic. He realizes she's right, his usual strategy is to clam up. Avoid confrontation. It solves nothing.

When he's merged the truck into the queue leading to the ferry toll booth, he turns to her and says, "I'd like that just fine."

SIX

Denver sits at a cluttered desk, sorting through bundles of papers, setting some aside and adding the rest to the bin to be taken out to the burn barrel. He heaves a sigh, tosses a handful of papers back onto the stack on the desk, and slumps in his chair.

The kitchen door slams and after a moment, Dallas appears in the doorway to the den. He tosses a bundle of envelopes and flyers onto the desk in front of his brother. "Mail," he says, taking his hat off and wiping the sweat off his forehead with his sleeve.

"Like I need more bills," Denver scowls.

"They ain't all bills."

"Well, they ain't valentines."

Dallas drops into the armchair next to the door. "So? Any more thoughts on sellin' Rocky Duster?"

Denver opens the bottom desk drawer and pulls out two glasses and a bottle of Chivas Regal. He splashes whiskey in both glasses, pushes one across to his brother, and takes a swig before answering. "I guess we'll have to. I talked to Hazen this afternoon. He wants to pay part in hay."

"If it's good hay and he don't want yer pecker for it, why not?"

"Yeah, it's good hay, some haylage, some hundred-pound bales of second cut twenty-five percent alfalfa mix, at a helluva good price. And we need it. Maybe better'n all cash. Don't think we could get hay around here at the price we've agreed on for his. There'll be a cost in gettin' it down here, though.

It'd be quite a few trips with the flat deck, so, cheaper to get it shipped. Still a good deal. But we also need cash. And we still need to economize."

"Could switch from Chivas to Johnny Walker Red."

"Hell, we're not *that* desperate. Not yet anyway. But hydro's going up again. Price of feed's up again. Price of horses, down. I think we're gonna hafta cull. Jesus! I hate to think of that."

"We can let the hands go. Hire again in the spring."

"We can't do that, Dal! Jimbo and Eddie, they might go on their own; they've got other prospects, but the others? Wilson? At his age? Where'd he go?"

"Not our problem."

"Put them out in the street? Have the cottage empty? Just to save a few bucks?"

"When they're too old to do the work, they're gonna hafta go anyway."

"Hell, no! We'll quit payin' them if they want to retire once they're drawin' their government pensions but they can stay in that house …"

"You kiddin'? Where's the guys we hafta hire to replace 'em gonna live?"

"Dunno, haven't figured that out yet. Maybe convert the mare barn if we have no mares coming in for breeding. Or maybe set up a trailer."

"How's it our problem, if they ain't looked after their retirement?"

"It's just the moral thing to do. They work for next to nothing—"

"It's always been like that."

"Yeah, always has been, but that's changing. We could start that RRSP matching plan that was discussed at the last Cattleman's Association meeting, but it won't help the old guys much. Like I said, we'll quit payin' them if they want to retire once they're drawing their government pensions, but they can live here as long as they want." He takes a swig of his Chivas. "Least we can do. I already talked to them about it. I won't go back on my word."

"So, we could afford that matching plan yer talking about? And we're runnin' a retirement home for old, wore-out cowboys?" Dallas clucks. "We got a money tree I don't know about?"

Denver scowls.

They sit in silence for a minute. Dallas clink-clink-clinks his gold pinky ring against his glass, then says: "We could take in boarders again. It's a pain in the ass but if we git a good deal on the hay, we can make money on it. Only five horses comin' in fer trainin' so we got stalls. And if we ain't layin' off any hands, we might as well have work for 'em. Fill up the barn."

"Yeah. That would help our cash flow. Let's put a notice up at the feed store next time we're in town. Tack shops too. I'll put something on Facebook and update our website, put an ad on Craig's List." He sips his whiskey with a grimace. "Lord, I hate to see Rocky go."

"Hardly anyone's doin' live cover no more and he's gettin' older. His value's in a downward spiral. We could get set up to collect semen. That would open up a huge market, not just limited to mares close enough to be hauled here. They're shippin' semen all over the world."

"Well, it'd be nice to think ol' Rocky's semen would be that sought after, but it would take a lot of money to get set up. Money, and work. There's advertising, office work—you gonna do it?"

"Maybe send him somewhere else and have them collect."

"Yeah, maybe. Still stressful for Rocky, though, having to leave here. And no use collecting unless you got buyers for it."

"Well, we won't git buyers for it if we don't have it to sell."

"That's a fact, Dal," Denver shoots the rest of his Chivas. "I just can't get my head around doin' all that right now. Don't get me wrong. I'm not sayin' it's a bad idea."

"We can't breed our young mares back to Rocky so we're gonna need another stud by spring, anyway. We should go have another look at that colt the Douglases have. He's well bred, goes to Doc Bar pretty close up on his dam's side, don't he? But he ain't cheap."

"We don't wanna go cheap. Already made that decision. We got a rep for good horses and want to keep it that way. But it's the wrong time financially to be buyin' a high-end stud."

"So, we ain't got the cash flow to buy a stud, or to git set up to collect from the stud we got so we could sell more breedings, but we can run a retirement home fer old cowboys."

"Back to that? Tell me, what do you want to do?"

"I want to buy that colt from the Douglases."

"We just can't spend the money now, Dal! We got that balloon payment coming up. Selling Rocky covers that, our operating expenses, plus gets us enough hay to see us through to spring. Nothing left over to buy that colt. But how about next spring we take a couple mares to him, sort of a trial to see what his babies are like. For the rest of the mares, we find a few studs we like, buy semen and A.I.'em. Never know, might get a promising stud colt outta that."

"We might not, though. Horses as well bred as that colt don't come along every day. What if we decide down the road we should buy him? If they put trainin' on him, the price will have went up. Plus, they'd of sold him by then, most likely."

"I know it's a gamble, but we really don't have the money."

"Damn! I'd wisht I had that colt here now, so I could start him."

"Why don't you buy him, then?"

"Now I gotta pay fer a stud *we* need fer *our* ranch outta *my* pocket?"

"You already got your own business, your training business. Buy him in that company. Triple R'll feed him and he lives here; in exchange, he breeds our mares."

More clink-clink-clinking of the pinky ring. "That might work. Still need to sell Rocky, though."

"Yup, doesn't seem to matter how many times we roll this around, and much as I hate the thought of uprooting him, sending him away from the only home he's ever known, sellin' him now we got a good offer makes sense. Wouldn't have to, if we could move Dad back home. He hates that place, tiny room, hardly any yard, can't even go out the door unless someone's with him. It's no place for an old rancher, and it's costin' a bundle besides. But that's somethin' else that can't happen." Denver clicks his tongue. He rubs his face and gives his head a vigorous, two-handed scratching that does little to ameliorate his headache. "The drought. Then Mom. Now Dad. Rocky Duster. Our old mares. Everyone gettin' older. Even Tippy. Seems like yesterday she was curled up asleep in my slipper. Doubt she'll make it through another winter. Would sure be nice if somethin' good came along for a change."

"Don't worry 'bout Dad, half the time he don't even know where he is. My ass is more picked 'bout Trisha."

"Trisha's not your problem."

"The hell she ain't! Well, she's part of *our* problem, anyway. How much d'you think we could rent yer house fer if she wasn't in it, speakin' of our cash flow? Dunno why you don't evict her."

"I'm hoping she'll do the right thing and move out voluntarily."

"We're talkin' about Trisha. When's she ever done the right thing?"

"Don't worry, I'll get her paid out. Already talked to the bank about a loan. Personal loan, nuthin' to do with the ranch. You can quit pissin' 'n' moanin' about it and bringing it up at every opportunity," Denver says sharply. Then he takes a deep breath, blows it out through his mouth, and continues more quietly, "You're right, though. Sure the hell wish she never moved onto the ranch."

"I warned you," Dallas continues, "like always, you wouldn't listen."

"You got a short memory. Who brought her here in the first place?"

"Yeah, well, I'm not the one who got sucked into marryin' her, am I?"

"Do we have to keep rehashing it?"

Dallas scowls, drinks his whiskey, then says, "Least you don't own this place. Better git shed of her before you do. Before Dad passes. Once he goes…"

"I don't want to think about that!"

"You better think about it, though."

They sit quiet again. Dallas vigorously scratches the back of his head, then says, "So, when do we ship them old mares?"

"We're not going to ship them! Those old girls gave us dozens of beautiful babies and this is their home. I won't put them through the hell of being shipped for a few bucks."

"Can't let go of Rocky. Can't lay nobody off. Can't let go of a few crocked old mares. Can't even get shed of yer ex! Why Dad set it up so yer the manager, I'll never fuckin' know! This is typical! You lay down a bunch of rules and then bugger off on yer judgin' gigs. Leave me runnin' the place but won't let me do what needs doing."

"Well, some things I'm not going to change my mind on, and shipping the mares, or any horse, is one of them!" Denver scowls.

Dallas slams his empty glass down on the desk. "So, if we ain't gonna ship them, what *is* yer idea of a cull?"

Denver takes a few deep breaths, calming himself so he can respond to his younger brother without the argument escalating. He laces his fingers together behind his head, leans back, swivel rocks in the high-backed office chair and looks out the window. On the road across the valley, he sees Old Man Halbe, miniature in the distance, back hunched, heading to the mailboxes, his Heinz 57 shuffling along behind. It's their daily outing, half a kilometer each way, even though Mr. Halbe is nearing ninety, and Cisco

The Fifth is the same in dog years. The familiar routine is beautiful and sad at the same time. He breathes a sigh, then straightens and pours them each another Chivas. "We'll have to shoot them, I guess. That way at least the wildlife rescue can use the meat."

"Hell, *we* can use the meat." Dallas barks a laugh, picks up his glass and gets to his feet. He goes to the door and turns back. "At this rate, it might come to that! But don't worry, we still got beef in the freezer. If Wilson ain't started supper yet, I'll see if he'll do up some spuds. I'll fire up the barbeque and throw some steaks on. And unless you dream up a better idea overnight, phone Hazens tomorrow and let 'em know we'll take their offer on Rocky Duster. And git him the hell outta here before you change yer mind again."

SEVEN

DENVER HUNCHES FORWARD over the steering wheel, slowing as he approaches a clapboard building that looks to have pushed up out of the dirt like a lopsided mushroom. Along the side of the building, this year's weeds mix with dead ones from years past. Above the canopy over the windows along the front, two-foot-high letters in weathered paint read "Dot's Diner" and a sandwich board on the boulevard declares it's Licenced! and has Home Cooked Meals! and The Best Pie North of Kamloops!

It looks like a lousy place to eat but the parking lot's crowded with enough vehicles, including eighteen wheelers, to suggest otherwise. He pulls in, heading through to the potholed gravel lot around back. It's been unseasonably cool and rainy; the potholes are full of water, and there are muddy puddles everywhere. He steers the truck to a clear area near the bushes at the back, avoiding potholes as much as possible to give the horse in the trailer the least amount of grief. "Sorry, ol' man," he mutters, "I know you been in there a while. I wouldn't stop, but I'm fadin' and need a coffee and a piss."

He opens his door, slides out of his seat to the ground, then puts a hand on his hip and bends to the side, giving his back a stretch. A couple of satisfying crunches in his backbone result. He tips his head to one side and then the other, working the stiffness out of his neck. With his cowboy hat on the seat, he gives his head an all-over, two-handed scratching, then rubs his face before re-settling the hat, closing the door, and making his way to the front of the building. The cowbell over the door jangles as he steps inside.

The room is filled with chatter and the clatter of plates and cutlery. TV monitors are silently running a B.C. Lions game and *Global BC News*. He heads to the men's room before coming back to find a seat.

A couple of orange-and-white-shirted servers circulate through the tables; another is behind the counter, putting the makings of a fresh pot of coffee in the Bunn. The tables are all taken, but there's an empty stool at the counter between a pony-tailed guy in a grey wool logger's sweater and a pimply young man with Plaza Bowling emblazoned across the back of his shirt. He slides onto the stool and pulls the menu out of the clip behind the sugar, ketchup, A1 Sauce, salt and pepper, and glances through it. He's hungry, but worries about Rocky. He wants to get him to his new home without too much delay, so he decides he'll just have coffee and test the claim about the pie. That'll be quick.

A clean mug is placed in front of him with a question, "Coffee?"

He says, "Yes, please!" Then he closes the menu and looks up to see a pretty blonde doing the pouring. "Astrid" is embroidered above the breast pocket of her shirt. His eyes widen and he sits straighter.

"Astrid!" he says.

"That's my name! Slingin' hash is my game!" she says cheerily. She looks up and they make eye contact.

"You're from Nanaimo, right?"

"Do I know you?" Her brow furrows.

He shakes his head. "No, I guess you don't." Movement in his peripheral vision attracts his attention and he glances down the counter. A man at the far end is leaning forward to see past the other diners, shamelessly watching. He returns his attention to Astrid, and continues, "Let me introduce myself. My name's Denver."

"And you already know I'm Astrid," she says, and smiles.

"You used to work at a pub near the exhibition grounds in Nanaimo?"

"Yup, the Highwayman," she nods.

"I saw you there last year. When I was back a couple months ago, they said you'd moved. The girl—Sharon?"

She nods again.

"Sharon told me your name and that you moved. She thought you went to Prince George."

"That is where I was headed, but then I got this job, and, well, here I am. You sure must have a good memory for faces."

"Well, you had a black nose."

"Oh! The guy in the cowboy hat was you?" Colour floods her cheeks. "How embarrassing!"

"Naw, it was cute! And it was only one of the things that made you memorable." He smiles and gives her a wink. "Can't believe I've run into you! I'm sorry I didn't make the trip sooner."

"Denver?"

He turns when the man from the end of the counter pushes in beside him and sticks out his hand. "Hank Hazen. I'm guessin' yer here to deliver our horse."

Something in the other man's body language, his intensity, sends Denver's guard up. He gives Hank's hand a quick shake and says, "You're guessin' right."

"Well, ain't this a coincidence!" Hank continues. "How long'd it take you to make the trip?"

"Let's see. I left about eight," he looks at his watch. "Ten, goin' on eleven hours. Horse'll be as glad to get outta the trailer as I was to get a coffee." He lifts his mug for a satisfying couple of swallows.

"You wanna follow me out to our place? I'm just headin' there."

"Well, I do want to get the horse settled in, but a slice of cherry pie won't take too long." He locks eyes with Astrid again and smiles.

"I'll wait." Hank's eyes narrow. "Yer plannin' on stayin' overnight ain't you?"

"I am."

"Well, we got room at the house 'n' Bridey, my mother, she's expectin' you. We'll git the hay loaded tonight, and you can git an early start in the mornin'."

"Well, thanks! That sounds real good."

"Okay. Goin' fer a smoke. See you outside." With a nod, he goes to stand at the cash register.

Astrid goes to the front desk and rings in Hank's bill.

As he turns to leave the cashier counter, Hank says, "Don't be late gittin' home, honey! I'll be waitin' up!" He pushes out the door and at the bottom of the steps, holds up, turns and looks back in as he lights a cigarette.

A man's voice from the kitchen calls out, "Order up!" as two meals are placed on the ledge at the pass through. Another server comes behind the counter to get them, and stands for a moment next to Astrid. Although their backs are to him, Denver overhears snatches of their conversation.

"…you hear him, Franny?"

"Everyone heard him."

"Grrrr!"

Franny picks up the orders and as she turns to carry them off, says, "He's persistent, I'll give him that."

Astrid comes back to take Denver's order. "So, cherry pie you said?"

"Yes, please."

"Would you like it warmed up, with a scoop of ice cream?"

"Now, that sounds perfect."

Astrid busies herself getting the pie ready while Denver drinks coffee and starts to feel human again. Then she sets the pie and a little napkin-wrapped bundle of cutlery in front of him, and asks, "I know you're in a hurry. Want the bill right away?"

"Yeah, please." Their eyes meet; he takes a deep breath and says, "I hope you don't think I'm too forward, but would you have breakfast, or at least a coffee, with me tomorrow morning? I'd like to take you for supper, but I have a long dr…"

"Yes!" she cuts him short.

Now there are other customers at the till waiting to pay; one rings the bell impatiently. Astrid lingers for a moment, then fixes a smile on her face and goes to deal with the bell ringer. Done at the register, she comes back; as she puts his bill on the counter, she looks up under her lashes with a grin.

More plates appear on the shelf at the pass-through and again the cook calls out, "Order up!" Astrid gives Denver another smile before turning away, picking up the meals and taking them out into the booths.

Denver works a piece of pie with melting ice cream onto his fork, then notices there's a piece of pink paper under the bill. It's a Post-It Note with Astrid's name and phone number. He glances toward the door and sees Hank on the other side, smoking, watching him. They make eye contact. Denver gives him a nod, then tucks into his pie, feeling even better than merely human.

* * *

The next morning, Astrid's in the corner booth at the end of the row of windows facing the road. It's only six-thirty, but the diner is busy with the usual breakfast crowd. Franny stops in her rounds with the coffee carafe to top up Astrid's mug, and says, "So, who is this guy you're waiting for again?"

"That cowboy who was here yesterday. His name's Denver. Franny, you must have noticed him! Tall? Good-looking? He sat at the counter. He was up here for something about a horse, he was delivering a horse to Hazens."

"I vaguely remember seeing a guy with a cowboy hat at the counter, but it's not that unusual, you know, and we were awful busy right about then. Jeez! How'd you hook up with him?"

"He remembered me from Nanaimo. I guess I should say, we remembered each other."

"Oh, he's a friend from home?"

"Not friends. I never even talked to him before. He was just ... well, you're going to think it's dumb. It was when I was working at The Highwayman. He was only in the pub for a few minutes, but we, well, we sort of made a connection."

"But you never spoke to each other? Just looked? Like your eyes met across a crowded room?"

"See? I told you you'd think it was dumb!"

"No, not dumb. It's nice! Romantic."

Just then, Franny looks over Astrid's head and out the window where a truck loaded with hay and towing a horse trailer is slowing, its turn signal on.

"I think that must be him, Astrid," Franny nods toward the parking lot before hurrying off.

In a few minutes, Astrid sees Denver come along the sidewalk and up the steps, then push through the door. He stands just inside as he scans the room. When he looks her way, she gives a little wave. He's smiling as he comes and slides into the booth across the table from her.

"Good morning," he says, fixing her with sparkling blue eyes.

"Good morning."

"Sorry I'm late. I wanted to leave before anyone got up, but Mrs. Hazen was in the kitchen when I came out and insisted on giving me coffee."

"It's okay, you're not late, really, I'm only on my second cup. And I got your text."

"Well, I'm sorry, anyway. I would a-hundred times sooner've been here having coffee with you."

Franny appears at their booth again, this time with a menu and a mug for Denver, which she puts in front of him and fills with fresh coffee. "Good morning. You must be Denver. I'm Franny."

"Nice to meet you, Franny," Denver says.

"Astrid always has two poached eggs on multi-grain, but I imagine you'd like a minute to look at the menu and see what you fancy?"

"I dunno, maybe just tell me,"— he gives them each a smile— "what's good here?"

"Everything. I recommend the Chokerman's Breakfast if you've got a big enough appetite," Astrid tells him. "Probably won't have to eat again until tonight."

"Chokerman's Breakfast it is, then."

"How do you want your eggs?"

"Over easy, please."

"Over easy it is!" Franny nods, picks up the menu and scurries off.

"So. For some reason I half expected you to show up at Hazen's last night."

"Oh… I suppose you heard what Hank said as he was leaving the diner. I guess everyone in the place heard it. Grrr! He says stuff like that so often, people are actually starting to believe we're boyfriend/girlfriend. Just to be clear, we're not. I have my own place, and I only see him when he comes in here."

"Lucky for me," Denver says. He reaches across the table and gives Astrid's hand a rub. "Still, I wasn't sure you'd be here."

"Oh!" Astrid feels heat rising and knows her cheeks must be turning pink. "Well… I… why wouldn't I be here?"

Denver shrugs. "I don't know. Maybe you'd think, what a cheap bastard! And maybe you agreed to meet me just to be nice."

"Well, it wouldn't be very nice to agree and then not show up, would it?"

"Still. Coffee or breakfast? Can't get much cheaper than that! The guy must really be a flake."

"It's fine. Nice, actually."

"Now you really *are* just being nice! I'd love to take you for supper, but I planned to drive up, drop the horse off, and go right back. It's a long drive, and the AGM of the Nicola Valley Cattleman's Association is tonight. I'm the Department of Agriculture liaison, so I have to be there. Otherwise, I'd cancel."

"I know you have horses—you have cattle too?"

"It's a big ranch. An old ranch. An old herd. The land's semi-arid, really not suited for anything but grazing. Even at that it takes about twenty acres a head. We raise some hay where the land's flat enough, but we can only do that because it's irrigated. The rest is more or less like it's been for a thousand years. Inhospitable for most creatures. As you might imagine, since it's named Rattlesnake Ridge."

"Have you lived there long?"

"All my life. What about you? What're you doing in Dark River? It seems like a big change, to leave Nanaimo and come so far north."

"Well, there was nothing keeping me there. Like I said yesterday, I didn't plan to stay in Dark River. I was headed further north, Prince George, maybe even Smithers, but I stopped for something to eat here. There was a help wanted sign in the window, I asked about it, they hired me, and here I am."

"You still going to move on? Or is this stop permanent?"

"No, not permanent. When my hours get cut here, which they've already told me will happen when the tourist season's over and the mill shuts down, I won't make enough to cover my rent. If I can't find another part time job, I'll have to go somewhere else. I don't know where, though." She fusses with her cutlery, takes a drink of her coffee, then says, "Talk about a flake! To someone like you, so settled in your life, I must sound like a lost cause."

"Hmm," he shrugs, "no, not a lost cause. Maybe just footloose and fancy free."

"Oh yeah, that's me, footloose and fancy free. Well, footloose anyway."

"I don't know what else I'd do, or where I'd go, either, but I do sometimes think about leaving the ranch." He settles back against the upholstery with an odd expression, looks out the window for a second, then looks back at her and says, "You know, I've never said that out loud before."

Franny comes back and sets their orders in front of them.

"That was quick," Denver says, "thanks."

"Everyone who comes in here is on their way to somewhere else," she tells him, "so, we try to get 'em on their way as quick as possible. Secret of our success."

"Seems like a good plan. Plus, really? This is enough for two."

"Better tuck in!" Franny says with a smile. "Eat what you can, and I'll put the rest in a box for you." She gives Astrid a wink, and scurries away.

Denver spears one of the sausages with his fork, cuts off a section and puts it in his mouth. As he chews, he looks at his watch, then swallows and says, "I'm sorry, I hate to rush through breakfast, but I really do have to get on the road."

Astrid dumps her eggs on her toast, cuts into them so the yokes drool out, and slices off a bite-sized piece. "Well, if you have time to eat your breakfast, I'll overlook it if you fill your face while I'm talking at you!"

He laughs, but takes her at her word, and attacks his food while she tells him little things about her life, like the big dog she had as a child. They chuckle together when she tells how often she fell out of bed because of him. "Rinny started sleeping with me when he was a tiny puppy, but in a few months, he weighed more than I did. My bed was so small, he took up most of it. He'd squirm around and off I'd go."

She asks him questions he can answer in a few words. Very soon, Denver has done his meal justice, puts down his fork and when Franny returns to ask if they'll be anything else, he says, "No, thanks, just the bill." She has it ready and puts it on the table.

Denver says, "Much as I hate to say it, I have to roll. I'll pay and then hit the can. If you don't mind waiting, would you walk me to my truck?"

Astrid nods and they both slide out of the booth. Astrid goes outside to wait. When Denver comes out, he takes her hand and they make their way to his truck, parked among the big rigs in the back lot. He swings the driver's door open before turning to her and saying, "Thank you, Astrid."

"Oh! Thank me? Well, you're welcome I guess, but I should thank you, for breakfast."

"I know it wasn't much of a date, bein' so short, but I'd have to say short and sweet. Can I call you?"

"Umm. Yeah, of course. You have my number. But… I mean, don't take this wrong, but, umm, you live so far away."

"Well, I come up here once in a while."

"You do?"

"No, I don't," he admits, "but I will. If you say I can see you again, I will."

"Okay."

"Okay?"

"Yes. Okay." She feels a stirring deep inside and can't maintain eye contact; she drops her chin and studies her feet, looking up under her lashes.

"I'll leave here a happy man if you give me just one kiss," he says softly, tugging on her hand. She moves close and their lips meet; gently, softly. He puts his hands on her hips and pulls her, unresisting, against him for another, lengthy kiss as she slips her arms around his waist.

A Kenworth with a Euclid on the flat deck pulls into the lot; the driver gives a treble blast on the air horn and hoots out the open window. Astrid jumps away.

"Aww, that was awful nice!" Denver breathes. "I wish that yahoo never came along, but if he hadn't, I might still be kissin' you tonight! And I really do need to get on the road." He climbs into the driver's seat and closes the door. He fastens his seat belt as he starts the engine, then powers the window down and says, "I'm a happy man! I'll call you." He coaxes the shifter into gear, gives her one last toothpaste-ad grin, and pulls away.

Astrid clasps her hands, lacing her fingers together, and brings them to her mouth. Forefingers on her lips, she watches the truck and trailer pull out of the lot and turn onto the street. She's still watching when it turns onto the main thoroughfare. Then she drops her hands, takes a deep breath and says "Wow!"

EIGHT

Astrid's in the barn. Since she's been living at the Double H, she's helped around the barn a little, tidying and sweeping mostly. She has extra time today, so she'll work in the tack room and even clean tack, starting with Hank Senior's saddle. It will be a nice surprise for him when he gets back from his business trip, a little thank you for letting her live at the ranch in exchange for helping Mrs. Hazen—Bridey, call me Bridey—and sometimes doing the morning feed. Hank Senior doesn't want her doing more barn chores than that. Not that she'd mind mucking out stalls; she isn't bothered by the manure, but he worries that because she's not horse savvy, she might get hurt.

Hank Senior and Hank Junior. Of course, they don't call themselves that, just Hank and Junior. Or sometimes Hank Junior refers to his father as Senior. But she can't bring herself to refer to them that way, even though Junior is Hank Junior's actual middle name. Henry Junior Hazen. It's a cumbersome name, and confusing. She vows that when she has a baby, she won't name her Astrid. Who would want to be called Astrid anyway? Can't even shorten it to something cute. Then she reminds herself it's very unlikely she'll ever be a mother, since people have their babies in their twenties. Or at least before they're her age. And she doesn't even have a boyfriend. A huge change would have to happen in her life, soon, too, for her to have a baby. It's probably not in the cards for her. She tells herself to quit thinking about it.

She refocuses her attention on gathering up bridles to be cleaned and hangs them on hooks over the sink. It's just as well they don't want her to do more barn chores, because Fletch needs the work, especially during the mill shut-down. So, her only task is to give the horses in the barn their morning feed. It's not much of a chore, since Fletch leaves each horse's allotment in front of its stall the night before, and she just shoves it in the feed door as she passes through the barn to start her morning run. The horses always nicker to her. She likes that.

Now that she lives here, she sees Fletch every day. She still isn't comfortable with him, even though she now knows why he always has his hand under the table when she's serving him at Dot's. It's deformed, and he hides it: in his pocket, in his jacket, behind his back and of course, under the table. Birth defect, Bridey said. It's not really all that noticeable, just a little crooked and with fingers smaller than they should be, that he can't straighten. But he's self-conscious about it. So, she feels empathy for him. And the animals all like him, that's in his favour. Still, it's creepy how he materializes out of nowhere when she least expects it, never saying more than two words, just staring.

She sweeps the tack room, then fills the sink with warm water, and gets the little tote with the saddle soap, leather balm, and sponge off the shelf. There's special polish for the silver conchos. She'll use it on the bits, too, careful not to get it on the part that goes in the horse's mouth.

She pulls the saddle rack with Hank Senior's saddle on it to the sink and sets to work. Smells of saddle soap and leather are pleasant. The leather balm smells good, too, and moisturizes her hands at the same time. Overall, the whole barn experience is pleasant.

There are many nice things about living on the ranch, but there are drawbacks, too, the main one being the long commute for her two or three shifts a week at Dot's. And not having her own place is taking some getting used to. But her room is in the lower level of the massive log house, opening off a short hall from the family room. There's a bathroom next to it, and in the family room, a TV bigger and much better than her old one, with cable even. Only Hank Junior spends any time there, and he's not around much. She comes and goes using the basement door, so she doesn't disturb Mr. Hazen and Bridey by going through the house. The realization comes to her she's like one of those thirty-somethings moving back into their mothers' basements. The Boomerang Generation!

When Hank Junior suggested the arrangement, she thought it was charity, following as it did on the heels of her hours at the diner being cut. Then she met Mrs. Hazen. Bridey. Bridey was always a dynamo, Hank Junior told her, but her multiple sclerosis has taken a toll. It's better than it was, though, as for a time, she was wheelchair-bound. The disease ebbs and flows. There's no telling how long her current good health will last. So, Astrid is needed here. It's a godsend for Mrs. Hazen, and a life saver for her. She'll miss Bridey when she has the money saved to move on.

She can't help but wonder if she'll have to move on sooner rather than later. Both Hanks left yesterday. They're meeting with a land agent in Edmonton. They haven't said much, other than some billionaire is buying land, they're talking, and any deal would have to allow the Hazens to stay on as ranch and mill managers. It would just be an injection of capital, so the Double H can make equipment and infrastructure upgrades. Besides adding to the pavement and constructing a new covered area at the mill, Hank Junior wants to build an indoor riding ring next to the barn here, so he can keep training horses over winter.

Hank Senior isn't sold on the idea. He thinks the mill is all right as it is and doesn't like the prospect of signing away the property to get a covered riding arena that would see so little use, with just the two of them riding in it. Or three, once Astrid gets going, he said with a wink at her. She can almost hear Hank Junior arguing it's like a loan, but with no payments; it doesn't make sense to worry about the title changing hands when they die, and without being able to ride here, he'll have to take horses south to train because if he takes the winters off, they'll never be serious contenders for the big money to be made on the cutting horse circuit. In his view, it's an investment. Besides, why did they buy Rocky Duster if not to breed competitive horses? Did they need an expensive cutting horse stud for the old man to go trail riding a couple times a week?

From the chill that's pervaded mealtimes ever since she arrived, Astrid surmises the arguments go on more often than just in her hearing. And now they're off to meet with the investor despite Hank Senior's misgivings. She supposes it makes sense to hear what they might have to offer.

They'll only be gone a few days, but she's glad to have Hank Junior and his grabby hands gone. It's a nice break, even though he's really only around during the day. Most evenings, he's gone. He says he works out at a gym and spends time with his buddies in Prince George. Won't admit he has a girlfriend. Keeping his cards close to his chest, he told Bridey when she teased him about it. Don't worry, Bridey, he told her, when I find the right one, I'll bring her home to meet you.

But why does he always go to Prince George? Surely these buddies of his would be just as happy staying closer to home, and there are bars, even places to dance, in Dark River. Astrid's gone to the one called Nashville North with Franny and her husband a couple of times. Lots of the girls were pretty. With his looks and charm, Hank Junior could have his pick even if he wasn't known to be the heir apparent to the biggest employer in town, yet he always goes to Prince George instead, making it really late when he comes in, if he comes home at all.

Then it occurs to her: maybe he goes to gay bars! That's something he wouldn't want the locals knowing about! He's got the looks, she'll give him that. He's not tall, maybe five foot nine, and like a lot of short men, he's well built. Compact. Muscular. Powerful-looking and masculine. But rather than handsome, she thinks pretty describes him. Fine features, clear, fair complexion, finely drawn dark brows, long dark lashes, rosy lips. He has a way of making a woman feel as if she's the center of the universe, desirable and sexy. They melt when he turns his big brown eyes on them. She's seen it often, and it happened to her! But guys? She's never seen any interaction between him and another guy that would lead her to think ...

Then she tells herself: *you're nuts, Astrid. He's as straight as they come, an aggressive alpha male.* Around here, they'd call him a man's man, and maybe it's just her West Coast liberal mind set that makes it impossible for her to overlook his attitude toward women.

But besides the conversation she overheard on her first day at Dot's, there are constant other misogynistic comments. Bitching about equal pay for the "Lesbos" that work in the yard. Maternity leave. The office "gals" that are always, in his view, either in heat or on the rag. Maybe he's not sensitive enough and she's too sensitive, but when she wonders if she should dismiss those kinds of remarks because he doesn't really mean them, she reminds herself he *does* mean them. It's who he is.

Anyway, since she met Denver she hasn't given Hank as a boyfriend any thought, something she's tried to make clear to Hank, yet he's still always grabbing her, slapping her butt, pulling her into awkward hugs— too familiar and a nuisance. She grits her teeth and tells herself it's just teasing. If she makes an issue of it, will she lose this job? Which is more than just a job, but a nice place to live besides?

It's satisfying in a primal way to live on the ranch. It's so different from life in the city. Quiet. Skies full of stars. And the animals! Cats appear when least expected. Two are friendly enough to pet, especially when they gather around the feed room waiting for their daily dole of kibble, but the other three, all that she's seen so far anyway, are wild.

There are three Pygmy goats, a nuisance, impossible to keep in the pasture, running all over the place and climbing everything, including the cars. They do look cute bouncing in and out of the Gator, though! They're friendly and like to be petted, too, but petting them leaves her hands stinking of goat. Also, they head butt, so caution is needed.

Maybe even better than the horses, there's the big Newfoundland dog, Buster. He reminds her of her childhood pet, Rinny. Maybe that's why they connected from day one. When she's outside, he's with her.

There's also the sight, sound and smell of cattle, out in open range since spring, now in the home pasture. Hank calls it a small herd. To Astrid, it looks like hundreds. Mixed in with the cattle are the horses. There are a lot fewer of them; Hank says twenty or so, brood mares and youngsters not old enough to be ridden. There are shelters, the loafing barns, they can go in at will.

Four horses live in the main barn: two young ones in training, the big gelding Hank Junior rides out around the ranch, and Rocky Duster, the stallion Hazens bought from Denver. Breeding season is in the spring, so Rocky won't join the mares until March. In the meantime, he's got the stall nearest the tack room, with the biggest adjoining corral.

Hank Senior rides Rocky a few times a week, either in the riding ring or out on trails, even over to the mill. He's not really into cutting horses. That's Junior's thing. Hank Senior does like to ride out in the herd to chase cows, though. He says he does it to remind Rocky he's a cow horse. Bridey says the real reason is that her husband likes to play cowboy.

Even from the tack room, she can hear the horses munching their hay, moving in their stalls, occasionally blowing softly, even their funny grunting as they poop and pee. It's peaceful. Buster is up on the couch, asleep. Astrid's humming as she works and sings snatches of songs she remembers her mother singing. She suddenly becomes aware of it, and wonders when she last felt like singing.

A big part of the reason for her high spirits is that Denver's coming Sunday. She lets her mind slideshow their brief time together the day after he delivered Rocky. That breakfast at Dot's. But mostly, that kiss! That sweet, soft, kiss, huddled in the shelter of the open door to his truck. As with all the times she's thought about it since, the memory is stirring. Not a boyfriend, not yet, but—? He's educated, well-spoken and has nice manners and gentle ways. They have similar views on religion and politics. He's even tall! From what she's knows of him so far, he's everything she looks for in a man.

She pushes the saddle rack back, returns to the cupboard, and is bending over to organize things on the bottom shelf when she hears Buster's tail thumping. She glances up to see he's raised his head. The back of her neck prickles with the "someone's watching" sensation. She tells herself it can't possibly be Fletch. She would have heard him. Still, she can't stop herself from turning.

He's standing a few feet behind her, his heavy brows drawn together, those piercing black eyes unblinking.

"Fletch! You startled me!" Realizing she'd been bent over at the waist and he must have had a fine view of her ass, she feels blood rushing to her face.

"Sorry," he says, and goes to the fridge to get a can of Coke. Holding it in his twisted hand, he uses his good hand to pop the snap top, and drinks nearly half at a go. Then, with a nod in her direction, he leaves, his heavy boots somehow silent as he heads down the alleyway and out the back. His ATV starts, revs a couple of times, then roars away.

As always happens when he creeps up on her, a chill courses through her and she shivers. A goose walked on your grave, her mother would've said.

NINE

Astrid opens the Zero Clearance refrigerator and re-arranges contents until she finds the jar of mayonnaise. She puts it on the island next to Bridey, who's perched on a stool, shredding cabbage for coleslaw. "How much longer for the roast, do you think?"

"What's it at? A hundred 'n' thirty-five degrees? Not much longer. The thermometer will sound when it reaches a hundred and forty-five, and it can come out. It'll come up another ten degrees and be just perfect." Bridey scoops a dollop of mayonnaise onto the mound of shredded cabbage in the bowl in front of her. "You say you never made Yorkshires before?"

"Not that you'd recognize them," Astrid grins. "My mother and I both tried many, many times, but they almost never turned out. Tasted good, but never rose. We called them Yorkshire pucks."

"Well, this is my mother's recipe. She was a war bride, and you know the English and their roast beef and Yorkshire puddings! They turn out every time. You'll see. So. Equal parts egg, milk and flour is key. You've already got the eggs and milk whisked together and waiting on the counter. Was it a cup of each?"

"Pretty close."

"Okay. I think it's been twenty minutes. Whisk in a cup of flour, just until the lumps are gone. And then leave it on the counter again. It should sit there another ten or twenty minutes."

Astrid gets the flour bin from the pantry, measures out a cup, and whisks it into the egg-milk mixture as instructed.

"My mother would've loved a recipe with guaranteed results," she says.

"We haven't talked about your family, Astrid. I should've asked you before. Your mother's passed?"

Astrid feels her throat tighten and can't do more than nod.

"I'm sorry. She must not have been very old. What about your father?" Bridey asks quietly.

Astrid shakes her head.

"Brothers? Sisters?"

"No." Astrid's voice breaks. She goes to the cutlery drawer, gets knives and forks, and takes them to the dining room table. Once back in the kitchen, she asks, "So, what's the oven temperature for the yorkies?"

"Four hundred and fifty degrees. Don't wait for the meat to come out, heat the other oven instead. Get the muffin tin from the rack in the bottom cupboard beside the fridge. That's right. Then, just enough oil to cover the bottom of each cup. Oil's in the pantry. And into the oven for five minutes. Only five! Then pull it out and pour batter into each well, quickly return it to the oven and set the timer for twenty-five minutes. If they're starting to show a little black, they're ready to come out. Not before. And don't open the oven until then!"

When the Yorkshires go in the oven, the potatoes are ready to be mashed, so Astrid drains them, saving the water for gravy per Bridey's instructions, and gets to work with the masher.

When the meat thermometer sounds, she opens the oven. Steamy heat pours out along with the tantalizing aroma. She dons oven mitts, pulls out the roaster, removes the roast and sets it on the carving board, covering it with a tent of aluminum foil to rest, and sets the roaster back on the stove, ready to make gravy.

There's a clatter at the back door and the two men come in. Hank Junior sidles into the kitchen, passing too close behind Astrid, casually giving her ass a squeeze. "Stop it," she says, and squirms away, giving him a look; as always, he just grins and winks. Bridey focuses her attention on stirring her salad and pretends not to notice, but her amused grin gives her away.

Hank Junior goes to the cutting board, lifts the foil from the roast and works a piece of meat loose, then chomps it, licking his fingers, smacking loudly.

"Get your dirty meat hooks outta there, Junior!" Bridey chides, still grinning. "Go wash up and then come and carve the roast."

Hank Senior comes to his wife, bends and kisses her temple. They squeeze hands briefly. "Have I got time for a quick shower?" he asks.

"Yes. Just as long as it really is quick. Supper'll be on the table in a few minutes."

"Senior can carve the roast," Hank Junior says, "I need a shower worse'n he does." He heads off down the hall to his room.

Hank Senior shrugs, goes to the sink to wash his hands, then sets about carving the roast.

When the meat, potatoes, coleslaw and herbed carrots are on the table, and the Hazens are seated around it, Astrid sets the basket of beautifully browned, hollow, softball-sized Yorkshires in the middle, then sits.

"Well, lookit that!" Hank Senior says as he spears a Yorkshire and pours gravy on it. "What a nice meal you gals made! You really put yourselves out."

"We wanted to make a nice home cooked meal for your first Saturday back," Bridey says. "No big deal, thanks to Astrid's help."

"Well, I can't take any credit." Astrid's beaming nonetheless.

"Don't be so modest, Astrid," Bridey says.

"She's a keeper," Hank Junior says as he grabs two Yorkshires, reaches across in front of Bridey for the gravy boat, and douses everything on his plate. "Empty," he says, waving the gravy boat at Astrid.

She feels a stirring of annoyance. Couldn't he let Bridey have the gravy before using it all? But Bridey doesn't seem to mind, so why does it get her back up? She gets to her feet and takes the gravy boat into the kitchen to refill it. When she returns, she sets it next to Bridey.

"I ran into Bev and Walter at the Co-Op this morning, Bridey," Hank Senior says as he loads carrots, potatoes and gravy onto his fork. "They want to have us over for a meal and some cards before they head south for the winter. Bev asked how you're doing. I told them Astrid's here helpin' you out. I couldn't tell them your last name, Astrid. I've heard it a few times, but just don't quite git a handle on it."

"Ingebritson," she tells him. "Inga.brit.son. Ingebritson."

"Unusual name."

"Norwegian," she says, feeling heat creeping up her neck. When the question of whether she's related to Senator Ingebritson doesn't follow, she breathes a sigh of relief.

"So, you eat those fish they cure with lye?" He smiles, deepening the crinkles at the corners of his eyes as well as his tiny dimples, his dark brown eyes warm.

Astrid returns the smile. For the first time, she sees a resemblance to Hank Junior. He's a bigger, older version, still in good shape for his age. And both Hanks have the same mesmerizing eyes. "Umm… Er…" she stutters, then says, "Lutefisk, yukkk! No. My mother was German, so it was meat, meat, meat, *spätzle* and *Knödel*. Knödel's dumplings. Bread dumplings were my favourite. The only Norwegian dish we had was lefse, which she made for my father. I liked it, although according to my father, it was never as good as what his mother made."

"What's spetezilla? Lefsah?"

"Spätzle is just noodles, really, usually fried in butter. And lefse is like a wrap made with potatoes and flour."

"Well, the spätzle and lefse sound good. Not so sure about bread dumplings."

"They're better than they sound, a good way to use up stale bread and a great way to eat gravy,"—Astrid gives Hank Junior a look— "so you'd love them, *Junior*. Spätzle is an everyday dish, but lefse's kind of a big project. We always made it around Christmas time. I love it buttered, with turkey rolled up inside."

"Well, let's make some this Christmas!" Bridey gives Astrid such a warm smile Astrid says, "Let's!" She doesn't add, "if I'm still here."

Once they finish eating, Hank Junior wastes no time leaving. From the window over the sink, Astrid sees his Chevy Silverado stop at the top of the driveway, its V-8 engine chortling as he waits for a passing car, then roaring as he pulls out onto the highway and accelerates away. Hank Senior goes for his shower, leaving Astrid and Bridey clearing up the kitchen.

"Junior didn't say where he was going, did he?" Bridey asks. She slides up onto a stool at the island and starts scraping leftover coleslaw into a container.

"No, but I think he had his gym bag with him."

"He sure goes to the gym a lot. He could tell us that's where he's going, though. You might want to go with him sometime."

"Umm, no, it's fine, I don't want to go. He's offered to take me, but I've tried gym workouts before. Not for me." Astrid opens one of the dishwashers and starts loading cutlery.

Bridey sighs. "I guess I shouldn't expect him to tell me where he's going. He could live somewhere else and we wouldn't know, after all. Could you get me a couple more containers, please?"

"It's none of my business, but why doesn't he? Live somewhere else, I mean? Most kids can't wait to get out on their own."

"Him too. He lived in the Lower Mainland for a few years, you know young people, nothing going on around here, this is Hicksville, can't work for the old man, he rides him too hard. Blah blah. Typical! Then when he was ready to come and work with his dad, it seemed pointless for him to pay rent in town, with just the two of us in this big house and the mill practically right across the road. And the horses he trains are here of course. With his room at the opposite end of the house from ours, we barely know he's there; he comes and goes as he likes. We never hear him come in."

"You don't hear his truck?"

"Well, with our room on the back of the house, and if I'm laying on my good ear and Hank has his hearing aids out, we could probably sleep through a tornado."

"Mmm, well, his room's right above mine. Sometimes I hear him thumping around up there."

"It wakes you?"

"Sometimes." Astrid shrugs. "It's not his fault. I'm a light sleeper."

"Well, I'll tell him to be quieter! He should take his boots off at the door."

"It's no big deal," Astrid tells her. She gets leftover containers out of the cabinet, puts them on the island next to Bridey, and returns to loading the dishwasher.

"I'm going to talk to him about it. He shouldn't come tromping through the house with his boots on anyway. Hank always takes his off, Junior can too. I don't know why I have to keep after him about it! But boys will be boys. They don't see the dirty floors." She clicks her tongue, and snaps the lid down on the Tupperware she put the coleslaw in. "I want to send these leftovers to Fletch, Astrid. Wrap up a few nice slices of beef, and you can take them to him while I finish clearing up."

Astrid stops loading the dishwasher, straightens, and looks at Bridey.

"What is it?" Bridey asks, "something wrong?"

"It's just—I really would rather not go over there now. You know, alone. It's getting late. And, well, Fletch gives me the heebie-jeebies."

"Oh. I see."

"It's stupid, I know …"

"No, I'm used to him but if I hadn't known him all his life, I might feel the same. Claire felt like that too. More than that, she really didn't like him and she sure never made a secret of it."

"Claire?"

"Yes, Claire. She had your job. Left last year."

"Oh really! Hank's never mentioned her. Why'd she quit?"

"No, she …"

"Don't tell me! Lemme guess," Astrid grins, "she married a cowboy, moved to his ranch and now all her troubles are little ones!"

Bridey laughs. "That's an old one!"

"From my mother. A comment in her high school yearbook."

"Ahhh! And is that what you're hoping for?"

Astrid shrugs. "I thought so. Now I don't know." She thinks of how Bridey and Hank Senior look at each other and still hold hands after forty years. "The way you and Mr. Hazen are, yes, I'd like that. But I think all the good ones got snapped up in their twenties and all that's left is the dregs." Then she blushes, remembering too late that Bridey's only son would be in the 'dregs' category. "I don't mean Hank Junior, of course …"

"Oh, don't worry, I know Junior's not perfect," Bridey says. "Far from it. It's okay you're just friends. But some of those guys that married young are probably divorced by now."

"I don't know, I've thought about that too. Maybe a good idea to get a 'previously enjoyed' husband, one that's already trained! But then I wonder if it isn't too much like my second-hand car—I'd just be taking over someone else's problem."

"Well, there's that. But that Denver fella that's coming tomorrow seems a decent sort. And getting hay isn't his only reason for coming all this way. He could've had it shipped for less than the cost to make what, three? More?

trips with his big, gas-guzzling truck, you know. In fact, I believe he was planning on having it shipped, except of course when he brought the horse up, it didn't make sense to haul back empty. Then for some reason, who knows what," Bridey grins as she catches Astrid's eye, "he changed his mind."

Astrid can't deny she hopes Bridey's right. She feels her cheeks warming and she's embarrassed. To change the subject, she says, "So, you were talking about Claire?"

"Fletch'll have to microwave this." She scrapes gravy out of the roaster and onto the Yorkshires in the Tupperware container. "But Claire. Well, we thought she and Junior would get together. They seemed to be getting on well. I mean, they never let on, but they were, er, a *couple*, but we knew. Hard not to notice such things when you all live in the same house, even one this big!" She colours a bit, then heaves a sigh. "I don't know why they didn't just admit it. I liked her. She was like a daughter. I miss her."

"I'm sorry. Did you want another child? A daughter?"

"We had a daughter."

"Oh?"

Bridey bites her lower lip, brow furrowed, before continuing. "She drowned. In the river at the bottom of the horse pasture."

"Oh, my god! How awful!"

"It's the most awful thing imaginable," she says quietly; then sighs, "but it was decades ago. Little Heather. She was just five years old. I almost don't remember what she looked like." She heaves another sigh. "Junior says I should leave it in the past, where it belongs. Hank says it's not healthy for a person to grieve so long. They're probably right." She gets up, clutches her cane and hurries off to the bathroom.

Astrid is flooded with sadness, imagining what it would be like to lose a child. Much worse than an abortion, a child born and loved for five years! She wonders if it's even possible for a childless person to comprehend. She fights off tears as she busies herself around the kitchen, trying to think of what to say when Bridey returns.

She's saved making a decision on that score, though; when Bridey returns, she picks up the conversation as if little Heather hadn't been mentioned. "Hank and I had gone to Vegas and Claire wasn't here when we got back. Didn't even leave me a note. Junior said she'd told him she was heading to Prince Rupert to meet up with friends who had a sailboat, planning to spend a few years sailing around the world. I was sure they must've had a spat for her to just run off like that. But Junior said they'd parted on good terms, it was just that the boat was only in Rupert for an overnight and she had to leave in a hurry or miss out. They'd agreed between them that we'd store her things, and she asked him to say good-bye for her, since she'd be out of cellphone range. Junior wasn't as bothered about it as I was. He claimed he was okay waiting for her to come back. He said if you love something, set it free."

"If it comes back it's yours, if it doesn't, it never was."

"That's it. I never thought I'd hear anything like that coming from him. He's always been so serious and, er, *detached*. Anyway, we packed up her things and Junior put them away somewhere. I haven't heard him mention her since, and no other girlfriend's been in the picture. I guess he's just not ready to settle down."

"Or maybe he really *is* waiting for Claire. But how could she run off to be on a sailboat for years? Trade thousands of acres of rain forest for a few square feet of cork bobbing out in the middle of the ocean? Talk about a change of scenery! I'd be throwing myself overboard by the third day!" She takes the roaster from Bridey and puts it in the largest section of the triple sink.

"Oh, don't wash that!" Bridey says. "Scrape the plates into it and put it on the stoop for Buster. He'll lick it so clean we won't have to wash it!"

They both chuckle; then Bridey's shoulders droop, and the humour slides from her face. "I still don't understand why she never said anything to me about leaving." She straightens, takes a deep breath, and looks up at Astrid, mustering a smile. "I'll go with you to Fletch's. We'll take the Gator, and go through the bush. Ready?"

"I'll go get the Gator."

Astrid goes out to the equipment shed. She's already had driving lessons on all the ranch vehicles (the main thing is knowing where to look for the keys), including the pick-up with the stick shift, but has only driven the Gator (having no visor or floormats, the key is under the seat) a few times. She's getting comfortable with it, although every time she gets behind the wheel she mentally curses the designers for the lack of leg room. "Built for no one with an inseam longer than thirty-two inches," she mutters. She checks to be sure it's in neutral, presses the brake to the floor and turns the key. It coughs, grumbles a bit, then starts. She releases the e-brake and drives to where Bridey's waiting on the sidewalk. Astrid takes the box with the food and stows in in the back. When Bridey's settled in the passenger seat, they start off. Buster, huge tongue lolling, runs happily ahead as Astrid drives the Gator down past the barn and into the wide alleyway separating the individual paddocks from the home pasture.

It's nearing sunset and the large swath of cleared land that is the pasture is preternaturally still. The wind that blew steadily all day has died. There are wisps of mist rising in the far distance, marking the location of the river. The horses and cattle are quiet, except for the lowing of some of the cows and the occasional relaxed blowing of horses as they pull hay off the big round bale in the feeder, or nibble at the short grass nearby. Everything's tinged with rose-grey highlights of fading daylight. Passing so close overhead they can hear the swishing of its wings, a raven yells *Hawk! Hawk!* as it returns to the forest to roost for the night.

"Man, that startled me!" Astrid says. "What a big crow!"

"It was actually a raven, not a crow."

"Oh! How can you tell?"

"Well, ravens are much bigger than crows, the size of a tall, skinny chicken, although you might not realize how much bigger they are unless you see them side by side. Course they're seldom side by side. The saying goes, if you see one, it's a raven. If you see a bunch, it's crows. But you can't always go by that." Bridey steadies herself by holding the grab bar with both hands as the Gator lurches over the rough spots.

"Funny, when Junior was little, he used to yell back at them. 'You're not a hawk! You're a raven!' He'd throw rocks at them. Never came near to hitting one, of course. His dad and I'd laugh and he'd scowl. He was such a serious little man." She bites her lower lip. "You know, I haven't thought about him yelling at the ravens for a long time. Now he's older than we were then, yet it seems like yesterday."

They've reached the end of the alleyway and Astrid slows the Gator to navigate a particularly rough section leading into the gloom of the forest.

"You like mushrooms?" Bridey asks.

"Love them. Why?"

"There's a couple of really good chanterelle patches in through here. Just about the season for them. If we get some rain, it'll bring them on and we'll come and look. I'd love a feast, and it would be nice to get some in the freezer."

"Chanterelles? I've never heard of them."

Bridey's dark eyebrows rise and then she chuckles. "I keep forgetting you're a city kid! Chanterelles are easy to identify, nice yellow mushrooms. When they're in season, you'll see signs all over the place for mushroom buyers. Fletch picks and sells them, but he always brings us some, too. This year, with you here, we'll get our own again! I love going out in the woods, but of course, I can't go alone, and neither Junior nor Hank will take me. Claire didn't like it, either. She was happy with what Fletch brought. They're so good! In butter sauce, with onions and parsley? To die for! Okay, Fletch's place is just to the left up ahead."

Buster has run ahead and as Astrid steers the Gator around rusting machinery and into the small clearing surrounding the trailer, cats go scurrying in all directions. The bolder ones remain perched on boxes and discarded furniture under the deck, eyeing the dog, and the human visitors, warily.

"Hank said Fletch had a lot of cats," Astrid remarks, "but I didn't imagine this many!"

"He's always loved cats, from the time he was little. I feed them when he's away. I'll have to get you to do it now."

"He goes away? You mean, he travels?"

"Well, not like vacations. He works outside the country sometimes."

"Really? Doing what?"

"Security, whatever that means. Once, he worked for an American mining company in Venezuela or Columbia. Somewhere in South American, anyway. He was gone nearly a year that time. He's been to the Middle East a couple of times. Makes good money, and I guess it's a way to keep the wolf from the door. He works for us, too, of course, and as you can see, he doesn't have an expensive lifestyle. His big expense is feeding all these cats! He started taking care of them when he was maybe seven or eight. It's gross, but he and Junior used to collect road kill to feed them."

"Eww!"

"I know! Revolting! But boys will be boys, and when those two little 'troubles' were out with their wagon and shovels 'hunting' road kill, it kept them out of my hair for hours. And, Fletch loved the cats. Wouldn't see them go hungry. Needs must, I suppose. His parents were, you could say, not inclined to buy cat food. We took him some once but the next day, he came back with it, saying he couldn't accept it. That little boy, humping the twenty-pound bag of cat food all that way through the bush!" She makes a *tsk* sound and shakes her head. "He had bruises he said he got from tripping over something. Wasn't the first time he 'tripped over something'."

"Oh." Astrid says, letting the enormity of that sink in.

"To my everlasting shame, we turned a blind eye. It was thirty years ago. Back then, I suppose we thought it was none of our business how other people raised their kids." She shakes her head again. "Well, that was then. Wonder where he is. He usually comes out when he hears us drive in."

"Maybe he went with Junior."

"Maybe. But then his ATV would be here. It's usually parked beside his truck. He must be out in the bush, or more likely, down at the old gravel pit, shooting cans."

Fletch's pick-up is in the driveway by the steps leading up onto the deck. Astrid navigates around a discarded barbeque, pulls up next to the truck, turns the Gator off and sets the e-brake. Bridey makes to get out.

"You sit," Astrid tells her, "I'll go." She gets out of the driver's seat, takes the box and goes to the door to knock. After a few moments, she knocks again. Still no answer.

"Just go ahead and take it into the kitchen," Bridey calls out.

A painted metal sign screwed onto the door declares: "Nothing in this house is worth dying for." Astrid points to it, and calls back, "You sure it's okay?"

"God yes, it's okay, we're as good as family."

The door is unlocked. Astrid pushes it open, sticks her head in, and hollers: "Hello!" When there's no answer, she steps inside. The door opens directly into the kitchen; she goes in and sets the box on the counter.

There are a few plates and a mug drying on a rack in the sink, and a frying pan with congealed bacon fat on the stove, but otherwise the kitchen is clutter-free. It's open to a small dining area and the living room is just past that, visible through cut-outs in the dividing wall. Everything is tidy. Not at all what she expected.

She takes a few steps toward the living room, curious to see how Fletch lives. She knows she shouldn't go further, but the pull is strong. *Ignore it,* she tells herself, *how many times did Mom tell you being nosey would get you in trouble one day? That curiosity killed the cat? But it's not like I'm going into his bedroom or snooping through anything personal. I'll just have a quick look,* she promises the mental image of her mother, *no more than a minute.* She takes the last half dozen steps.

Furniture and carpet are worn but clean. There's a gun rack over the chesterfield, filled with rifles. Posters of various sizes depicting busty women in various states of undress plaster the walls. There's a large TV, the old projection type, with a VCR and Xbox connected to it. There's dust on the coffee table but the *Soldier of Fortune* and *Guns and Ammo* magazines are in a tidy stack. Nowhere is there an empty beer can or a dirty ashtray.

Bookshelves next to a gun safe at the far end of the room hold thick tomes: Jeep and Chevrolet S10 repair manuals. There are novels, too: Nelson DeMille, Stephen King, James Patterson. Stieg Larsson's *Millennium Trilogy*. A couple of the *Game of Thrones* books. Half a dozen Tom Clancy novels. Next to a shiny silver pistol on the end table, a paperback copy of *Rainbow Six* is folded open, worn enough to indicate it's a favourite. "Dumber than a bag of hammers, eh Hank?" she mutters.

And there are dozens of VHS movies, many of them home made, the obvious reason there's still a VCR. Odd for a single guy not to have the latest, biggest, brightest HD-est TV. Bridey said he makes good money. But obviously, buying cat food accounts for only a fraction of his spending. He's a gun nut. Probably has the latest, biggest, loudest shiniest guns in that locked gun safe. Smart enough to enjoy Tom Clancy, but a gun nut. *Ugg.*

Her attention is drawn to the poster on the dining room wall. The young blonde woman is wearing nothing; she's got her head thrown back and has an expression of ecstasy on her face. She's masturbating with a pistol.

Double ugg. A smart, sicko gun nut. No wonder he gives me the creeps.

Then she can almost hear her mother saying, *'You're snooping, Astrid!'* Her mother's right. Besides, Bridey must be wondering what's keeping her. She's about to turn when the back of her neck prickles. She stiffens and her guts clench. The last time she had that feeling, he was right behind her. She takes a deep breath and slowly turns.

But no one's there.

Then she notices a large black cat on top of the refrigerator watching her, ears flattened, eyes large with dilated pupils making them nearly completely black.

"How did I miss seeing *you* when I came in?" she mutters, and begins breathing normally again. She goes back to the kitchen, takes the box of food to the refrigerator and opens it. She shifts enough beer to make space, and stacks the containers next to a pizza box.

"Aren't you one mean-looking little Halloween cat," she says in what she hopes is a kitty-soothing voice, watching the cat warily in case it should launch. But it doesn't move a whisker or make a sound, just stares. She shuts the refrigerator, takes the now-empty box in one hand and scurries to exit the trailer.

When she's back in the Gator, she tells Bridey about the cat on the fridge. What she doesn't tell her is how much it reminded her of Fletch.

TEN

Astrid's tidying up the kitchen after starting a pot of chilli to go with the cornbread she made for the Hazens' supper, when Denver's truck, towing a flatdeck trailer, pulls into the driveway, passes the house and continues to the hay sheds by the barn before stopping. Denver gets out and looks up at the house. Wiping her hands on her jeans, she heads out the door. She's trotting across the yard when she sees his grin and realizes she must appear way too eager given they've only had one, very brief, date. She slows to what she hopes is a casual saunter.

"Hi," Astrid says. She stops, and shoves her hands into her front jean pockets.

"Hi," he responds, pushing away from the truck. "Why're you standin' way over there?"

She moves toward him, pulling her right hand out of her pocket and extending it as if for a handshake. He takes it, but with his left hand; pulls her to him and wraps both arms around her waist, pulling her close for a lengthy, fervent kiss.

He whispers, "I've been dreamin' of that for weeks."

"Ohhh!"

"Was that too much?"

She shakes her head.

"Well then, how 'bout you pull your other hand outta your pocket 'n' put both arms around me?" His voice is husky. She blushes, but reaches both arms up around his shoulders. He pulls her in tight and then they're kissing again until, breathless, they break apart.

"Well, that was worth the trip!" he breathes, stroking her back. Then he's looking over her shoulder, toward the barn. He gives her a squeeze before releasing her and calling out: "Hello?"

Astrid turns in time to see Fletch's back disappearing into the barn. "It's the neighbour," she tells Denver, and calls, "Come say hi, Fletch!" But he doesn't reappear. "Must not've heard me," she says.

"Mmm. Well, let's go see Rocky."

Astrid leads the way into the barn, where Fletch is in a stall, sifting manure out of the sawdust bedding and tossing it into the box of the Gator. He stops at their approach, drops his right hand to his side, and stands propping up the manure fork.

"Fletch," Astrid says, "You remember Denver? He used to own Rocky Duster."

Fletch nods but makes no move to come closer. Denver holds out his hand, and takes three steps into the stall toward him, saying, "How do, Fletch! Didn't meet you the last time I was here. Astrid tells me you've been takin' good care of my horse." He almost has to pick Fletch's hand up from his side before Fletch reaches out for the handshake. "I sure do appreciate it! Lord, how I miss that boy! The place just isn't the same without him."

"He's a good horse," Fletch says. "Always polite. Better manners than some of the mares and nice 'n' clean in his stall."

"Glad to hear it!" Denver comes out of the stall, turns back and says, "Well, I'm just gonna say hello to him, and then I'm the lucky guy that gets to take this lovely lady out for supper. Nice to meet you." He turns and follows Astrid toward Rocky's stall.

The horse in question has his head over the stall door and is looking their way. He bellows a whinny that reverberates through the building.

"I think he remembers me," Denver chuckles. "I'm not kiddin', I really miss the ol' bugger. Had him since he was born, you know." He goes to Rocky and rubs his forehead, slides the door open far enough to slip into the stall with him, and spends moments just stroking and talking to him in soft tones. Then he looks at Astrid, who's watching through the grate along the stall front, and says, "He looks terrific."

"Fletch likes him. As I told you, I see him in his stall grooming him, a lot."

"Well, it shows." He's stroking the horse's neck, running his hand along his back and rump. "Could you get me a brush?"

Astrid nods, ducks into the tack room, comes back with two dandy brushes and hands them over the door.

"Thanks."

"You know," Astrid begins, in barely more than a whisper, "I'm surprised at Fletch."

"What do you mean?"

"Well, I think it's the first time I've heard him speak in sentences."

"Oh? Really? Maybe he just doesn't know how to talk to women. Especially beautiful ones!" He sets to work using both brushes up and down Rocky's near foreleg, then looks up and says, "If you want to comb your hair or whatever ladies do before a date, I'll just be a few minutes. I'll unhitch the truck and come up to the house to say hello to everyone before we head out."

"Don't hurry. I need to change. But why don't we take my car?"

"It's okay, I need to gas up anyway, and it's simpler without the trailer. I'll be up shortly."

* * *

Denver is having difficulty focusing on driving, as he keeps glancing over at his passenger, wondering how she can be even prettier than he remembered. They chat amiably, renewing their acquaintance, adding detail to the basic facts of their lives as discussed in their brief time together weeks earlier and telephone conversations since then. She tells him she's running every morning, getting more fit so she's able to go further afield, and how peaceful and soul-satisfying it is, running the myriad trails through the forest.

"Hank Senior says the trails were already there when he bought the property all those years ago. He says they're ancient game trails, made bigger by the horses and cattle. I've seen deer often, but he says there's elk, moose, bears and even cougars. Thankfully, I've never seen any of those! Although he says they've probably seen me!" She chuckles nervously. "We've talked about what I should do if I come face to face with any of those. Mostly I just try to make enough noise that they hear me coming, and get out of my way!"

"Sure is a lot different than out on the open prairie, where I live," he says. "Although I guess we have elk and moose too. Not so many bears, mostly up in the more wooded areas. Biggest worry around our place is rattlers!"

"Oh! Are there lots?"

"Yeah, lots, I guess you'd expect that, with Rattlesnake Ridge Ranch bein' the name of the place. But they pretty much stay outta the way."

"Don't they bite your horses?"

"It happens, but not often. Last time I remember anything gettin' bitten was when I was still in high school. So, yeah, gotta be twenty years ago."

She's quiet for a moment, and he realizes he's just given her a good idea of how old he is. Is she doing the math? She looks so young! Younger than he remembered. *Will she think I'm too old for her? Am I too old for her?*

"Hank Junior's promised we'll take horses out on the trails, too," she tells him, without skipping a beat. "He says he'll ride one of the youngsters and let me ride his gelding. His horse is big, but he's gentle. I'm looking forward to it."

"Nice," Denver says.

"So, your ranch. Your whole family lives there?"

"Well, at one time or another. My mom died."

"Oh, I'm sorry."

"Yeah, thanks. It was sudden." He shakes his head. "Really hard on all of us, but Dad most of all. He's in a care home now. Still have my younger brother, Dallas, livin' on the ranch. And of course, my ex-wife, if you call that family. Had my own house on the ranch, but until she gets out of it, I'm back livin' in the big house. I'm so goddamn modern, moving back into Mom and Dad's. Least I'm not livin' in the basement!"

Astrid laughs. "Funny, I've been thinking lately that's what I'm doing! And I *am* in the basement! Of course, Hazens aren't my parents, but Bridey's such a mother type, she almost seems like it. Or more like an aunt, I guess."

"What about your family? Where are they?"

"My mom's passed away. I never see my father. And that's how I want it."

"Oh?"

"The turn's just up ahead," she says.

He pulls in to the Riverview Motor Inn parking lot and finds a spot near the entrance to the restaurant. He gets out and starts to go to her door when she comes around the front of the truck. He takes her hand and gives it a squeeze, liking the feeling of her squeezing back.

With the tourists mostly gone and the mill shut down, the restaurant isn't busy. They're seated promptly among the few dozen patrons in the section next to the windows overlooking the slow-moving black water river the town was named for. She orders the Greek platter and a glass of house white. He orders the prime rib special and a pint of draft Labatt's Blue.

When the food comes, Astrid eyes the enormous, blood-oozing slab of meat on his plate, and says, "I'm finding you get lots of beef on the ranch, imagine you do, too. I'm surprised you ordered it."

"True, there's no shortage of beef on your plate when you raise your own. But since my sister Abilene moved away, it's just us men, and no one likes to cook. Most times, in the summer anyway, we just throw something on the grill. Wilson, he's like family, he always did help around the house, and when Mom passed and Abby left, he took over completely. He prefers the frying pan. If he makes a roast, he cooks the livin' bejesus out of it 'til it's as dry 'n' hard as the heel of your boot." He takes a pull of his beer, saws off a chunk of beef and pops it into his mouth. "Mmm, mmm, mmm! Melts in your mouth!" he says. "Don't get me wrong, we don't complain about Wilson's cooking. Whoever complains gets the job, was Mom's rule."

"Smart lady!" Astrid smiles. "I'm no cook either, but I made Yorkshire puddings that turned out just like that," she points to his plate. "Bridey's recipe."

"Are you getting on okay there? I mean, I know I got no right stickin' my beak in your business, but I gotta say I was a bit discommoded when you told me you moved in there."

"Discommoded?"

"Discommoded." He chuckles. "Dad always called that one of Mom's ten-dollar words. She used it in many ways. Dallas and I *discommoded* her quite often. At least I heard the word a lot. Once I was old enough to look it up, I realized she never actually used it correctly; close, sometimes, just not quite right. But I never told her." He chuckles again, takes another draught of beer, then continues sombrely, "Dad worshipped her. He thought he won first prize when she chose him. She came along a little late in his life, and was so much younger. We sure didn't expect she'd be the first to go."

"It's awful," she says.

"You know, I don't usually say 'discommoded', it just pops out once in a while. When it does, it reminds me of her."

"So, it's a good thing. Kind of a keepsake."

"That's a nice way of looking at it! Thanks!" He takes another bite of prime rib, and chews thoughtfully before continuing. "It was nearly two years ago. Just before I went to Nanaimo and saw you that first time. I nearly bowed out of that show because of it." He shakes his head to clear the memory. "I'm glad I didn't! I might not've met you! Or at least I wouldn't've had the nerve to introduce myself when I did." He smiles at her, cuts off another piece of meat and loads mashed potatoes and gravy on it before putting it in his mouth. He chews, swallows, then continues, "But anyway, I still expect to see Mom around every corner. Wonder how long it takes for that to go away. What about your mother—how long since she passed?"

"Coming up on twenty years."

"That's rough. Cancer?"

She spears a dolmade and swipes it through the avoglomadi sauce before popping it in her mouth, then washes it down with sip of wine. "No," she says, shifting in her seat. She notices a drip of sauce on her sleeve, wipes at it with her napkin, and asks, "Why were you 'discommoded' about me moving to the Double H?"

His biggest niggling concern about her moving is all the time she'll be spending with Hank. But he can't say that. He'll come off sounding insecure and whiny. So instead he says, "Well, it's way out in the bush. What if something goes wrong?"

"We do have phones. We're even in cell phone range, as you know."

"Have I been calling you too much?"

"No, silly!"

"Should I keep on, then?"

The shy grin she gives him as she nods tells him she knows he's teasing. He reaches across the table and gives her fingers a brief squeeze. "I guess I worried, you know, about your job situation too. How you'd get along."

"I won't pretend the free room and board isn't a godsend. And it's good, so far anyway. Junior rubs me the wrong way. Bridey thinks he's cute, teasing me, but sometimes it crosses the line. Still, he's not around all that much and I really like Bridey. Hank Senior is nice, too, a real gentleman. Too bad his son isn't more like him! But it isn't permanent. They pay me, not a lot, but

I still have three shifts a week at Dot's. The pay at Dot's sucks, too, but tips are good. I have no expenses except my cellphone bill and gas for my car. As soon as I have enough money saved, I'll be moving on. I took a course, a year long course, executive office assistant, plus a bunch of computer stuff. I thought I'd have no trouble finding a job, a *career*, with that under my belt. And here I am, still a basement-dwelling waitress, at my age. But there's hope. A friend in Nanaimo thinks there might be a job opening up in her office they might let me interview for, so possibly I'll go back there."

"Why wouldn't they let you interview?"

"Oh, that came out wrong. I meant, I might go and interview for it. Depends on whether I, you know, *qualify*, with the courses I took." There's a little tick at the corner of her eye. "But thanks!"

"Thanks? For what?"

"For worrying." She concentrates on her roasted potato.

He studies the planes of her face, high cheekbones, small straight nose, smattering of freckles across her cheeks. Wispy curls escaping from her casual up-do are sun-bleached nearly white. She's left the top two buttons of her shirt open, affording a view of smooth skin, an alluring glimpse of the soft swell of her breasts…

He sees her drop her chin, look up under lowered lashes and then look down again, blushing. Actually squirming. *I'm too intense,* he realizes, *and it's putting her off, like staring at a timid dog. How can a woman who looks like she does be uncomfortable with a man looking at her with appreciation? Okay, lustful appreciation? And how can she possibly be unattached?*

That day in the diner, he nearly didn't ask to see her because he was sure someone so beautiful must be taken. Then Hazen horned in, looking like an alpha dog with his hackles up, seeming to confirm it. If he hadn't overheard her exchange with Franny, he never would have had the nerve to ask to see her the next day. With that, and seeing her that first time in Nanaimo, and over a year later, finding her in a diner a thousand kilometers away where he never would have been except by chance—it's as if the stars aligned and it was meant to be.

If I thought there was a god, he thinks, *I'd thank him for setting her in my path.*

* * *

Astrid's watching as Denver backs his truck up to the gooseneck flat deck, now loaded with big plastic-wrapped round bales firmly strapped down. It's dark, but there's a light on the back of the cab shining down into the box, and he hitches up the trailer with practiced ease.

He climbs down out of the box into the driver's seat, and gets Astrid to confirm the brake and turn signals are working. Then he leads her to the tack room, where he writes on the white board: "Fletch. Thanks for loading the haylage. Buy yourself a beer! Denver." He uses one of the magnets to hang a twenty-dollar bill beside the note.

"That's good of you," Astrid tells him.

"Well, I wouldn't want him to work for nothing."

"Still, it's something I'm sure he doesn't expect."

"I doubt he has high expectations about anything." Denver gives his head a short shake as he clucks.

"Oh? Why do you think that?"

"You weren't here when Hank came in."

"What did he do?"

"Nothing, really. It's more his tone. There's an odd, umm, *dynamic* between them, just kind of a feeling I got. We were having a nice chat until Hank came in, and then Fletch's whole demeanor changed. I think he was *discommoded*." He chuckles as he pushes his wallet back into his hip pocket. "I'd've rather talked to Fletch. He's an interesting guy. What happened to his hand, do you know?"

"Born that way."

"Hmmm."

"He's self-conscious of it, because of how it looks, but also, I think, because of the way it kind of twitches sometimes, like when he goes to reach for something. He tries to hide it. I didn't notice it until I moved here, although I saw him at Dot's quite a lot. I think he was surprised when you shook hands with him and didn't say anything."

He takes Astrid's hand and pulls her to him. "What would I say?"

"I don't know. Ask him about it or something. Doesn't help that Hank Junior calls it his hook."

"Well."

"I know. It's mean," she shrugs. "But he says it's nothing, he's been calling it that since they were kids, and Fletch doesn't care."

"What makes him think Fletch doesn't care?"

"Well, he says things like that, and Fletch never does anything. Calls him dumber than a bag of hammers, a freak with a hook, eyes so squinty he could be blindfolded with dental floss, and so close together he only needs half a pair of sunglasses, stuff like that, then he says something like 'You know I don't mean nuthin' right Fletch' and Fletch doesn't say anything."

"Hmm. That's what I mean, an odd dynamic. Looks to me like Fletch could beat the snot outta Hank, but he just takes it."

"He's used to it, I guess. Maybe Hank really doesn't mean anything by it and Fletch knows it. But you think Fletch is interesting? He gives me the willies, always sneaking up on me and every time I look at him he's staring at me. It's like… like a cat, staring at a mouse."

He barks a laugh, then says, "Sorry, I was just picturing you as a little mouse when I see you more as a kitten! I guess it's not funny you feel that way, though. I'll bet he likes you, and once you get to know him, I think you'll like him, too. Anyway, enough about other people." He pulls her up tight against him, nuzzles her neck and whispers, "I had a nice time tonight. I don't want this day to end."

His whiskers are rough; she realizes it must have been many hours since he last shaved, but it's only a fleeting impression, and the sensation is oddly erotic. She doesn't pull away. She doesn't want their time together to end, either. Then he's kissing her ear. Jaw. Then her mouth, tongue exploring. His hands drop to her hips and he leans back against the wall, pulling her with him.

After a time, he gently pushes her slightly away and strokes her cheek. "I better go. I got a long drive ahead," he says, kissing her gently, "I want to see you again. Next week?"

"You have more hay to pick up?"

"I'd come even if I didn't have hay to pick up, if you wanted me to."

"I want you to."

"Good!" He takes her hand and brings it to his lips to kiss the knuckles, then leads her to the truck and opens the passenger door. "Hop in. I'll give you a ride up to the house."

At the dooryard, he stops the truck and nudges the gearshift lever into park.

"Are you sure you shouldn't take Bridey up on her offer to stay over?"

"No, babe, I wouldn't get any sleep thinkin' of you, downstairs, all alone. And you may not have noticed, but Hank was not real supportive of the idea." He pulls her close and whispers, "It's gonna be a helluva long week!" Then he covers her mouth with his before reluctantly releasing her, settling back in his seat and clicking his seatbelt on.

Astrid opens the door and slides to the ground, then leans in and says, "I hope you're not too tired to drive safely."

"I'll be fine. If I find I'm gettin' tired, there's a rest stop south of Dark River. I'll pull in there and sleep for two or three hours. *If* I can fall asleep, for fantasizing about you!" He nudges the shifter into low. "Good night. I'll call you tomorrow, babe."

Astrid closes the door and steps away from the truck. The big diesel engine chortles, then truck and trailer pull away. She watches until she can't see the lights any more, then walks up to the house. The light by the front door is on, but once she turns the corner to go to the lower level basement entry, it's full dark, and there's barely enough moonlight to see the path. The smell of cigarette smoke wafts up and when she rounds the second corner, she finds Hank standing by the stairs leading down. He drops his cigarette in the gravel and grinds it out under his boot.

"What're you doing here?" she asks.

"Smokin'."

"I see that, but why *here*?"

"Why not here?"

She clucks, then agrees, "Why not." She steps off the path to go around him. "Goodnight, then."

He takes her arm, pulling her up short. "Yer out late."

"After dinner, we went into the lounge for a nightcap." She pulls her arm out of his grasp.

"Nightcap down in the tack room, too? It was gettin' a little steamy, wasn't it?"

"Were you *spying*?"

"You know, there's windows. If yer gonna have a knee wobbler, you should turn off the lights. I saw you from the patio."

"It wasn't—oh, bugger off!" she hisses, and tries again to step around him.

He cups her shoulders and says, "Astrid, you know I like you." He leans in for a kiss. She turns her head so his kiss lands on her jaw.

"Stop it!"

"Come on, honey, be nice. I bin waitin' so long." He buries his face in the hollow of her neck. She squirms; he holds her tight against him and nuzzles her, his lips soft on her neck.

"What're you doing? Quit that!"

"Not so loud! You'll wake Bridey."

"Maybe I need to wake Bridey! Get off me!"

After a heartbeat, he says, "Goodnight," releases her and pulls away, walking back along the house and out of view around the corner. In a moment, the front door slams.

She takes several deep breaths, then goes down the stairs into the basement to her room. Damn Hank anyway! This is an escalation from his usual pawing. Should she tell Bridey? No, Bridey would laugh it off. *He made a pass at you? Boys will be boys.*

Is the only solution to quit this job? Right now, that would put her in a bad spot. Her bank account is growing, slowly but steadily, and with her expenses so low now that she's living at the Double H, she'll soon have enough put aside to take her through until she can find another job. Until then, she can manage Hank Junior. She won't let him discommode her!

She slips out of her jeans and socks, then unbuttons her shirt and examines the sauce stain on the sleeve. Another top that has to be washed before she can wear it again. She tosses it into the clothes hamper along with her panties, gets into the oversized T-shirt she sleeps in and goes to the bathroom. When she's brushing her teeth, she glances up at her reflection in the mirror and notices a dark spot on her neck about the size of a quarter. A hickey? Hank! Damn him! How will she hide that in her Dot's Diner shirt? Or is that the point?

Then Hank's cigarette-foul breath and unwelcome advances are forgotten as she sees the rash-like reddening of her cheeks. Whisker burns. Those she didn't get from Hank! She feels a renewed stirring of desire as she remembers the smell of Denver, masculine aftershave with undertones of horse and sweat. Sandy-haired and tanned, clear blue eyes twinkling, kissable mouth always on the edge of a grin, he has the kind of looks she's always been attracted to. And his hard male body! Wide-shouldered and tall enough she has to tip her head back for his kisses, making her feel petite and feminine in his arms. The lovely sensation of muscles rippling under her hands, the taste of his mouth, his lips soft while the hard mound of his penis strained against two pairs of jeans. No knee wobbler, but definitely a dry hump! She imagines their bodies intertwined, no jeans separating them...

"Whew," she says to the mirror, "Astrid, my girl, when was the last time you were this turned on? I think you need a cold shower!" She realizes it's going to be a long week for her, too.

She sets the timer on the exhaust fan for fifteen minutes, starts the shower, pulls her T-shirt off over her head, and when the water's warm enough, steps in.

ELEVEN

IT'S RAINED, SOMETIMES hard, for a couple of days and now, despite the bright sunlight, the day is chilly. Fall is in the air. Perfect for chanterelles, Bridey says. Fletch confirmed they're coming up, and offered to bring them some, but Bridey wants a mushroom-picking outing. So, they don warm jackets, Astrid loads three twenty-liter white plastic buckets in the back of the Gator, and they set out. Buster runs ahead, beside and all around, as usual.

Part way into the forest, they turn off the main trail that leads to Fletch's onto a narrower path Astrid might not have seen if Bridey hadn't directed her onto it. Although overgrown, it's open enough for the Gator. Bridey soon points out the first patch of frilly orange-yellow mushrooms.

"Oh my god," Astrid says, "they're so bright! And isn't that patch pretty!" She stops the Gator and they both get out. Astrid is concerned about Bridey walking in the uneven terrain.

"Just give me your arm, Astrid," she says, "I want to pick at least a few, just to get my hands in the dirt. And I'll show you how to pick so you won't damage the mycelium, which is their roots. Actually, a network of fine roots. If you damage it, they may not come back again next year."

Astrid follows Bridey's instructions, pretty much how she would've picked anyway, then holds one of the larger mushrooms up to her nose. "Hmmm. It smells kind of good. Like apricots or something. Can I taste?"

"You can eat them raw, but they're peppery, and some people get an upset stomach from them. But a little taste? Sure, go ahead."

"Do they have bugs?"

"Not usually."

Astrid takes a small bite, rolls it around in her mouth and spits it out. "Definitely don't need to eat 'em raw," she says, "bugs or no bugs."

"Don't worry," Bridey says, chuckling at Astrid's screwed-up face, "you'll love them once they're cooked."

She helps Bridey back into the Gator, then picks all she can find in the first patch. Buster, who's been off exploring, comes crashing back through the undergrowth to stick his nose in, but he loses interest and soon runs off again. After picking what she finds within twenty or thirty meters of the Gator, the first bucket is nearly full.

"This really is a great patch!" she grins at Bridey. "They're so easy to find!"

"They are, now. Wait until more leaves fall, not so easy to find then. But today, it's as easy as it gets, and we'll have the buckets full before long. It'll take us way longer to clean them and get them in the freezer than to find and pick them. It looks like it's going to be a good year for them."

Astrid starts the Gator and they continue through the forest, stopping here and there to pick, and the pails are full when they come to a barbed-wire fence that Bridey says separates the home pasture from Fletcher's land.

Bridey points out the wire gate, and says, "You open that gate and we'll go home through the pasture. While we're down here, I'll show you where there's a little beach by the river. You might want to swim there next summer."

"Should we wait for Buster?" Astrid asks as she opens the gate.

"No, he'll find us," Bridey clucks. "That dog! I don't know why Hank got him or why we have to keep him. I love dogs, you know. I wanted a Corgi, but Hank insisted we needed a bigger dog, like a guard dog. But he slobbers too much and sheds too much fur, can't have him in the house. And he doesn't stay home. Some guard dog, out roaming around the bush half the time."

"Well, if it helps, I like having him around."

"He's taken a liking to you, too."

"Knows I like him, I guess. He spends a lot of time with me. It's true, though, he's usually with me when I start out on a run, but soon takes off. Sometimes he doesn't show up again until I'm almost back at the house!"

Astrid drives the Gator through, then closes the gate behind them before continuing. After a few meters of well livestock-trodden forest, they emerge onto the cleared pasture area, then follow a low ridge until they come to another, much wider trail leading back through the trees and down an embankment to the river, stopping on a semi-circle of sandy gravel next to the water. There are horse and cattle tracks and plenty of both types of manure everywhere.

"This is where the livestock comes to water. Nice, eh? We never have to worry about watering them, at least until the river freezes. That won't happen until maybe January, and sometimes where the current's fast, it doesn't freeze over at all. The narrower part over there, where the bank's steep," Bridey points left, "is deep and a good swimming hole. It's usually shallow where you see the rocks and that's where the cattle and horses go across, in the summer," Bridey says. "Before the rain, we could've driven across, but it'd be dicey now. We don't need to cross anyway, it'll take a day to clean the mushrooms we've got and get them in the freezer." She leans back, looks around, sighs deeply and says, "Let's just sit for a bit."

They sit in silence, watching the dark water slide by. A family of Canada geese, two adults and half a dozen juveniles, comes bobbing along on the other side. Just as they get across from the Gator, Buster comes crashing down the far bank and into the water, startling them. They all take to the air with splashing and a clatter of wings and excited honking.

The dog crosses at the ford easily despite the high water, swimming when he needs to, then comes up beside Astrid and shakes. "Damn it, Buster!" she cries.

Bridey doesn't seem to notice; she just sits staring sightlessly across the water. After a moment, she stirs and says quietly, "This is where Heather drowned. On her fifth birthday."

"Oh!" Astrid gulps; her throat constricts, and her eyes fill.

"She was down here with Junior and Fletch and somehow fell in. Fletch came running up to the house to get me. J-Junior stayed here. He tried to save her, but,"—Bridey chokes back a sob— "the coroner said she must've hit her head on a rock. We found her little body there—" she points to a stand of willowy shrubs at water's edge where the river curves.

Astrid reaches across to rub Bridey's arm, to draw her into a hug, but the older woman stiffens and turns away, shoulders heaving, sobbing quietly. After a bit, she turns back. Wipes her eyes on the back of her hand. She says in barely more than a whisper, "you'd think I'd be past that by now."

"Maybe you never get past something like that," Astrid says gently.

Bridey heaves a sigh. "I used to come here every year on her birthday. Now even on my good days I'm not strong enough to drive this thing and the truck can't get through here. I always wanted to build a little shrine, just a gazebo or something, but I've been overruled. Neither Hank nor Junior will bring me here any more. They say it's too hard on me. Maybe they're right." She looks unseeing at the willows, yellow leaves dancing in the slight breeze as they fall. Then, in barely more than a whisper, says, "I can't stop thinking about her last minutes. Did she panic? Did she almost make it and then slide back? Did the current pull her under? Was she afraid? Did she know she was going to die? Or did she just slip and hit her head before she went in and not even know what was happening?

"The boys were so upset, they couldn't tell us much. I guess they were in shock or maybe they just didn't see what happened." Her tears flow freely now, but without the gut-wrenching sobs. "*I should've been watching her* but instead I was in the house baking a birthday cake. A damn cake! I'd shooed them out of the house, made the boys take her with them. I didn't know they'd go down to the river! I didn't want her to know I was baking a cake, didn't want her to see it, so she'd be surprised! I had little charms to put in it so there'd be a prize in each piece. Agg!" She wipes her nose on her sleeve. "They all tell me I'm not to blame, but I can't forgive myself, and I can't forget. I don't want to forget. Is that wrong?"

Astrid ponders the question before responding, "I don't know."

They're both silent for a bit, the only sound the water cascading around rocks, and bird song. Then Astrid takes a deep breath, and says: "I still think about my mother every day. I wonder about her last minutes, too. If you're wrong, then so am I."

TWELVE

IN THE FRONT room next to the kitchen of the big old farmhouse, Dallas and Hank Junior are on the couch and in an armchair respectively. Denver's in the leather swivel recliner that was his father's favourite, now his. He swirls the Chivas in his glass, then says, "So, Hank, it's sure good of you to deliver the last of our hay. But I'd've thought you'd be too busy, what with runnin' the ranch, and the mill besides."

"Well," Hank says, "like I told you, the mill's still shut down fer annual maintenance. We needed a bunch of replacement stuff, blades 'n' so on, also we bought another big gen set and a compressor. I can save a bundle pickin' it up myself instead of payin' shipping and I ain't busy, so, I thought, might as well save you guys a trip instead of haulin' down empty."

They've had supper: fried pork chops, mashed potatoes, boiled-to-mush carrots, and Wilson's famous biscuits. Wilson also made his signature gravy: flour and milk in the pan drippings. Denver suggested he didn't need to go to the trouble of making gravy. Wilson just snorted and said, "I know you don't like my milk gravy, but you ain't the only one eatin' 'n' you don't have to put it on yer spuds 'n' if you got any more complaints you kin have the job."

No one had any complaints and there were no leftovers. The gravy boat and even the pan the gravy was made in, were scraped clean, which Wilson said proved his gravy was not so goddamn bad. Of course, it helped they'd worked outside all day at the usual chores and then moved the semi-load of hundred-pound hay bales into the hay shed. Supper was late, and they were ravenous.

Once the hands deposited their plates in the sink, Wilson shooed everyone out of the kitchen so he could clear up. Hank said he wanted to talk to Denver and Dallas about a business opportunity, so the three of them moved into the living room. Now they're waiting to hear what Hank has to say.

"We ain't exactly on the way to Vancouver." Dallas points out.

"No. I could take the Cariboo instead and save a couple hundred klicks, but it ain't as good a road and I can make up the time on the Coq instead of goin' down the Canyon." He takes a long swig of his beer, then belches. "Good supper. Think I'll see if Wilson'll come and work at my place. Meals've gone downhill since Bridey don't cook no more."

"I thought Astrid was helping out," Denver says. "She seemed pretty pleased with learning how to make Yorkshires."

Hank snorts and says, "Well, let's just say cookin' ain't what she's best at." He chuckles and swigs his beer.

Dallas frowns at his brother's sharp intake of breath, turns to Hank and says, "So, you said you wanted to talk to the two of us. Some business deal? But yer dad didn't come with you?"

"Yeah, well, er, Senior ain't in on this. He's gittin' ready to retire, he's come down with the old fart fear of spendin' money and has a death grip on his wallet."

"Shit, Hank, if you're looking for a cash-in partner, you came to the wrong place." Denver says.

"Let's hear him out," Dallas says. "What's the deal?"

"Here's the thing. We're all ranchers, you know we're up the pipe if there's drought. Lookit what you run into, hadda buy hay this year 'cause yer pasture's the shits, hadda start feedin' early and couldn't raise enough hay of yer own. We were lucky, we got rain, but you either gotta git more irrigation or yer gonna end up buyin' what you need again. That's a cost you can't control. And if somehow no one wants yer horses no more or you git one little case of mad cow and have to destroy all yer cattle? Nuthin' to sell. No income. Still got bills to pay, though. Course I also got the sawmill, but I'm at the mercy of all kinds of other shit there. Carbon tax. Gas. Hydro. Stumpage up, down and sideways. Everyone always wantin' more money fer doin' less. Got no control over those costs. Just startin' to recover after the pine beetle, and now all the fuckin' fires, and the Americans threatening to scrap trade deals, renegotiate the softwood lumber deal, which sucked for us in the first place, they wanna come back and make it worse? So, what I'm lookin' at is diversification." He leans forward, arms on his thighs, and starts peeling the label off his bottle. "Diversification is the key to buildin' wealth. I'm lookin' to buy into real estate. Apartments. In Toronto and Vancouver."

Denver sits back and swivels his chair.

Dallas sits up straighter, leans forward and says, "Well, I'll be go to hell. How're you gonna do that?"

"We got a big investor gonna give us a lot of money. I mean a lot. They're lookin' fer other properties. Might be I could git 'em innerested in yer place. How much money, you might ask? Five, six million maybe? Yer thinkin' too small."

"We're not lookin' to sell," Denver says.

"Sometimes sellin's yer best move. You get paid out now, make a deal to stay on. So nuthin' changes, except you get *paid* to manage the place 'n' now you got a bag full of money to invest, besides. You come in on this here apartment deal of mine, and start rakin' in a share of the rents. High rises. Lots of units. You wouldn't believe it, them city folks're shelling out a thousand bucks a month fer a lousy seven hunnerd square footer."

"Really," Dalla says, exchanging a look with his brother.

"And there's another perk," Hank continues. "They pay a finder's fee, so anyone else you bring in, you get another bag fulla money. And a percentage of what they make, too. You'll be *mull-tie* millionaires." Hank drains his beer.

When Dallas gets up and goes to the kitchen to get another beer for Hank, Denver sits swivelling his chair, frowning. The back door slams, and they hear Dallas say, "Hey!"

"Where's Denver?" Trisha bursts into the room with Dallas at her heels. "You still haven't got my water heater replaced and on top of that, now my goddamn car won't start!" She glares at Denver, then backs off a bit when she notices Hank getting to his feet. "Oh, hello," she says.

"Er, Hank," Denver says, "meet my ex."

Hank takes the few steps toward her and extends his hand. Her frown evaporates, replaced by a coquettish smile as she takes his hand. "You'd think I don't have a name," she says. "I'm Trisha."

"Hank Hazen. Glad to meet you." Keeping her hand in his, Hank adds, "*Very* glad to meet you! Know what I wanna know?"

"No," Trisha says with a giggle, "what do you want to know?"

"I wanna know where you bin all my life."

Denver snorts and says, "I hate to interrupt, but we're in the middle of something, Trisha. And I told you, your problems are just that, yours."

Trisha pulls her hand away from Hank's, tosses her hair back over her shoulder and pushes past him to stand over Denver. "Well, like it or not, you're my landlord and I have a right to hot water, so it *is* your problem. I have to work tonight, couldn't shower, and now I've got no transportation because my car, which was already a piece of shit when you bought it for me, thank you so much, won't start!"

"Listen, Trisha," Dallas says, "We're busy right now, but I know the fun don't start at The Red Pony 'til you git there, and we don't want to keep the boys waitin'. So how 'bout I loan you my truck fer tonight. Tomorrow, call a plumber to bring you a new water heater and we'll pay fer it."

Trisha snorts, then her posture relaxes; she turns and says, "Okay." She steps back around the coffee table to stand next to Dallas, then glares at Denver and says, "But you're getting off light, *Mister!*"

Dallas hands Hank the beer, roots in his jeans for his keys, and holds them out to her. Trisha takes the keys and turns to Hank with her sweetest smile, saying, "Nice to meet you."

"The pleasure's all mine," he says.

She studies him for a moment before turning and walking, hips swaying, back through the kitchen.

When they hear the door slam shut behind her, Hank gives a low whistle and sinks to his chair. "How'd you let *that* git away?"

"More like, how'd he let her sink her hooks into him in the first place," Dallas says. "If yer smart, you'll steer clear."

Hank twists the cap off the new bottle and takes a deep draught. "Oh, don't worry," he says, giving Denver an intense look, "I don't need to drive a thousand klicks for pussy."

A series of loud clangs comes from the kitchen, as if something had to be shoved into the cupboard with the other pots and pans several times to make it fit, indicating in a not-so-subtle way what Wilson thinks of that comment.

Dallas shrugs and says, "Good thing you got other business, or your trip was for nuthin'. We don't own this place." He picks up the bottle of Chivas and tops up Denver's glass before refilling his own and settling back on the couch.

Hank's brows rise for a second, then he narrows his eyes. "Oh?"

"No. The ol' man owns it."

"Might he be interested in this deal?"

"Don't know," Denver says, and sips his drink. "We'll talk about it and get back to you."

"Well, you'd be fuckin' stupid to pass this up."

A door in the back hall slams, punctuating Wilson's opinion of that remark and signalling that he's gone to his room.

"Like I said, we'll talk it over." Denver pulls a pen out of his shirt pocket and flips open the magazine on the side table, ready to write in the margin. "What's the investor's name? Where're they located? Website?"

"Oh sure, it's, ahh, just some rich dude. American, I think."

"You don't know his name?"

"No, I don't know his name. I've been dealing with his agent, which is Prairie Equity and Wealth Management. Run outta a little shit hole town in Saskatchewan, believe it or not. Go ahead and Google it. Don't want to wait too long though; this opportunity won't be there forever! I only got a few weeks to line things up and then they'll start lookin' elsewhere." He chug-a-lugs his beer and gets to his feet. "I'll shove off now. Thanks fer supper." he says, and heads out to the kitchen.

Denver and Dallas walk him out; they shake hands all around, and watch as he climbs into the cab of the Kenworth, starts the big diesel, and drives off.

As the tractor-trailer moves away, Dallas says, "Did you really have to sit there lookin' like you got a mouth fulla shit?"

"Something about him rankles me."

"Oh, no shit, I wouldn't of guessed." Dallas absently kicks a rock.

"You don't get a bad vibe off him?"

"No."

"No? Well, I do, and I'm pretty sure he doesn't like me any more'n I like him." Denver says, turning and going back inside.

"Well," Dallas says as he follows him up the steps, through the kitchen and into the living room, "yer not likin' him don't mean we can't do business with him." He resumes his seat on the couch, works his feet out of his boots and puts them up on the coffee table, then picks up the remote and clicks the TV on.

"I dunno," Denver says, "this deal of his sounds too good to be true, and you know what they say about deals that sound too good to be true. He should've had more facts with him if it was a serious proposition. And how snotty he got when I pressed him on it? And there's a time crunch? *We'll* be millionaires? He means *he'll* be a millionaire, 'cause of course he gets a finder's fee if he signs us up. Hank Hazen is out for Hank Hazen and no one else." He sips his drink and swivels the chair. "I don't get it about delivering the hay, either."

"He wanted to talk to us about his deal."

"He didn't have to come here to do that, he could've told me about it up at his place and had all the documents to show me, and I could bring you up to speed when I got home. Or, all it would take would be a phone call and you'd've gone up with me."

"He was goin' to Vancouver anyway, like he said. Save us the trouble of getting' the hay ourselves. Cost, too."

"Save us the trouble, won't take anything for it 'cause he was headin' this way anyway, my ass! This doesn't feel right."

"Well, I think it makes sense. And fer his deal—why can't we git involved and git finder's fees, too? Sounds pretty sweet if you ask me. We might git a bunch of other ranchers around here signed up, make ourselves a bundle pretty quick, too!" Dallas says.

"Sounds like a pyramid to me, and you know the only ones who make it big in those deals are the guys at the top. Everyone else is just workin' for them. You'd take advantage of our neighbours, make money off them like that?"

"You don't know it's a pyramid and if it turns out to be a good deal fer them too, why not?" He picks up the remote and mutes the TV. "And delivering the hay? It's a friendly gesture, might make us more receptive to his deal. You can't blame him fer that. Not a big deal for him, like he says, they got that rig idle with the mill shutdown anyway."

"Yeah, I get that part of it too. But why? When we first made the deal, I told him I'd be arranging to have the hay shipped. He didn't offer their rig then. Hell, I'd've paid him to deliver it! He didn't even offer before I went up for the second load, and the mill was shut down then. I think he only came up with the idea after he found out about me and Astrid. Remember his remark that cooking ain't what she's best at? And driving a thousand K for pussy? Those were shots at me. He's lucky I didn't kick his ass. One more snotty comment and I would have."

"So, now it's you and Astrid? You seen her what, once? Twice? You think he's jealous of that?"

"Maybe it just pisses him off that she doesn't like him."

"Why'd he be jealous if they have nuthin' goin' on? You said you got a feelin' she's holdin' somethin' back."

"I think there's things she hasn't told me about herself yet. We don't know each other that well, that's all. I'm sure she's no two-timer. She loves Hank's mom. If she was Hank's girlfriend, she wouldn't go with anyone else for fear of hurting Bridey, if nothing else." He tosses back the rest of his Chivas. "Nope! I don't trust that smarmy li'l fucker and I don't like doing business with people I don't trust."

"You give Astrid a pass for holdin' back, don't know each other that well, but you know Hank even less and it's enough for you to decide he's a smarmy little fucker? I don't like passin' up an opportunity 'cause you got a bad feelin'! We should at least see what it's all about."

"We don't have to waste the time. We're the fourth generation of Danielsons on this land. Are we going to sell? Not fuckin' likely."

"Denver, fer chrissake think about it! What if we have another year like the last couple? We don't have another Rocky Duster to sell to see us through. You said yerself we're gittin' up to the limit on our line of credit, and you don't want to go to the bank and see 'bout gittin' the limit increased 'cause it's already dicey keepin' up the payments. Dad always said, time to sell a horse is when you got a buyer. Maybe that's true fer the ranch, too. What're we gonna do, wait till we wanna retire and then sell? Maybe there won't be a buyer then. If we sold now, you could buy a smaller place, just a horse farm. You don't like the cattle business anyway. And I could get my training barn set up, maybe in Texas or Arizona. We ain't fuckin' tied to this place."

"Are you kidding? We're not tied to it? This place is part of all three of us, a big part! And it's a legacy for future Danielsons!"

"Future Danielsons!" Dallas snorts. "Looks to me like we're the last of the Danielsons."

"Abilene's only twenty-eight. And even me or you could still have kids. Dad was older'n me when he married Mom."

"Abilene's gonna have kids? Not likely. And I'm not interested in gittin' married, are you?"

"We don't know what the future holds."

"Ahh, I git it! Yer thinkin' of marryin' Astrid!"

"Too soon to tell if me and her will get there, but it's not out of the question. Anyway, we can't do anything 'til Dad passes. We can't get him to sign a Power of Attorney with the Alzheimer's, you know that. We'd have to go to court for a committeeship, which takes time. And would we really serve it on him? Kick him in the teeth like that?"

"He'd've forgot about it two minutes later."

"So that makes it okay?"

Dallas shrugs.

Denver shakes his head and studies his younger brother, wondering for the thousandth time how they could have had the same two parents, or how he's spent decades with the man who so often seems like a stranger. "Okay," he says, putting his glass down and rubbing his face, "say we decide it's no big deal, tomorrow he won't remember anyway, which, by the way, I am never going to agree to, but say we get a committeeship and sell this place, Trisha would get a big hunk of it. You know I've got to get her sorted out first. Or maybe you don't give a shit I'd come out of it with nuthin' but my dick in my hand?"

"Course I care, but Trisha *is* entitled to somethin'."

"I've already offered her enough she could buy a place in town and she won't take that, wants alimony on top, for chrissakes. She's happy livin' in my house for nuthin', part-time server at that sleazy bar, and full-time party girl. She did dick all around here for five years, never drove a fuckin' truck or fuckin' helped Mom. She was supposed to do the payroll and you remember how *that* went! She's not entitled to a share of the ranch!"

"Don't matter whether you think she's entitled or not, it's the law."

"I'll fuckin' get rid of her somehow that doesn't involve the ruin of this ranch! Or, if she's going to insist on getting half my share, she'll have to fuckin' wait. The courts can't force a sale, they can only attach *my share*. All three of us have to agree to sell and that'll happen *never*."

"Well, Abby and I might vote against you on that."

"Wouldn't matter. The two of you can vote all you want. The way Dad set it up, unless all three of us agree to sell, it doesn't happen."

"Maybe we need to sell for you to get rid of Trisha."

"If she's determined to get a share of the ranch, she'll have a long fuckin' wait! And I'll tell you something else, that water heater you so gallantly said we'd pay for is the last fuckin' dime I put into that house until she's gone. I don't care if the fuckin' thing falls down around her fuckin' ears!"

"Okay! Okay! Yer right. Yer the guy with the college degree so of course yer *always* right! Jesus fuckin' Christ!" Dallas hits the button to turn the TV sound back on, then runs the volume up a couple of notches. After a moment, he mutes it again, and continues: "You really got a burr under yer saddle today. I think yer the one that's jealous! Jealous of Hank 'cause he's livin' up there with her."

"He's not living with her!"

"Same house, anyway. Cozy, eh? Last time I seen you all discommoded over a girl was Trisha. I'd of thought you'd of learned yer lesson!"

"This is different. This feels different."

"You got a bad feel, you got a different feel, somethin' don't feel right! Damn it, Den, when're you gonna start usin' yer head?"

Denver jumps to his feet. "I'm going down to do night check." He strides through the living room and out the kitchen door, slamming it behind him.

Moments later, he comes back in and says, "Sorry, Dal. You're right. It's fuckin' Hazen, he picks my ass. Let's talk to Abby. See what she thinks."

THIRTEEN

"So," BEGINS THE man who's the oldest, and putative leader, "there's a couple reasons I called this meeting." He sips his brandy while letting them wait, and looks with satisfaction around the great room which, together with the billiard room, takes up the entire center front of the sprawling log building. It's two storeys high, with wall-to-wall, ceiling-to-floor windows affording a view of the grassy area and the driveway leading to the gate in the chain link fence where the forest begins a kilometer away. Fire crackles and sputters in the massive river-rock fireplace. Moose and deer heads, bear skins, cougars, and even an entire rare white bear First Nations Peoples call a Spirit Bear incongruously mix with abstract and surrealist paintings and pop art. An art aficionado would recognize an original Picasso. An original Dali. An Andy Warhol Marilyn Monroe diptych. *Not bad for a guy with a grade eight education,* he thinks. He paid attention. Taught himself to talk and act like an educated man. When he jokes about how much richer he'd be if he hadn't stayed in school so long, it's only half in jest. He's a self-made man. Except for—well, there's no one still alive to remember his first business partner. He empties his glass and pours more.

A tall, muscular man dressed in black stands beside the staircase leading to the second storey, his back to one of the doorways into the hall giving access to the kitchen and the rest of the ground floor rooms. Earlier, he brought in the tray with a bottle and glasses and set it on the coffee table in front of them, but no one would mistake him for the butler.

Clusters of sofas, chairs and tables are arranged on thick area rugs. The three of them are at the grouping nearest the fireplace.

"Well? No party planned, so what is it? That girl?" the bald man asks.

"Yeah, that's obvious."

"Ahh! Good looking?" the obese man asks.

"Nice ass?" the bald man wants to know.

"You can judge for yourself, later." The leader swirls the brandy in his snifter and takes a sip before continuing. "She's been here a while, healing, putting on weight. She wasn't in good shape when she arrived."

"Is she okay now? I mean, for tonight?" The heavy-set man's double chin overflows his shirt collar and quivers as he speaks. "I don't care if she's skinny if she's all we got."

"Don't worry, Bruce. You can fuck her tonight, we all can, but goddammit, she should've been ready before now. She was at the cabin too long. Way too long. We have to put a stop to that."

The bald man gives Bruce an accusatory look and says, "You better not fuckin' hurt her. You got no self control, never did! You go last." He pulls a handkerchief out of his pocket and dabs at his eye.

"Fuck the hell off, why am I always getting sloppy seconds? I'm a partner here, same as either of you!" Bruce starts to hoist his mass out of his chair.

"Sit down, Bruce," the leader says, "he's just protecting our asset. I'm sure he didn't mean to disrespect your, er, *preferences*. Okay?"

"Mffft!" Bruce grumbles. He flops back down, his chair squawking in protest.

"You have to fall into that chair like that?" the bald man snaps. "You're gonna break another one!"

"Cheap, crappy chairs!"

"Next one you break, you pay for. You'll find out they're not so cheap!" the leader says. He swirls his brandy, then takes another sip and continues: "The second reason, the main reason, is of course the videos. You've all had a chance to watch them. Now we have a proposal to discuss. It means getting girls, willing girls."

"Yeah, I figured the reason for the videos was something like that," the bald man says, still mopping at his eye. "Dozens of girls, 'ceremonial wives'. Sounds great, but I watched the video…"

"Probably more than once!" Bruce interjects.

"Yeah, more'n once. Didn't you? Anyhow, they've got some nasty-looking old broads. Who wants to fuck those old boots?"

"That's what the hooded robes are for!" Bruce chuckles.

"Not all old boots!" the leader says, "they've got some nice pussy too. I met with the Illustrious Leaders and took part in a Communion Ritual. You guys have no fuckin' idea! I get a chubby just thinking about it. Hell, I'm getting a chubby now!" He sips his drink before continuing. "And, you can fuck them more often than just at rituals. The big boss gets more pussy than you ever dreamed of. They come running when he crooks his little finger, think he's doing them a favour!

"But we didn't just talk about fucking. We talked about how to recruit. Prime candidates are runaways who can be picked up hitchhiking and at the bus depot, and divorcees, not just widows. And the bible thumpers. They already drank the Kool-Aid, so they're low-hanging fruit. The ugly ones, they don't move up to True Believer status, just fill up the meeting hall and the collection plates!"

"So, the runaways. The hitchhikers," the bald man begins as he leans forward, takes the bottle from the table and splashes more brandy into his glass. "Right off the street and upstairs?"

"Well, no. It takes time. We treat 'em good. Give 'em a place to stay. A job, something in one of our businesses. And a divorcee or widow, maybe she needs a new roof on her house and can't afford it? All she has to do is sign it over and it's all taken care of. As long as she's a member of the church, she lives there, and can't fuck, er, *thank* us enough!" They all have a laugh, and drinks are topped up all around.

"It'll take time before they're ready to make the jump from Ordinary Congregation to True Believers, of course," the leader continues, "but we got time. I, for one, am not planning on kicking the bucket anytime soon.

"Meantime, we still use the pros for the rituals. Gradually integrate the True Believers until we have enough so there's no need to fly those high-priced cunts up from Vancouver. Delete that cost center! Once we get rolling, they're not only begging us to fuck them, but signing over their property, bank accounts, even their pay cheques! We audit them to make sure they're complying, like Scientology. Once they're in, they can never get out. They sever ties with biological relatives and we become their family. And there's the dogma about apostasy. Apostates are pariahs. They lose everything if they leave, so they're in for life."

"Even Scientologists get out," Bruce points out.

"Yeah, a few. Not many, though, not enough to worry about. And we got a perfect set-up for the communion rituals here. The three of us will be the Illustrious Leaders, with you, Bruce, doing the preaching. All we need is a place in town for meetings of the Ordinary Congregation. Maybe your church, Bruce? You think your congregation would convert? That would give us a real good start."

"Maybe. But what about the men?" Bruce shakes his head, setting off a storm of ripples in his chins. "Can't get rid of the men in my flock."

"There's men in the video, didn't you see them? They take part in the rituals, too, just The Mingling, though. There'll be some sheeple that actually believe it's a church and will never be more than Ordinary Congregation. They go to meetings, never take part in the rituals, never come here. There'll be men in that mix. And plenty of men will want in *only* because of the rituals. We'll have a steep buy-in, half a million? Men who don't have cash, they can sign property over to us and buy in that way."

"Not all our members want willing girls," the bald man reminds him.

"Yeah, those Red Pill guys." He shrugs and takes a sip of his brandy. "We'll have some attrition there. But I think it'll be more than offset by new guys coming in."

"Your, er, *acquisitions* guy's gonna be redundant."

"We have to stop that anyway. Every time he gets a new one, the heat's back on. Townspeople out beating the bushes. Fuckin' cops asking questions. Drags on for months. If he gets really active again, we might end up with another fuckin' special task force."

"How do we stop him? Nothing's worked so far." The bald man's eye is flowing freely now. "Damn it!" he says, then balls the cloth up and just keeps it against his eye. "That cabin is too close for comfort. And if they catch him, are we sure he won't sing? I know you won't like it, but you have to realize we may need a permanent solution."

"That's not an option! Never will be! I think he'll, uh, *embrace* our new direction if we let him in here."

"Him? In here? Our members are all well fixed. All upper crust." The obese man shakes his head. "No offence, but he's just a ... just such a redneck!"

"*You* think that, but women seem to like him."

"Yeah, he's a natural-born pimp all right, but I sure as hell don't see him as a leader."

"Well, he might grow into the job. For now, something has to be done about that cabin. I offered him a seat on the board."

"What? Without running it by us?" Specks of saliva spray from Bruce's lips as his voice rises an octave.

"It's the same deal we made with Max."

"Yeah, but Max had to buy in! Is he going to buy in too? He doesn't have money!" Bruce's voice is back to normal, but his shoulders haven't relaxed. "Far as I know, he doesn't own any property, either. Are we going to *give* it to him? You might be okay with that, but I'm not going to have my share of this club watered down again, for nothing."

"No, it won't be given to him, he'll have to earn it."

"I don't like it!" Bruce snipes. "How's he going to earn it?"

"We'll figure something out." The leader sips his brandy and gives Bruce a glare to end the debate. He picks his cigar out of the ashtray and re-lights it before continuing, in a softer tone. "We're going to be bigger than the parent church. They don't have a lodge like this. Which brings me to the second part of this deal, something I came up with that the parent church hasn't thought of. Call this lodge a multi-use facility, great place for the church rituals, and the rest of the time, it's still a private members club. Men don't have to join the church, they can just be members of the lodge like before, but there'll be more, er, *lively activity* to interest them. Lots of girls, all the time, not just now and then. Remember those ceremonial wives? They not only fuck us, but they fuck anyone we tell them to. Men can get dressed up in their hunting gear, kiss their wives good-bye, come and spend their vacation 'hunting' here. Hell, they can actually *do* some hunting! We'll expand that. There'll be a charge for the rooms. Use of the four by fours. Some of our guys can train as guides. We'll get some of the gals trained to do massage. We'll have members from all over the world. There's lots of details to be worked out, but think of it this way: it's two separate things. The church angle, besides being very lucrative on its own, supplies the bodies to run the gentlemen's club. It's going to be a big business. It won't happen over night, but I'm excited about this. We're going to be billionaires, my friends."

"So why do we want to be affiliated with the parent church? What's in it for us? Why not just do our own thing?"

"We could, Bruce, but they've got a bunch of stuff already in place. For one thing, they're a recognized religion: tax exempt! And, they're set up to do the real estate transfers, any washing of money that might be needed, anything to do with finance, through a company called Prairie Equity and Wealth Management. It's their shell company, started by Al Capone, believe it or not, that's how long they've been up and runnin'. So, we tap into that. We use their hymnals, they've already got their own bible, prayer book, liturgies… nothing you'll find in your library, Bruce. There'll be reciprocal visits for communion rituals. I foresee franchises world wide. There's an infinite pool of prospects. Don't underestimate the power of the sex drive in a healthy male! Think about it! Maybe we go spend a few weeks in a compound like this in South Africa. Brown Sugar, anyone?"

"Oh, *ye-a-a-hh!*" the bald man says. "The booties on those black beauties!"

"That's right! Don't think small, gentlemen!"

They're quiet for a moment, not thinking small. Then the bald man shakes his head. "I don't get it. If they've been at it so long, why're they just branching out now?"

"Not sure exactly, but all three Illustrious Leaders were replaced a couple years ago. You probably heard about it, it's not every day there's three murders in a town with a couple thousand people."

"Yeah, I seem to remember. Never solved? I think it was on Cold Case Files."

Bruce shakes his head. "Didn't know it had anything to do with religion, though. If they assassinate their leaders …!" He shudders.

"I wasn't told why they were whacked, just that it wasn't by their own people. The new leaders may not have thought of franchising either, if we hadn't approached them. That's thanks to Max, and it's one of the reasons he's more'n just an ordinary member." He raises his glass in salute to the man in black standing at the bottom of the staircase, then drinks the rest of his brandy, stubs his cigar out and stands. He hoists up his pants, grabs his crotch and leers, "Well, you guys discuss it. I'm going to go do something about my chubby."

FOURTEEN

Astrid's watching out the window as the Greyhound pulls into the depot. There are several men in cowboy hats, jeans and jean jackets on the walkway, but one draws her eye. Denver! Her heart speeds. He's scanning the windows; she waves, then realizes the windows are tinted and he can't see in. She's flooded with anticipation; it's a trial to wait for the other passengers, frustratingly slow, as they fuss with their bags and block the aisle. When she's finally out, she squeezes past the crowd milling around right at the door of the bus, and hurries to him. Before she can say a word, he's pulling her into his arms and lifting her off her feet to kiss her. When he finally puts her down, he doesn't release her.

"Would you mind just standin' like this for a bit?" he whispers as he nuzzles her neck, "otherwise it'll be obvious to everyone how glad I am to see you."

"Oh! I..." she says. "Er...! Thank you for letting me come."

"Letting you come? You think I'm doing you a favour? I hate that you live so far away. I'd like to see you every day. It'd be a helluva lot better than spending hours on the phone and not being able to do this." He kisses her ear, then her mouth.

"I think *this* may be adding to your predicament," Astrid whispers with a giggle.

"I haven't stopped thinkin' about you," he whispers back. He grins sheepishly, rubs her shoulders for a moment, then eases away. "Hank threw a kibosh into my plans to go up for hay a couple weeks ago like I said I would, but I could've come up to see you last week."

She bends to pick up her duffle bag before answering. "I know. I told you Bridey and Hank Senior signed up for a seniors' tour to Reno. Well, Bridey had a lot to do before leaving and wanted help. Insisted, really. She's fallen a few times, even with changing from her cane to her walker, and doesn't feel safe driving, of course. The irritating details she wanted to deal with before they left! They're only going for two weeks, she didn't have to take the printer paper over to the lady who's doing the posters for the Christmas craft sale that's two months away. Why did she even offer to do it? Stuff like that. But she refused to give me time off and I wouldn't want you to come if I could only spend so-called 'after work hours' with you. There actually are no after work hours! I'm at her beck and call twenty-four seven. You know, she's sweet, but I'm beginning to see she *is* a bit of a control freak. She flew off the handle when I pressed her for the time off. Really shocked me! That's a side of her I haven't seen before! Just a couple of days off, for heaven's sake! Still, she's been so good to me, I couldn't say no. And anyway, when you said it was okay for me to come and stay here while they're away, it didn't make sense for you to make the trip up." She sighs. "I'm sorry. I'm making it sound like the situation is horrible. It's not. I'm just venting."

"It's okay. Sounds like you got reason."

"Maybe I just need a break! Anyway, I took them to the airport, drove from there to the bus depot and got on the next bus, which was only going as far as Kamloops. I wish there was one that was going to Merritt, so you could've picked me up there."

"It's okay, babe, I'd rather come here since it means I get to see you an hour sooner." Denver kisses her again, then takes her bag and leads her along the sidewalk to the parking lot and his truck.

"At least I wasn't driving. I don't have snow tires, and we ran into a squall near Clinton. Imagine, already! The highway was terrible! The driver had to slow right down. That's why the bus was late. I'm sorry if it's meant a long wait for you."

"It would've seemed like forever, even if it was on time." He squeezes her hand before releasing it to open the passenger door and stow her bag behind the seat. Once she's settled in, he closes the door and goes around to climb in behind the wheel. "Are you hungry? Should we get a bite before we hit the road?"

"Well, I *am* hungry, but how far is it to your ranch? I'm looking forward to seeing it."

"It's about an hour and a half and it's already late. I'll give you the nickel tour tomorrow. How about we have supper here..." he stops mid-sentence and turns to her. "My apologies, babe. I was going to say, get a room and head to the ranch tomorrow. How wrong-headed! We've only seen each other a couple of times. Please don't think ... we can drive out after we eat. Or we can get two rooms ... I don't want you to think ..."

She stops him with a kiss, then feels her face grow warm as she looks deep into his eyes, pushes her inhibitions aside and whispers, "I know we don't know each other very well, but ... Room first. One room. Then supper."

* * *

Astrid's starting to come awake. It's still dark, but the thin light of pre-dawn squeezes in around the edges of the heavy draperies. She keeps her eyes closed, enjoying the comfortable warmth of the big male body next to her, luxuriating in the memory of the previous night's lovemaking. When she opens her eyes and turns to look at Denver, he's awake, lying on his side, looking at her.

"Good morning," she whispers.

"Good morning, beautiful," he whispers huskily. "If I'm dreamin', please don't wake me." He lifts a hand to stroke her cheek, the fine blonde hairs on her arm, then trace a line up across her shoulder to her collar bone and down beneath the blanket to her nipple, fingertips light as butterflies. A pleasant shiver courses through her.

He draws her into his arms and kisses her. At first the comfort of warm skin on skin along their whole length is enough, but as they explore each other's bodies, desire builds and soon they are pressing together with urgency. She feels the weight of his penis against her thigh becoming rock hard, then straining against her as he moves over her, his muscular thighs urging her legs apart. Her hips rise to meet him; their thrilling joining, still so new, somehow feels familiar and right. The little sounds they make express pleasure, gaining in intensity as they move together in the ancient dance. Slow and luxurious at first, increasing in tempo until they're swept away in the all-over body rush, and collapse.

After a time, he whispers, "Oh, babe, you don't know what you do to me! But... Is it okay for you? Is there something else I should do? Something else you want me to do?"

"*Okay?* Oh! You think because I'm not a screamer..." she runs her palm over his nearly hairless chest, "it's great, you're great, believe me. Just because I'm kind of quiet doesn't mean I'm not enjoying it. But you don't make a lot of noise, either. Just a few little 'oh gods'."

"Well, I know *I* enjoyed it. That's lame! I loved it. In fact, I was shoutin' 'OH MY FUCKING GOD!' in my mind."

She laughs.

He draws her into his arms and tickles her before they kiss and relax, just cuddling, again.

"More good news, we can sleep together, I mean, actually sleep, besides the great sex. And there's lots of time for me to learn how to get some 'oh gods' outta you!" Denver whispers. "You're a beautiful, wonderful, fabulous woman. You fill me up."

"Oh, Denver! You're a beautiful wonderful fabulous man."

"I'm beautiful?"

"Yes. Beautiful. And handsome too, of course."

They kiss and then cuddle some more. After a bit, she pulls away a slightly and whispers, "I guess we should get up."

"I guess."

"I'm going to shower," she says, and feels his eyes on her as she slides out from under the covers.

"Mind if I join you?"

* * *

By the time they get down to the hotel breakfast room, everything except coffee and juice is cleared away. They check out, get Sausage McMuffins and potato patties at the McDonalds drive-through, and roll into Rattlesnake Ridge Ranch just as the hands are coming out of the house to get back to work after lunch, or what they call dinner. They cluster around as Denver introduces them.

Eddie is the youngest; so handsome, with smooth brown skin, long black lashes any woman would die for, and black eyes. His dark forelock falls forward over his brow when he removes his hat and half bows as he takes Astrid's hand. "Ma'am," he says.

"Hello, Eddie," she says, "Denver tells me you're a bull rider!"

"Tryin' to be."

"He's crazy enough," the older cowboy with the moustache says. "You know, still young enough to b'lieve he's immortal."

Barney and Shane both appear to be in their late forties, with tanned, weather-beaten faces and hair so salt-and-pepper it's not clear what its original colour was. Shane pulls the toothpick out of his bushy walrus moustache and says, "Welcome," his bright blue eyes twinkling. Despite a missing tooth, his smile is infectious and it's easy to believe he means it.

Barney hangs back; he doesn't smile, but nods politely.

"Dallas around?" Denver asks.

"Him 'n' Jimbo went up the line. Didn't come in fer dinner." Shane replies, sticking the toothpick back in his mouth. "They got them yearlings brought down, though."

"Okay, good. You three can work 'em a bit this afternoon. Any of you got time to bring Daisy and Melody in? I'd like to give Astrid the royal tour."

"I got time, if Eddie'll float the ring," Shane says. "Want me to saddle 'em?"

"Yeah, thanks, that'd be great. Mom's saddle on Melody, I guess. We'll be back in a bit." He takes Astrid's hand and leads her onto the verandah, stopping to introduce her to Tippy, who's laying on a mat thump-thump-thumping her tail, before going inside.

* * *

"Aww, lookit that!" Shane says with a sigh. They're watching their boss and his new girlfriend walk up to the main house, and see Astrid crouch down to make a fuss over Tippy. The old dog licks her hand. "She sure puts me in mind of Iris."

Barney scowls. "If that don't push Trisha right off her perch, I'll eat my shorts. Her horse, too."

"You'll eat her horse?" Shane asks.

"Smart ass. You know what I mean." He fishes a can of Copenhagen out of his shirt pocket, opens it, pinches a wad and inserts it between his cheek and gum.

"Well, I'd pay money to see you eat yer shorts. But Trisha never gave a hoot about Melo."

"Don't matter. I just hope she don't see nuthin'."

"What if she does? What's the worst she can do?"

"Oh nuthin' much, just git herself some shyster lawyer and skin him fer half the Triple R."

"You fergit, Barney, the kids ain't the owners."

"Not yet, you mean."

'Well, that's so," Shane allows, "but it *is* good he's movin' on, buddy. You know how close he was to his mother. It laid him low, and I b'lieve he's still grievin'. Not surprisin' he picked that one, lookin' so much like her. On top a that, Trisha kickin' the stuffin' outta him? This is good fer him."

"Well I hope the hell there's more to her'n good looks," Barney says, and sends a dark stream of snoose into the dust at his feet, "or he's ridin' fer another fall."

"She's pretty. I like her," is all Eddie says.

* * *

When Denver and Astrid come into the kitchen, they find a wiry little bald man in worn jeans and tromped-down cowboy boots busy clearing away the noon meal, dishtowel over his shoulder. He looks up when they come in, smooths the few hairs across his shiny dome, and comes around the table to take Astrid's hand. "You must be Astrid," he says. "I'm Wilson, chief cook 'n' bottle washer. Hardest workin', most unappreciated body on the place."

"Hello, Wilson," Astrid giving his callused hand a squeeze, "I've been looking forward to meeting you. Denver's told me so much about you."

"That so? Likely pis...er, *complainin'* 'bout my cookin'," he grouses, scowling at Denver. "

"No. Well, maybe a little. But mostly he talks about how he wouldn't know what to do without you," she smiles, first at Denver, then at Wilson. "I hear you've been here over forty years."

"Yup. Hell, I was here when Dan was a bachelor 'n' said he'd stay that way. Then he met Iris. Them kids wasn't even born yet when I signed on."

"So, you saw them grow up! All the mischief they must've gotten up to! I bet you've got some stories to tell."

"Hey!" Denver exclaims.

"You know so much of the history of the ranch," Astrid continues with a smile at Denver, "knew his mother. Remember his father as he was all those years ago."

"Knew his granpappy too!"

"Well, I hope you'll tell me all the old stories. And while we're at it, maybe teach me some of your recipes. I'm helping Mrs. Hazen, and she's taught me a few things, but all I've really got down pat so far is Yorkshire puddings. Bridey's—Mrs. Hazen's—foolproof recipe."

"Is that so! Well," Wilson's grin deepens the lines that run all the way from the corners of his eyes down to his jaw. His bushy white eyebrows bob up and down as he gives Denver a smug look, tugs his jeans up over non-existent hips, and says to Astrid, "I'll git you to show me that recipe, then, and yer welcome in my kitchen any time!"

They hear him whistling as they go upstairs to Denver's room, where he puts her duffle bag on a chair and his hat on the dresser before closing the door and drawing her into his arms. "We do have an extra room for you, babe, but I'm hopin' we don't need it."

"We absolutely don't need it! Unless it bothers Wilson, you know, us not married and sharing a room."

"Seriously? Mom lived here before her and Dad got married. I was on the way when they tied the knot. Wilson would think I was either queer or sick in the head if I let you sleep alone." He kisses her, then whispers in her ear, "You realize we're all gonna be in love with you by supper time."

"Oh, Denver," she chides. But she suddenly feels warm and knows she's blushing. "Anyway, are you sure about me riding a horse? I've never done it before."

"You're not riding Hank's horse?"

"Haven't yet. He's been too busy." Astrid sits on the bed and gives it a bounce, causing the headboard to thump against the wall.

"Have to put a pillow or something behind there so it can't do that," Denver says. He pushes her down and lies half beside, half on her.

"Do we have time for this?" she whispers.

"Well, no. You're right, Shane'll be waitin'." He sits up. "As nice as it would be to spend the day in bed with you, we can't count on weather like this at this time of year, so we better take advantage of it. If it was snowing north of Clinton yesterday, we could have a blizzard tomorrow. I know you people from the Island find it hard to imagine, but we often have snow in September. Doesn't stick around, of course."

"I guess this winter up in Dark River will be quite an eye opener for me!"

"Yup, I'd say so." He gives her arm a rub. "Also, I have time to take you out around the ranch today, but I might not tomorrow. Some folks're coming, they're interested in a couple of yearlings, so I may be tied up with them. You can hang out with us, of course, but you might want to just spend some time with that book you brought for a while. Do you mind?"

"A bottle of wine, some trail mix, and a good book on the verandah overlooking this fabulous place? I don't mind! Is it a good prospect? The buyers, I mean?"

"Yeah, they're pretty serious. They've bought from us before and did well with those horses. Hadn't heard from them for a couple years, then out of the blue they called up and said they wanted to come and see what we got now. Coming back for more is always a good sign."

"Your horses must be really good."

"We think they are. Kinda rare, Paint cutting horses, but they come from Quarter Horses, after all, and the ones we breed, if they don't show enough cow sense, go on to be good all-around riding horses. But I'd be lyin' if I said the favourable exchange rate on the U.S. dollar didn't play a big part." He gets up and pulls her to her feet. "Your jeans are fine, but you'll need boots. Maybe Mom's will fit you. We haven't cleared out her things yet. Started to, but it bothered Dad too much. Guess we could do it now, since we can't bring him for visits any more." He sighs and gives his head a slight shake.

Astrid sees the flicker of sorrow that crosses his face, realizes he's feeling the weight of the loss of both parents, and doesn't know what to say. "I have big feet," is all she can come up with.

"Mom would say you have a good understanding," he says, brightening at the happy memory. "She was as tall as you. I bet a lot of her things will fit you." He leaves the room and in minutes, returns with tall black boots. The tops have row upon row of red stitching in a kind of leaf design, and there's red piping along the scalloped top and the pull tabs.

"They're beautiful!" Astrid says. "So fancy!"

"Not all that fancy by today's standards! You should see what they've come up with now. Sparkles. Flowers embroidered on the toes. All kinds of nonsense."

"Well, I like these. What size are they?" Astrid asks, looking inside the shafts. "Oh, I see ... ten and a half. Should be good." She pulls them on and stands. "Perfect, Denver!"

"Nuthin' better'n boots that're already broke in!" He grins, kisses her again, then takes her hand and leads her out to the yard, pointing out the various buildings as they go. The biggest is the barn and its attached shell of a building, the indoor riding arena. The barn is similar to Hazen's, but with more stalls, and at the end of the alleyway there's a gate leading into the covered riding area. The windows are only to admit light, just narrow strips running along the top of the walls. There are pens at the far end, and Denver explains those are for the cattle used when they're working the cutting horses, or if they're roping. Eddie's on a small tractor, pulling something around the dirt area, levelling out the lumps and bumps.

There are numerous small paddocks outside, each with its own little shelter. In the alleyway between the barn and the paddocks, Shane stands holding the horses. Melody is the smaller of the two, gleaming coppery gold and white with a blonde mane and tail and blue eyes.

"Oh, my god!" Astrid exclaims, stroking her shoulder, "She's gorgeous!"

"She's an own daughter of Rocky Duster. Her full name is Rockin' Melody. We always try and name his babies after him, somehow. Her dam is Honky Tonk Melody, who's an own daughter of Honky Tonker's Boy, so she's well bred top and bottom."

"Er ... Top and bottom?"

"Sire and dam, on her pedigree. Sorry, babe, I ran off at the mouth there. I guess I don't have to give you my sales pitch! She'd practically sell herself, anyway. We've had a few people interested in her, but I can't bring myself to let her go. Makes Dallas crazy! She has Rocky's good temperament, and is such a pet, she's nice to keep around. I'll keep her for you, now," he says. He loops an arm around her and gives her a quick squeeze before taking Melody's reins from Shane, and asking her, "Can you see how much she looks like her dad?"

"Nnnn, no. Well, maybe. He's more brown, and she looks like polished copper. But he does have the same kind of markings. Like lacey white doilies all over! I love it!"

"Yeah, her coat pattern is called overo, basically a dark horse with white spots, same as Rocky. Tobianos are the opposite, like that mare." He points to a horse with large patches of black on an otherwise white body. "But they're all purebred Paints, even Daisy, here, and as you can see, there's no white on her except for her feet."

"And what's her, umm, her other, fancy name?"

"Rockin' All Day-Zee." He chuckles. "Corny, huh? If you come up with any suggestions for names, write 'em down. We're runnin' out. Although I guess we won't need 'em any more. We have a few foals due next spring, but after that ... well, maybe you can help Hazens name theirs." He clicks his tongue and then turns to instruct her on how to mount.

Despite being about the same height as his mother was, Astrid's legs are longer, and the stirrups have to be let down. Shane astutely looks away as Denver spends extra time fussing to place her thighs where he says they ought to be. Once she's settled, he shows her how to hold the reins.

"Don't pull on the reins, Astrid, just keep 'em nice and loose. Hold onto the horn if you feel unsteady. You won't have to steer; Melo will follow Daisy. We'll just walk, though Melo may jog now and then to keep up, but you just sit quiet. She won't do anything awful. If you say whoa or lose your balance, she'll stop." He takes Daisy's reins from Shane and swings up onto her back with practiced ease. "Okay?"

She nods.

"Okay. Just give a cluck and a little nudge with your heels, and she'll follow along behind me." He turns his horse down the lane between the corrals, heading toward the open pasture beyond them, with Astrid on Melody a few paces behind. When they get to the gate, Denver opens it and closes it again once they're through, all without dismounting. It's not clear to Astrid how he gets Daisy to pivot carefully around the gate so he doesn't have to dismount, or even let go of it.

"How'd you get her do that?"

"When you're as lazy as I am," he says with a grin, "you make sure and teach the horse things like what to do at a gate. Also, I'm steering her with my legs."

There's a worn path leading across the open grasslands and they follow it down a ravine, and then along the barbed-wire fence next to the road. The sparse prairie grass is bleached and desiccated except for a green strip along what must be a seasonal waterway at the bottom of the ravine. The soil is so parched it's turned to powder. Even as slow as they're going, their horses' feet are raising dust. There's the frequent rattling of grasshoppers stirred up by their passing, but no noise or vehicle exhaust taints the air.

Melody plods along after Daisy as predicted, her head nodding with each step. Astrid finds herself relaxing, and just lets her hips undulate with the four-beat, swaying motion. The rhythmic movement of the horses; their smell; and the sweeping views of the wide open blue skies above rolling hills dotted with sage are intoxicating. The day is warm enough the riders soon stop to take off their jackets, and Denver dismounts to help Astrid with hers.

"Aren't you worried about snakes?" she asks.

"No. What made you think of snakes?"

"Well, the noise those frickin' giant grasshoppers make. I've never seen such big grasshoppers! The first one I heard really startled me! I thought it was a snake, and the ranch is named for them, after all. And you did say a horse got bitten before."

"Yeah, I probably shouldn't've told you about that. The hoppers've been thriving the past few years. They like the heat and drought. They'd be even worse if it wasn't for the snakes. Don't worry, the rattlers aren't aggressive. They don't strike unless you step on them, and the horses are careful. The one that was bitten was a foal."

"Aww! A baby?"

"Yeah. Silly mare shouldn't've taken her baby there."

"Is that the rattlesnake ridge up ahead?"

"No. My house, the one Trisha lives in, is just on the other side of that hill. The ridge the ranch is named for is way out behind the old house. It's rocky and steep, and even more barren than this. Faces due south, so it's ideal snake habitat. They can have it. Don't worry, we're not going there today."

"Couldn't your family have named the ranch something, well, that made it sound like a nicer place?"

"Danielsons didn't name it. The story is, everyone knew about the ridge where all the rattlesnakes lived, and the ranch was just the Danielson place. Then people started calling it the Danielson Place at Rattlesnake Ridge. Grampa said back then, the ranch was a town on its own. Made its own ropes, had its own smithy— even a saddle maker. Great Grandma, she was a Reichel. See? I have a bit of German in me, too! She taught the ranch kids their three r's. Then the neighbours' kids came for schooling and people started having their mail sent here so they could pick it up when they came for the kids, and soon there was a post office. Preacher came once a month and held a service in one of the bunkhouses, before they built the chapel. Afterwards they always had a big potluck dinner."

"So, even a chapel! What happened to all that?"

"Fire. Everything but the big house burned down. Lucky no people were hurt. Then that red brick church over on Old Smithy Road was built, Merritt had the schoolhouse and the post office, so they never did replace everything."

"I really envy you your connection to the land. And family. I don't even know my grandmother's maiden name."

"Well, not everyone cares about stuff like that. Abby has no interest in the ranch; she never cared much for the horses, even. And Dallas? He likes the horses, and he's good with them. Too good, I guess. He talks about going to Texas, so he can make big money as a trainer. He'd sell the place in a heartbeat and never look back. Then there's me. I think about leaving every once in a while, but I can't imagine living anywhere else. I don't know how three people with the same parents can be so different." Denver finishes rolling their jackets and tying them behind their saddles, then swings back onto his horse. "Ready?"

Astrid nods and they start up the hill out of the ravine, when they hear a vehicle on the road and a red sedan comes into view, slows and stops. The driver gets out and stands hands on hips, looking their way.

"It's Trisha," Denver says, reining Daisy back beside Melody. "We're not stopping." Instead of continuing along the trail next to the fence that goes to the top of the hill, he turns Daisy's nose away from the road and onto a lower trail. Melody follows, but before turning away, Astrid sees the small woman's pretty face is twisted in an expression of such malice it causes her to draw in a sharp breath. She stiffens involuntarily; Melody breaks into a jog and doesn't walk again until her nose is on Daisy's tail.

Astrid thinks, *if looks could kill.*

* * *

Hank flips onto his back and reaches his cigarettes and lighter off the night table. He opens the pack, takes a cigarette out and lights it, drawing deeply and exhaling loudly as he leans back against the headboard and lets out a long, treble fart. "Not bad for a half-inch speaker, eh?" he chuckles.

"You're a disgusting pig!" the woman next to him grumbles.

He snorts, then reaches his arm across her and pulls the covers up over her head. She makes gagging sounds and struggles; he pushes the covers back down to bare her breasts, and delivers a stinging slap.

"Ow! That hurt! What was that for?"

"A sample of what's to come if you don't get yer little sugar shaker outta here. I told you, you ain't hangin' around here. Gittin' late. Time you hit the road."

"Are you kidding? You think I spent all day driving up here just to meet you in a bar? No dinner even, just lousy chicken wings? Then spend one night with you, and drive back? What's the big rush? You said your folks aren't due home until tomorrow."

"Don't bitch, it's just my policy. Girls never stay overnight. It's a long drive, so I made an exception in yer case. It don't mean yer stayin' another night."

"I imagine there's a steady stream of females lining up to fuck you? I got news for you, you weren't that fuckin' good! I should of known you'd have a tiny dick when I saw how small your feet were! Oh yeah, you're going to 'rock my world' all right. You're not even as good as my husband!" She rolls so her back is to him, pulling the covers with her. "Hmmpf!"

"Well," he snorts, "that dick sure made you moan 'n' squirm." He swings his legs off the bed and stands, pulling his briefs, then his jeans on and buckling the belt. Tendrils of smoke from the cigarette held in the corner of his mouth curl up his cheek into his eye, causing him to squint. He draws deeply on it before setting it in the ashtray and pulling his shirt on. "Come on, time to move along. I got things to do and if you ain't ready to go when I am, yer gonna hafta hitchhike back to town."

She sits bolt upright. "What? How can you even suggest that? Isn't it the highway right out there where all those girls have gone missing?" She gets out of bed and comes close, cupping her breasts, presenting them to him. "Besides," she smiles seductively, softening her tone, "you can't tell me you don't want to play with these some more. We have the house to ourselves. How about tonight we put on some music, you get comfortable, and I'll dance for you."

Hank picks up his cigarette and puffs for a moment, enjoying the nicotine fix and the tantalizing view of her Barbie Doll body. "I was just kiddin'. No reason fer you to go today. I'll go down to the barn 'n' do the mornin' feed 'n' you go see what you can rustle up fer breakfast."

"You want me to make breakfast? Can't we go out to eat? Maybe that place you say you go to all the time, Dot's or whatever?" She drops her hands to her side, sets her mouth in a pout.

"At least make coffee. If it's not too much fuckin' trouble. You *can* make coffee, can't you?"

She turns away from him and starts toward the ensuite, then turns and glares. "This is a poor fucking way to treat me and I don't like your tone. I think I *will* go home. You go ahead and do whatever you have to do that's so *fucking* important and I'll hitchhike back to my car. It's on you if I get murdered!"

"You ain't gonna get murdered."

"Bet none of those girls thought they were going to get murdered, either!" She snorts, then goes into the bathroom and slams the door shut behind her. A second later she opens it again, sticks her head out and gives him another withering look, then says, "And lose my phone number, asshole!" She slams the door again.

"You didn't have to phone me," Hank calls to the closed door. Then he shrugs and goes to the kitchen to make a pot of coffee. He's perched on a stool at the island, drinking coffee and smoking, when she comes into the kitchen towing her suitcase, and sets it at the door. He admires her narrow waist and flat stomach, the tempting swell of her ample breasts in her low-cut T-shirt, the way she fills out her snug jeans.

She glares at him as she pulls her jacket on.

"You ain't mad, Trisha?" Hank cajoles. "I said I was just kiddin' and I never meant it when I told you to hitchhike. I know about this road, I'd of never let you hitchhike! I'm sorry if I hurt yer feelin's. Didn't mean to. Come on, pretty girl, have a coffee, we'll go somewhere for breakfast, like you said. Not Dot's, someplace nicer. Grab a coffee now, and we'll take a run in to Prince George, have brunch, do a little shoppin'. I'll buy you somethin' nice, you know, a little thank you for comin'."

The tension flows out of her body. Her frown relaxes and is replaced with a smug grin. "Okay." She puts lays her jacket across the suitcase, flips her hair over her shoulder and comes to sit on the stool Hank's pulled out for her. He fills a mug with coffee, then sets it on the granite in front of her, slides the carton of Half & Half next to it and hands her a spoon. "Sugar," he says, kissing her forehead as he pushes the sugar bowl from the center of the island so it's within her reach, then resumes his seat on the stool beside her.

"So," he says, "you mentioned yer husband."

"Yeah?"

"You ain't divorced?"

"No, or he wouldn't be my husband," she clucks. "Duh-uh!"

"I have to know where I stand, Trisha. I … I'm … You know that's the only reason I told you to go. I don't want to, you know, let my feelings grow. If I do, then what happens to me if you make up with him?"

"Don't worry, I am *so* done with that asshole. On top of everything, he's picked up with someone else. Day before yesterday, I saw them out riding, and *she* was on *my* horse!" She gives her coffee a stir and sets the spoon down on the granite with a clatter.

"You still love him!" he says with a sigh as he gets up to refill his mug.

"I do not! It just pisses me off she's pushing in there."

"Yeah," he allows, "but he calls you his ex, and you said you split up over a year ago. Why ain't you divorced?"

"Money, what else? He hasn't offered me enough. But he will. And since he's parading his floozy all over the place, the price just went up."

"What d'you think you can get?" Hank asks, turning with the carafe and topping up her mug before resuming his seat on the stool. "You know he don't own that place."

"He doesn't? Oh! The old man!" Her shoulders slump and the frown returns. "So. I guess there's nothing until he dies."

"Just how old is the old man, anyway?"

"I don't know. Eighty, maybe eighty-five? He could live for another ten years!" she heaves a sigh.

"Didn't you tell me he's nuts, has the Altimers? How long's he had it? The Altimer's?"

"Hmm. He already had it when I first went there, and that was five years ago, so, six or seven years? He didn't go into the home until after the old bitch dropped dead, though. Why?"

Hank drains his coffee and gets to his feet. "Ready to go? I just gotta run down and feed the horses. I'll be ten minutes." He puts his arms around her and nuzzles her ear, whispering, "You know, about before… I'm sorry."

"You should be."

"Can you forgive me?"

"Maybe."

"Please? I just… well, you know, you're so different. So different, so special, so beautiful! I was worried you only wanted a one-night stand and I… well, my pride."

"Okay."

He cups her chin and brushes her lips with his, then turns and heads out the door, a bounce in his step as he trots across the yard.

FIFTEEN

FRANNY SLIDES INTO the booth next to Astrid, heaves a sigh, and says, "Thank *gawd* that's over," as she pulls her feet out of her shoes and reaches down to give them a quick massage.

She's referring to the hectic shift they just put in that saw the three servers run ragged. There'd been a relatively slow supper hour and then about nine, when the diner is usually quiet and they were starting to put things away, two big groups, both needing tables pushed together, came in within minutes of each other. After the customers were gone and the door was locked, there were still tables to bus, so they're finishing up late.

The third server empties the last of the coffee into three mugs, then brings them to the booth and slides in across the table from Astrid. "Is it always like this on a Friday?" she asks. "It's been so slow all week you could've handled it on your own, Franny."

Astrid frowns. All week? She's new, and she's been working shifts Astrid could have been booked in for?

"They're here for the curling bonspiel, isn't that what they said? Prob'ly be busy all week-end," Franny says. "We made good tips, though. It's hard keeping track of everyone, especially when they start moving around. You handled it well, Jen."

The lock on the door rattles even though the 'OPEN' sign has been turned off, and they look up to see the owner, Lester Cline, come in. He locks the door behind him.

"Girls," he says, scowling. "Late night?"

"A big crowd came in shortly before closing," Franny tells him.

"So, all three of you had to stay past the end of your shift?"

Al's face appears at the pass through and he says, "Could've just turned the customers away, would you rather we did that? I asked the girls to stay. It was a mess. I had these girls help Suki clean up the kitchen, so I could get into the office and do the receipts, since you wanted them tonight."

"You want to pay their extra wages?" Lester gives Al a return frown, then pulls a handkerchief out of his pocket and dabs at his eye.

"The deposit's not quite ready," Al says, mouth set in a hard line as he turns away.

Lester heads toward the kitchen, pushes the door in, and says to Al's retreating back, "I'm booked for surgery to get this goddamn blocked tear duct repaired on Monday. I won't be back until Wednesday night. You'll have to …" The door at the far end of the kitchen leading to Al's office and the private back room closes behind him, cutting off whatever else he's saying.

"Old Les Inclined," Franny says conspiratorially, "Less inclined to part with a dime than anyone you ever knew. Wouldn't put it past him not to pay us for the extra hour and a half."

"Doesn't he have to?" Jen asks.

"Has to, but might not. Make sure you're keeping track of your hours and match 'em up to your pay stubs. Cheap bastard. You've seen him take pies, Astrid?"

She nods.

"Ol' Les Inclined has a catering contract with some lodge. That's where the pies go. Other stuff too. Sandwich trays. All those bins of stuff for the steam table. Salads and roasts."

"I wondered," Astrid says.

"Of course, the cost goes against Dot's, everything's written off as spoilage, like when his buddies come in," Franny says, "a tax dodge I guess? Just make sure his wife doesn't try to put it on your meal ticket. She charged me for pies once, an 'honest mistake' of course." She takes a sip of her coffee. "Speaking of his wife, the two of them are total opposites, right Astrid?"

Astrid nods and glances uneasily through the kitchen to the back room to confirm the men are still behind the closed door.

Franny continues without skipping a beat, "Him so tall and skinny, and she's barely tall enough to go down the green waterslide at the Dark River Aquatic Center and so round she'd get stuck if she did. So round she doesn't even have an ass, well, unless you call a giant camel toe an ass"—she chuckles and takes another sip of her coffee before continuing—"Can almost understand why he's such an ass grabber. Make sure you don't let him corner you, Jen. It's not accidental."

"I'm surprised you've put up with it for so long, Franny," Astrid says. This is the same pep talk Franny gave her when she started at Dot's months ago, and the admonition against getting cornered by Les has proven warranted. But when Franny delivered her orientation speech back then, she seemed to be half joking. Now there's a bitter edge to her voice and no humour in her eyes as she finger-combs her short, salt-and-pepper hair.

"Well, what can any of us do about it? Not many jobs in Dark River," she says, and sips her coffee. "Bill got laid off two weeks before the mill shut down, and this is the longest shutdown we remember. Longer than they need to do the maintenance. We're worried there may be more layoffs, and that he might not get called back when it starts up again. There's a shortage of logs because of all the fires, and there's talk they're scaling down besides. Maybe they're only going to call the young guys back. You know, Hank Junior's fan club."

"I need the job, too," Jen says, "although if it wasn't for Les giving me a good deal on a room, it wouldn't fuckin' be enough to keep me afloat."

"A room?" Astrid asks.

"Yeah. In an old house over behind the Plaza. I have my own bedroom and there's a common kitchen and living room, cable tv included. Not a fuckin' palace, but …" She worries a few strands of dark hair until they come loose, looks at the hair for a moment, then shakes it off onto the floor. "I'm the only one living there right now, though. Les says there'll be other girls coming."

Franny gives her a sharp look, and when the girl ignores it, says, "Didn't I just sweep the floor?"

Jen shrugs. "Yeah. So?"

"So, don't do that!"

"What?"

"Don't put your hair on the floor."

"Okay!" Jen mutters something under her breath, then pinches another few hairs between thumb and forefinger, twists them, and continues as if Franny hadn't spoken. "Like I was sayin', Les says other girls will be moving in soon. I hope so. It's fuckin' lonely, me not knowin' no one in town. Least Les drops by now and then, to make sure I'm okay."

Astrid wonders why that last comment gives her pause. Maybe he's just being kind and caring, but that would be a side of him she hasn't seen, and he's an ass grabber—would he do more than just grab Jen's ass if he had her alone in the house? She'd say something if he did, wouldn't she? But both she and Franny have given him a pass on the ass grabbing, just try and make sure to stay out of his range, because they need the job. Would Jen? Would she give him a pass on even more?

"So, you're new in town?" Astrid asks.

"Yeah," she says, squirming, "hey, can I smoke now that we're closed?"

"No," Franny says, "you still have to go out the back."

"Fuck it, I'll wait then," Jen says, "it's just that a cigarette goes with coffee and I haven't had a smoke break for a couple hours."

"Go have a smoke, then. Take your coffee out with you."

"I said, I'll wait."

"Speaking of coffee, this is undrinkable," Astrid says. She slides to the end of the bench. "I'm gonna take off. If you aren't going out for a smoke, do you want a ride, Jen?"

"No. Les said he'll give me a ride on the days he's here."

"Really?" Franny frowns.

"He's all right, you know," Jen tells them. "I can't believe I run into him, just off the bus, waitin' for the bus to Vancouver, thinkin' 'bout savin' the bus fare and hitchin' instead. But he seen me, offered me this job and a place to stay, so I decided to hang here for a while. Might not be so lucky in Vancouver."

Franny nods but is still frowning; Astrid makes a mental note to suggest they don't discuss Mister Cline when Jen's around. She studies the girl's unlined face. She must have lied about her age to get a job where she serves liquor. Trying to be tough, with her artless ballpoint pen tattoos on her arms, hands, even her neck. And her attitude! But the chewed-to-nub nails, torn, bleeding hangnails, and dime-sized bald spots above her ears tell another story. *Poor kid,* Astrid thinks. *She probably needs the shifts more than I do, and obviously needed a place to stay. Maybe Les isn't so bad, ass grabbing aside.*

"Well, goodnight," Astrid says, sliding out of the booth and taking her mug to the dishwasher before going through the kitchen and out the back door.

She crosses the parking lot to her car and is unlocking the door when the throaty roar of a V-8 engine draws her attention. She looks up and sees tail lights speeding away. Hank? But he left Dot's hours earlier, before the crowd came in, so it can't be him. His is far from the only V-8 in this town of small houses and big trucks, after all.

As she pulls out of the parking lot, lights from a vehicle beside the Chevron station across the street attract her attention. They're promptly shut off, but not before she notices it's Fletch's old green and white Chevy S10 snugged into the shadows beside the west wall.

"This has gone on long enough," she mutters under her breath. She pulls into the service station lot, parks in front of the truck, gets out and goes to the passenger side window. He leans across and rolls it down.

"Everything okay, Fletch?" she asks.

He nods.

"All right then," she says, forcing a smile, "come up to the house for lunch tomorrow. We got left-over roast beef again, and I'm going to try out the bread maker, so unless something goes sideways, there'll be fresh bread for sandwiches."

His only response is to nod.

"Okay! See you tomorrow," she says, and exhales loudly as she goes back to her car. She even manages to give him a friendly wave before driving away.

The thought of him in the kitchen, silent, hulking over his plate, is cringe-worthy, but she hopes if she treats him like a normal person, he'll start acting like one. She tries to put herself in his shoes. Living alone out in the bush with only his guns and cats and Hank for company, he must be lonely.

Hank should treat him better, include him more, but she admits Fletch isn't an easy person to have around. She's tried Denver's suggestion of drawing him into conversation, but it's a struggle to find something—anything—to ask him about and he never initiates a conversation. That unblinking stare! And materializing behind her seemingly out of thin air!

Practically homesteading in the corner booth at Dot's is bad enough; now he's been showing up at other places unexpectedly. He's sneaky about it, like on her morning runs when she hears the ATV off in the distance and catches glimpses of camo movement through the trees. His truck parked half a block away from the Co-Op. Pulling in behind the Danton Creek gas bar near the mill, when she ran down there yesterday. Last week, he was parked in the alley across from the thrift store when she came out. And tonight, again, he's waiting for her to leave work. It's escalating. When does a stalker do more than just stalk? Is calling him on it the right thing to do?

Bridey assures her he's harmless. But he still gives her the heebie-jeebies.

SIXTEEN

HE SPRINGS THE padlock and pulls the chain away from one of the doors, opens it enough to get through, and pulls it closed behind him. He squeezes in beside the old Jeep hidden here, fumbles for the lamp and turns it on, noticing the light's becoming dim. He'll have to remember to get new batteries. He stands for a moment, letting his eyes adjust to the gloom, then gets the folding camp chair from the back of the Jeep, opens it and jiggles its feet into the dirt floor until it's secure before collapsing down into it.

He closes his eyes, leans back and rotates his head side to side, front to back, then takes several deep breaths. He always enjoys the smell of the old shed and doesn't have to look at everything so carefully displayed on the wall to feel profound calm wash over him. After a few minutes, he opens his eyes and allows his gaze to linger where it will.

The first thing he focuses on is the small backpack, the one with the little cartoonish stuffed animal clipped to it. He remembers the girl with her short black hair and budding little breasts. She was his youngest, maybe ten or eleven. Her little cooch was hairless and snug but his cock wasn't the first to plough it. She didn't struggle. Pinching her nipples, even biting, caused barely a whimper. He almost wouldn't have known she felt anything but for the tears running silently down her face. Even when he choked her out, she did nothing. It was as if she accepted it, maybe even welcomed it. The third time he choked her out, he didn't stop when she was unconscious. She was a no fun toy. The most stimulating part of his time with her was watching her body tumble in boneless cartwheels over the cliff and into the canyon.

All the others fought him, or tried to make like they could be friends, but at least they screamed when he bit their earlobes off. Eventually, they all pleaded with him to kill them. Some got their wish. Others moved to the lodge. He doesn't know or care what happened to them after that.

Here, the mental movies of what he's done, never far from his mind, seem the most vivid. It's a good time to masturbate.

He rises from the chair and passes along the row of purses hanging on the wall, lovingly stroking and taking a little trip down memory lane with each. Except for one, he doesn't know their names. They all tried to tell him their names, and it earned them an extra beating. He seldom remembers their faces, either, but he remembers vividly what they did together.

Then one of the purses falls to the floor at his touch. He feels a torrent of rage boil up inside and kicks it, sending it tumbling up against the end wall. The useless, stupid sluts! In the end, they don't fight hard enough. Squeezing the life out of them with his bare hands is hard work, and they can't put up a better fight? They just shit and piss themselves and die, leaving him with a mess to clean up. He doesn't mind the piss; at least it's pleasurable, but the shit's disgusting.

He returns to his chair, closes his eyes and fantasizes about things, new things, to do with the next girl. He visualizes using a spoon to scoop out her eyes. Is it hard to do? Or maybe cut her tongue out. *Yes, that's it,* he thinks. *That way she can still watch the other things I'll do.* He pictures holding the tongue with pliers while he slices it off. Imagines torrents of blood flooding the mouth. He'd have to make the cut quickly. What will he do with it once it's cut off? Maybe cook it and feed it to her later? Woo-hoo-hoo-hoo! He unzips, pulls his penis out and starts rubbing.

There's the added bonus that with their tongues gone, he won't have to listen to any annoying yammering. He can keep them longer.

And the rifle. Watching the last one squirm and cry and plead with him while his .22 was up her cooch—that was something! He didn't clean it for days, not until the smell of her had faded.

His anger rises again when he recalls how mad *he* was, how he pissed and moaned over her missing earlobes, the other little nips. Now it's impossible to get an erection. He's one to talk! He was fine with it, supportive even, and then, out of the blue, no more girls, just hookers? A church? Dress up in robes and have orgies? And he has to buy in? No more payment for the fresh meat he takes them?

"Fuck that!"

It was *his wife* who sent him to the nut house. Why did he allow that? But a few years of whining about how his mother always loved his sister best. How the little snot could never do anything wrong while he could never do anything right. Telling them what they wanted to hear. All those framed diplomas on the wall and they gobbled it up. All he had to do was agree to take some pills every day, and he got sent home, cured. As if he's going to take pills that make everything seem dull and flat. As if there was ever anything wrong with him in the first place!

He's felt the power of watching their lives slip away while he has his cock in them. Their life in his hands! Them pleading with him, him letting them think he might let them go, then watching pain and terror replace hope when he slices their nose, or maybe a piece of their lip, off. Nothing in the world can compare.

"Oh-h-h!" he moans. His penis is swelling now. He spits in his hand and rubs himself more vigorously. But it's not enough and doesn't stop the dark nub deep in the folds of his brain from bursting. Skinny legs, like tentacles, bloom, and other smaller black nubs start creeping out, growing as they move toward his eyes. Then they're filling his nose, swelling and clogging his mouth until his lips are forced open and they begin to tumble out. They're falling onto his penis, latching on with their long, skinny appendages. He jumps to his feet, sending the chair toppling, and swipes at them, but can't shake them off. They keep coming, their sticky little feet clinging to his foreskin. Growing. They're large enough now that he can see their faces. Soon they're all over him. He knows he has to keep them from covering his face or they'll smother him; already his chest feels squeezed and his lungs can't draw in enough air.

He turns to the nearest purse, opens it and thrusts his face inside. Inhaling the scent reminds him of the girl and what they did together. The spiders retreat until at last they're all re-absorbed and The Mother is again curled up in her parlour deep inside his brain. But instead of a quiet nub, round and smooth and as featureless as a marble, he can see her eye, and her legs aren't completely folded in. He knows she's just biding her time until she ripens and her babies burst forth again.

He straightens. Closes his eyes. Takes deep breaths until his lungs re-inflate.

His need has become undeniable.

SEVENTEEN

ASTRID'S IN THE kitchen clearing away the makings of the cucumber sandwiches she and Bridey had for lunch, when she sees a black sedan turn into the yard and drive up to park by the garage. The goats come bounding into the driveway. In seconds they're up on the hood of the car, then they bounce up onto the roof. An obese man in a rumpled gray suit climbs out, shouting angrily and waving his arms to shoo the goats, who watch him as if amused. He manages to chase them off by swatting at their legs, but they immediately hop back up again. Red-faced, he throws up his hands, then lumbers toward the house, shoving Buster out of the way with a swift jerk of his tree-trunk thigh.

Astrid goes to the door and meets him there. "Sorry 'bout the goats," she says.

"Don't know why… they still… keep those!" he says, puffing at the exertion of the arm waving and climbing the few steps to the door. He sticks out his hand. "Hello."

"Hello."

"I'm Pastor Green. Remember me?"

"Umm, sorry, no. I'm Astrid." She shakes his hand, surprised to find it's soft and sweaty and limp.

"Yes, I know. You really don't remember me? I've seen you at Dot's."

"Oh, sure," Astrid agrees rather than prolonging the discussion. And when she thinks back, she does recall an obese man barely able to squeeze into a booth.

"I heard you were here," he says, pulling at her hand and holding it moments longer than necessary and giving it an extra little squeeze. "I'm a friend of the family. I heard Bridey was under the weather, so I thought I'd stop by. Is she up and around?"

"Well, she's up, anyway. She's in the family room. I'll tell her you're here." She struggles to look him in the eye rather than staring at the quivering jowls spilling out above his shirt collar that make him appear neckless.

"I know the way, I'll just stick my head in," Pastor Green says as he pushes past her.

Astrid steps aside to let him pass, wipes her hand on her jeans to rid it of his sweat, then follows.

"Bruce! Hello!" Bridey, wrapped in a crocheted throw and propped up by toss cushions, smiles and pulls herself up a bit at seeing him, then directs him to an armchair. She picks up the remote control, turns the TV off and says, "Astrid, this is our dear friend and the pastor of our church."

"Glad to hear you still think of it as your church," Pastor Green chides.

"I know, we hardly ever go now. Hank spends so many weekends at that lodge of his, and I don't like to drive. I'll have to get Astrid to start taking me again."

"I'm just teasing, Bridey. I know you're a good Christian woman, despite not attending services very often. You're missed, that's all." He reaches across and gives her hand a squeeze.

"Oh, thank you, Bruce!" Bridey smiles and seems to have perked up. She turns to Astrid and says, "Astrid, would you make us a fresh pot of tea, please?"

"Of course!" Astrid agrees, and returns to the kitchen to make tea the way Bridey taught her (hot the pot and so on). She hears them chatting, Bridey saying she enjoyed the trip, but she must have picked up a bug on the way home.

"Toxic air on the airplane," Pastor Green says.

"A cold, nothing serious, although it's been hanging on longer than usual."

More chatter. Then there's laughter. The pleasant sounds of an old, comfortable friendship. It was good of him to stop by to visit Bridey, and Bridey's happy about it. He must be okay. Pushy, but okay.

When the tea is steeping, Astrid puts the pot in its crocheted cozy on a tray with cups, milk, sugar, lemon and spoons. As an afterthought, she adds a packet of Rich Tea Biscuits, and delivers the tray, pushing aside the Kleenex box, books and remote controls on the lamp table to set it within easy reach of both Bridey and Pastor Green.

"Will you be here for a bit, Pastor?' she asks. "I have my shift at Dot's this afternoon and if you're going to stay, I could leave early. I'd like to do some shopping before I go to work. I don't like leaving Bridey alone. But Mr. Hazen and Hank Junior might not be home for a couple of hours."

"You go ahead, dear, I'll be fine," Bridey says.

"Well," Pastor Green says, reaching for the biscuits, "I don't mind staying until Hank gets here."

"You don't have to," Bridey says. "Honestly, Astrid worries too much."

"What if you take another fall?" Astrid asks. "You could be on the floor for hours. And what if you really hurt yourself?"

"I'm glad Astrid has good sense even if you don't, Bridey," Pastor Green tells her. He's worked a couple of biscuits out of the box and shoves them into his mouth, chewing and spewing crumbs as he says, "I'd like to say hello to your husband anyway, so I'm happy to stay."

"Well that would be nice, Bruce," Bridey says, "if you're sure it's no trouble? We do have some catching up to do. Did Hank tell you Junior brought a girl home? It's the first time he's shown an interest in anyone since Claire left, so we're thinking it's serious. They are so cute together! So much in love! I've never seen Junior so smitten. Of course she's pretty, a very pretty girl. Such a tiny, sweet person. I just wish she didn't live so far away. I might get grandchildren yet!"

Astrid thinks, *why does she always refer to Trisha as a tiny sweet person?* She forces a smile and says, "I'll be on my way, then. Text me if you think of anything you need me to pick up while I'm in town, Bridey. Nice to meet you, Pastor Green." She turns and escapes down the stairs to her room to change into her Dot's Diner shirt before setting out.

Not for the first time, she wonders how Trisha made such a good impression, and tries not to feel hurt. It's as if Bridey thinks 'tiny' and 'sweet' go together; it makes her feel big and awkward, and seems like an insult, especially after Bridey's reaction the first time she saw Astrid's shoes on the tray at the door. She'd laughed, *Can't tell your shoes from Junior's, ha ha! What size are they, anyway?* She has to admit that next to Bridey's size fives, they look like clown shoes. Since then, Bridey can't seem to resist mentioning what she calls Astrid's Number Tens at every opportunity.

Of course, Trisha *is* tiny, or at least short. But surely not sweet! She remembers the look of intense malice on her face as she stood on the road watching them ride by.

She must be showing her good side to the Hazens. When Hank Senior mentions her, he sounds as smitten as his son, in a platonic way of course, and her relationship with Hank Junior is boiling ahead at breakneck speed. He's already bought her a new car. Somehow, girls like Trisha get guys to buy them cars. How do they do it? If she was tiny and sweet, with size five feet, would Denver want to buy her a car? She couldn't accept it even if he did. She's not like Trisha. She's not a gold-digger. She'd like to push that uncharitable thought away, but can't. She's enjoying it with the smug certainty of her moral superiority.

When she found out Hank and Trisha had hooked up, it was supper time. Knowing he'd be in the kitchen, she phoned the landline at the Triple R to tell Denver the news. He was silent for a moment, then burst out laughing.

"Well," he said between guffaws, "he was warned! He deserves everything he gets!" When he held the phone away for a moment and told the others in the room, there was a burst of raucous laughter.

Although muffled as if Denver had his hand over the mouthpiece, she heard Wilson say, "Them two deserve each other." Then Dallas said, "Who's driving a thousand K for pussy now!"

Denver would be mortified if he knew she'd heard that, and it worries her. Is that what Dallas thinks she is, just pussy? Is that, in fact, all she is to Denver? Surely not. It doesn't feel that way. If that's all he's after, he can get it closer to home. It would be hard to miss the 'come on' looks one of the new boarders, twenty-something Megan, gave him.

Megan, who besides riding well and having a nice horse, would fit Bridey's definition of tiny and sweet. She's pretty, too. Plus, she has a good job. Astrid wanted to dislike her for all those reasons, but she was so nice, she couldn't. And Denver seemed oblivious to the looks she gave him. But then, Astrid was only at the ranch for a couple of weeks and anything could've happened after she left. That's such an unhappy thought, she pushes it out of her mind.

She wonders if Trisha will spend Christmas at the Double H when Astrid's at the Triple R. When she suggested it to Denver, saying she wouldn't worry about Bridey then, as Trisha would be there to help Bridey if need be, he laughed and said it would be interesting to see how *that* worked out, but since it's a reasonable idea, it would not be like Trisha to agree.

Regardless of what Hank and Trisha do, she has to work something out so she can be away from December twentieth to January fifteenth. Denver's asked her to stay that long. If it was a regular job, she wouldn't be entitled to vacation, but it's more an informal agreement and so it shouldn't be a problem. Hazens really need to find someone else anyway, because she can't be there twenty-four seven forever. But Bridey's hissy fit when she wanted time off for Denver's visit that time makes her nervous about asking. And as for Dot's, she already took her earned vacation time, and more, for her last trip to Merritt. Booking more time off might mean she doesn't get scheduled back in. If she loses either job—well, she'll cross that bridge when she comes to it.

Bridey might be disappointed rather than mad that Astrid won't be in Dark River for Christmas; they'd talked about making lefse, but that was before Denver invited her to the Triple R. She can get around that by making the lefse ahead of time. It would be nice to take some to the Triple R, anyway.

Astrid's missing Denver so much it's almost physically painful, and it seems an eternity before they'll be together again. He's in the States now. He has shows, some big ones where he's only one of a bunch of judges, in California, Arizona and Texas, and won't be home for weeks. It's good for his reputation, and great that he's so in demand and booked up; the judging has been a lifesaver, with the drought making finances tight at the ranch, and the looming financial hit of his divorce.

But him being away for so long is a worry. Astrid imagines how others must see him: tall, well-built, with that wide smile, either in one of his casual western sports coats for smaller shows, or one of the snazzy suits he wears at the A-ranked shows and awards ceremonies. In the photos Wilson showed her, he's so movie-star handsome it took her breath away. Seeing him in the flesh, those beautiful horse girls must feel it, too.

He has a string of other shows beginning late January, so they're planning to be together for the entire four weeks or so in between. For today, Astrid will stop by the tack shop in Deep River in hopes of getting ideas for gifts. Maybe being surrounded by all the horse stuff and thinking of what he might like will fill the emptiness.

Why am I feeling this way? she wonders. It feels good being with him, and she knows she likes him. Really likes him. But is she in love with him or is her brain playing tricks on her, making her think she has strong feelings for him because he would be her ticket to the good life? Why does she worry about him meeting some beautiful horse girl at a show, or taking up with Megan? Why does she constantly wonder what he sees in her, a basement-dwelling waitress with big feet who can't even ride?

Sometimes I wish I'd never met him. Afraid to give my heart. Afraid not to. How can something feel so good and feel so bad?

EIGHTEEN

ASTRID TROTS ALONG a game trail through the forest. It's late for her run, but the morning was grey and drizzly with some snow mixed in; she got busy with other things, and it wasn't until there was a sunny break mid-afternoon she decided to go. A bit of snow was still in evidence, half-melted skiffs in shady spots here and there. Chilly, yes, but good running weather. The sunshine was irresistible. She pulled on fleece-lined tights, a fleece vest over a long-sleeved T-shirt, and a jacket. Thinking she might find new chanterelle patches if it's not too late in the year, she stuck a plastic bag in her jacket pocket, called Buster, and the two set out. Now she's warmed enough by the exercise to think the vest was a mistake. Maybe the jacket, too.

This is not her accustomed route. *Let Fletch try and follow me this time*, she thinks, chuckling to herself. *I left hours later than usual, and I'm going somewhere I've never gone before!*

Instead of going east or north, she went west across the highway and headed into the bush along an obvious trail, ignoring the 'no trespassing' signs. She's not trespassing. The land all belongs to Hazens, and Bridey told her with a warm smile that she can go anywhere her number tens take her. Hazen Sawmills is on this side of the highway, and the trail she's on should come out at their sort yard. Old tracks and horse manure along the way tell her this is the trail Hank Senior uses when he rides Rocky Duster.

Soon, the sun disappears, and what she can see of the sky through the canopy of tall cedars and native firs is a uniform stainless-steel grey. The pungent scent of the wet underbrush is pleasant, but the temperature is dropping; her breath forms vapour clouds, and there's a promise of more snow in the air. Her tights are soaked through, and now her legs are starting to feel chilled. She wishes for waterproof running pants. So far, she hasn't been lucky enough to find a pair at the thrift store, but now that she's running enough to warrant the expense, she'll order some on line. For now, she's glad she wore warm clothing, but even with the fleece, she's beginning to look forward to a soak in the tub.

She's about to turn back when she sees another way through the forest that looks more open and appears to lead directly back. She leaves the trail she's on and cuts through snags and shrubs to get to it, following it for a while before realizing it isn't really a trail, as it's petered out.

Now she can't see how to get back to the original trail and she's not sure where she is, other than still west of the highway. She shoves her hand in her pocket to get her phone with its compass app and GPS, and finds only the plastic bag. She remembers now. She left the phone on the end table in the family room, charging.

Buster went bounding off through the bushes shortly after they started out, and hasn't been back since. He'll likely catch up with her soon, but will he stick with her, and lead the way home?

Thinking she must be close to the highway, she's not worried. She picks her way through the trees, avoiding steep areas, heading steadily east so she'll soon come to the highway, or at least cross another trail. Hopefully one with horse poop!

Finally, she skirts a rocky outcropping, climbs over a mossy log, then climbs again before coming out onto what seems to be an old lane. She amends her initial impression. It can't be a lane. Driving through here wouldn't be possible, with the outcroppings of bedrock and branches closing in on all sides. She stands with hands on hips, taking a bit of a breather while she decides which way to go. She locates a light spot in the clouds that must be the sun and concludes east must be to her right. She starts to turn that way, when she notices a structure of some kind a bit further on. It's the wrong direction, but it doesn't mean backtracking too much, so she decides she might as well check it out.

The size of a single car garage, the building's made of hewn logs chinked with some whitish clay-like substance. It appears derelict, and very old. Could it be a homesteader's cabin? There are two doors meeting in the middle, with a chain through the handles, and oddly, a padlock. Fletch doesn't lock his house. Hazens don't lock theirs. Why is this building locked?

Intrigued, she pushes through the bushes crowding up around the shed, hoping for a window. There is one on the back wall, but it has something over it on the inside. There's a small door next to it, and it's ajar, held in that position by many seasons of tall weeds and branches growing through and around it. Peering through the narrow opening, she sees a vehicle. An antique truck? Old logging equipment?

She'll ask Hank Senior about it. When it comes to the mill and its history, he's a fount of information. He loves talking about how it was when he first came to Dark River as a young man, started working as a faller, and made his own way to owning a vast tract of land, the mill, and the ranch. He'll know about this shed and that thing, whatever it is. She needs a closer look. By pulling weeds and breaking branches away, she frees the door to open it wide enough to squeeze in.

Inside, it's gloomy, but there's enough daylight coming through cracks to see that what she thought might be an old truck, is a Jeep, dull olive-green and khaki camouflage with open wheel wells and big, knobby tires. It looks like something from an old movie, but it's dirty and there's a small cedar branch stuck in the grille, still green. It hasn't been parked here and forgotten. It's been used, and not that long ago.

She realizes she's in someone's garage. The forest trails can be confusing; maybe she ran away from the sawmill instead of toward it. This can't be Hazens' Jeep or she'd have seen it around before now. Besides, there are plenty of other, more logical, places to park it.

She's about to leave when she notices the wall on the far side of the Jeep. It looks like there are purses hanging on it. *Purses?*

As small as the vehicle is, it fills the shed. The front bumper has a large motor on it—a winch—which butts up against the front wall. There's a narrow space along the passenger side; she turns sideways and skiddles through.

Behind the Jeep there's a folding camp chair, tipped on its back, bright white with a stylized maple leaf and the words "Canada 150" emblazoned across the back. It seems odd, but she doesn't give it much thought, as her attention is drawn to the wall.

Yes, there are purses. Each on its own nail. She moves the chair and steps around it to get a closer look. There are backpacks, too, some hanging, some on rough shelves underneath. She takes the nearest purse off its hook and opens it. Inside are things any woman's purse would contain: lipstick, mints, Kleenex, two Tampaxes in a hard plastic case. No wallet or I.D., but there's a small, thin book with a bank logo stamped in gold on the cover. When she opens it, she sees it's for a savings account. The last entry is nearly forty years ago.

Her mind races. Did someone find purses along the road or in rest stops, and collect them over the years? No. More likely they belonged to someone who died, and her kids put them here instead of donating them to a thrift shop.

Intrigued, she closes the purse and returns it to its nail, then reaches the next one down. It has a similar assortment of contents, but without the bank book. Of course. A person would likely only have one bankbook.

The third purse has a wallet and a cellphone. More recent, then. The phone's dead, but in the wallet, oddly, there's cash, a Visa card, a bank card—and a driver's licence.

Claire Charlie's driver's licence.

Claire Charlie? Did Bridey ever mention Claire's last name?

Her brain feels blasted for a split second and then begins whirling as the implications flood through it.

She notices other things: a watch, a fanny pack, other purses. How many? Ten? More? Some are vintage, some mouse chewed, some are worn; and some, pristine. One child-size backpack has a little Hello Kitty stuffy clipped to its zipper. The sight of the cheerful little cartoon kitty almost brings her to her knees and a bolus of cold dread settles deep in her gut as she realizes what she's stumbled on.

"No! No no no no no!" she cries.

Then she hears something, and holds her breath to listen. It sounds like an ATV. And it's getting closer. Has Fletch found her, after all? Should she show him this...

No! He couldn't have followed her over the rough terrain she came through to get here. If he's coming here, it can only mean he knows about this place. Terror stabs through her like a hot wire. Her heart pounds. *Run!*

The ATV stops outside the double doors and chortles as it's turned off. The chain on the lock rattles.

She won't have time to get around the back of the Jeep so there's no way to get to the narrow door she came in, except over the Jeep.

The door swings open.

* * *

Denver's in a hotel room in Amarillo, Texas. After dinner with some of the show committee members, he begged off a tour of the Quarter Horse statues, saying he's seen them before, thank you, has some email to catch up on and will turn in early. Now he has his laptop open on the desk in front of him.

He's looking through the show schedule, tomorrow's classes, names of today's winners. He's also pulling up the results of shows in other states. Some of the horses are relatives of Rocky Duster. There's a filly whose sire was full brother to Rocky, but there are none of Rocky's offspring. Not surprising this far from home, but they do show up here and there, Washington State, occasionally in Oregon and California. Rocky Duster's sons and daughters doing well in competition makes the Rocky Duster babies the Triple R has for sale worth more. So he keeps track.

He laces his fingers together behind his neck, leans back in the chair and thinks of Astrid, wondering if it's too late to call her. It's after ten in Dark River. She's likely in bed.

He wonders why he's even thinking of calling her, as they'd had a long, steamy phone conversation earlier. A phone fuck. But that's a misnomer, as it makes the wanting of her, this constant wanting of her, worse instead of better.

At the oddest times, he's swept away with memories of their weeks together. From the bittersweet visit with Dad at Mayberry Woods when he didn't recognize his own son, kept calling Astrid Iris, and cried when they left, to the raucous fun around the big kitchen table at mealtime. In the evenings, cards: whist, poker, stook, everyone laughing and joking. Spirits were high then, thanks to the sale of not two, but four horses, one of them a pricey five-year-old Dallas was training, but also thanks in no small measure to Astrid. Wherever she went, she lit up the whole room. Wilson was smitten from day one, and even Barney was seen with a pleasant look on his face. Being near her is like basking in sunshine, and he's not the only one who feels it.

When he should be concentrating on other things, even important things, his thoughts are of her. He keeps losing track of what people are saying and has to keep asking them to repeat themselves. At the show today, he had to refer to the order of go repeatedly.

He thinks about how he was drawn to her the first time he saw her at the pub in Nanaimo, and how what she looks like, smells like, feels like, stirs intense desire. Is it really just physical attraction?

Dallas keeps telling him to slow down, that there are lots of fish in the sea, that it's too soon to tie himself to someone he barely knows, because he's on the rebound. Denver has to admit Dallas nailed it when he accused him of being like a lovesick teenager. But he doesn't think he's on the rebound. His marriage was over before he saw Astrid the first time, and he's not Dallas. He doesn't want a series of conquests. He wants commitment. He wants Astrid.

He decides to just send her a quick text, which won't wake her if she's already in bed. She'll see it when she looks at her phone first thing in the morning and know he was thinking of her. 'Sweet dreams, babe,' he dictates, 'miss you. Love you.' Then he looks at the text, reconsiders, and deletes the 'Love you' before hitting send.

When she was at the ranch those two weeks, he felt a growing pull. The more time they spent together, the more he wanted to spend time with her, and he never tired of looking at her. How many times did he interrupt his work go to her on some pretext, just for a kiss? The more they made love, the more he wanted to be making love, feeling her sensuous body against his, her velvety softness pulsating and hot! He knew he was in lust, but it wasn't until she left he realized he was also in love.

He hasn't told her yet. He doesn't want it to be over the phone and it can't be in a text. He feels a surge of emotion as he thinks about how he will tell her. As soon as he sees her? (I missed you so much! I love you!) While they're kissing before they make love? (I love kissing you. I love *you*.) After? (I love you.) Is it too soon? Does she feel the same? What if he simply says "I think I'm falling for you" so if she doesn't say she loves him, too, it's easier to walk it back? *No, that's foolish pride and dishonest,* he thinks. *I love her. I'm not going to soft peddle it.*

His reverie is interrupted by the chime alerting him to new email. He opens his mail program and sees it's from Dallas: *'You know Wilson's been poking around in his memry for a while. Tonite he bugged me so much I Goggled it. Came up with this.'* and a link. Big deal, he thinks, probably just a big, long-winded groaner-joke, which aside from solitaire, is the limit of Wilson's interest in the computer. Is it worth the trouble? It's late and he's tired. But he decides to have a look, and clicks on the link. In moments, there's an old newspaper article headlined "Senator Convicted of Fraud Charged with Wife's Murder" on the screen. The name jumps out at him. Ingebritson.

So that's what she's holding back!

No longer tired, he speed-reads the article. Then he gets another Chivas from the honour bar, pours it over fresh ice, and settles in to re-read the article.

NINETEEN

WAVES OF SHOCK course through her when she sees who's in the doorway.

He smiles and says, "Look who walked into my parlour!"

"Hank! I was just…"

"Just what?"

Even in the gloom of the shed, Astrid can see the maniacal gleam in his eyes. His tone and body language tell her she won't be able to play stupid and talk her way out. She's going to have to make a run for it and he's between her and the open passage. Her only option is to climb over the Jeep, and she needs to do it fast.

Even if she makes it over, will she be able to squeeze through the small door before he can get around the far side of the Jeep? What if he just goes outside and catches her there? If he does go around the outside, can she make it out the front door before he realizes what she's done and comes back? She might be able to outrun him, but she has to get out first, and right now, over the Jeep is her only option.

She turns and bolts for the front of the Jeep, leaping to put her left foot on the tire. She vaults up but her foot slips and the sheet steel of the hood clangs as she crashes down only partway across.

He catches her by the hips and pulls her off the Jeep, then wrenches her arms behind her. She yells, squirms, tries to kick him. "Let me go! Let me go!" she shrieks. She rams back against him, shoving him into the wall with all the power her runner-strong legs braced against the wheel can muster. Purses and backpacks tumble around them.

"Hmmpf!" is all he says. She thrashes and screams but can't break free. He drags her, stumbling awkwardly, dislodging more purses as they go. He kicks the folding chair aside and hauls her around the back of the Jeep.

As he pushes against her she can feel his erection on her buttocks. He presses his forearm against the back of her neck, forcing her head against the Jeep, and strokes her buttocks with his free hand before slipping it inside the elastic waistband of her tights, sliding it around front and into her crotch. She grinds against his arm, trapping it between her body and the Jeep, flails her elbows, kicks. She can't shake him off; kicking him with her soft running shoes barely annoys him, but it's enough to make him grunt and push away. He pulls his hand out of her pants and traps both her arms, reaches a rope out of the Jeep and ties her hands behind her. Then he swings the spare tire away, opens the rear door, picks her up and hoists her inside as easily as if she were a toy. He climbs in on top of her, puts the end of the rope over a pipe at the roof and pulls it tight, wrenching her arms painfully up, forcing her to fold nearly in half. She manages to bite his hand as he stuffs a cloth in her mouth, but he just snorts. He pulls a cloth bag over her head, then pushes her over onto her side. Something rough and hard and smelly like old carpet is pulled over her.

The Jeep rocks as he settles in behind the wheel. She hears him fussing with something; after some grumbling, the engine starts. He backs the Jeep out of the shed, then stops and gets out. She hears him talking. Is someone else here? But it's only one side of the conversation. He's on the phone. Then she hears the ATV start up. After a moment, it's turned off; the doors slam and the chain rattles, as if he locked the ATV inside the shed. Now he's back behind the wheel of the Jeep. After a three-point turn, they're off along the trail she thought was too rough for a vehicle.

She concentrates on quieting her mind, knowing she must memorize the turns, how long they travel in each direction, and try to get a sense of the type of terrain, because as soon as she has a chance to run for it, she'll need to at least have some idea of where to go.

Despite constant lurching and tilting, nothing stops the Jeep. She's tossed around and every jarring bump delivers an excruciating jerk to her arms and shoulders. It's a relief when they turn left and out onto the smoothness of asphalt. She calculates that they're north of the ranch. There are different road sounds for a second. The bridge over the river? Likely. So they're north of that, too. And soon, the Jeep slows and they're making a right turn, meaning they're east of the highway.

Now she can hear pebbles striking the undercarriage. It's a gravel road. It's hard to judge how far they've gone on the winding road that seems to be steadily uphill, before there's a left turn, and the Jeep plunges down a steep decline. It bounces and rocks and then lurches back up onto a flatter trail. The vehicle grumbles its way along, branches scraping sides and top, and at last, comes to a halt.

The back door opens and the carpet is pulled aside. Astrid is hauled out and half dragged, half pushed along a rough path and up a couple of steps. She tries to flail her way free, but he jerks the rope up, sending red hot needles of pain through her shoulders. Then she's held up against a wall while he fumbles with something that sounds like a chain. The door creaks open and she's given a hard shove that sends her sprawling. With her arms still tied behind her, she's unable to break her fall and lands flat, striking her chin and propelling the air out of her lungs in a whoosh.

She's still gasping for breath when he kneels on her, his knees rooting into her thighs as he unties her hands. There's the rattle of a chain and cold steel is fastened around her left wrist. She's jerked up into a sitting position and the cloth bag is pulled off her head. She gags and coughs as she pulls the rag out of her mouth.

They're in a dark little room that smells overpoweringly like a combination of something long dead and an outhouse.

He pushes her down onto her back, her left arm held up over her head by the shackles, and starts pulling at her tights. "Okay," he breathes, "go ahead! Fight all you want!"

"Don't do this!" she says, pushing against him. "We're friends!"

"Friends!" he snorts.

His phone chimes. He ignores it and her flailing and screaming; his strength is astonishing as he lifts her hips to work her tights down. By the time his phone stops ringing, he's got her tights and panties down at her ankles. He unzips and frees his erect penis, pulls her knees up and forces them apart. "Friends," he breathes, and pushes in between her legs.

"Stop it! Stop it!"

"Go ahead. Scream all you want," he growls. She bucks vigorously but it only serves to increase his excitement. "Ahh!" he groans, and forces himself inside her.

"Gaaahh! Gahhh!" She thrashes and squirms with revulsion and disgust; his guttural caterwauling grows in intensity and volume as he rams her again and again.

His phone rings, a different ring tone this time. He shoves harder, faster. The ringing stops. He's just ejaculated and collapsed on her when it starts up again and he mutters, "Fer chrissakes!" He kneels up, pulls the phone out of his jacket pocket and answers it.

Astrid yells, "Help! Help!"

He snorts and hits her face. It's a slap with an open hand but even so, it's hard enough to stun her and bring tears to her eyes. He says into the phone, "*What?*" He's quiet for a heartbeat, then gets to his feet, hoists his pants up and goes outside, closing the door behind him.

She gets up off the filthy mattress, fighting off gut-wrenching sobs, trembling so violently she's scarcely able to pull her tights back up as waves of revulsion wash over her. She's nauseous, clenches the muscles in her pelvic floor again and again as if that might expunge the assault.

Then she gives herself a mental shake, knowing this could get worse and she needs to use her brain if she's going to get out alive. She pushes her revulsion to the back of her consciousness and scans the cabin for anything that might be of use. Now that her eyes have adjusted to the low light, she sees it's a rough shell of a building, two by four studs with no interior finish, just cladding on the outside. Scarred wood floor. There's firewood in the opposite corner next to a small pot-bellied stove. A frying pan hanging on a nail. An oil lamp. All out of reach. The half-meter long chain won't be helpful unless he puts his head against the wall so she can get it around his neck. In other words, it's useless. She wrenches at it again and again, knowing it's futile but unable to stop herself.

Next to the mattress, there's a twenty-liter white plastic bucket. The label on it reads 'E.D. Smith Cherry Pie Filling', the same as the ones Dot's gets their pie fillings in, the same as the pails she picked chanterelles into. She recalls putting the empties out beside the back door, free for the taking. This one has been used as a toilet, the source of at least some of the stench. Whoever was here before was held long enough it's nearly half full. Who was it, the girl that went missing months ago? Where is she now? She still hasn't been found, but no body either. Is she still alive? Is this an indication he might not kill her?

But she knows who he is, and she's found his trophies.

He has to kill her.

Maybe just not right away.

His footsteps thump on the step outside the door; she expects him to come back inside, sucks in a huge breath and steels herself for another assault. Instead, the chain rattles as if the lock is being fastened. In moments, headlights on the small window illuminate the interior of the cabin, and she hears the gerwer-gerwer-gerwer of the Jeep's engine turning over. Then it chortles to life and drives away.

Darkness closing in around her, she collapses onto the mattress and is no longer able to hold the gut-deep, incapacitating sobs at bay.

* * *

In Texas, Denver listens to her cheery voice saying "This is Astrid! I can't get to my phone right now but if you leave a message, I'll call you as soon as I can!" He leaves another voice message and wonders why she hasn't returned his call.

TWENTY

Astrid awakens with a jolt. It's no longer inky dark in the cabin. The night was long; if there was moonlight, none found its way into the cabin. It was so dark she couldn't see her hands. She alternated between her brain being virtually shut down as she wailed despondently, and then racing with ideas, possibilities, solutions.

She tried desperately to get the chain loose. She wrenched and jerked and pulled and screamed at the chain as all the others before her must have done. The structure creaked and the walls seemed to flex, but the chain held. She gave up and crumpled to the floor.

Was there any hope of rescue? Who would miss her? Denver is thousands of kilometers away, not even in the same country, and while he'll wonder why he can't reach her by phone, what can he possibly do? If he reports her missing, the cops won't begin a search for a while and she'll be dead long before anyone finds this cabin.

Hazens will miss her, and maybe they can get the cops on it sooner, but they won't report her missing if Hank Junior convinces them she left voluntarily, like Claire.

What about work? When she doesn't show up and doesn't answer her phone, they'll call Hazens. Will Hazens realize she's been abducted, and report her missing then? Not if they believed the lie.

At some point, she fell into an exhausted asleep. Both shocked that she had slept and frantic she'd squandered valuable time, she jumps to her feet.

There's no way of knowing the time. Light from the gap in the rag over the window is silvery. An indication the sun hasn't risen yet? Or is it just that it's a gray, drizzly day? At best, the reason is that it's before sunrise, but at this time of year, that only means it's before eight. Eight o'clock! How much longer before he returns?

She's flooded with the memory of the rape. She can almost smell his stinking breath filling her nostrils, the weight of his body pinning her, his penis violating her. Waves of revulsion wash over her again.

Then her mother is in her head, saying, *so? You survived. Now you have to get out of here.*

But I can't! Bridey will report me missing and someone will come and get me.

You don't know that, and it will be too late. He'll be back before anyone can find you and you won't survive what he's going to do next.

Succumbing to the urgency of needing the toilet, she draws herself up, works her pants down, and squats over the E.D. Smith Cherry Pie Filling bucket. There's no means of wiping other than using bedding. She grits her teeth and employs the corner of the tattered quilt. She realizes it's not the first time it's been used that way, and that she'd wrapped herself up in the filthy thing overnight because she was cold. She knew it smelled bad, but at least in the dark she couldn't see the stains.

Okay, her mother says, *put your disgust at the filthy quilt with the memory of the rape, and lock it away. You can agonize over it again another time.*

She stands, fixes her clothes, and looks around, hoping for an idea.

First, the chain. It's attached to a two-by-four stud by a ring like the ones in the barn for tying horses to, with four screws through the plate. The shackle on her wrist is held in place with a padlock. Maybe she could get it to spring open if she had something to stick in the keyhole. She sees a few nails with heads sticking out; she's tall enough to reach one, but can't loosen it. Even if she could, it wouldn't be fine enough to fit in the keyhole and she isn't sure she could pick the lock if it was. Still, it would be good to have a weapon, however feeble. A jab in the eye with a nail might not stop him, but it would hurt him, and it would certainly slow him down. There's a chance it would infuriate him and make matters worse. She'd be willing to take that chance if only to get some licks in before... *Don't think about it!*

The ceiling is just the underside of the roof: strips of boards with enough nails sticking through to suggest shingles layered on top, supported by rough poles. There's daylight and fresh air coming though where the poles meet the walls. If she can get loose, she might be able to get out over the wall. Nonsense! There's no way out through the roof any more than through the walls.

The window! Could she fit through? Not likely. If she gets stuck, she's doomed.

She sinks to the mattress and sobs. After a moment, she gives herself a mental kick and tries to gather her wits. First things first. Worry about getting the chain off, then worry about getting out. In fact, once she's loose, at least she'll have a fighting chance. She could wait for him behind the door and hit him over the head with the frying pan! But not if she's shackled to the wall. Can she somehow get a piece of firewood and use it to work the chain loose, or at least pry out a nail? Even if she can't get loose, if she got a piece of firewood, hid it under the mattress, she could use it to hit him over the head and get his keys. She thinks of using her jacket to throw and snare a log, but with her arm shackled, she can't get it off.

It'll have to be her tights. She wiggles out of them; holding one end, she tries flinging them, first by one leg, then by the waist, but they just flutter uselessly and it accomplishes nothing. Of course! She needs something on the tights to give them weight. But what? Nothing other than the bucket half full of sewage is at hand, and she doesn't want to fling that. It'll have to be her shoe. She removes one, and using its laces, ties it to the end of one of the pant legs. Holding the end of the other pantleg, she swings. The shoe flies off, hits the wall and lands on top of the firewood, out of reach.

"Can't lose this one," she mutters, taking off her other shoe. She makes a hole through the fabric at the ankle hem by working it over an exposed nail, threads the shoelace through the hole, and ties the second shoe securely. Now she casts the shoe again. It hits the wall and lands on the firewood. She carefully hauls it back in, but it falls off the woodpile without snagging anything. She casts again. This time, it hits the wall behind the firewood and she notices the frying pan hanging there jiggles. The oil lamp on the shelf above it, though, wobbles dramatically. She thinks, *I don't need the lamp, I need* ... Then she realizes the lamp is, in fact, exactly what she needs.

After dozens of tries, the lamp only wobbles close to the edge, only to maddeningly be knocked back again with the next throw. It's teetering there now, closer than ever, and she's optimistic the next cast will do the trick. She organizes the tights, winds up and gives an extra hard swing.

The shoe flies off, bounces on the wall beneath the lamp, and comes to rest next to the stove.

Astrid collapses to the mattress. She hadn't checked to make sure the shoelace hadn't worked loose. Now she can't reach either shoe, or anything else.

Despair settles over her in a thick fog; she pulls her tights on and closes her eyes. *I'm going to die,* she thinks. *He's going to come through that door any minute and kill me. There's nothing I can do about it. I wonder how he'll do it, if it will hurt. How were the others killed?* She imagines being stabbed. Strangled. Shot. Worse, being tortured to death. She's overtaken with sobs.

Her mother would tell her not to be such a drama queen. Her mother again! Her mind wanders back to when she was a little girl hiding in her bedroom while her parents screamed at each other downstairs. Her narrow little bed was too close to the floor to hide under, so she made a fort between it and the wall by pulling the mattress over and draping blankets down like a tent. It didn't completely drown out the sounds of the fighting, but did muffle them. It was her safe place. She could build the fort within minutes of a fight starting. If it went on long enough, she'd fall asleep and still be there in the morning. If it didn't, it was only a matter of a few minutes of tugging the mattress back the other way, and she could be in her bed when her mother came in to hug her and tell her everything was all right.

The mattress!

Astrid jumps to her feet, pulls the quilt aside, and tries to lift the mattress. As thin as it is, it's quite heavy. Lumpy, stained, probably decades old, it's like nothing she's ever seen before, with a gridwork of rusted metal buttons. She's able to raise it part way off the floor, but it's stuck along the top, fastened there with nails driven through the piping. She tugs at it, then heaves, and with a rip, the nails pull through the aging cloth and the mattress comes loose. She stands it on its short edge, and shoves it toward the wall. It strikes the shelf, but doesn't dislodge the lamp.

"Damn damn damn damn!" she wails. Now the mattress is leaning against the wall, just under the shelf. If only she could lift it again! But chained to the wall, she can't reach. Can't reach *with my hands,* she amends her thought. She lies on her back on the floor, shackled arm over her head, and is easily able to put her feet against the mattress, even with knees bent. For possibly the first time in her life, she's glad to have long legs. She pushes. Pushes. One final shove and the shelf dislodges, sending the lamp tumbling to the floor almost right beside her, smashing the glass and spilling the lamp oil.

She nearly cries with relief.

The metal collar around the top of the oil reservoir has four clips that held the chimney in place. They're fine enough to fit in the slot in the screw, but not sturdy enough to turn it. If only they were regular screws instead of Phillips! But if she can carve away enough wood to loosen the screws a little, it might still work.

She selects a triangular shard of glass, wraps it in a corner of the quilt, and sets to work. By stabbing its sharp point into the wood next to one of the screws holding the chain in place, she's able to use it like a knife. She begins paring wood away from the screw. There are four screws, but she hopes that with two loosened, she'll be able to get the chain free. Even as soft as the old wood is, it'll take time. *Better get to it then, girl.*

TWENTY-ONE

HANK IS SITTING at the bar in the billiards room of Spirit Bear Lodge. Max is alternately shooting pool and manning the bar. He's been mixing Cuba Libres and acting like he's just hanging out, but Hank isn't fooled. He knows if he tried to leave, Max wouldn't allow it. He was rude when he blocked him from following him upstairs when he took the girl's lunch up, even used some signal Hank didn't see to set his ugly dog to guard him. All he knew was that the dog sat up, alert, staring at him. When he tried to outstare the mutt to see if it would back down, it raised its hackles and growled. It didn't take its eyes off him until Max came back.

Totally unfair. He has to see her. Needs to see her! The black nub deep in his brain has been squirming and stretching its legs for days. Barely even quieted down after the session with Astrid, the old bastard cutting that short made sure of it. Even admiring the bite mark on his hand, remembering Astrid's teeth clamping down on it as he was shoving the rag in her mouth doesn't help. Now the black nub is bigger. Its eyes are starting to glow. It's starting to whisper. That's new, and damned unpleasant, like being in a room full of people, all of them whispering, but you can't quite make out what they're saying. He's sure if he had time with the girl upstairs he could do something to make it stop. He's the one who got her for them in the first place, after all. All he wants is a poke. Maybe tease her a little with some love bites. Can't do more than that, not here. But Max ignores his arguments.

He ponders overpowering Max. He thinks he's as fit and as strong as Max is, but Max has size and reach on him. He'd have to take him by surprise. And then there's that big ugly dog of his, just lying on the dog bed. It looks like it's sleeping, but perks up whenever Max moves, and its posture during their staring contest gave him pause. He abandons the idea. Or at least puts it on a back burner. If Max goes for a piss or maybe takes the dog out for a piss—but that hasn't happened yet. How far would Max go to keep him from leaving? He's packing, but would he shoot him? Can't rule it out.

Even if he snuck outside, even with the V-8 in his truck, would he get to the fence before Max's five-liter Mustang caught him? He wouldn't have time, or the keys, to unlock the gate. If he crashed through it, would it wreck his truck? Does he care, as long as it keeps on going?

A better idea would be to get into the little cabinet by the back door where the keys for the Lodge's vehicles are kept, then get into the garage and find the right vehicle … which one? The Hummer, maybe. Or better, the Range Rover they use to pick up the high rollers from the airport. It's got the remote code for the gate programmed in. If the timing was right, he could get out and close the gate before Max's Mustang got there. Max would never crash through the gate with that. He'd be kilometers away in the Range Rover before Max even got his gate key out. But there's no chance of getting to the garage, never mind getting the Range Rover out, before Max would be on him.

Max will just have to be unconscious. Or dead. Hank's Bowie knife is wherever Max puts things he steals from guys like him, but there are knives of all sizes in the kitchen. There is also the little knife Max used to slice limes for the drinks, small but deadly if used right. An opportunity will present itself. He'll bide his time. For now, he sits at the bar sucking back Cuba Libres and watching Max fool around, making impossible shots.

"You like her?"

Max just frowns and racks the balls.

"You fuck her?"

Max breaks, scattering balls in all directions, ignoring Hank.

"She's got a nice tight little cunt," Hank says, "I mean the one upstairs, not Astrid. You ain't met Astrid. Not much in the way of tits, but she's got legs that go on furever. She's nice 'n' tight too, but a little dry." The scowl on the other man's face makes it clear there'll be no male bonding. Not that he wants to bond, anyway. He just wants to put the big ox at ease.

He swivels on his stool, watches Max run all the balls on the table with only a couple of misses , and amuses himself by imagining ways of immobilizing him and making him watch as he slices up the ugly dog. Then he chuckles out loud when he visualizes Max with the lime-slicing knife sticking out of his eye. Max gives him a befuddled look, prompting a derisive snort.

He flicks the big TV on, finds a rerun of *The Walking Dead*, and after watching for a few minutes, says, "It's past lunch time. I'm hungry. If those assholes don't show up soon..."

"There's trays in the bar fridge. Chips in the cupboard. Help yourself," Max tells him, and sinks one ball in the side and one in the opposite corner with one shot.

"Well whaddaya know, Igor can speak," Hank says with a snort.

Max's nostrils flare and his frown deepens, but aside from that, he doesn't react.

Hank chuckles and thinks the big ox might not be a problem after all. If he had any balls, he'd never let an insult like that pass! He gets off his stool and goes around behind the bar, looking through the bottom cabinets, opening and closing doors. He notes the paring knife on the cutting board next to the sink. Eureka! The big ox not only has no balls, but no brains either, or he wouldn't have made the mistake of leaving that knife where Hank could get it, and then send him back here unsupervised. It's almost too easy. He pulls out a bag of chips and rips it open noisily, sending chips scattering about. "Fuck!" he says loudly, then bends over to pick them up, slipping the knife into his boot as he straightens.

* * *

Denver, in Arizona now, listens to Astrid's greeting again. He pushes against the notion that she's screening calls and choosing not to answer. *She wouldn't do that*, he tells himself, *there must something wrong.*

He doesn't have a cell number for Bridey or Hank Senior, or the number for their land line. He wonders why he doesn't, and realizes all their phone conversations, except for those with Hank Junior, have been on the landline from his office at home. So although he's reluctant to do it, he grits his teeth and calls Hank Junior. It goes to voicemail, and he leaves a message.

Then he Googles Dot's Diner, gets a Yellow Pages listing, and calls. A woman answers, "Dot's Diner! Best Pies North of Kamloops!"

"Hello. Is Astrid there please?"

"No."

"Do you expect her in today?"

"Just a sec." He hears the woman yell out, "Is Astrid booked in today?" Then she comes back on the line. "Yeah, but she ain't in 'til four. Can I help you?"

"I just wondered— I haven't been able to reach Astrid…"

"Like I said, she ain't here till four."

"Yeah, I know, but when she comes in, could you tell her I called?"

"Sure. Who's this?"

"Denver—"

"Okay, *Denver*,"— she cuts him off— "what's your last name? *Sandwich*? What's the message? *Hold the mayo*?" The line goes dead.

"Goddammit! Goddammit!" he pounds his fist on the desk. She's not the first person to think they were being pranked when he's tried to leave a message, just the most frustrating. But it doesn't matter. He's being alarmist. Hank will call him back, and there will be some reasonable explanation for her telephone silence. Maybe she lost the phone. Dropped it in the toilet. Or it just died. No. If her phone was dead, she'd have charged it by now. If it was broken, she'd find another way to call him.

It crosses his mind he should call the RCMP. Then he imagines the response he'd get when he told them he's concerned because he hasn't been able to reach her by phone since yesterday. Maybe he'll call hospitals during the supper break.

Now you're really *being alarmist,* he tells himself.

He heaves a sigh, rubs his face, and leaves the show office, hurrying through the crowds of spectators milling about and exhibitors with their horses waiting for their turns in the ring, to the arena where showmanship classes are in progress. With an effort, he ignores the frowns of the scribe and the whipper-in, both obviously and justifiably annoyed at a judge delaying the show to make a phone call.

* * *

"Gotta take a leak," Hank says as he slides off the bar stool and heads for the hall. He checks to see if Max is watching, but Max is looking out the window. He wonders if this is his chance to leave, but then the big man puts his cue down on the table and follows him, his big ugly mutt right behind him. "Now yer followin' me to the shitter?" Hank hisses back over his shoulder.

Max ignores him and instead of turning left to follow Hank, he turns to go and unlock the back door. The old fucks have arrived. They're all talking at once as they haul provisions in, like it's a complicated job they can't accomplish without discussing it among themselves. "Buncha cackling hens," Hank mutters.

Finished in the washroom, Hank Junior comes back to the billiard room, gives each of the men a glare and says, "Took you fuckin' long enough. Didn't you think I might be gettin' hungry?" He slides back onto his seat at the bar. "Plus, I got things to do, and instead I'm sittin' here all fuckin' day."

"Yeah, we know what things you've got to do, Junior," Hank Senior says. "That's why you're here. She better not be damaged!"

"She'll definitely be gettin' hungry by now, but she ain't damaged. I didn't do nuthin', just fucked her."

"I know you slapped her. I heard it! I told you not to hurt her!"

"You don't tell me what I can 'n' can't do, *Dad*," he snorts. "I didn't hurt her. She wanted it. She liked it. She's been teasin' me fer months, you seen her. And remember, I didn't have to call you and tell you I had her."

"Of course you did, or you wouldn't have! You didn't know if she was supposed to work yesterday and even if she wasn't, Bridey would've missed her. I told her she's staying with a friend in town for a few days. She was pissed, but it shut her up." Hank Senior shrugs his jacket off and hangs it on the deer antler coat rack at the end of the bar.

The tall bald man goes behind the bar and gets himself a beer. "What does everyone want?" he asks.

"I'll have a Steamboat Lager, Les," Pastor Green says. "When's the food going to be ready?"

"Max," Les says, "Go put the bins with the chicken wings and potato skins in the oven to warm, wouldja? Bruce here is in danger of starving."

"Bring me a plate of the cold wings when you come back," Pastor Green calls after him. He takes the beer Les hands him and goes to sit at one of the pub tables next to a window.

Hank Senior gets a beer and stands beside his son at the bar, his face grim. "Junior, do you realize what you've done?"

"Yeah, I saved our asses by makin' sure she didn't go to the cops."

"Saved our asses? You fucked up big time! We would've been able to come up with some way to explain it to her, and life would've gone on as usual. But not after this! She's not some mutt you picked up at the side of the road, Junior! Her disappearance won't be easy to explain. That cowboy'll have questions, and she'll be missed when she doesn't show up for work. She'll be traced to us!"

"So? Just report her missing. She went out for a run and never came back. That's the truth anyway."

"So, you don't mind cops, search parties, swarming all over our property? Not worried about them finding anything?"

"They can't come on our property!"

"How could we stop them? What possible reason would we have for refusing to let them search the trails where she was running? And now two girls connected to you have disappeared. You don't think you'll be a prime suspect? You don't think they're already looking at you for Claire, with your record?"

"Yeah, my record's sealed, you know that, except for the last one," Hank Junior snorts, "and that was a lie. She was tryin' to trap me, she dropped the charges, didn't she? And Claire! Her family reported her missing, we gave the cops the sailboat story and that was the end of it. If they had anything on me they'd of arrested me by now."

"They still have time. It's not just cops, either. That fuckin' P.I. from Vancouver who's been investigating on his own dime still comes sniffin' around every few months. He's been at it, what, ten, fifteen years? Like it's his life's work."

"If Astrid was really missing, you'd of reported it last night," Les says, frowning at Hank Senior. "Why didn't you?"

"You know why he didn't," Bruce snorts, "he's protecting his pup, as always. But it's not too late. Just say she went for a run this morning and hasn't come back."

"I don't want cops crawling all over the place!" Hank Senior exclaims, "least not until we clean out that shed. She found it. Searchers will too. We could solve that problem PDQ but it would be better to make it so she's not missing, just moved on, like Claire. So, two girls who knew Junior moved away. That's nothing unusual."

"Yeah! Les can change the schedule so no one expects her, tell everyone she quit. And we tell the cowboy she left with someone, a trucker maybe, or maybe we should say she left to be with the cowboy. Yeah, that's better," the younger Hank smirks, "the heat'll be on him, then. Let him talk his way outta that! And we tell Bridey she left to be with him. Load up her car with her things and put it over the cliff with Claire's. Won't be found for a thousand years. End of problem."

"Sure, Junior, great idea," Hank Senior says as he sinks to a bar stool, "except the cowboy isn't even in the country."

"Oh." Hank Junior fidgets. "Well, good! So she went with him."

"He's judging horse shows. He's got travel records and a hundred people fuckin' know she isn't with him."

Les gets chip dips and plates of cheese and pepperoni out of the fridge, sets them on the bar, bumps the fridge door shut with his hip, and says, "Besides that, he's already phoned the diner looking for her."

"So?" Hank Junior shakes his head and lifts his hands in a 'so what' gesture.

"So? Jen took the message and told Franny and everyone else who was sitting at the counter about his call. Thought she was clever, calling him Mister Sandwich or Denver Sandwich or something. I'm surprised the stinky's even heard of a Denver sandwich. So fuckin' proud of herself for bein' so smart it was the first thing she told me when I picked up the food." Les hikes his pants up. "Now that I think about it, maybe I should put Denver sandwiches on the menu again. You know, retro diner stuff. Maybe it's time to redecorate, make it a Fifties theme. What do you think, guys?"

"Jesus, Les, this isn't the time!" Hank Senior scowls. "Junior! Any more bright ideas?"

"I'm on the hot seat? I gotta solve this?" Hank Junior whines. "You three shoot down every idea I have? How about comin' up with some ideas of yer own? Like maybe she went with him before he left fer the States and he offed her then? He could've phoned to make it look like he's innocent." He shoves pepperoni bits in his mouth.

"He was already in Texas when she worked her last shift." Hank Senior says.

"We can say she didn't work that shift. Les can change the…"

"Don't forget about Franny. Her and Astrid are close. Astrid would've told her when the cowboy left and she'd know Astrid didn't go with him. We have to pick up Franny, too?" Les massages his neck. "Won't take a detective, even the fuckin' janitor can verify his alibi. *Jesus*, Junior."

Hank Senior gets to his feet and paces to the window at the end of the room and back, hands on hips, worry pinching his face. "You might as well accept it, we're not going to stick this on Danielson," he says, shaking his head. "Why've you got such a hard on for him, anyway?"

"If you ain't noticed, he's an arrogant bastard, him and his high-priced horses, travellin' all over judgin' shows, expectin' everyone to kiss his ass. I saved his bacon, buyin' that crocked old horse and then he moves in on my girl? I'm done with her, too. I'll send her over the cliff with the car." Hank drains his glass, slams it down on the bar and as he pushes it toward Les, says, "Hit me."

"Don't tempt me!" Les says. "Fuck, you're stupid. Don't you get it? The first place the cops will look is the Double H. You're both gonna be wearin' orange jumpsuits for the rest of your lives. And you, pretty boy, you better buy the large economy size of Vaseline, 'cause you'll be sportin' a size eleven asshole."

"Fuck you! You're the bigshots, why not just buy her off!"

"I'm not interested in putting up any money to get your ass out of a sling, Junior. Wouldn't work, anyhow."

"Hey, Les," Pastor Green calls out, "how about bringing one of those trays over here?"

Les pushes a tray along the bar toward Pastor Green, who scowls, but thumps down off his stool to get it. He takes it back to his table and starts shovelling handfuls of cheese cubes into his mouth.

"Well it's not just my ass," Hank Junior says, "it's all of yers too. Don't fergit, I caught her snoopin' through the shed."

"So?" Les asks.

"So? And you call me stupid! She was snoopin' through everything."

"Again, so? Why do we care? What's the deal with the fuckin' shed, anyway?"

Max brings in two plates of cold chicken and puts one on the bar and the other on the pub table in front of Pastor Green before taking a seat at the far end of the room.

"Where's the dipping sauce?" Pastor Green asks. "Hey, Max! Didn't you bring the dipping sauce?"

"Forget the fuckin' sauce, Bruce," Les hisses. "What do you mean, she was snooping through everything, Junior?"

"You're hoping for mummified ears, or tits maybe? All of 'em had purses. Or backpacks. That's what's there."

That comment draws Bruce's attention away from the chicken wings and the colour drains from his face. He turns to Hank Senior and asks, "You knew about this?"

"Who d'ya think started puttin' them there?" Hank Junior says, as he shoves his glass across the counter at Les. "Am I fuckin' cut off here?"

"It was before DNA, and anything with I.D., I took out," Hank Senior says. "Destroyed everything after that. I haven't thought about it, haven't even been there in years. I guess you have, though, eh Junior?"

Hank Junior shrugs.

"I take that as a yes." Hank Senior shakes his head. "Did you at least dump any i.d., any personal stuff? Any combs with, say, hairs in them?"

Another shrug.

"Well, it doesn't make any difference. Now that they've got touch DNA, the purses themselves are probably enough."

The room falls quiet except for the sound of Pastor Green sucking the meat off a wing and smacking his lips. He starts in on another wing, and says, "I doubt there's anything there that would incriminate me." He looks at Hank Senior. "Is there anything that would lead back to me?"

"Well, I don't think we have to worry about the fuckin' shed," Hank Senior replies. "It's not a big deal. We can clean it out easy enough. End of problem. Move Astrid here. It's secure, and Max is here. Then we torch the cabin. She has no family. I'll handle Bridey, then we just need something to get Danielson out of the picture."

"Not a good idea, moving her here," Les says. "She doesn't know Junior's connected to us, aside from the obvious. She doesn't know about this place.

We should keep it that way. Just let her go. Like Bruce says, you two are the only ones who have to worry about that shed and the cabin. Maybe only Junior, even. It's on your property, Hank, but you wouldn't necessarily know about it. You can rescue her, be the hero! Remember Robert Willy Picton? His brother was a partner in that pig farm. How many women did he do there? Forty? More? Don't tell me his brother didn't know what was going on! But he never spent a day behind bars. So, if we torch 'em both, even if she says there were old purses or whatever, no way to prove it once it's gone."

"So, you think we can just let Junior take the fall?"

"Why not? He's the cause of this mess."

"If you think I'm gonna take the rap, yer fuckin' nuts," Hank Junior snarls. "They'd wanna know where the bodies are. You bail on me, I'll tell 'em."

"Yeah, I guess that shouldn't surprise anyone," Les says, "but don't forget, you're expendable."

"Don't *you* forget, Les," Hank Senior says, "he's my son. I'd get over it, but Bridey! She still thinks she's going to have grandchildren. No telling what she'd do if he disappeared. May never recover. She goes to Nechako Manor, starts blabbing, one of the shrinks might start listening. Do we whack her too? Either of you wanna do it?" He looks around the room. "Didn't think so. We don't have a choice, we have to come up with a solution that doesn't involve a stack of bodies. Besides, are we willing to give up the church racket? The millions we'll make? We can still go ahead on it, just have to figure out a solution and put this behind us." He looks from Les to Bruce. After a moment, they both nod. "Okay," he continues, "end of discussion. We sink or swim together."

"You ain't gettin' permission to torch my cabin!" Junior's voice is shrill.

"We don't need permission," Hank Senior growls.

"You fuckin' bastard!" Hank Junior shouts and jumps to his feet, taking two quick strides toward his father. "Yer gonna mess up my deal?"

Max stiffens and takes a step to intercept him.

"Sit the fuck down!" Hank Senior says, waving Max off.

Hank Junior snorts, looks around the room, then goes back to his seat on the bar stool.

"You got nobody but yourself to blame," Hank Senior tells him. "You were mean from the day you were born and a liar from the time you learned to talk. That road kill story? Might've been true at first, but by Christ that stretch of highway was unbelievably fuckin' lethal for dogs!"

"You guys had a thing goin' on before I ever did."

"Ancient history, and nothing that could come back at any of us after all this time, unless someone does some excavating out back. Once we got this place, we never took another girl. We all sleep just fine."

"Oh yeah? How about ol' Les here, tryin' to grab up that woman last year? Sure botched that, didn't ya, *Mister* Cline? I'm surprised no one recognized you from the police sketch. Better not wear that stupid hat no more. And none of you turn down the fresh meat I bring you, do you?" Hank Junior snorts.

"That was just an impulse!" Les exclaims. "An opportunity presented itself. No big deal. And we only take the ones you bring to save *your* ass, fuckwit," Les says.

"What a crock that is! Every one of you, you can't wait to git yer dicks in 'em. Don't fuckin' tell *me* there's nuthin' in it fer you!"

"Every time you grab one, we're back looking over our shoulders until the heat dies down. How long d'ya think we'll keep bailing you out? There's a limit. I've reached it."

"Don't start that again, Les," Hank Senior says as he stops pacing and leans a hip against the pool table.

"You torch my cabin," Hank Junior snarls, "I'll build another one."

"Maybe you become a permanent guest here."

"You wouldn't! Bridey wouldn't let you!"

"You don't think so?" He pushes away from the pool table and comes to stand over Junior. "Don't you remember? She's the one who committed you! I just wish the hell we'd left you at Colony Farm."

"You fuckin' bastard."

"You're sick. Colony Farm didn't cure you, and it seems like the meds don't work either. We already decided we had to do something about you. This just moves it up the agenda." Hank Senior's shoulders slump; he takes a deep breath, picks up his beer and goes to sit at the pub table across from Pastor Green.

"You can't keep me here!" Hank Junior exclaims. "I'm workin' on a deal."

"Oh yeah, one of your deals," Les says. "This should be good."

"It *is* good. You know Danielson inherits that ranch when the ol' man dies? It's worth millions. You said to be a partner here I hadda buy in. That's how I'm gonna do it." He fixes a sincere look on his face and locks eyes with Hank Senior as the lie slips easily from his lips. "The money will come to you."

"You think he's going to give you the money? No one's that stupid," Pastor Green says.

"Well, I wouldn't be so sure about Danielson, but I don't need to git the money from him, anyway. His ex will git a big divorce settlement. I only have to git the money from her."

"That's iffy. You gotta get the girl, wait until the ol' man dies, then convince her to give you her settlement money?"

"I already got the stupid little twat eatin' outta my hand."

"Yeah, you sure do, Junior," Hank Senior snorts. "All it took was a car, some jewelry, what else? She'll dump you as soon as someone comes along and offers her more."

"You ain't givin' me enough credit."

"I've seen plenty of self-centered, manipulating little hoes like her, that's all."

"Don't worry, I'll keep her long enough. If I'm her husband, even common law, her big cash settlement is mine if *something* happens to her"—he chuckles—"And the ol' man has one foot in the grave already. How long do people with Altimer's live, anyway?"

"Alzheimer's, idiot." Les says.

"They don't live long, but still longer than you're gonna want to wait," Pastor Green opines.

"He's already had it six or seven years."

"Hmm. Well, he likely won't live a lot longer, then," Les says, "but you're still an idiot."

"We're off topic," Hank Senior intercedes. "Back to Astrid."

"Yeah, Astrid," Les says. "I say she needs to stop breathing."

"That is *not* going to happen," Hank Senior slams his beer down. "Put that idea out of your head. She can live here for the rest of her life."

"I say let's do that, bring her here," Bruce says, "why wouldn't we? She's talent, like any of the others. I'd like to fuck her. Bet you guys've thought about it, too."

Hank Senior frowns at Bruce and seems about to say something, but instead slides off his stool and goes to get his jacket off the rack. "It gets dark early, and besides that, they're forecasting snow. I don't want to be driving around out in the bush in a blizzard. Les, come with me. We'll go get her, bring her here, and put this behind us."

Junior gets up and starts for the door.

"I said Les, not you, Junior."

"Yeah, well, I'm comin'. Been cooped up here all fuckin' day as it is." He strides toward the doorway, but at a nod from Hank Senior, Max blocks it. Junior nearly bumps into him. Max is a head taller and Junior has to step back to glare at him. "Outta my way, Igor," he growls.

Max stands his ground, silent, unmoving.

Hank shrugs and as if backing down, turns away. Then he bends, pulls the knife out of his boot, and slashes upward in one swift movement as he straightens.

Max reacts instantly, jumping back, but not far enough; the knife catches the waistband of his jeans and slices into his T-shirt, then finds flesh. Max's left hand shoots out and clamps down on Hank's wrist. He puts his full weight behind a right that connects with Hank's chin and follows it up with another right to the gut. As Hank collapses to the floor, the dog leaps into action, grabbing his knife arm in her teeth with a growl. The knife hits the floor and Max kicks it out of Hank's reach, then quickly backs away, hand on his belly.

"Tell yer stinkin' mutt to let go of me!" Hank Junior screeches.

"Did he get you? Did he get you?" Hank Senior cries as he hurries to Max.

Max pulls his hand away from the bloody circle that's rapidly growing on his shirt and lifts the shirt to examine the cut.

"It's nothing," Max says. "Just a scratch."

Hank Senior leans over and prods the wound, then straightens and says, "Hand me some of those napkins, will you Les?"

Les comes out from behind the bar with a handful of napkins and passes them to Hank Senior, who uses them to staunch the bleeding so he can get a clear look at the laceration.

"Well, it's more than a scratch, Max, but it hasn't penetrated the abdominal wall. It needs stitching up, though. Pastor, you help Max get a dressing on this, then take him to E.R. will you? Les and I need to get a move on."

"Me?" Colour drains from the Pastor's face. "I'm no good at that sort of thing!"

"You're not good at that sort of thing." Hank Senior says flatly. He glares at the Pastor, shakes his head and says, "Okay, fine. Les, you take him."

"It's okay," Max says, "we got butterflies in the kit. That'll do. I can look after it. You and Les go ahead."

"Yer worried about him? What about me? Lookit his fuckin' dog!" Hank Junior thrashes but the dog just growls and hangs on.

"Okay, girl," Max tells the dog. She lets go of Hank's wrist but continues to stand over him.

"What the hell's wrong with you, Junior?" Hank Senior demands. "You could've really hurt him!"

"Well, his fuckin' ugly mutt really hurt me! Lookit this!" He holds out his wrist, displaying puncture wounds. "Who the fuck does he think he is? He's been lordin' it over me all day! I had enough!"

"I'll tell you who he is, he's the Lodge Manager, and he works for *me*. He was acting on my orders."

"What the fuck?" Hank Junior struggles to his feet while the dog growls quietly. He glares at Max and demands, "Call off yer fuckin' dog, Igor!"

At a sign from Max, the dog goes back to her bed by the door.

"My mistake, Boss," Max says. "Shouldn't've left that knife where he could get it."

"Now we gotta lock up the knives?" Hank Senior grabs Junior by the back of his collar and propels him out into the great room and to the bottom of the stairs before letting go. "You've really gone off the reservation this time, Junior. You're staying here. And since you can't be trusted around sharp objects, I'm locking you in your room. I'll deal with you later."

TWENTY-TWO

AFTER A TIME, the edge of the shard dulls. Astrid turns it and continues, using the new edge. When all three sides are dulled, she selects another shard and keeps carving, enlarging the hole little by little, ignoring the myriad little cuts from handling the glass.

Every few minutes, she tries to turn the screw, and when that's not effective, gets to her feet, holds the chain in both hands, and reefs on it to see if it's possible to break it out. Finally, it looks so close to coming loose she lies on her back, puts one foot on the wall on each side of the stud, holds the chain in both hands and body lifting off the floor, leans all her weight into it. The last little bit of wood gives way; the chain comes free with a clatter, and she hits the floor with a thump.

With a joyful shriek she leaps to her feet and dances in celebration. Then she's brought back to reality when she steps on a piece of glass. She drops to the floor and takes the injured foot in both hands. There's blood seeping out around a glass shard. She pulls the shard out. It's a painful wound, but thankfully, not deep. It's a reminder she's not out of the woods yet. Literally.

With no means of telling time, she doesn't know how long it took to work the chain loose, but judging by the position of the light from the one tiny window, it's been hours. It's mid-afternoon, if not later. He could be coming back at any moment; in fact, it's surprising he hasn't been back before now. While she's better off now than when she was chained to the wall, she'll still be in for a fight against a much stronger foe. She must get out of the building.

Careful not to step on glass, she takes the few steps to the woodpile, gets her shoes and puts them on before examining the structure more closely. There's no interior finish other than a bunch of dried furry rags hanging around the top. Some are so old and blackened it's impossible to tell what animal they're from, but a few are newer. She gasps when she realizes there's only one animal that comes in tabby stripes with white paws. Have these cats all been killed in a torture or sacrifice ritual? Are girls an escalation from that? She's read about kids, boys usually, having a morbid fascination with dead animals, then graduating to killing, first animals, then people. With a horror of realization, Bridey's tale of the boys collecting road kill comes to mind.

It doesn't change anything, Astrid, her mother's voice in her head brings her back to reality. *Get to work.*

Her first thought is that she might be able to take the door off its hinges, but the door opens out, so the hinges aren't accessible. Maybe she can smash it out. With the bag over her head, she didn't see how it's locked, but it sounded like a chain and padlock, maybe like what was on the shed where the Jeep was parked.

She launches herself against the door several times, shaking the entire structure, but the door holds. Then she tries kicking it near the knob like she's seen on TV, but all that does is give her leg and hip a nasty jolt, and the door stubbornly remains intact.

She goes to the window and peers out. Branches from overhanging trees cover it almost completely. The window would be easy to take out, as it's only held in place by a few nails, but it's too small an opening to be of use. She'd be lucky to get a shoulder out.

She turns her attention to the walls. The cladding isn't plywood, but rough horizontal boards, each overlapping the one below it, nailed to uprights all the way along. Is it possible to pound them enough to loosen them? She's getting the cast iron frying pan from its nail on the wall, thinking to use it like a hammer, when she sees the hatchet behind the firewood.

"Oh. My. God!" she exclaims as she pulls it out. It will be much more efficient for pounding at the wall than the frying pan would be. And if he comes back while she's still trapped, she has a decent weapon and a fighting chance! But she'll have to be determined to make her first swing a lethal one, because if it isn't, he will overpower her and … With an effort, she pushes the mental image of the hatchet buried in her face out of her mind.

She realizes she dismissed the window as an escape route prematurely. The opening, too small as it is, can be made bigger more easily than starting a hole elsewhere. She uses the hatchet to pry the window out, then delivers a solid hit to the next board down, right next to the stud. The board comes away enough to be promising. Another good hit, and there's a bigger gap between the stud and the board. It's held in place by nails in the next stud over. So, she moves to that stud and does the same thing there, and then the next. Back and forth, back and forth. Finally, the board swings out from the last nail and hangs against the wall.

The next board is easier, but it still eats up precious time before it's broken out too. Now there's enough space for her to get through. Should she take out more boards, or climb out now? Her instinct is to save precious minutes and get out now.

The plastic bucket is taller than the cooler, enough that by standing on it, she should be able to get a leg over the opening in the wall. She thinks of the satisfaction she'll get dousing its contents over the whole damn cabin, starting with the stinking, filthy quilt, and picks it up by the wire handle.

Then she stops. *I'm still out in the bush,* she thinks. *I don't know where I am or how to get to safety. This filthy quilt might save my life. Slow down! Think everything through.*

The lamp and the stove both require lighting. With luck, there's a lighter, or at least matches, here somewhere. There's nothing left on the shelf, but when she finds a Bic lighter with the newspapers in the wood pile, she nearly cries.

On top of the cooler, there's a flat of water with three full bottles in it. She pulls them free of the plastic shroud, opens one and drinks a third of it at one go.

Inside the cooler, mildew and stink, but there is a brick of Crisco, only partly used. She puts it with the water bottles in the plastic bag she thought she might need for chanterelles—was it only yesterday?—and stuffs in as much newspaper as she can. Then she tosses the hatchet and the bag out through the opening in the wall before draping the quilt over it.

Should she should burn this house of horrors down? There's newspaper, firewood, and the pond of lamp oil soaking into the floor. It would be easy.

But this is evidence. She needs to get away and bring the police back. Besides, there are huge fir trees all around, with their dry, dead branches hanging close over the shed. It would start a forest fire. Aside from killing countless wild creatures, she might not be able to outrun it.

Picking up the bucket, she holds the bottom and swings it in an arc, splattering everything but the corner she's standing in. The stench is an assault, but despite gagging, she feels a rush of pleasure.

Once it's upended, she stands on the bucket, grabs the studs and puts one leg over the boards. With a little hop, she's astride the board. Then she struggles to get her other leg through the opening. *It's just so damned long! But then if I wasn't for these ridiculously long legs, I'd still be chained to the wall.*

She takes her back number ten in her hands and pulls it toward her enough that it comes through the opening. She's sitting on the board with both legs out the opening now, glad for the padding afforded by the quilt under her bum, but her upper body is still inside. She flips over onto her stomach so she's bent in half, draped over the board; then she slides down, gives a little kick against the wall, and drops.

The ground is uneven and she lands awkwardly, tumbling backward. A sharp pain shoots through her left arm and she realizes she fell on a nail. It's projecting out of the board about an inch, so the wound isn't deep and isn't anywhere near anything that matters. Nothing else is damaged, no broken bones or sprains. And she's free!

She picks up the hatchet and hangs it from the elastic loop that adjusts the waist of her jacket. It's heavy and skews her jacket to the side; she'll find a better way of carrying it later, but now, she pulls the quilt to the ground, puts the plastic bag full of newspaper and water bottles on it and purses it up.

She hears something and stands still, not even breathing, to listen. It's the sound of a vehicle, and it's coming closer.

Hank!

She flings the quilt pack over her shoulder and runs into the bush.

* * *

Hank Senior stands with his phone to his ear, leaning against the driver's door of his truck. The door to the cabin stands open, and a short distance away, Les is stomping around and swearing. "Son of a bitch! Son of a fuckin' bitch!" he says, "How the fuck did she do this?" He holds up a shattered board before tossing it aside.

Finally, someone answers and Hank Senior speaks into his phone. "Problem just got bigger. Place looks like a wild animal was in it, and she's gone...

"No, we can't torch it now. Is that your first thought? Just a minute." He holds the phone away from his ear to speak to Les, who's come to stand beside him. "You find something?"

"No. Just, I think she's hurt. There might be blood. Hard to tell with the rest of the crap."

"Blood? Like a pool of blood?"

"No. Only a few spots. Enough to slow her down, maybe."

"Hmm. Well, the Pastor's more worried about someone finding this cabin than with us finding Astrid."

"Maybe he's right."

"He's not right, for fuck's sake. No one's found this place in decades, and if anyone did find it, they'd think nothing of it. But if Astrid tells the cops about the, er, other shed before we have a chance to clear it out, and about what happened here, even if there's nothing left but a pile of rubble, we're in trouble."

"Junior's in trouble, you mean."

Hank gives him a dark look, waves him off and returns to his call. "We *will* burn it, Bruce, just not right now. Think about it. Even if it doesn't start the woods on fire, the smoke would be seen, and there'd be firefighters crawling all over. They'd find her, or she'd find them...

"Yeah, I know you think Junior's the only one whose ass is on the line, but you heard him, he'll sing...

"You wanna do it? You really think you can? You saw what he did to Max. He'd gut you before you...

"He doesn't have a knife now, so are you thinking you'll go and do him before he gets one? Like right now?

"No, Max won't do it. Just get your ass in the saddle and come...

"Yeah, I know you can't hike anywhere, your gout 'n' all, but it's nearly dark. We need you to bring flashlights…

"No, Max can't bring them; he's injured for fuck's sake…

"Oh? Max says he's okay? That's good, but he's never been here and doesn't know how to find this place. You have to bring him…

"I don't give a fuck how mad your wife's gonna be if you're late! She won't kill you, but if you don't get your fat ass here *now,* I will. Bring flashlights, gps, the walkie-talkies…

"What? Sure, bring food if you must. And coffee, I suppose. And Bruce? Tell Max to bring his dog."

He hits 'end', shoves his phone back in his pocket, and says to the sky, "Idiot!"

TWENTY-THREE

AFTER HER INITIAL panic to get away from the cabin, Astrid slows her pace. Was she too hasty? Should she circle back and see if the vehicle she heard was someone coming to rescue her?

Then she reminds herself anyone driving through the bush this late in the day, following what's barely even a track, knows about the cabin and is not a rescuer. If not Hank Junior, someone equally bad. Fletch? Are they in this together? She can't afford to stay and see who it is. If she does, she'll be close enough to be caught. She doesn't like her chances of fighting either of them off, even with the hatchet. She picks up her pace again.

When she thinks she's a safe distance away, she stops for a breather. She's grateful for the water, and focuses on how lucky she is to have escaped instead of thinking about her empty stomach. Or the cut on her foot that pains her with every step. Or the dull ache in her arm where the nail pierced it.

She left the cabin at least an hour ago, and she's been running steadily downhill. Or, running where she can, as steadily as she can, given the ups and downs of the topography. She's climbed over snags and crawled through dense thickets, so it's been a workout, made more awkward by the quilt "pack" that bobbles around and won't stay gathered up, and the chain dangling from her wrist. She hauls the quilt bundle off her shoulder and sets it on the ground, then goes a few steps away and squats to urinate.

She's pulling up her tights when she notices a spot of bright orangey yellow under the leaf mould. When she carefully peels back the leaves, she discovers a patch of chanterelles. Food! *Bless you, Bridey,* she thinks.

She searches the area for more mushrooms; despite concern about stopping for too long and allowing anyone who's following her to catch up, she realizes the chanterelles are a valuable food source she can't afford to pass up, because it's already late in the day and she might not get to safety until tomorrow. She pulls the newspaper out of the plastic bag and fills it with mushrooms.

Remembering what Bridey told her, as hungry as she is, she resists the temptation to eat them raw. The last thing she needs is a stomach ache or diarrhea. Is it safe, is she far enough away from the cabin now, to make a fire and cook them? Stay here overnight maybe? Daylight is fading fast. No, she should keep going until it's too dark to see. If she makes a fire now, the smoke could lead him to her. She bundles everything back up and sets out through the bushes again.

She has to assume whoever came in that vehicle is looking for her. Has she left a trail he can follow? The duff on the forest floor is better than dirt as far as not showing tracks, but she's scraped moss off logs by sliding over them and broken branches when they've snagged on the quilt or her clothes or the damn chain! She's crossed boggy areas with lovely big patches of skunk cabbage she noticed only in passing as she struggled through muck that sucked at her feet, leaving a trail a blind man could follow. Hiding her tracks hasn't been uppermost in her mind. It's time she paid more attention. At least it's nearly dark now. Can he track her in the dark? It would be a lot more difficult, for sure, so she's likely safe until morning. And from here on, she'll be more careful.

When she comes to a small stream, she refills the nearly empty water bottle. There are still two unopened bottles, but she thinks it wise to get water when she can. She jumps across the rivulet, then realizes she should follow it. It might meander, but it won't go around in circles, and can be counted on to go steadily downhill. It likely connects with the Dark River. Where she goes once she gets to the river, she's not sure. Up river to the highway? But what if Hank gives up tracking her through the bush, guesses she'd head for the highway or go back along the road, and sees her there? It's not safe.

Does she dare go to the house? As much as she gives him a pass for bad behaviour, Bridey won't think what he's done this time is just boys being boys. She will help. No way of knowing if the house is upstream or downstream, though. The only thing for certain is that the highway is upstream. So, downstream, then. No way of knowing how far away the river is. With luck, there's another ranch or farm before she has to go that far.

Then she remembers every fugitive-chase scene in every movie she's ever seen, where the trail ends at a creek. This one's not very deep. She can walk in it and leave no tracks. Not even a dog can track her! Plus, it might feel good on the cut on her foot. If she can stand the cold.

It'll be full dark soon. She'll find a sheltered spot, make a fire both to cook the mushrooms and for warmth, and worry about wet feet then. She steps into the water, shudders at the cold, and heads downstream, just as snow begins to fall.

* * *

"It might help if we had something of hers, you know, to give Delilah the scent of," Max says, "but she's a guard dog, not a tracker. I've never even tried tracking with her. I don't know how to set her on a trail."

"Just give it a try," Hank Senior tells him. "Show her something in the cabin, maybe?"

"You think she'll be able to figure out whose scent we want her to pick up, with shit and piss on everything?"

"I know. What else have we got, though?"

"I guess we can try." Max takes his dog up the steps and into the cabin. She sniffs everything with interest, looks up at him several times as if puzzled about what's going on, and just keeps on sniffing.

When it becomes obvious the dog doesn't get the idea, Hank Senior says, "There's some tracks in the dirt near where we parked. Maybe she'll be able to pick up the scent there." He leads Max, with the dog at his side, through an opening in the scrub brush and shows him the imprint of Astrid's runner.

The dog sniffs and trots around, and when she sets off into the bush, Max follows her.

"I'm going with Max," Hank Senior tells Les and Bruce. "You guys fan out, see if you can find other tracks. Since Bruce neglected to bring the walkie-talkies and the cellphone coverage is spotty, don't go too far. We don't need anyone getting lost."

"I brought Max," Bruce says, "so I've done my part. I really need to get home."

"We can use all the help we can get, Bruce."

"Well, I can't go into the bush! Besides, you guys have hiking boots. Lookit these!" He points to his shoes.

"Jesus, Bruce! Loafers?" Les asks. "You couldn't've put on a pair of boots?"

The Pastor purses his lips and frowns. "I have gout, remember!"

"Oh yeah, how could we forget?" Les snorts and shakes his head, then turns and starts toward a slight break in the undergrowth east of where Max went.

"Just make yourself useful for a change!" Hank Senior hisses at the Pastor. He puts the keys to the Tahoe in his pocket and follows Max. He hasn't gone far before he hears a shriek and turns back. Pastor Green is in a heap on the ground just a few meters into the bush.

"I slipped," he says. "I think I busted my ankle."

"Let's have a look," Hank says, and Bruce squirms so his leg is out in front of him. Hank hands him the flashlight, then pulls the sock down and palpates the ankle. He says, "Well, if it's broken, it's not displaced. More likely a sprain. Let's get you up. I'll help you into the truck. You might as well go home."

"I can't drive!"

"Either drive, or stay here until we're ready to go."

"I'm in pain! I have to get to a hospital! I need to get it X-Rayed. Max can take me!"

"We need Max here. The Tahoe's an automatic. You can drive with one foot."

"You don't understand!" The Pastor wails. Tears spill down his cheeks.

"No, *you* don't understand. Get yourself out of here, or stay. Those are your options. End of discussion," Hank hisses. "I'll help you to the truck now, or you can stay where you are until I come back." He turns and walks away.

"But it's starting to snow! The ground's already wet! My legs are getting cold!"

Hank Senior snorts and continues walking away.

"Okay!" Bruce calls out. "Okay! I'll go!"

Hank comes back, helps Bruce turn and get on his knees and then stand. With an arm around Hank's shoulder, Bruce hobbles to the truck, huffing and puffing and moaning with every step. At last, he pulls himself into the driver's seat. Hank hands him the keys; he starts the engine, gives Hank a black look, turns his tear-streaked face away and drives off without another word.

Hank mutters under his breath, "Jesus H. Christ! Useless as tits on a bull!" Then he hurries into the bush to catch up with Max.

He doesn't have to go far. Max is standing, hands on hips, whistling for his dog. In a few minutes, they hear her crashing through the brush and she comes back to sit beside her master, panting happily.

"She went through stuff no human would go through," Max says. "I think she's just having fun."

"Oh well. It was worth a try. Maybe we can pick up her tracks ourselves," Hank tells him, and starts into the bush, playing his flashlight beam along the ground.

Max follows, using his flashlight to scan both sides of their pathway, and finds a small broken branch. "Something went through here," he says, pointing it out. "Could've been my dog, though."

"Nope! I think we're on the right track," Hank says, pointing out more partial impressions of running shoes further on. They're able to follow, picking up tracks here and there, until they get to a marshy area where their feet get sucked into the mud.

They shine their flashlights around, and Hank says, "I can't believe she plowed through that!"

"Looks like she did, though."

Delilah goes in up to her belly before Max calls her back.

"Well, we're not going, not in the dark, anyway."

"Go around?"

"Hmm. No way of knowing how big it is."

It's been snowing lightly for the past half an hour or so, and now the flakes are becoming larger; it's getting too dark to see anything outside the beam of their flashlights, and they decide against going further.

"Ready to go home, girl?" Max asks the dog. She gives a happy *youww!* and runs ahead as they return to the cabin.

Les is waiting in his four-by-four. "Where's your truck, Hank?" he asks as he steps out of the driver's seat. "You're damn lucky I didn't leave, thinkin' you guys were gone."

"You know we wouldn't leave without telling you. Surely to god you wouldn't leave without telling us!" Hank says.

"Well, where *is* your truck?"

"Lardass fell and hurt his leg. I sent him home."

"Didn't really think he'd help, anyway, did you?"

"No. But we needed him to bring Max." Hank Senior shucks his jacket and tosses it in the back seat of the SUV. He pulls out a Thermos, screws the lid off and pours coffee into it, taking a grateful draught, and offers it to Les. Les takes the cup as Hank says to him, "He remembered the coffee and the chicken wings. Would've been nice if he remembered the walkie talkies."

"Typical," Les says.

"I've been thinking. Maybe we don't need three leaders."

Les gives him a narrow-eyed look before saying quietly, "I've been thinkin' that for a while."

"We're on the same page, then. Let's talk about it when this is behind us. But for tonight, we have to call off the search. We'll start again first thing in the morning."

Max has put his dog into the cargo compartment and now comes up beside the other two men.

"The dog couldn't find anything?" Les asks.

Max shakes his head.

"Fuck, so now I've got a muddy mutt in my truck to clean up after, for nothing!"

"I'll clean it," Max says.

"Don't blame Delilah," Hank warns. "She's not a tracking dog. I'll bring Buster tomorrow. He's not a tracking dog, either, but he likes Astrid, often goes out in the bush with her. He might try to find her if he picks up her scent."

* * *

A dog barks. Buster? It seems far off, but it's hard to tell; sound is so dampered when it's snowing. It sounded a little like Buster. Not quite his usual deep bassoon *woo-woo-woof*, but close. Maybe it was wrong to leave when she heard the vehicle coming! It could even be a formal search, with tracking dogs. Should she go back?

Still, it might be Buster. If so, he'd be with Hank Senior, because Buster steers clear of Junior and Junior never takes him anywhere. But still. It *could* be Junior. And it could be Fletch, too; Buster likes Fletch. Can she take the chance? If he'd only bark again, maybe she could tell.

But the dog doesn't bark again, and she decides it didn't sound like Buster, not really. It must be a tracking dog and, in that case, she *should* go back. But won't the dog find her? Maybe it can't, because it lost her trail when she went into the stream! She starts trotting back.

Then she holds up, thinking, if it was Search and Rescue or RCMP or even just ordinary citizens like the search group she joined way back when, wouldn't they be calling for her? She remembers they were given an area to search, and told to call the girl's name, often and loud. If she could hear the dog, she should be able to hear a search party. Besides. This is a long way from where she was abducted. Why would they even start searching here?

She holds up and stands quietly, listening, but hears no barking dogs and no one calling her name. She overrules the part of her that desperately wants to believe it's Search and Rescue, turns, and continues down the mountain.

It's soon dark enough she can't see where she's going. It's not safe to continue. She stops for the night, hoping it's far enough from the cabin that a fire won't be seen. The Bic flame throws enough light to see a deadfall. It looks like a tree that blew over, exposing its roots and leaving a fair-sized divot. There's a nice bit of shelter there, and that's where she'll make her fire.

She breaks off small branches and tents them over a crumpled wad of newspaper, puts the Bic to it, and is relieved when it catches easily. When the fire's low enough, she spears chanterelles onto a stick, uses her finger to wipe a bit of Crisco on each, and roasts them over the coals. She doesn't leave them there long, though; ravenous, she eats them when they're barely sizzling. To say they don't taste good would be an understatement; bitter and astringent, if she didn't know for sure they were edible she would have spit them out.

She lays out newspaper to stand on and warms herself while her shoes and socks are steaming on rocks near the fire. When the socks feel dry, she puts them and her shoes back on, and makes a bed of newspaper. She hooks the quilt over the roots, places rocks around the edges to hold it down, and squeezes herself in. Light from the low flames of the nearby fire flicker across the quilt. At last, even knowing how perilous her situation still is, she falls into an exhausted asleep.

When she awakes to thin light of morning, she discovers the snow that was falling when she went to sleep had become heavier overnight. The quilt has a layer of fluffy snow on it.

Breakfast is chanterelles cooked the night before. She walks a few steps away to urinate and move her bowels. *Newspaper has more than one use,* she thinks, tearing off a few strips, rumpling and rubbing them together to soften them. Finished, she shakes the snow off the quilt, bundles up her things and starts out again. How much further is it to the river? The snow isn't deep, but it's enough to make the going slippery, especially in the steep downhill parts. Of more concern is the obvious trail she's leaving. The sunlight coming through the trees is wintery-pale. Will it be enough to melt the snow and erase her tracks?

The chanterelles haven't stopped the hunger pangs, and she's rationing them in case she doesn't find more. It's late in the season, they're already close to rotting, and now, buried under snow and leaves, hard to find.

There are other edible things Bridey showed her: salal berries, blackberries and huckleberries. Also Oregon grape, both the berries and the leaves. The leaves look like holly, so she would never have thought to eat them, but Bridey told her the young, soft leaves are good and taste like potato chips. Then there's skunk cabbage, which Bridey claimed the First Nations people called famine food.

There are no young, soft Oregon grape leaves at this time of year, though, and the old leaves are nasty. She's not hungry enough to eat them. Not yet, anyway. As for berries, she's found some; this late in the year they're desiccated and hard as stones, but she eats them despite that. She knows she might be passing up other edibles, and wishes she'd spent more time taking Bridey foraging. But then, she never imagined her life might depend on it.

Fortunately, she has water. Oddly, her mother's image keeps popping into her mind. *You can live for days without food,* she's telling her, *as long as you have water. But you have to keep moving.*

TWENTY-FOUR

Denver can barely keep his mind on judging. He begged off socializing with the show committee again tonight. Why? Just so he can mope around the motel room? Spend more time agonizing over Astrid, wondering why he can't reach her by phone, why she hasn't returned his calls? It's worrisome, especially since Hank hasn't called him back, and when he called Dot's the second time, they told him she'd quit.

He called Dallas earlier. They had ranch business to discuss. As usual, the discussion devolved into a disagreement. Despite that, with his thoughts on Astrid, he found himself telling Dallas he hadn't been able to reach her by phone since Wednesday morning. "So?" Dallas said, "This is only Saturday. What's a few days? She's probably just busy." He added rather tactlessly, "She's no doubt got other things going on in her life even if you don't."

At least he agreed to go into the office and get him the phone number for Hazen's Ranch. He dials it now. It rings half a dozen times before Bridey answers.

"Hello?"

"Hello. Is that Bridey?"

"Yes."

"Bridey, it's Denver. Denver Danielson. How are you?"

"Oh, hi, Denver! I'm okay, thanks. How are you?"

"Well, I'll be better when I get in touch with Astrid. She hasn't been answering my calls. When I called Dot's yesterday, they told me she was booked in at four. When I called again then, they said she'd quit. I had no idea she was planning to do that!"

"Neither did I."

"She's still not answering her cell. Is she home now?"

He can hear Bridey take a few breaths, then she says, "You don't know?"

His heart thumps. "Know what?"

"Oh, Denver, I'm sorry, I hate to be the one to tell you…"

"What? Tell me what?"

There's silence on the line for a heartbeat, then Bridey says quietly, "She quit her job at Dot's because she moved away. With a man. A trucker, I think."

Denver draws a sharp breath. His guts clench and a rush of anguish courses through him. He's unable to speak for a moment. Then asks quietly, "Do you have a phone number for her new place?"

"No."

"Do you know the guy's name? Or where he lives?"

"She didn't tell me anything. All I know is, she wasn't here for a couple of days. They told me she was staying with a friend. Hank and I went to town this afternoon, did a little shopping and had supper at Dot's. The owner is a friend of ours. He told us Astrid quit her job because she was moving away to live with a guy she met at the diner. We were only gone a few hours, but when we got home, her car and all her things were gone."

His heart thumps.

"She hasn't called me and she's not answering my calls, either. I don't understand it. I don't think she was angry with me. I thought we were getting along well!"

"Sorry, Bridey," he rasps, "I have to go." He touches end call, drops the phone on the night table, and flops down on the bed, covering his face with his hands and taking deep, gulping breaths. Then he rolls over to bury his face in the pillow, his body wracked by sobs.

* * *

Astrid is picking salal berries into the plastic bag. It's a good patch of berries; there are still quite a few that aren't dried to hard lumps. She wants to eat her fill and harvest as many as she can find before moving on, because this is the first patch she's come to with berries that aren't all like stones, and there's no guarantee there will be more.

When she found the skunk cabbage bog, she tried pulling one of the plants out by the roots. Despite struggling with it and even reaching down into the muck nearly to her elbows, the root stubbornly refused to let go and all she got for her trouble was arms coated in cold muck, and skunk cabbage stalks. They looked good enough, sort of like a large, flattened green onion. She was hungry enough to eat a green onion, so she started chewing the tough stem.

She quickly regretted it.

Her lips, tongue, gums and the insides of her cheeks felt as though they were being pierced with thousands of needles. Although she spat it out instantly, hours later she can still feel the burn. *I'd like to have a chat with whoever told Bridey skunk cabbage was edible,* she thinks. But then, Bridey said the roots were edible. She didn't say the stems were, too.

Is it because she's so ravenous that she's beginning to enjoy the salal berries? They have a peculiar taste, but are mild and kind of sweet, and the burning sensation in her mouth is fading along with her hunger pangs as she shovels them into her mouth as fast as she can strip them off their stems.

An odd, snuffling sound alerts her; she straightens and looks around.

In another salal patch a couple of hundred meters away, a bear raises its head.

Astrid is jolted by an adrenalin rush; she's frozen into inaction for a heartbeat, then her instinct is to turn and run. But she remembers Hank Senior saying that although bears look clumsy they can easily outrun a human and if she met one on the trail, to remember running may trigger its prey response. She commands her number tens to stay put.

What should I do? I remember what he said not to do, but what did he say a person should do?

The bear didn't look large when it raised its head behind the salal patch, but when it moves out into a more open space and stands up on its hind legs, it looks enormous! It seems to be sniffing the air, as if to confirm it smells something. *That something,* she realizes, *is me.*

Then it drops back on all fours and starts huffing and snorting, swinging its head from side to side. When it starts pawing the ground like an angry bull, Astrid utters a choked sob and is barely able to overrule her flight instinct.

She checks behind her to make sure she isn't going to fall over something, and starts slowly backing away. "Nice bear... good little bear... isn't it time for you to be hibernating? Don't make eye contact... dogs don't like that... maybe bears don't either... I won't hurt you if you don't hurt me... You can have this berry patch..." She's talking under her breath, more to bolster her courage than to convince the bear to leave her alone.

Now the bear seems to be clacking its jaws. Its ears are laid flat back. A sign of annoyance in horses and cats—bears, too? Astrid's heart leaps to her throat and she lets out a little squeak when it darts forward a few steps, but it stops up. The relief that floods through her is short-lived; it charges again, astonishingly fast, but once again stops and comes no closer.

She wills herself to take deeper breaths, not to scream, and starts backing away again. It's all she can do to stop herself from turning and running. She reaches for the hatchet. She hadn't bundled it up in the quilt as she'd planned to; she'd only kept it out because she found it useful to hack her way through dense parts of the bush. *I have the hatchet,* she thinks, *and the chain on my wrist. I'm not completely unarmed.*

As she puts more distance between herself and the bear, it seems to calm a bit, and then after what seems an eternity, it turns and bounds off through the bush.

Astrid's knees buckle and she collapses to the forest floor, oblivious to the prickling of the deadfall she landed on. Huge gulps of air can't stop her sobs, but she quickly gets back on her feet, not wanting to be even more helpless than she really is if the bear comes back. But the forest remains quiet and the bear seems to have moved on. Still, it's unnerving. She keeps moving in the opposite direction from the bear's retreat, but constantly scans her surroundings and can't stop fearful glances back over her shoulder as she continues down the slope.

My god, she thinks, *what Hank Senior said about bears being fast is right! There is no way I could've outrun him. He bounded through the bushes and over the deadfall almost like it wasn't there!*

When I get back to civilization, I'll have to write a book.

TWENTY-FIVE

BRIDEY'S STUMPING HER way through the yard, pruners in hand, cutting back perennials and shrubs in preparation for winter, heaping the cuttings on the sere lawn for Fletch to pick up with the Gator and take to the burn pile.

She turns her face to the glow of the sun coming over the trees on the far side of the driveway and closes her eyes. It feels good to be doing something useful to stave off the dark, and her garden was ugly. All those dead and dying plants! The plants going dormant signals the approach of the long dark, and on top of that, Astrid's gone.

"But I must get this done, Astrid or no Astrid," she mutters, and gets back to work, clipping and pulling, switching back and forth from the small pruners to the long-handled loppers. She's worked her way back to the front steps when she hears a car turn off the highway into the driveway and looks up to see an RCMP cruiser. It pulls up onto the concrete in front of the garage; the officer gets out and approaches her.

"Good morning, ma'am," he says.

Bridey cocks her head and looks at him with narrowed eyes.

"I'm Constable Villeneuve. Are you Mrs. Hazen?"

She frowns and nods.

"Mrs. Hazen, I'm checking out a missing person report."

"A missing person?"

"Yes, Astrid Ingerson. I understand she lives here, and works for you?"

"*Ingebritson! Inga-brit-son!*"

"…Okay… Is she here?"

"She's not missing, she moved away."

"Do you know where she moved to?"

"She met a man and moved away."

"Did she leave a forwarding address? Phone number?"

"Who says she's missing?"

"We got a message on our anonymous tips line. Normally we don't get reports of missing person on dat line. Might be a prank, but we have to check it out." He pulls a pen out of his pocket, clicks it and holds it over his notepad. "Does she have family? Friends? What about a boyfriend?"

"A boyfriend? Of course, she has a boyfriend!" Bridey snorts. "What do you think? I just told you, she left with her boyfriend."

"Do you know his name?"

She shakes her head.

"How about other boyfriends, maybe a bad break-up?"

"He's gone."

"Do you have his name and phone number? We just want to make sure dere's nothing to dis report. You know the reputation dis area…"

"They should build a new highway. I don't know why they don't build a new highway."

Constable Villeneuve's posture relaxes as he studies Bridey, and then says gently, "Do you have his name, maybe his phone number, ma'am?"

The door opens, and Hank Senior comes out.

"What's this about, Officer?" he asks.

"Are you Mr. Hazen?"

"Yeah?"

"I was just explaining to your wife I'm checking out a report, a woman who was working for you, Astrid Ingerson, has gone missing."

"Ingebritson!" Bridey snarls.

"Sorry. Ingebritson."

Hank comes down off the stoop to stand between Bridey and Constable Villeneuve. "My wife must've told you, she ran off with some guy. A trucker, we heard."

"Moved, yes. I still want to contact her. Her ex-boyfriend also. Your wife was just going to get his phone number for me."

"Well, I'll save her the trouble. I have it." He digs his cell phone out of his shirt pocket, looks through it, and reads out the information while Constable Villeneuve writes. Then he asks, "Have you checked with her work?"

"Our information is dat she worked here, for you."

"She did, but she also had a job at Dot's. You must've seen her there," he narrows his eyes, "there's where the cops are when you need 'em, sittin' around eatin' donuts at Dot's."

Constable Villeneuve returns his stare and hands him his card, "I've been to Dot's," he says. He goes to his cruiser, opens the door, then turns and adds, "If you hear from her, please have her call me."

"We sure will, Officer," Hank says, and puts an arm around Bridey.

Constable Villeneuve gets back in his cruiser and drives away, and as they watch him leave, Bridey says, "He must be French. Did you hear that accent? I think he's French. He's so young and handsome! So bright!"

"Not bright, Baby. As dark as every cop is. A cop is a cop is a cop," Hank says, "and no sense of humour, besides. I wonder who reported her missing. Must've been... unless... you didn't, did you?"

Bridey shrugs his arm off her shoulder and sinks to the seat of her walker, shaking her head. "She's not missing. She moved."

"You told Danielson that, didn't you?"

"It upset him."

"Well, nobody likes to be jilted, but he's a big boy. He'll get over it."

"He wanted to know the trucker's name. Do we know his name?"

Hank purses his lips and frowns, then says, "I never met him. You're the one who told me about him, remember?"

Bridey frowns and her eyes narrow. She cocks her head and says, "Oh."

Hank looks around the yard, at the shrubs that are scalped and the heaps of leaves and branches, and sighs. "How long have you been out here, Baby? Were you working out here in the dark?"

"I can't lay in bed all day! I have things to do!"

"I know." Hank pulls her to her feet and takes her arm. "Let's get you back in the house. I have to go, and I don't want to be worrying about you being out in the cold."

"Astrid was helping me," Bridey says.

"I know, Baby, I know. Don't worry about your flower beds. I'll have Fletch deal with the rest." He kisses the top of her head. "And Baby, if you're going to come outside, please get dressed first. At least put on shoes."

* * *

"Thanks, Franny. I appreciate it. Dunno what's keepin' those guys." Hank Senior watches as Franny tops up his coffee. "Looks like it's busy out front. Last thing you need is us in here."

"It's okay, Mr. Hazen." She returns his smile. "And it *is* busy. I wish Astrid hadn't just run off, no notice or nothing. It's just lucky Jen was available on short notice. She can use the extra shifts, but she's not as much help as Astrid was."

"Did Astrid say anything to you about what she was planning?"

"That she was going to live with a trucker? No, never. It's odd. I don't remember her ever getting particularly friendly with any of 'em. She seemed to be head over heels for that cowboy. And you'd think she'd at least call me back. She's even ignoring my texts."

"Well. I wouldn't know for sure, I'd have to ask my wife, but I think she had at least one other guy on a string. I'm away from home a lot, you know, but I seem to remember Bridey saying something about Astrid having a guy stay the night. Parked his semi in the yard overnight, anyway."

"Really? That surprises me." Franny shakes her head. "That *really* surprises me."

Did I oversell it? Hank wonders. *I should back it off a little.* He says, "I guess everyone has their secrets. But maybe Bridey was mixed up."

They're interrupted when Les comes into the room ahead of Pastor Green, who's hobbling along on crutches. The Pastor props the crutches up against the wall and grunts and groans his way onto the nearest chair. Les walks around behind Hank to sit on the other side of the table.

"Bring a couple more mugs, Franny," Les tells her, then turns to the other two and asks, "Anyone want something? A Danish? Pie maybe?"

"Not for me, thanks," Hanks says.

"I'll have a slice of apple and a slice of raisin. Don't warm 'em up, but put a couple scoops of ice cream on 'em," Pastor Green says.

Franny looks at Les, who says, "I'll have a cruller. And bring a thermal carafe of coffee, too."

Franny hurries off.

Hank says, "You'll spoil your supper, Bruce. Ruby'll be pissed."

"A little pie won't spoil my supper. I might not get any, anyway, maybe I should eat here. What's the special today, Les?"

"Same as every Monday, meat loaf. Comes with coffee and pie, as if you didn't know. Why don't you have supper at home?"

"Ruby's pissed at me. I've been spending too much time at the Lodge, she says, and then I get hurt when I'm up there, to boot."

"Jesus!" Les says. "You'd think she'd be happy, not having your ugly mug around the house."

"It takes more'n that to make her happy. And now that I'm incapacitated, she had to hire the neighbour kid to do yard clean up, and she let me know what she thinks about wasting money paying for something I should've done. As if my accident was my fault!"

"You're not going to be on crutches forever. Aside from that, what's wrong with her?" Hank asks. "She's not crippled, for chrissakes. When I left this morning, Bridey was out getting her flower beds ready for winter. Her MS is bad lately, but she still manages to garden."

"Yeah, Bruce," Les contributes, "you're pussy-whipped. When was it Ruby got your balls, anyway? Back in high school?"

Franny returns with a tray, cutting off any angry retort from Pastor Green. She sets the carafe, mugs, cruller and two plates of pie à la Mode on the table.

"Thanks, Franny," Les tells her, "shut the door on your way out. No one is to disturb us."

Once Franny's gone and the door is secured, Hank says, "So. The contract with The Children of Noah is at Ken's office. He says it looks okay, but he'll go over it in detail and let us know of any changes we should write in. I'm sure it's going to go ahead, so I ordered prayer books, a couple of those liturgy books, and for starters, three red robes and ten black ones. We don't have to pay for ours. We sell the black ones for $250."

"What's our cost?" Les asks.

"Let's just say the sheeple will pay for it. The first purchase covers 'em all." He shares a grin with both other men before the humour slides from his face and he continues, "But, back to our problem. No sign of her yet."

"I don't think you need to waste any more time tromping around out in the bush looking for her," Bruce says. "It's been what, five days? Six? It's been cold. She must be dead by now, or if she isn't, she soon will be."

"I was thinking we should hire a spotter plane," Les says. "See if we can find a pilot we can trust. Wouldn't have to tell him we're looking for a person, or maybe just that we heard there's people out in the bush wantin' to start forest fires, or—I don't know—something."

"Naw," Hank cuts him off, "that's a non-starter. If she saw a plane, she'd try and attract his attention, and any pilot in the world would report it. No one could keep their mouth shut about something like that. Not unless he was, maybe, one of our members. Wonder if any of our guys has a plane? We can look into that. Maybe we should build a landing strip at the Lodge, too. Not for this, of course, but for the future. Then guys that have their own planes can fly in."

"Yeah," Les says, "and I can fly up with the food and not have to ride with *him*."

"I'll go without you next time," Pastor Green says. "Let you burn your own gas. Think about that."

"We won't have so much prepped food to take up once we get rolling," Hank Senior says. "We'll staff our own kitchen. But I didn't mean to get off topic. Back to Astrid. You know how hard it is to see anyone in the forest when you're on the ground. Absolutely impossible from the air. If she gets out to the clear-cut, maybe."

"How about you 'n' Junior take the horses and dogs out into the clear-cut and see if there's any sign," Les suggests.

"I thought you said the dogs were no help either of the other days," Bruce says, "so why would it be any different in the clear-cut? Useless slobbering mutts." He wipes melting ice cream off his chin with the back of his hand.

"Junior stays at the Lodge. Aside from him being, er, *unpredictable*, if she saw him, even if he was with me, she'd run the other way," Hank says. "And I told you, Max's dog isn't a tracking dog. Buster isn't either. I hope that useless slobbering mutt roots you a good one right in the ball sack next time you come by the house."

"He's tried," Bruce says.

"Lemme guess," Les says, "he couldn't find it?"

"Up yours," Bruce says, frowning at Les.

"I warned you," Hank Senior tells him.

"I'm just sayin', I see why Junior doesn't like him."

"He doesn't like Junior either," Hank Senior reaches for the carafe and tops up his mug. "We didn't lose her trail until she went into the creek. Don't think we'd've got that far without the dogs. Dunno how long she walked in the creek, we followed both sides through some rough terrain but couldn't pick up her tracks again. Goddamn snow made it impossible, remember?"

"Bruce wouldn't know," Les growls. "He was never out of sight the car. Second day, he stayed in bed."

"I'm injured, you asshole!"

"Yeah, Nancy, you have a sore foot. We know."

"Like to see you go tromp around out in the bush with a bruised ankle!"

"Let's stay focused," Hank says. "Buster and Delilah are both good dogs, even though they couldn't find her. End of fuckin' dog debate."

"Aw, gee, bruised ankle!" Les scowls. "You were less than useless even before you landed on your ass. Can't walk from here to the car without stopping for a rest. You're getting worse and worse. About time you went on a diet, don't you think?"

"Why not ask your wife the same question? And at least we don't look like we just escaped from Auschwitz! My glands…"

"Yeah, yeah, your glands. I think I'll put an end to you eatin' on my 'spoilage' account. I see dollar signs flying away every time you come through the door."

"You *cheap* bastard!" Spittle flies from the Pastor's lips as his voice rises in intensity. "You're going to charge your best friend for something that costs you *nothing*?"

"Cheap? *Me*?"

I really don't need a preacher, Hank thinks. *I'm beginning to think maybe I don't need a food guy, either.* He raps on the table and says, "Guys! For fuck's sake, you're like a couple of ten-year-olds! Have you been nattering at each other like this since high school? Give it a rest!"

Les scowls but relaxes back, takes a sip of coffee, squirms in his chair and then asks, "How long d'you think it would take her to get to the clear-cut, Hank?"

"Hmmm. It's rough terrain. Rocky, lots of steep drop-offs. No trails. Difficult going, even for the horses. So, even if she didn't end up going in circles, six or seven days."

"So, she likely isn't out there yet?"

"No, I don't think so. And if she is, I'd never get through on the horse. The lop 'n' scatter's worse than the bush, although some of the older slash has been machine-piled for burning, so there are some roadways made through it. You think she'll cooperate and stay where the horse could go?"

"If she saw you, she'd come to you."

"Dunno. She might not stick around to see if it's me or Junior. She'd be expecting him, after all."

"Can't outrun a bullet," Les points out. "Just sayin'."

"I'm not fuckin' gonna shoot her! But if by some chance she's made it out to the clear cut … Well, I might as well give it a try. If I'm gonna try the logging roads, I don't need the horse. I'll take the Hummer tomorrow."

"More likely it's a body you're lookin' for." Bruce shoves another forkful of pie and ice cream into his mouth. "Why do we have to do anything?"

"You just sit 'n' do nothing, Pastor. You're good at that." Les says, and continues, ignoring Pastor Green's scowl. "By the way, I told the staff here the story we decided on. When cop came snooping around, that's what they told him."

"That fuckin' cop was at my place, too," Hank says, "talking to Bridey. She says she told him the trucker story. She can be loopy, as you know, but she's also believable. Especially since she thinks it's the truth."

"I hope that cop isn't gonna be a pain in the ass! Not content takin' Franny's word for it, he came and talked to me, too." Les takes a bite of his cruller, chews thoughtfully, washes it down with coffee, then says, "But he's got no reason not to believe us. I think that's the end of it."

"I wouldn't be so sure," Hank says. "He's seems to be doin' the job. He wanted Danielson's name and phone number. I said we didn't know him well, only met him once, and that his name is Dennis Daniels, an honest mistake. Gave him the number for the Danton Creek field shack, which of course is shut down. Hope he doesn't come back to me on that. But I'm more concerned the cowboy won't accept the story."

"So what if he doesn't?" Pastor Green studies his plates as if willing more pie to appear. "Didn't you say he's working down in the States?"

"Yeah. Still." Hank drums his fingers on the table. "Just now I told Franny I thought Astrid had another boyfriend. Planted a seed, to get her thinking that way. And, something Franny said, that Astrid's ignoring her texts, got me thinking. I wonder where Astrid's phone is."

"Wouldn't she have it with her?" Bruce asks.

"Of course not!" Les hisses. "If she had it, don't you think she'd've called someone before now?"

"Junior wouldn't've let her keep it," Hank assures them. "So, why don't we lay this to rest once and for all. Find her phone. If Junior doesn't have it, it must be boxed up with her things. We can send texts to everyone who's been trying to contact her."

"Ahhh!" Les leans back and grins. "Great idea! We'll just say she's happy with her new man because he has the biggest cock she's ever had. Tell 'em she'll drop by if she's in the neighbourhood. Meantime she's getting a new phone, and will let them know her new number when she has it."

"Something like that," Hank grins and nods. "Let me look after it."

TWENTY-SIX

IT'S ALREADY QUITE late, later than she usually starts out, but Astrid is reluctant to leave her camp. Yesterday, she came out of the tall fir and cedar trees and looked down across a vast, cleared area littered with fallen trees and branches, with only small deciduous trees and low shrubs, mostly leafless now, in among the tangle.

Clear cut. Hank Senior told her about it, but this is the first time she's seen it. He said the British Columbia Forest Service started requiring loggers to scatter the branches from the felled logs, what he called slash, instead of piling and burning like they always had. Then, when the province was ravaged by forest fires, all that dead wood on the ground made a heavy fuel load and a barrier fire crews couldn't get through. So now it's to be left scattered for two years, then piled up and burned like before. "Like there won't be a forest fire during those two years! And they even want us to put roofing felt or tar paper over the slash piles to keep the wood dry," he'd said. "Afraid we won't be able to git 'em to burn otherwise. Wonder how we ever managed without their input!" He'd snorted and added something about over-educated young punks sitting at desks with nothing better to do than to come up with ridiculous ideas so it's tougher than ever to make a profit logging.

Besides scatter making the going tough, there was nothing she recognized as edible. After half a day, she came to the older section with the slash piled in heaps. Still nothing to forage, but at least hiking was easier.

When she found a pile with tar paper over it, she stopped for the night. She pulled out enough branches to make a good-sized den, and it was dry inside. Once she was in, she pulled branches down over the opening, and snuggled into her quilt, no longer noticing its smell. It made a decent shelter. She felt protected and safe and slept better than she had since leaving home.

She ate the last of the chanterelles the day before. Now she's run out of berries and hasn't found more. Worse, since leaving the creek, she hasn't found water.

Besides the throbbing pain from the puncture wound on the back of her right arm, her sore foot, and the shackle that's rubbing her wrist raw, the hunger pangs constantly gnaw at her insides. There's nothing other than a lump of Crisco to eat this morning. She opens the little paper packet and looks at it. Then she stuffs the walnut-sized piece in her mouth, moving it around with her tongue, enjoying the sensation of it melting. *Delicious! Why didn't I think of eating it before?*

But it's the last of her food. She studies the waxy paper it was wrapped in, and thinks she might be able to eat that. It still has some Crisco on it. She licks it off.

As has been happening more and more often over the last couple of days, she fantasizes about Bridey's roast beef dinners. Yorkshires smothered in gravy! Buttered carrots! Mmmm, butter! And Dot's cherry pie with ice cream. She pushes the thought of the E.D. Smith Cherry Pie Filling bucket at the cabin out of her mind and forces her thoughts on Denver instead. He'd had cherry pie with ice cream the day she met him.

"Denver! Are you wondering why I'm not answering my phone? Are you looking for me? Don't be stupid, he's so far away, what can he do? At least he must have reported me missing. And now I'm having a conversation with myself!"

She's lost track of the days, but surely by now they've missed her at work, called Hazens, and they must have reported her missing if Denver hasn't. Someone should be looking for her. They must be! Maybe she should just stay here, where she has this good shelter and lots of firewood, and wait to be found.

They must be sending out planes. Helicopters even. Maybe it's too hard to see her, a little black blob in the middle of hundreds of acres. A signal fire would be smart! She could light one of the slash piles! Out in the open, and with the snow, it's not going to start a forest fire, and someone's bound to see the smoke and come to check it out. But what if Hank Junior sees it, and comes before rescuers reach her?

Where are the rescuers, anyway? Why hasn't she seen, or heard, any planes or helicopters? Have they given up already?

How many days can she afford to wait here, where there's nothing to forage? She's already light-headed and doesn't have nearly her usual energy, or strength. It's difficult to clamber over deadfall she probably could've jumped the first day. She sits to rest frequently, and when she gets up again, she's often confused as to which direction she came from. Every part of the clear-cut looks like the rest.

Yesterday, she went back along her trail and might have gone the wrong way for hours if she hadn't come across a heavy steel cable, likely something the loggers left behind, laying in the dirt. She remembered crossing it earlier and only then realized she was going the wrong way. It was a stark reminder that people who get lost often wander in circles. If she does that now, with no food or water, she will die. But if no one comes for her, she will die where she is.

Following the creek, she was confident she wouldn't be going in circles, but she had to leave it when it went into a gorge. She must have strayed too far away from it, and hasn't been able to pick it up again. She was hoping to find it in the clear-cut, but hasn't yet.

At least out here, she can judge direction from the position of the sun. At this time of year, it's low in the sky. She will be careful to always have the sun ahead of her. The bigger problem is that she has no more water.

Eating snow didn't quench her thirst, and chilled her from the inside out, as if she wasn't already cold enough! Thinking to make drinkable meltwater, she filled the plastic bag with snow, gritted her teeth, and not quite able to force herself to put it next to her skin, placed it under her vest. That strategy, like eating snow, just made her miserably cold, and the bag leaked besides.

Her next idea was to fill the plastic bottles. Setting them close, but not too close, to the fire worked well but a bottle full of snow only resulted in a couple of swallows of water.

Then she piled up snow on a branch near enough to the fire to melt, and caught the drips in a bottle. That proved best; not something she can do while on the move, but she can make enough each night to get her through. Water, yes, you can live for a long time without food if you have water. But it's the lack of food that's making her weak and light-headed.

The will to go on is becoming hard to summon; she knows she must, though, and forces her body to rise, steadying herself by holding a branch until the dizziness she now experiences every time she gets up passes.

For the past couple of days, she hasn't been making a bundle out of the quilt, but wearing it like a cape instead. It's warmer and her hands are free, making climbing over logs and down steep declines easier. The empty plastic bag makes a decent hat and keeps the snow off her head.

"I must look ridiculous! Ridiculous! Ridiculous!" she shouts, and giggles at the mental image. Then she can't stop laughing until, exhausted, she collapses into the snow, and cries. She's sleepy. Starts to feel warm. Dozes off.

With a jerk, she awakens. She's read enough about the physiology of freezing to death, or dying from exposure, to know that going to sleep is dangerous and the warm feeling is an illusion. Why had she succumbed to it? She forces herself to get up, and finishes packing the quilt.

Yesterday, she made pockets for the water bottles by ripping holes in the threadbare top layer of the quilt big enough to slip them inside. She made a smaller pouch for the few remaining berries, but then ate them without ever putting them in there. So today, except for the water bottles, the pockets in the quilt are empty.

More rips in the quilt form a holster for the hatchet. It's still within easy reach and it's much better not having it tugging at the hem of her jacket, bumping her leg with every step.

Checking to be sure the paper from the Crisco is still in her jacket pocket, she gathers up the quilt, settles it across her shoulders, knots the corners under her chin, and looks around. The sun is still not far above the horizon, so if she keeps it to her left, she'll be heading south. Promising she won't stop to rest until the sun is directly above her, she gathers up her chain and starts off.

It's colder today than yesterday. The dark clouds on the horizon hold the promise of more snow. It's becoming difficult to push the thought of dying to the back of her mind. "How much more can I take? How much longer can I keep going? Surely I'll find someone, or a house, or come to a road before much longer."

She hasn't gone more than a few dozen steps when she stops in her tracks. There, starkly black against the snow, is a pile of scat. She's puzzled and stands looking at it for a moment. Was that there yesterday? Then her heart thumps. *That was not there when she made camp!*

Her brain disengages; forgetting it's impossible to outrun a bear and that running might trigger its prey response, she bolts, running as fast as she can. When her quilt snags on a branch and clotheslines her to a halt, she turns, pulls the knot loose and jerks on it, shouting, "Shit! Shit! Shit-shit-shit!" The branch it's snagged on flexes, but the quilt doesn't come free.

"Gaaahhh!" She leans all her weight into it; it breaks free, sending her scrambling backward. She gets her feet under her before falling, but she's at an embankment, and too close to the edge. The ground sloughs away under her and she goes tumbling down, down, down.

When her eyes open, Astrid finds she's pitched up against a stand of leafless bushes, partly buried in dirt. She's left the clear cut behind. There are dark firs and cedars towering above the bushes here. It's snowing. Not soft, fluffy snow like before, but more like tiny hailstones. *Sleet*, she thinks. *Just what I need.* It stings. It was the cold and wet on her face that woke her.

Her body, sore before, now seems to be nothing more than a vessel of pain. She's got a raging headache. Working her arm out from under a clod of turf, she touches her forehead. There's a large bump. Headache explained. But she can move her arms and legs. Nothing's broken.

She attempts to sit up, but collapses back to the ground; tries again, and makes it partway, propping herself up on an elbow. For dizzying minutes, she surveys her surroundings, brain muddled in confused thoughts. *Where's my quilt?* she wonders, *my quilt! My quilt! My quilt!* and tries to remember how she got here.

It comes back to her in a rush: the bear dung, running, falling. She's at the bottom of a steep slope; a cliff, really, extending as far as she can see both left and right, near-vertical and vegetation-free for the top thirty meters or so. There's a gravelly pile at the bottom, festooned with clumps of bushes, grass and black soil. *Those must be sections of the top, like the one that broke away under me*, she thinks. *If I fell from there, no wonder I'm sore all over.*

Then she sees her quilt. It's snagged on a root, waving teasingly in the wind like a flag near the top of the embankment she has no chance of climbing. The white plastic bag bounds away across the scree like a living thing, carried off by the wind.

Without the quilt, she has no warm shawl. No shelter. No hatchet. No water.

She lies back down, and thinks, *I can't go on. This is where I die.*

TWENTY-SEVEN

Save a four-hour drive by waiting three hours to get on a one-hour flight, Denver thinks. One airport is the same as the next; bigger or smaller, the only difference is size. They're full of the same people: parents with tired, cranky children; business travellers oblivious to everything but their laptops; teens with earbuds sprawling across multiple seats or with legs stuck out so everyone has to walk around them. Behind the counters, the same check-in clerks serve the same demanding, unreasonable customers.

A motel room is a motel room, whether it's roomy and modern and has an honour bar, balcony and Jacuzzi, or badly out-dated décor, stained curtains, and barely enough room for the bed. These last always seem to overlook the parking lot, or worse, the outdoor patio for the bar, with drunks caterwauling until two a.m. and the bass from the third-rate local band boom-boom-booming through the building. They all meld together in Denver's mind. *It's the weariness of living out of a suitcase,* he thinks, *but it's never hit me so forcefully before.*

Thankfully, the Rancho Murieta Equestrian Park in California has on-site accommodation for judges. Denver is there for a week-long reining futurity and derby, and shares the two-bedroom suite with another judge, a fifty-something mustachioed good ol' boy named Gus, whose family has been in South Texas since the Mexican Wars. Denver knows him slightly from past shows, and has always been drawn to him, initially because of his resemblance to Shane.

Like Shane, Gus is a little rough around the edges, but so amiable no one cares. Also like Shane, he's a talker, with endless stories of his antecedents, and a humorous world view. He says: "Are you *shittin'* me?" every few sentences. Despite his initial misgivings at having to share a room when he doesn't feel even slightly sociable, Denver is surprised to find he's enjoying the company.

They've gone to a local bar two evenings in a row. Gus is gregarious, genuinely interested in everyone and talks to everybody. Denver joins the conversation enough to seem engaged. It helps pass the time.

But the hours between bedtime and dawn are long, and he's sleeping only fitfully. Much of the night is spent staring at the ceiling, wondering how he could have been so wrong about Astrid. How could he have thought she had feelings for him? But she was so soft, so welcoming, so loving. He mentally replays the awful phone conversation with Bridey over and over, until he's not sure he remembers it accurately.

It's too painful and humiliating to talk about; he's certainly not going to confide in strangers. Besides, he's not sure he could get through it without blubbering like a baby. When he told Dallas, he just summed it up in two words: 'We're quits.' Dallas shucked it off. Not even an 'I'm sorry', just 'Oh, well, life goes on.' *He never understood what she meant to me,* Denver thinks, *but still, you'd think he could be a little sympathetic. At least he stopped short of telling me not to be discommoded because there are lots of fish in the sea.*

This night, Gus and Denver got a pizza on their way home from the bar. It's on the coffee table in front of them, and they're having a beer to wash it down before heading to bed.

"Big pro jackpot tomorrow," Denver says.

"Ay-yuh, gettin' to the part of the show that's innerestin'." Gus fusses with his boots to remove them, then puts his feet up on the table near the pizza, wiggling his toes. "Gads, that's better," he says with a chuckle. "Hope the smell don't kill ya!"

Denver gives his head a slight shake and says, "Can't be worse than the stench of black olives on your half of the pizza!"

"An acquired taste!" Gus chuckles and takes a swig of his beer. "Should be some high-end competition tomorrow."

"Yeah, not just the pros, either; I like the ammies too. Some of 'em could give the pros a run for their money." Following Gus's lead, he works his own boots off and puts his feet up on the other side of the box.

"You talkin' 'bout that little lady on that Doc O'Lena-bred stallion? Wouldn't kick her outta bed fer eatin' crackers!" Gus manages to stuff nearly half a slice of pizza in his mouth in a few bites, chews thoughtfully, then says, "You ain't much of a talker, prob'ly 'cause it ain't easy to git a word in edgewise when I'm around, but I know yer straight. Tonight, them gals was buzzin' 'round you like bees to honey, looked to me like you were in fer a threesome, and you come back here fer pizza 'n' beer with this ol' geezer? I figger you must have someone special waitin' on you back home."

"I did."

"Past tense? Well you know, gittin' back on the horse is the best cure."

"That's what they say."

Concern furrows Gus's brow. "Is it recent?"

"Saturday."

"Are you *shittin'* me?"

Denver's face is grim. He gives his head a slight shake.

Gus puts his feet back on the floor, leans forward and sets his half-eaten slice of pizza on the box lid. "I don't mean to pry, but I can put a few things together. It ain't a death, or you wouldn't be here. But sometimes a break-up is worse 'n' I'm guessin' from how you look, it wasn't yer idea. You musta bin on the road when you got the news."

"Yeah. At WestWorld, for the Arizona Paint Horse Classic."

"Tell me she didn't dump you in a text!"

"Nope. Just quit answering the phone."

"That's it?"

"Well, when I couldn't reach her, I phoned the lady she worked for. She told me."

"Are you *shittin'* me? A *third party* dump?" Gus gets to his feet, kicks his boots out of the way and goes into the kitchenette. He comes back with two fresh beers. Handing one to Denver, he sits down and says, "Now let's hear it. All of it."

"Not much to tell," Denver says, but once he starts talking, the words flow; he's surprised how much was bottled up, and that he's able to talk about it. Gus listens intently, nodding and grunting where appropriate as he finishes off the pizza.

"I still can't believe I could've been so stupid. Couldn't imagine her bein' a two-timer. Couldn't see her for what she was. My brother did. I was blind, I guess." Denver says at last. "I was going to ask her to stay with me, not to go back to Dark River after Christmas, come with me on the road." He clucks and shakes his head. "That's how fuckin' clueless I am."

"We-e-ll," Gus drawls, "here's my two cents worth: that li'l gal owes you a face-to-face. In my book, the only thing you done that some might call stupid is to take that Bridey woman's word for it. What I'd do if I was in yer boots is haul ass up there 'n' git it straight from the horse's mouth."

"Bridey doesn't know the name of the guy she left with, or even where they went."

"Astrid still has her phone, doesn't she?"

"It just goes to voicemail."

"Hmmm. She must have friends, at least someone at that diner who can tell you more! Won't be easy 'n' you might git nowhere 'n' you might not like what you find out, but at least you'd be doin' somethin'. I say, forget 'boot the rest of this show. Git the show committee to call up an alternate. Tell 'em it's a fam'ly emergency, which it is, 'n' git yer ass back home."

Denver slouches back in his chair, closes his eyes, and takes several deep breaths, blowing out through his mouth.

"We-e-ll, you know what they say 'boot free advice, it's free 'cause that's all it's worth," Gus says, getting to his feet and walking to the door of his room. He turns and says, "It's late. We got an early mornin'. Try 'n' git some sleep."

Once in bed, Denver goes over the story as he told it to Gus and marvels that far from being embarrassing, telling the older man about it was cathartic. He tries to remember word for word what Bridey told him. What is it that makes him keep running through it in his mind? Is he taking masochistic pleasure in suffering? Wallowing in the hurt?

Then, with a start, he realizes what niggles at him. Bridey said *they* told her she was staying with friends, and when they got home from town, *her car and all her things were gone*. Why wouldn't Astrid tell Bridey herself if she was going to be away for a few days? And why would she leave her car behind when she went to visit someone? She thought so much of Bridey; like an aunt, she said. She wouldn't leave without saying good-bye. She'd have introduced a boyfriend to her, too. *It doesn't jive,* Denver thinks. *Why am I just realizing this now? I don't know what, or why, but Gus is right, I need to go there and find out more.*

He gets his laptop, searches for available flights, and books a seat on the 10:15 a.m. Southwestern Airlines flight to Vancouver.

TWENTY-EIGHT

RINNY IS RUNNING around the yard, easily keeping ahead of Astrid. He's got her ball and seems to think having her chase him is more fun than watching her practice a'larries. But she really needs to practice. All the girls at school are way better at it than she is. As the new girl, she needs to join their game if she's to be accepted, and she's so inept they laugh at her. She can't blame them. She's a klutz. Her long legs just won't do what she wants them too. The other, shorter-legged girls can even do their a'larries as they march forward across the concrete play area, while she can never get past six a'larry, and then only on the spot.

One, two, three, a'larry! She flings her leg over the ball, but her timing and ball control are off. She can't catch the ball again. It bounces off the concrete and down into the playground. The other girls continue: four, five, six, a'larry, seven, eight, nine, a'larry, while she has to run after her ball on legs that won't move. The ball is getting further away. If it gets where the boys are kicking the soccer ball around, one of them will grab it and throw it further, or pretend not to have it, and she won't get it back until next recess, if at all.

Now she's on the ground and Rinny's licking her face, his breath ripe with the smell of horse manure. He's always so excited when he finds some on their hikes. Where did he find it in their yard? But it's not their yard. It's big, way too big, plus the schoolyard is there. But of course it's their yard, now with a pool. Rinny's been in it and he's dripping water, ice cold water on her.

Now her mother is bugging her. *Astrid. Get up. You can't sleep.*

But I'm so tired. She's in her bed, where it's nice and warm, and it's cold in her room so she doesn't want to get out from under the big furry blanket, even though it's heavy. Now the blanket's gone and Rinny's licking her face again.

Astrid! Her mother's voice again. *ASTRID! GET UP!*

Her mother's command breaks through into her conscious mind and forces her out of her dream. She awakens with a start, looking up into a huge, black, furry bear face. Terror shoots through her like a lightning bolt.

But its tongue is lolling out ... It almost looks like it's smiling ...

Buster?

"Oh my god!" she cries, "Buster!" She throws her arms around him. He pants happily and stands patiently while she pulls on him to get to her feet. When she's up, he goes bounding off a few feet, then turns to look at her. "Is that the way home, Buster?" she asks. "Are we close to home?"

As if in answer, he gives one throaty woo-woo-woof! before bounding off through the low bushes and into the trees. She stumbles after him and in a few meters, finds he's led her to a well-travelled game trail. Further along the trail, there's a barb-wire fence. Buster ducks under it. Judging by the streamers of black fur on the barbs, he's done this before. Astrid struggles through between the top and middle strands. A bit further into the bush, there's horse manure—old, but still promising—and now she hears a roaring sound she realizes is the river. She forces her number tens to keep following Buster and finds him waiting on the river bank. On the other side is the sandy shingle. They are at the ford.

The river, although not running as fast as when she and Bridey were there weeks ago, is still high. But Buster is a big, water-loving dog; he's undeterred, and wades in, stopping to look back at her as if to say, *are you coming?* She hesitates, fearing the cold, the strong current. But she has to chance it. No one will find her here any more than when she was out in the forest and she has no way of letting anyone know where she is. She latches onto his collar and scruff, and splashes in beside him.

The going is treacherous. The rushing water, paralyzingly cold, pushes at her. Her feet slide on the rocks. Astrid is grateful for Buster's solid presence. Then the bottom drops off abruptly and she slips under the surface. She has a death grip on Buster's scruff, though. He's a powerful swimmer, and tows her along. The current carries them further down river, but as they near the opposite side she can touch bottom again, and Buster pulls her up on shore. She collapses face down onto the ground, the cold slicing into her like needles, too exhausted to move.

Buster shakes, then sits and waits for her to get up. After a moment, he comes and pushes at her, relentlessly goading her, whining while pushing his nose hard into her neck and sides and licking her face until she summons all her strength, leans on him and gets up. Her clothing soaked through, shivering violently, she can barely make her muscles obey, but she grips Buster and he tows her up the short embankment, along the path through the trees, and out into the pasture.

The barn, visible in the distance, looks to be kilometers away but beyond it, on a slight rise with a backdrop of dark evergreens, the sprawling log house has smoke issuing from the chimney and the windows are alight. The sight is nearly enough to collapse her knees. Tears flow down her cheeks. Buster trots ahead; she forces her number tens onward, losing her balance from time to time, startling the horses as she stumbles through the herd.

The barn is closed and she's too weak to push the heavy sliding door open. She goes around and forces herself the final two hundred meters up to the house.

She lurches up the steps and leans on the doorbell button but doesn't wait for someone to answer; instead, she turns the knob and stumbles against it, sending it crashing against the wall. A blast of warm air and tantalizing dessert aromas assault her. Her knees give out.

TWENTY-NINE

BRIDEY'S AT THE stove, humming as the pot of blancmange she's stirring starts thickening nicely. She turns the burner off. When she was a girl, her mother made blancmange whenever there was too much milk to drink before it soured. Now Bridey makes it even if the milk isn't close to souring, and enjoys the warm, bright memory. She relaxes back against the counter to survey with pride the neat rows of pudding, all in the matching fruit nappies she inherited from her mother. She sighs.

Mother always put a dollop of strawberry jam in each dish; it would sink to the bottom and once the skin formed on top, you wouldn't even know it was there until you ate down to it. Mother called it the sweet surprise, wait till you get to the Sweet Surprise! *Isn't it funny how such little things connect you to the past,* she thinks.

Junior never liked the jam. Too sweet, he complained. *You don't have to eat the jam, Junior,* she told him. *Leave it out or I won't eat any pudding at all,* he said. She kept putting it in, because Heather liked it. Maybe she should have left one dish, just for him, with no jam. But it was her one act of defiance. They'd been butting heads since he was old enough to talk, and so often she felt as if he came out on top. How did a child manage to do that?

She still adds jam, each dollop reminding her of her precious little girl. How pleased she was when she got to the sweet surprise at the bottom of the dish! How her pretty little face would light up! It's a warm, bright memory.

There are few warm, bright memories of Junior. Bedtime stories, mostly. Fairy tales. But even then, he was never snuggly. When she was sitting on his bed leaning back against the headboard, with him barely able to stay awake as she read to him, he'd squirm away if she pulled him into a hug.

He liked Hansel and Gretel, especially the part where the children fool the witch and push her into the oven. His favourite book, though, was The Spider and the Fly, the illustrated version with the creepy Vincent Price lookalike spider. How did it go? She remembers the words, and as she spoons pudding out of the pot into bowls, recites with a sing-song voice: "Will you walk into my parlour said the Spider to the Fly, will you walk into my parlour said the Spider to the Fly, will you walk into my parlour said the Spider to the Fly…"

The doorbell rings. The door crashes open. Bridey turns to see Astrid stumble in, staggering as far as the first stool, bumping it and sending it crashing into the one next to it. Then she collapses to the floor with a clatter.

"Oh my god!" Bridey cries, grabbing her walker and coming to bend over Astrid.

"It was Hank, Bridey! Junior! He…he…"

"Oh my god, Astrid! What are you doing? You're all wet! You're dripping all over the floor! Get up!" With Bridey's goading and her hands on the side bars of the walker, Astrid pulls herself up.

"You have to get out of your wet clothes!" Bridey tells her, but Astrid is swaying, and sinks to the seat of the walker. Bridey scolds, "You're filthy! Look at your dirty shoes! What is wrong with you?"

"Cold…"

"I'll get a towel." and she goes into the laundry room. When she comes back, instead of a towel, she's got the terrycloth robe Astrid recognizes as Hank's.

"No, no, no," Astrid moans.

"What…? What's wrong with this? Don't take it, then!" She tosses the robe on the floor, but then thumps her way down the hall to the linen closet. When she comes back with an armload of towels, she pulls off Astrid's shoes while muttering, "Dirty… Dirty…"

Astrid, shivering so violently she's barely in control of her muscles, struggles to get out of her jacket. Bridey pulls the sleeve off over the chain.

She wraps towels around Astrid's head and shoulders, then prods her to get up and leads her to the family room couch.

"Why have you got this stupid chain? Quit that jiggling! I need Hank!"

"Police!"

"Police? I'll get Hank. You'll have some nice blancmange."

Astrid heaves a sigh, and closes her eyes, and slumps back against the cushions.

Bridey goes to the wall-mounted land line in the kitchen, lifts the receiver and touches speed dial. After a few rings, Hank Senior answers. "What is it, Baby?"

"Come home! Astrid's here."

"Wha..."

But Bridey has already hung up. She pours blancmange into a bowl, adds a scoop of strawberry jam, takes it into the living room and sits on the couch beside Astrid. "Hank will be here soon," she tells her.

A woman's voice comes from behind them. "What's going on?"

Astrid looks up and sees a short, pretty woman standing in the doorway. She's in a bathrobe and has a towel, turban-like, on her head.

Bridey says, "I thought you were having a nap, Trisha."

"I took a shower and was just lying down when I heard all the fuss. Who is she? What's wrong with her?"

"She's cold."

"Oh? Cold?" She pulls the towel off her head and uses it to fluff her hair. "What's for dinner?"

"I'm waiting for Hank."

"Well, I'm hungry. I haven't eaten since breakfast."

"Go!" Bridey snaps. She puts the bowl down on the end table and urges Astrid to sit up slightly, propping a cushion behind her. Then she perches beside her and picks up the bowl again.

"Trisha?" Astrid asks. Her shivers are becoming less violent as she warms up. She takes the bowl from Bridey; its warmth starts a tingling in her fingers.

"Yes, Astrid, she came to see Junior," Bridey says, "but he's at the Lodge."

"Well, he isn't staying there. He's coming back tonight." Trisha frowns. "Astrid ... is she ..."

"I told you to go!" Bridey snaps.

Trisha snorts, stands defiantly for a moment, then turns and retreats to the kitchen. Astrid manages to spoon up the warm pudding despite her spastically-shaking hands, and her insides begin to feel as though they're glowing. When she gets to the jam in the bottom, she groans. "Mmmm!" She manages to smile and Bridey beams.

"We'll have a nice cuppa, and then you rest." Bridey takes the empty bowl from her and goes to the kitchen where Trisha is perched on a stool at the island. Puddings pushed to one side, she's smoking, knocking her ashes into a cup.

"Couldn't find an ashtray," she says. "You're still making pudding? You already have so much."

"There's an ashtray on the stoop," Bridey tells her. "If you're going to smoke, go there. I need this!" She snatches the cup away from Trisha, takes it to the sink and scours it before putting it back on the counter by the stove.

"Go outside? It's cold and I just got out of the shower!" Trisha grumbles, but at the look she gets from Bridey, goes out the door and comes back without the cigarette. "Who is that girl? Is she the one who dumped my ex and ran off with a trucker?"

Bridey fills the kettle and plugs it in, then gets the teapot, keeping her back to Trisha and ignoring her questions as she fusses with tea things.

"Hank phones me every day," Trisha says. At that, Bridey turns to look at her, frowning at the smug grin on her face as she continues, "I know what goes on around here." Then her grin dissolves and she frowns. "Hank said Astrid is the girl who was living here. She was dating my ex."

Bridey's only response is to turn back to her pudding and mumble under her breath, "Jam. Jam."

"So? What's she doing here? Where's the trucker? She want her job back?"

An ambulance turns into the driveway. Bridey recognizes it as the one from the mill, and as it pulls up to the house, sees her husband in the driver's seat. She pushes her walker out the door to greet him on the stoop.

"How'd she get here?" Hank Senior asks.

"Astrid, you mean? Why are you driving that?" she points to the ambulance.

"Baby, who else?"

"Trisha. She's here. She's all wet and came inside with muddy shoes!"

"*What?*" Hank hisses. "Trisha's *here*? And she's all wet and has muddy shoes?"

"Not Trisha!" Bridey scowls.

"Oh. Astrid's wet ... Has Trisha seen her?"

"Of course. We both have."

"Jesus H. *fuckin'* Christ! Just when you think it can't get any worse!" He paces back and forth across the stoop, stopping to kick Bridey's garden shoes into the corner. "Okay. Nothing we can do about it. You just stay mum, Baby, I'll look after it." He holds the door open, takes her arm and gently propels her inside.

As he comes into the kitchen, he holds up for a moment and surveys the scene. There's scarcely a clear space on any surface. Bowls, drinking glasses, coffee mugs, even dog food cans overflowing with pudding are everywhere. The sinks are heaped high with dirty saucepans. Clothes, shoes, towels and a bathrobe are on the floor. He clicks his tongue, sucks in a breath, and goes to Trisha.

"Hey, Trisha!" he beams, giving her a hug. "Good to see you! Didn't know you were coming."

"Hank invited me, said to wait here. He'll be back tonight, and tomorrow, we're going to Prince Rupert to get the ferry to Vancouver Island."

"Oh?"

"Yeah, he's taking me on a vacation! We're gonna drive down island to Victoria, get the Anacortes ferry, then take the Coast Highway to San Francisco."

"Yeah, that sounds nice. He didn't say anything about it to me, though, and something's come up. He's needed at the Lodge a little longer."

"Oh. Shit."

"Don't worry, Trisha, I gotta go up tonight, and I'll take you. You can leave from there."

"I don't know ... Is it that place out in the bush Hank talks about? No shops, no entertainment. I'll bet it's cold! Does it even have indoor plumbing? Maybe I should just wait for him here."

"Well, definitely no shops, but there's a pool and a hot tub. I think you'll be pleasantly surprised! It's closer to Prince Rupert, too. No arguing, now! Go get dressed, get your things, get ready to leave."

"Can we eat dinner first? I'm hungry."

"Help yourself to all the pudding you want."

"No!" Bridey shrieks.

"It's okay, Baby, you can make more."

"Don't worry," Trisha scowls, "I don't want it anyway. Isn't there real food?"

"Just grab a bowl of pudding to tide you over. In an hour, we'll be at the Lodge, and the food's good there."

"I'll wait."

"Okay. Can you be ready to go soon?"

"Yeah. I never unpacked."

"Good. Go and get organized, make yourself all pretty for Junior. Why don't you text him and tell him you're on the way? I'll let you know when we're leaving."

Trisha nods, slips off the stool and heads down the hall.

Hank Senior waits until he hears the door to Junior's room close, then turns to Bridey. "Now for Astrid," he exhales loudly, then puts an arm around his wife. "You know this isn't my fault," he says.

"Hot the pot." She frowns and shrugs his arm off her shoulders.

Hank Senior goes to the counter, picks up a mug, and fills it with tea. He pulls a small bottle out of his pocket, opens it, and adds some of its contents to the cup. He stirs three teaspoons of sugar into the tea, then takes it into the living room, Bridey following.

"God, Astrid," he says, as he sets the mug on the end table, "You're a sight for sore eyes! Where've you been? You really had us worried!"

Astrid struggles to sit up, but only manages to get part way. "It was Hank. He…"

"Don't try to talk. Save your strength. You need to have your story straight when you give your statement to the police. They're going to meet us at the hospital. I brought the ambulance, Astrid, I'm going to take you. The mill's still shut down so there's no staff. No first aid personnel. My certification isn't current, but I've taken the St. John's Ambulance First Aid courses a few times over the years. We'll be at the hospital before the first responders from the Danton Creek Firehall could even mobilize."

Bridey helps her sit up, and Hank hands her the mug. "Drink this. It's very sweet, but that's what you need." He strokes her arm. "You look like you've been through hell. You're going to be all right now. Finish your tea, then I'll help you into the ambulance. Bridey, can you put some of the winter sheets, the flannel ones, in the dryer to warm, please?"

Then he says to Astrid, "We should be ready to go in just a few minutes. I'll be back as soon as I've got the ambulance ready."

* * *

Astrid, feeling warmer, is trying to organize her thoughts so she can give the police a coherent account of what happened, when Hank Senior comes back with bolt cutters. He carefully positions the jaws on the padlock at her wrist, snaps it, and the steel cuff comes away. He clucks at the raw skin on her wrist, and says, "I'll bandage this once we get you in the ambulance." He helps her up, and he steadies her on his arm as they go to the door.

"Shoes," she says.

"We'll bring the things you'll need to the hospital tomorrow, if they keep you in. I don't think they will. I think they'll just check you over and send you home. But I want to make sure." Hank Senior tells her. When they get to the bottom of the steps, he picks her up and carries her to the open rear door of the ambulance.

"I can sit…"

"Nope, you're riding back here. I don't want you fainting in your seat half way to the hospital."

She feels weak, even a bit fuzzy-headed. Lying down sounds appealing. She settles on the gurney, while he goes back into the house. When he returns, he has the warmed flannelette sheets, and arranges them around her, paying special attention to her icicle feet.

"Oh-h-h," she says. She wants to thank him, tell him it feels wonderful, but can't form the words.

"You rest. Sleep if you can." As he fastens something across her upper body, her eyes fly open and she stiffens. "This is just like a seatbelt, Astrid. To keep you safe. Don't want you falling off this thing."

She relaxes into the warm, safe feeling and closes her eyes. Everything fades into a pleasant mist. She hears Bridey saying jam, she needs jam, and that it's too dark. The jam is too dark? Hank answers, but although he's right beside her, it's as if they are both far away.

She feels Hank taking her arm; he's applying something soothing to the sores on her wrist, and wrapping it. She looks at him, wanting to tell him about the cut on her foot, and the sore from the nail on the back of her arm that's still bothering her. She wants to say something, anything, but her mouth doesn't work and now her eyes don't focus. She's looking at his face but it's becoming blurred. He's shaking his head, and his mouth is moving. She thinks he's saying *I'm sorry*, but the words are faint, and it doesn't make sense and she can't be sure.

Then he's gone and the ambulance door bangs shut but it doesn't matter because she can't stay awake.

* * *

Hank Senior goes back into the house and tells Bridey, "Get that little nitwit moving, will you? If she asks where Astrid is, just say she's in bed downstairs."

"She's dark, Hank! Dark! She used to be bright, but now she's dark!"

"I know, Baby. Just remember, Junior loves her. I'll bet you'll be grandma before long!" He pulls her into his arms and kisses her. "I want you to get used to the idea they're going to have to stay at the Lodge, though."

"He won't want to stay at the Lodge."

"Well, it's either Colony Farm or the Lodge, and at least for now, it's gonna be the Lodge."

"But the baby ..."

"The baby'll come live with us. That'll be nice, won't it? A little munchkin, or maybe even two, running around here again? Our secret, though. Right? We won't tell anyone, only you and I will know. Remember that. We won't tell *anyone*, not even Trisha. *Especially* not Trisha. Right, Baby? If you tell anyone, we won't be able to keep the baby. Understand?"

Bridey nods, and he kisses her again before releasing her. "Now, go get Trisha."

THE DARK RIVER SECRET

* * *

Hank Senior backs the ambulance to the rear entrance of the Lodge, where Max and Junior wait. When he's at Junior's side, he says, "Take Trisha up to your room. Once she's settled in, I'll see you in the billiard room. Oh, and Astrid's cell phone? Make sure it's charged up. Now that we have her thumb to unlock it, we can get those texts sent."

Trisha comes around the other side of the ambulance and Junior goes to her, pulling her into an embrace. "Hey, baby! Change of plans! We're gonna stay here a couple days."

"Oh. Can we talk about it? Although this place doesn't look as bad as I thought."

"Let's get you settled in, then I'll give you a tour."

"It's getting late. When can we eat? I'm hungry and your dad said the food here's good. Believe it or not, your mother was making pudding for dinner. Enough for about fifty people. As if anyone would want to eat pudding out of a dogfood can!" She giggles. "You did say she's crazy!"

"Well, the food's definitely better here than at Bridey's, and this is a really nice place. It'll be like a honeymoon!"

"Nice idea, but for this to be a honeymoon, we'd have to get married."

"Well, maybe we should," he says. "If you weren't still married, we could get Pastor Green to do it. Maybe we can, anyway." He winks and kisses her before releasing her.

Max comes forward out of the shadows. Even in the dim porch light, the look of interest that crosses Trisha's face is unmistakable, and Hank Junior doesn't miss it. His face creases in a frown.

"Trisha," he says, "this big ox is the caretaker, Igor. If you need anything, you can ask him."

"Pleased to meet *you*," she tells him.

Max gives her hand a quick shake. "Welcome," he says, then steps back.

"I'll show you to our room." Hank Junior takes her arm and propels her to the door, then turns and says, "Get her bags, Igor," before pushing her inside.

"Never mind her fuckin' bags," Hank Senior tells Max once they're out of earshot, "Junior can hump them up later. Jesus H. Christ, I dunno why he thinks he can talk to you like that! Pastor's just as bad."

"It's okay."

"No, it's not! Junior I can understand; he's gettin' too full of himself. He's been acting like he's off his meds. But the Pastor should fuckin' know better. I'll set them both straight. I don't want you to keep takin' it. Okay?"

Max shrugs, but nods and says, "Okay."

"For now, just take the two small suitcases with you when you go to lock them in. I don't want them knowin' Astrid's here until we decide what to do with her. When you come back, you can help me get her upstairs."

Max trots off. While he's gone, Hank Senior climbs into the ambulance beside Astrid and gently slaps her face. She moans and turns her head side to side, but doesn't awaken.

Max is back promptly.

"She's still out," Hank Senior tells him. "Hope I didn't give her too much. She weighs next to nothing. I think we don't need to take the gurney up. We can carry her. Hell, *you* can carry her. By the way, Trisha isn't the only one gettin' peckish. We got food laid in yet?"

"Yeah, Les brought a bunch of stuff, the first half of the order for the week-end. He said he's gonna bring the rest tomorrow. Him 'n' Bruce were both here earlier."

"Oh? Bruce too?" he clicks his tongue. "Dammit! How's Jessica?"

"Split lip, little bit of a black eye, but nuthin' else where it shows."

"That *fuckin'* asshole! We got members coming this week-end, too." Hank shakes his head. "They didn't stick around?"

"No. They rode up together. Les wanted to wait for you, but the Pastor had to get back."

"As usual. If Les wasn't so cheap, he wouldn't car pool with him. I hope the fat bastard didn't eat everything."

"There's lots."

"Doesn't mean he couldn't eat it all! Anyway, let's get Astrid up to my room. Then we'll let Junior out. If Trisha wants to come out too, she can, but I need some private time with Junior to get him sorted out. He won't be happy when he finds out that instead of him leaving, now they're both staying."

"Yeah. He's been talkin' about how you'd have to let him leave when Trisha got to your place. I wish he *would* go. No offence, but I'm gettin' tired of watchin' the sneaky little bastard."

"I get it, don't apologise." He scratches the day's growth of stubble on his jaw. "I shouldn't've let him keep his cell phone. I thought it would be best to let him keep in touch with the little ho by phone until she got tired of his excuses and broke it off. Didn't expect him to invite her up. Even so, she could've been sent packing if she hadn't had the bad luck to see Astrid. Now we're gonna have to come up with a story for her disappearance, too. Goddamn!"

"Maybe she never arrived at your place. Lots of road between Merritt and Dark River. She could've gone off into a ravine anywhere along the way and no one would ever know. But Bridey..."

"Where Bridey's at right now, she'll believe what I tell her. I might be able to convince her Trisha was never at our place, but if someone else starts looking for her? That cowboy even? Now Claire, Astrid and Trisha, all connected to Junior, have disappeared?" Hank Senior shakes his head and blows out a long breath. He looks down at Astrid again, and smooths the hair off her forehead before unclipping the belt. He says, "I never would've believed anyone, especially a girl, totally unprepared, could survive out in the bush so long at this time of year."

Together, they pull Astrid into a sitting position, then Max hoists her over his shoulder and easily carries her to a second storey suite, where he puts her down on the bed.

"She's soakin' wet," Max says.

"Yeah. I guess she came across the river at the back of our place. Dunno how she managed that! Bridey should've had her out of these wet things." With a shake of his head, he clicks his tongue, then says, "Well, let's get her undressed."

They work together to get her vest, shirt, bra, tights and panties off while she's as limp as a rag doll. "What d'you think?" Hank Senior asks.

"Mmm, skinny, but nice. Athletic looking. Carpet matches the drapes. Her hair's pretty when it's clean, I bet."

"Yeah, she cleans up good. Plus, you can have an intelligent conversation with her."

"She'll be popular," Max says. "Need me for anything else?" When the older man shakes his head, he gathers up her wet clothes and leaves.

Hank checks Astrid's temperature. It's 36.3 degrees, just .5 to .7 degrees lower than normal. Not critical. And her breathing is regular. A good sign.

It was a risk giving her the GHB when she was in such bad shape; he wasn't sure how much to give her, and he breathes a sigh of relief that she's asleep rather than unconscious. He'll check her again in a half our or so. If he can rouse her then, he'll get some more tea, without GHB, into her. If she doesn't wake, he'll dress that angry-looking wound on her arm anyway; but for now, he's satisfied it's all right to leave her sleeping.

He shakes his head slowly as he studies her pale, gaunt face. He perches on the bed beside her and pulls a twig out of her tangled hair, then smooths it back off her forehead again. Not for the first time, he imagines her long legs wrapped around him. She really is something, a Nordic warrior goddess. In other times, she might have been a Viking shield maiden. She must be a tiger in the sack. He realizes the truth of what Max said, that she would be popular with their members. But he's not going to let that happen. He will keep her for himself. No way will he let that sadistic bastard Bruce anywhere near her. He's going to be a problem once they have ceremonial wives, too; they won't put up with being knocked around just because he can't get it up any other way. The time has come to think of a permanent solution.

He slides his hand under the covers and cups Astrid's breast. It's small, but then, she's lost a lot of weight this past week. It's likely going to be just perfect once she's fattened up. His penis stirs at the thought. He tweaks her nipple, takes his hand away before the urge to fuck her while she's in this drugged sleep becomes undeniable, and resettles the blankets. He wants her wide awake, a willing partner.

If she comes around as he hopes, he'll get a permanent live-in care aide for Bridey and move into the Lodge. He can easily go back every couple of days, even on short notice, if something comes up at the mill that he can't deal with over the phone. Bridey won't care. He'll tell her he's making a baby for her and as in the past, she'll be just fine with it.

His wife. So obsessed with babies. How unfair someone with such a powerful maternal instinct should be barren! And then to be refused for adoption! Those episodes aren't her fault, after all, any more than the MS is. The doctors have explained that the two can be related. Stress can set it off. This time of year is always bad. Her flowers dying. Anniversary of Heather's drowning. And now she loses Astrid. Astrid was so good with her. Goddamn Junior! But he knows the signs of an episode coming on: cooking pudding morning, noon and night; forgetting to get dressed; the confusion and crazy light and dark talk. They managed. Got their own babies, and managed. It's too late for them to be parents now, and he doesn't want the nuisance, but he hopes the fiction another baby may be on its way will be enough to keep Bridey content.

At first, being married to Bridey was exciting; magical; she was thrilled about every little thing and her exhilaration was contagious.

Mostly.

What he's come to know as her dark terrors, times when she is a completely different person, were fleeting; now they're more frequent and last longer. It feels like a life sentence with no chance of parole.

Then came the incident with the first girl, the first one they picked up hitchhiking. He remembers being so crazy in love with Bridey he hadn't even wanted to go to Les's bachelor party. Why didn't he stop them from raping that girl? Why didn't he stop Bruce from beating her? Why did he help them dispose of her body?

Because it was exciting.

There's that dark thing inside him that can't deny it.

The "date rapes" kept him sane during Bridey's terrors. It was easier to get away with it then. And for years now, the Lodge has kept him sane. Soon they'll have willing girls. Legal. And he'll have Astrid. He wouldn't change a thing.

Except Bruce. Bruce has to go. A problem for another day.

He studies Astrid's face, relaxed and innocent in sleep. He's always been nice to the girls and now he's going to keep this one. He's not being selfish; he's earned it. As the idea takes hold, he wonders about putting Bridey in Nechako Manor permanently. He visualises Astrid living at the Double H with him. Not right now, of course.

For now, it means another full-time resident here. Three more, with Junior and Trisha. Not without logistical problems. But they'll have to step things up when the cult starts to rock 'n' roll anyway. The weekly cleaners, ladies from nearby Tsilhqot'in Reserve, aren't allowed past the cardlock door to the second floor. One of the women from the Reserve comes every day to do what cooking and meal prep is needed, and Jessica cleans her own suite, but with more guests, they'll need more staff. Not just cleaners, but kitchen and laundry staff, grounds keepers, security. Fletch has skills; he works 'security' for mining companies. He'll put him and Max in charge of security.

Too bad the cult thing isn't starting up yet. It's going to be a while before they can shift any of those girls to the Lodge, except that runaway Les has living in his rental. Maybe she could be moved up here right away. And maybe Jessica will pitch in, in exchange for privileges. Timid little mouse! Still acts like she's being raped, every time. Only the Red Pill guys like her, and they probably won't renew their memberships once the Lodge goes in its new direction. Might be time for a complete re-structuring.

Might be time for Les to go, too. Les. Always jacking the food prices up, even though he pays his prep staff minimum wage and shorts them on hours to boot. On top of that, most of it's written off on Dot's spoilage account, so it costs him next to nothing! *Does he think I'll put up with it forever? Maybe he thinks I don't know what he's doing.* But that's another problem for another day.

When he got the news that Astrid had come home, then discovered Trisha was there, too, it seemed his plans were circling the drain. But Astrid hasn't been in contact with anyone but Bridey and Trisha, both taken care of. Things have worked out better than he could have hoped.

He takes one last long look at Astrid, then stands and, whistling softly, leaves.

THIRTY

"Thanks for picking me up," Denver says. "I could've rented a car."

"Naw, I needed a break from the doom 'n' gloom at the hospital, anyhow."

"How is Dad?"

"No recent updates, but not good. It's lucky you were on yer way home."

Airline connections to Kamloops or Merritt being what they are, that is, next to impossible, Denver planned to rent a car and drive, but he was met at Vancouver International Airport by his brother. The traffic from YVR is horrendous; the route is complicated and with Google Maps yammering nearly constantly, their conversation has been as stop-and-go as the traffic. It's just as well. It's a difficult conversation.

"Like I told you on the phone, he's had a stroke. One big one, 'n' they think he's been having more, little ones. He's in the stroke ward at the Royal Inland Hospital in Kamloops. They gave him what they call clot-bustin' drugs, powerful stuff. We had to agree to that, we made that decision without you, even though there's a risk it might cause bleeding in his brain, but he had to have it right away."

"I'd've done the same," Denver assures him. "We should just make a quick stop at home, then go to the hospital."

"Obviously yer going to see him, but it's doubtful he'll know yer there."

"I've kinda gotten used to it."

"Well, now it's worse. He hasn't spoken or even opened his eyes. They brought him in late last night, and they managed to rouse him enough to get him to cough, and he still squeezed Abby's hand when she asked him to, but when I left this mornin', he was what they call non-responsive." Dallas shakes his head. "Abby's takin' it hard."

"Well, she is his little girl, you know."

"I know. She says regrets not introducing him to Shelly, and now it's too late."

"It's tough. I took Astrid to visit him at the care home, remember, but he didn't realize who she was. Thought she was Mom. So, who knows what he'd make of Abby's wife."

"Yeah. I'm not even sure what I make of her wife." Dallas clucks.

"Better get used to it."

"I know."

"She's happy, that's what counts."

"I *know*. It's just, think of all the guys around town would love to hook up with either of them two gorgeous ladies, and they only got eyes for each other."

They ride along without speaking for a few minutes, then Dallas clears his throat and says, "We have a tough call to make, brother." He clears his throat again. "He can't swallow, isn't even able to swallow. The doc wants to know if we want him fed by a stomach tube, or if we just want him to have pain management."

"In other words, let him starve to death?"

Dallas is frowning, braking as the semi ahead of them suddenly slows. "Yeah. I guess that's what it is. It takes a long time, but I guess that's what it is."

"Does the doc think there's any chance he'll recover?"

"Anything's possible, he says, but if he does come to, it'll mean lengthy rehab. He says it'll be a marathon, not a sprint, and he'll have to stay there fer months, maybe a year. And even then, it's not likely he'll walk again. The best possible outcome would be fer him to learn how to live in a wheelchair. More likely he won't be that good. Might not be able to even feed himself."

"That's the shits. The total fuckin' shits." Denver gulps. "He would hate that. *I* would hate that, for him or for anyone. And with the Alzheimer's..."

"Yeah, the doc says that's a huge complication. And he hasn't said so in so many words, but it's doubtful he'll be alive long enough to starve."

"Have you talked to Abilene about it?" Denver asks. "What does she think? What do you want to do?"

"Abby and I agree, pain management only. Unless you got other ideas."

"I think I agree. But I want to see him, talk to the doc myself, first."

"Of course. Abby's there now. Maybe we should go straight to Kamloops without stopping at home."

"I guess that'd be best. I'll call Abby, give her our E.T.A., see if she can find out when the doc will be there."

* * *

Denver and his two siblings stand around the bed, trying to come to grips with the fact it's their father propped up there, connected to sensors, an I.V. in his arm, the plastic bag over his nose and mouth pulsating with each laboured breath.

"He had the nose thing for the oxygen when I left," Dallas says. "What's this bag?"

"They said he's getting most of his air through his mouth, because he's mouth breathing. So the oxygen in the nose wasn't helping," Abilene says. No contacts today; her violet-blue eyes are huge behind thick lenses. She pushes her glasses up. "It's dehumanizing, getting old. He was always so big and strong..." Her throat works as she quells her sobs.

"Has he opened his eyes? Or moved?" Denver asks, blinking back tears.

"No. Well, maybe his thumb twitched. I'm not sure."

"I feel terrible, knowing he's going hungry when we could have him tube fed."

"He's comfortable, sweetie," his sister tells him, "this is what he would want."

"But what if it drags on?"

"If there is any improvement, we can have the stomach tube done then."

"I wish I could talk to him!"

"You can," she says quietly, rubbing his shoulder. "We don't know if he hears us and knows we're here, or not, but he might." She sighs and finger-combs her short coppery hair. "If you want, Dal and I'll go for a coffee, give you some private time with him. Okay?"

Denver's lip is quivering. He nods. "Thanks," he says gruffly.

Abby squeezes his arm, then she and Dallas leave the room, closing the door behind them. Denver pulls a chair up beside the bed and takes his father's hand. The big hand, strong no more, feels like a warm bundle of sticks. He gives it a gentle squeeze. There's no answering squeeze. It's that, more than the sight of the once-handsome face gone slack, mouth hanging open, that hits him. He can't hold back the tears, and sobs. Then he collects himself, sits down and begins the last conversation he will ever have with his father.

"Dad, it's Denver. I want you to know I've met a wonderful girl! I know you'll like her. When I leave here, I'm going up to Dark River where she lives and I'm going to bring her back to the Triple R with me. She makes me happy, Dad, happier than I ever thought possible. Now I know how you felt when Mom came into your life.

"And Abilene. If she didn't tell you herself, she's in a good place, too. She has a job she likes, in Merritt. She doesn't live on the ranch, but I think she'll move back someday. She's in a loving relationship, and is happy.

"As for Dallas, well, he takes after you I guess; he's still playing the field, but when a girl like Mom comes along, I'm sure his bachelor days'll be over, too. We butt heads a lot—that's nothing new!— but mostly we get along.

"You know we've had a tough couple of years on the ranch, financially that is, but we haven't had to lay anyone off, and I think we've turned the corner now. We've been selling horses, gettin' good prices for 'em, too. That stallion you bred that you said was going to make a name for the Triple R, Rocky Duster? You know he won a lot of money while he was competing, and now his sons 'n' daughters are winning. Dal's a real good trainer, better than I could ever hope to be. He's got a couple of real promising Rocky Duster colts he's going to campaign next year.

"But the main thing I have to tell you is, I've always been proud to say you're my father. You gave me, *us*, the best life possible. We won the birth lottery, having parents like you and Mom, and growing up on that ranch! I know you had rough times, too; ranching's like that, but you always pulled through. Us kids always knew you loved each other and you loved us. Everything on the ranch has your stamp on it. I can't turn a corner without picturing you or Mom there. You have my promise we won't sell the ranch, it's one thing all three of us agree on." A brief twinge of guilt washes over him, knowing it's a promise he might not be able to keep, but if his father *is* in there listening, it's kinder than the truth. He takes a deep breath and continues: "I love you, Dad. I try to be the kind of man you are, the kind of son you can be proud of. I have to go now. Until I see you again, I want you to know that you are with me. You'll always be with me."

He gives his father's hand one last squeeze, and when he gets to his feet, he bends over him and kisses his forehead. Then he stands at the door, quietly taking deep breaths until he is composed enough to meet with his siblings and explain why he has to leave.

THIRTY-ONE

Astrid's awake, staring at her surroundings in the dim light, trying to make sense of it. She remembers being at home, and Bridey acting strangely. Pudding. Hank Senior. Trisha? Was it a dream?

No. There was the ambulance. This should be a hospital room, but it's not. The clock radio on the night table reads 6:40, and hospitals don't have clock radios.

But if she's not in a hospital, why isn't she in her own room at Hazen's? It looks like a hotel room. A high-end hotel room: large; nicely furnished; there's even a fireplace, but there's no phone or coffeemaker on the desk. So, not a hotel room.

I'm naked, she thinks. *How did I get naked? Where are my clothes? Where am I?* She gets out of bed and goes to the entrance door. It's locked. The knob doesn't turn and there's with no thumb turn, only a key card slot.

There's a closet, empty.

The third door leads to the bathroom, so she goes in and uses the toilet. A fuzzy robe hangs on the back of the door. As she slips into it, the sleeve rubs on something; she touches the sore on the back of her arm and turns to see it in the mirror. There's a band-aid on it. *When did that happen?*

She goes to the window next to the bed and opens the drapes. The view isn't the parking lot she was expecting, but rather, forest. It's snowing; the trees wear mantles of white and on the ground, tracks across the open space to the adjacent building look to be at least ankle deep.

At least the window isn't locked. When she slides it open, cold, fresh air scented with evergreen forest rushes in. She lifts out the screen and props it up against the wall, then leans out.

From what she can see, the building she's in is large. Judging by the windows, there are several other rooms like this one to her left, and half a dozen more on the second floor of another wing to her right. Below her window, there's a tar and graveled flat area, the roof of a single-storey part of the building, with air conditioning units and exhaust vents. So, she's on the second floor of a motel or lodge, out in the middle of nowhere.

Suddenly, she realizes where she is. It's *the* Lodge, the men's club Hazens talk about, where Mr. Hazen spends so much time. But if it's a men's club, why is she here? And why is she locked in? No hospital. No interview with police. And she's a prisoner again!

Rage boils up inside her. Bridey and Hank Senior are responsible for this! Damn them! She picks up the screen and shoves it out the window. It lands with a dull thunk in the snow on the roof below. The act of vandalism satisfies some of her frustration. She pulls a chair out from under the table and is about to toss it out the window after the screen, when the keylock rattles. She turns to see a man entering. He's carrying a tray with juice boxes, a coffee carafe, a mug, and a plate with a plastic cover. She looks him in the eye and pushes the chair out before backing away.

"Good morning," he says. The door closes behind him with a clunk, and he brings the tray to the table. "Your breakfast," he says, putting the tray on the table before closing the window and going to stand by the door.

"Who are you? Where are my clothes? Why am I here? Why am I locked in?"

"My name's Max. The clothes you had on when you came are being washed and will be returned to you. For your other questions, Mr. Hazen will come by in an hour or so. You'll have to ask him."

She is struck by how handsome this guy is; good looking, his dark hair cut military-style—and what a pleasant, kind expression he has. *Don't let that fool you,* she thinks, noting the scar that runs through one eyebrow, across the bridge of his nose, and ends on his cheek. Jailhouse tats on both arms. *He's got some hard miles on him.*

The breakfast tray! *The cutlery, can I get it?* But clearly, if she grabbed the knife or fork, Max would grab her, and overpowering him isn't an option.

No use trying to outrun him, either. Supposing she beat him to the door, what's on the other side? She'd never get out of the building.

"Come and eat. When you're done, you should shower and wash your hair." Then he points to the fireplace and asks, "Would you like me to light that for you?"

"I'm not staying," she says. She'd like to demand the return of her clothes and to be released, but can't quite force herself to refuse the food. Instead, she says, "You can go now."

"I'll stay until you're finished," he says mildly.

She looks at him and frowns, wondering what it is about him that's familiar. The way he moves, or something about his eyes? Then the smell of the food hits her; after days of starvation, her salivary glands react powerfully, gushing so forcefully it's almost painful and producing such an abundance of saliva she has to swallow several times.

She sits at the table and lifts the cover from the plate. There are two poached eggs, bacon, sausage, fried potatoes and an orange slice. On a separate plate, there's a stack of whole grain toast. Little packets of jam and peanut butter are scattered on the tray.

"What more could I want?" she mutters, and starts by piercing the eggs so the soft yokes ooze out, and dipping the toast. Then she forgets about everything but the food.

After Max leaves with the tray and dishes, Astrid takes inventory. The clock radio and the lamps on the night tables are bolted down. Pictures have no glass in the frames, and are attached to the walls. Window and shower glass is tempered. The bathroom mirror has a tiny logo in the corner identifying it as a Lite Glassless Mirror. No chance of making a weapon out of any of these, then.

Nightstand drawers contain a selection of sex toys including several sizes and colours of dildoes, vibrators in interesting shapes, gels promising to stimulate female orgasm, enhance female orgasm, delay male orgasm, produce a tingling effect, and taste like chocolate or strawberries. There are condoms that are the world's thinnest, or have pleasure-enhancing ribs, or promise to feel completely natural.

In the bathroom, she finds shampoo, cream rinse, several brands of shower gel. In addition to a man's electric razor and aftershave, there are tampons, toothbrushes still in their packages, toothpaste and mouthwash, hand lotion, body lotion, even foot cream. "Well, haven't we thought of everything," she mutters, "and not a glass container to be found."

In the open shelves at the bottom of the night tables, there are *Playgirl, Cosmopolitan, Hustler, Maxim* and *Playboy* magazines, as well as others she's never heard of, depicting bondage. One has a cover picture of a man with his back to the camera and a young woman facing him, chained to the wall, horror and fear on her face. It looks like a photo, an actual photo, and the woman is either a gifted actress or she's really being raped. With a sudden jolt, she almost feels Hank Junior on her, forcing her legs apart, pounding away at her, his stinking breath a suffocating miasma. She wails and sinks to the bed. It takes minutes of deep breathing before she can push the memory away and collect herself. She takes the magazines to the window and dumps them out.

Reliving the rape makes her feel violated again. Crossing the river may have cleansed her of his essence, but she still feels revulsion; dirty; like some part of him is still on her and in her. She starts the water in the shower, and when it's warm, drops the robe and steps in.

She stands under the water a long time, washing her hair, sudsing herself over and over, turning up the water temperature until it makes her skin redden, using the shower wand on her crotch. At last she feels clean, gets out of the shower and towels dry before slipping back into the robe and wrapping the towel around her head. When she comes out of the bathroom, she finds Hank Senior in weekend warrior hunting garb and with a day's growth of prickly gray beard sitting in the armchair.

"Hello, Astrid," he says with a smile, "you slept about fourteen straight hours. Feel better?"

"Why am I here? Why am I locked in?"

He gets to his feet and comes toward her. She backs away, but he follows and when she bumps up against the wall, he cups her shoulders, and massaging them gently, says, "Don't be scared. You're safe."

"If that was true, I wouldn't be locked in." She squirms out of his grasp and goes to the window, putting the table between herself and him. "I guess you know what your filthy, asshole, sick, degenerate, *criminal* son did to me! What he's done to all those girls!"

"I'm not sure what you mean by 'all those girls', but when you went missing, he admitted what he did to you. We spent days out in the bush trying to find you. I was so relieved, you can't believe how relieved I was when you made it back home! I brought you here to heal, and rest, after your ordeal."

"That's a crock, a total crock! Did you report me missing? No! Or there would've been more than just you looking for me and I wouldn't be here! I want my clothes, and I want a ride back to my car, and I want to leave *now!*"

"Your car's here, Astrid."

"Great. Thanks for breakfast. Now if you'll give me back my clothes, I'll be on my way."

"I was hoping you'd enjoy our hospitality a little while longer." He moves toward her again, but instead of coming around the table, he pulls out a chair and says, "Have a seat. It's lucky we aren't expecting another couple to join us for dinner, since we seem to be short a chair."

"Actually, forget about the clothes. I'll just borrow this robe. So I'll be going."

"I imagine you're thinking about going to the police."

"You don't really think there's any other option?"

"Well, what Junior did was wrong. Believe me, I'm pissed about it."

"You're pissed? *You're* pissed?"

There's a tap at the door, and Max is back with a plastic thermal carafe, two mugs, and small, plastic-wrapped packets of cookies. He sets the tray on the table. "Anything else?" he asks.

"No, we're good, thanks."

Max nods and leaves the room. Hank sits at the table and again beckons to the chair across from him. "Let's have coffee, and talk."

"I don't need coffee. I need my clothes and my car keys, and for you to let me out of this room."

"Well, I can't do that just now," he says as he pours himself a mug. "Are you sure you don't want some?"

Astrid snorts and leans back against the window ledge, glaring at the man she had liked so much, was it just yesterday?

"All right, then," his grin evaporates as his expression turns dark and his tone, menacing. "Here's what you need to know. You don't need to worry about Junior. I've taken care of him. Now my only problem is you. You might promise not to tell anyone if I let you go, but we both know that would be a lie. So, you will be here for the rest of your life. Which can be long and pleasant, or short and unpleasant, it's up to you. Understand?"

The intensity, the darkness in his eyes brings home the truth of what he's saying. He denies knowing Hank Junior is a serial killer, so he's given him a pass. At the very least, he's complicit. The realization hits her with a jolt: it's not just his son he's protecting! She won't be able to talk her way out of this, and she's dealing with people for whom nothing is over the line.

"I liked you," Astrid whispers. "I thought you liked me."

"I do like you, doll, of course I like you. We had some nice times, didn't we? And you can have a good life here," he assures her. "There's a pool with a big hot tub, a workout room, the food's great, and you don't have to lift a finger. You like the horses. There's a barn here, hasn't been used in years, but we can get it cleaned up, bring some of the horses from the ranch. We got near a hundred acres inside the fence, you can ride all over it. Or I'll build you a riding ring. You'd like that, wouldn't you?"

"I don't deserve this! It's not fair!"

"You thought life was fair?"

She crosses to the bed and slumps down, hunching over to look at her feet, squiggling her toes into the carpet.

"I know it'll take some getting used to," he says, more gently now, "but it's not all bad. We have parties, in fact there's one tomorrow night. You'll meet wealthy, powerful men. You'll be surprised when you discover who our members are. There are other girls coming, too, and sometimes some of them, like you, live here. When they leave, it's often with a rich man they met here."

"So, I'm to be a sex toy?"

"No. I have other plans for you."

"Such as?"

"You're mine, Astrid."

Her head snaps up and she meets his gaze.

"You're mine exclusively," he says. "Think of yourself as a second wife. You'll have status, and privileges. Do you want to travel? How would you like to fly to New York to shop? Paris, maybe? How about winters in Belize or Costa Rica?"

"And if I don't agree?"

"You don't have to decide right now. You liked me before; you will again. But you should know that the alternative is to be one of the girls here to *entertain* our members. And some of them have, let's say, *fetishes* you'll find less than enjoyable.

"I'll leave you the coffee. There should be Styrofoam cups in the cabinet under the desk. Eat the cookies. You need the calories. Max will bring your lunch in a while." He stands, picks up the tray with the mugs on it and goes to the door, where he turns and says, "I sent someone to get your things. But Astrid, I'd like to see you in something other than jeans and sweats, 'specially for the parties. I'll send up some flyers, Neiman Marcus, Victoria Secret, I think we have a couple others too. You go through and mark whatever you like. We'll get it ordered right away." He touches the scanner with his card, opens the door, then turns again and says, "I'm coming back to have dinner with you. And I'll be sleeping here." The door closes behind him, the lock engaging with an ominous whirr.

Sleeping here?

She slumps back against the pillows. Is there no way out? Is her only option to play along with him until he trusts her enough to take her somewhere? How long, how many years will that take? Where will Denver be by then? Will she ever see him again? Surely he'll have gone on with his life! In the meantime, she has to have sex with Hank Senior? She liked him, but she never thought of him that way!

She gets to her feet and crosses to the window, opening it and looking down. The window is her only avenue of escape. In the movies, they tie sheets together, anchor them to something, then climb down. It wouldn't be that hard! Luckily, although this is a second-storey room, there's the flat roof building below. It wouldn't be too difficult to get down onto that roof, and then just another drop. Neither is a big drop, more than two meters but less than three.

And from there, go where? And in a bathrobe? What if they don't give her back her clothes until tomorrow? He wants sex tonight. He's old, but he could still easily overpower her. Would he really rape her?

Of course, he would. He's willing to pass her around to other men to let them rape her. And apparently, he's not averse to killing her, either.

I don't have a choice. But I can negotiate. Forgive me, Denver, she thinks, and starts brushing her hair.

THIRTY-TWO

The cowbell over the door jangles as Denver walks into Dot's. It's after dinner and not yet supper time, so the diner isn't busy. Franny sees him and smiles. "Take that booth back in the corner," she calls, "I'll be with you in a sec!" Then she turns and says to someone on the other side of the pass-through, "Okay, I'm on my break!"

She pours two mugs of coffee and brings them, together with a plate of creamers, when she slides into the booth across from him. "You made good time! I didn't expect you for another couple of hours."

"I was up early. Drove straight through."

"Oh, no stops?"

He shakes his head.

"You want something besides coffee? You can still get breakfast, if you want. Bacon 'n' eggs?"

"You know, that sounds good, but I think I'd rather have a burger."

Franny jumps to her feet.

"Naww, Franny, you don't have to get it right now."

"Let me at least put the order in, so it can be in the works while we talk. Might take a while. They're making up a big catering order, so although it's quiet out here, the kitchen's busy. Cheese? Bacon? Fries?"

"All of the above plus tomato and lettuce, please."

Franny goes to the order window and talks to someone on the other side, then returns and slides back into the booth. "Denver," she says, "I'm sorry 'bout, you know, you and Astrid."

"Thanks." He takes a sip of coffee, then grins sheepishly. "You probably wonder what I'm doing here, if I've come to make trouble for her."

"Well—"

"I don't want to make trouble, Franny, but it's not like we were, like, casually dating and stopped calling each other. We had plans. I want to hear it from her, not Bridey Hazen, that we're through."

"She didn't tell you herself?"

"No. And nobody seems to know who the guy is, other than some trucker she met here. Do you know who it is?"

"No." Franny's brow furrows. "If it helps, I'm as puzzled as you. She never said nothing to me, either, just didn't show up for her shift on Friday, and Al said she called the boss and told him she quit. Me 'n' Al, we're both miffed. Thought she'd at least say good-bye. Besides, she was never cozy with any of the guys who come in here. You're the only guy she ever talked about. She was totally hung up on you. And she was looking forward to spending Christmas at your place."

"See, that's what I mean, we had plans. So, this guy, has he been here since? I mean, if he's here often enough for her to get to know him well enough to move in with, he must've been back."

"That's another weird thing. The 'frequent flyers', guys that pass through here every few days, have all been asking for her. I guess there's some who are only up this way every few weeks that haven't been in yet, but honestly," her voice drops to a near-whisper even though there's no trucker near enough to overhear, "mostly, they're a good bunch, but the only one we thought was easy to look at is married. And he only came in once in a while, not enough that we got to know him, really." She takes a deep breath before continuing. "I have to tell you, though, Mr. Hazen said there was a trucker who stayed at their place overnight."

"Oh." Denver focuses his attention on his coffee, breathes deep, and tries to slow his runaway thoughts.

"Sorry. All I can tell you is the same thing I told that cop. She left suddenly, and I was told she left with a trucker she met here. I guess if it was anyone, it would be him. I don't know his name and haven't seen him for a couple weeks. She never said anything to me about it, but I suppose if he's married…"

"Cop?"

"Yeah, a cop came around, said he was investigating a missing persons report. I assumed it must've been you who reported her missing."

"No, not me. Hazens, maybe?"

"But if Mrs. Hazen told you she moved away—"

"She wouldn't have reported her missing," Denver completes Franny's thought. "So. Who did?"

"Yeah, who did? None of us thought she was missing, we all thought she just moved away. So, unless she's got friends I don't know about—"

"I better go see that cop. Can I get that burger to go?"

"Yeah, and I have that cop's card in my purse. I'll get it."

* * *

Les Cline comes through the door just as Franny is handing Denver the box with his burger and fries in it.

"Thanks, Franny," Denver says.

"Oh! Here's that cop's card!" She pulls the card out of her apron pocket and hands it to him. "Let me know what he says?"

"I'll keep you posted." He gives Franny a grim smile, nods to Les, and goes out the door.

Les watches him cross the parking lot and get into his truck, then turns to Franny. "Who's the cowboy?" he asks.

"That's Astrid's boyfriend. Was her boyfriend."

"I didn't think he lived around here," Les scowls.

"He doesn't."

"What's he doing here?"

"He wants to talk to Astrid. She never broke up with him. No one seems to know this guy she supposedly left with. I don't get it myself!"

"You told him about the cop?"

"Of course. He said he wanted to speak to Astrid's ex-boyfriend, remember?" Puzzled at Les's scowl, she retreats behind the counter. "You here for your catering order?"

"I came in for lunch, but scratch that. I'll take the order now."

"We didn't think it had to be ready for another hour."

"Better get a move on, then," he barks, pulling out his phone as he storms around the end of the lunch counter. He hunches over his phone and speaks in low tones into it before pushing through the swinging doors into the kitchen. A heated exchange with the kitchen staff draws curious glances from the few customers.

Al, red-faced, appears in the pass-through window and he says, "Can you help in the kitchen, Franny? We gotta put a rush on this catering order."

* * *

Denver's the only one waiting at the Dark River RCMP detachment. He's had time to pace the slate floor of the lobby half a dozen times, sit to flip through the Prince George Citizen and a Gazette magazine from the stand on the end table, and check his email, before the civilian receptionist behind the window says, "Sir? Constable Villeneuve's here now. I'll buzz you in."

Denver stands, the door lock buzzes, and he pushes through into the squad room. There's one female and one male officer working at their desks. The trim, baby-faced male officer is standing, beckoning. Denver makes his way through the desks to meet him, and introduces himself.

"Have a seat," Constable Villeneuve says. "How can I help you?"

"I understand you're working on a missing persons case, for Astrid Ingebritson," Denver replies, dropping to the chair in front of the desk.

"I was."

"Was? You're not any more? You're not still looking for her?"

"It's not an active file."

"You found her?"

"No."

"Then why? I mean, why isn't it still an active file?"

"It was an anonymous report. No one ever came forward. We did some checking, turns out she just moved away." He swivels his chair, tapping the edge of the desk with his pen, then leans forward and asks, "What's your interest?"

"She's my girlfriend. Or at least was my girlfriend."

"Oh. You're the ex-boyfriend." Constable Villeneuve puts his pen down and begins tapping at his keyboard, studying the monitor. "Dennis Daniels. I tried to call you, but your phone number, it's out of service. I couldn't find a new one. I checked a few with dat name, but…"

"No, my phone number hasn't changed,"—Denver cuts him off— "and my name's *Denver Danielson*." Denver roots in his hip pocket, pulls his wallet out, and extracts his driver's licence, pushing it across the desk.

"Address current?"

"Yes."

"Phone number?" Denver tells him, and Constable Villeneuve frowns as he amends the information in the computer file. Then he asks, "When you broke up, you had a fight maybe? It maybe got a little physical?"

Denver bristles for a moment, then shrugs. "You're right to ask that question. No, we hadn't even had our first fight. It wasn't like that. I'm worried. That's why I'm here. I wonder if she's been hurt, if something"—he swallows the lump that suddenly materializes in his throat— "if something bad happened to her. I've been away for a while, we spoke by phone often, texted often. Here. See for yourself." Denver opens his phone to Astrid's messages and hands it to him, watching his face as he scrolls through. His eyebrows go up at a couple of points and Denver feels heat flooding his neck, realizing some exchanges are rather personal. But then, what could be a better indication of how good things were between them? After a minute or two, Constable Villeneuve slides the phone back across the desk.

"We had plans," Denver says, "she was going to spend Christmas, more than three weeks, with me. I guess lots of guys that get dumped think it was outta the blue, but this was so outta the blue I didn't even know about it! And this trucker she's supposed to have left with, no one can give me a name or even say where he lives. Her friend at the diner's baffled, and yet that's where she supposedly met him. She didn't say good-bye to anyone at the diner, either. It's like she just dropped off the face of the earth."

Just then, Denver's phone chimes its text alert, followed rapidly by a second text alert. He looks enquiringly at Constable Villeneuve.

"Go ahead." Constable Villeneuve says.

Denver picks up the phone and reads. His shoulders slump and he says, "Huh!" He opens the message and is quiet for a moment before telling Constable Villeneuve, "It's Astrid. She says, 'I've moved. I'm happy. I'm getting on with my life. You should too.' And Franny, her friend from Dot's. Franny just got a text from her, too. She must be on her phone now. Do you mind if I call her?"

Constable Villeneuve shrugs. "Go ahead."

Denver opens Astrid's text and touches the phone icon. After several rings, he hears her voice: "This is Astrid! I can't get to my phone right now but if you leave a message, I'll call you as soon as I can!"

Denver says, "Astrid, it's Denver. What's going on? Please call me. I really need to talk to you. Please!" He puts down his phone and sits quietly staring at his hands for a moment. The he looks up at Constable Villeneuve and says quietly, "I can't believe she didn't take my call."

"Well. Some people, dey just avoid unpleasant, er—"

"Sorry," Denver says, getting to his feet. "I guess I just wasted your time."

"It's okay," Constable Villeneuve says, "have a good day."

As if, Denver thinks; he replies with the customary, "You too," but Constable Villeneuve has already returned his attention to his monitor.

Denver leaves the Detachment, pondering Astrid's cryptic, heartless, impersonal message. He goes to his truck, sweeps a skiff of snow off the windshield with his forearm, then gets inside and starts the engine to let it warm. He folds his arms on the steering wheel and rests his forehead on them. The headache he thought had gone is back with a vengeance, resurrected by the wash of fresh emotion. Can that message really have been from her? But it must have been. Who else would have her phone?

Was she really seeing someone else while they were together? If so, she is really a gifted actress. All the loving, all the affection, all an act? *She really had me fooled,* he thinks. *The lying bitch!*

Well, Gus warned him he might not like what he found. The trip up here was for nothing. Time to go back home, check on his father, and then head south for his next judging gig. He nudges the gearshift into low and drives to the exit, turning left and following the signs to Highway 16 South, heading home.

Dark River is in his rear-view mirror when he realizes it never felt like Astrid was putting on an act. It felt genuine. Real. Honest and wonderful. He experiences a rush of guilt for thinking of her as a bitch. She was never anything but sweet, and wonderful. There's still something niggling at him, something that just doesn't feel right. Dallas criticizes him for being ruled by feelings instead of using his brain. Is that what he's doing?

He pulls over to the curb and shifts into neutral, grits his teeth and looks at her text message again. Getting on with her life? All the times they talked about plans for the future, and out of the blue she's getting on with her life with some other guy? It doesn't make sense. Maybe he's a glutton for punishment, but he didn't come all this way to leave without her telling him, face to face, that they're through. If not Bridey, then one of the Hanks must know the friend she was supposedly staying with, or the name of the trucker.

He puts the truck in gear, pulls an illegal U-turn, merges back into traffic and takes the next turn west, heading for the Double H.

The trip usually takes under an hour, but road conditions are poor, with the sporadic light snow having turned to icy snow pellets now building ridges. A Highway Maintenance truck that's plowing and sanding passes him, going in the opposite direction. As anxious as he is to talk to Hazens, he has to drive slowly, and the trip takes over an hour. Finally, daylight nearly gone, he pulls into the yard in front of the Hazen house. He gets out of the truck, gives Buster a scratch on his ears as he deftly avoids the dog's customary prodding of the gonads, and goes to the door. Bridey answers the bell.

"Hello, Bridey," he says.

"What're you doing here? Astrid's gone. She left with a trucker. Go away."

"Did she say anything, tell you his name at least?" Denver asks.

"No!" her dark eyes blaze, "I already told you, she's gone!"

"Is your husband or Hank Junior here?"

"No!" The tidy little person with the gentle expression and soft manners he remembers is gone, replaced by a scowling shrew, still in her soiled, rumpled bathrobe although it's nearly supper time. She starts to close the door, but Denver puts his arm out and pushes it back with more force than he intended. It bumps back against the wall.

A woman dressed in scrubs appears at the end of the hall. "Can I help you?" she calls out.

"It's no one," Bridey screeches, "he's leaving!"

"Did she leave anything for me," Denver persists, "a note, maybe?"

"No!" Lips pressed into a hard line, Bridey steps behind the door and shoves it hard enough to rattle the glass when it closes. He hears the click of the deadbolt. *She actually slammed the door in my face,* he thinks. But not before he saw that Astrid had, in fact, left something behind. Not a note and not something obvious. Something Bridey hadn't realized was Astrid's. Among the several pairs of cowboy boots on the boot tray just inside the door was a tall black pair with red stitching and piping.

He starts toward his truck, his brain flooded with jumbled thoughts. Would Astrid deliberately leave the boots behind? Maybe because she wouldn't be riding any more? But lots of truckers wear cowboy boots; she said she loved them, and that they were comfortable. It doesn't make sense she'd leave them behind, or if she did, it would only be because she thought she should return them. In that case, she'd have left a message.

He calls Constable Villeneuve. The harried-sounding receptionist who answers the phone says he's left the office. He can leave a message, but Constable Villeneuve might be a while getting back to him because he has four days off after today, and then will be back on nights. No, there's no one else looking after his files on his days off, except in an emergency.

He admits the news Astrid left cowboy boots behind wouldn't mobilize the troops. But he leaves a voice message anyway, and says it's okay to call, day or night.

He leans against his truck, welcoming the assault of the icy snow on his face and wondering about Bridey. She sounded like her old self when he spoke to her by phone a few days ago. What could account for the sudden dramatic change? People have moods, but this is more than a mood swing. It's not normal. The woman in the scrubs—a care aide? Like they had for his father before he had to go into the home?

With Astrid gone, Bridey would still need help, but a care aide? Did she need help for something more than her physical condition? The malice on her face and the venom in her voice! Those intense, unblinking eyes! And she slammed the door with maniacal strength. Mental illness? Has she had a psychotic break? Could she have done something to Astrid? She's so much smaller, it doesn't seem possible she could overpower her, but she knows more than she's admitting.

What can I do? What should I do? I just don't know.

He pushes away from the truck and goes down into the barn to see Rocky Duster. He doesn't turn the lights on, just slides the stall door open wide enough to squeeze in, and stands in the dark, scratching the horse's withers while speaking to him in low tones. The horse's familiar bulk, his smell and the silky hide under his fingers, is a comfort. He's finger-combing the short mane hair on the stallion's withers when he feels as though he's being watched. He turns.

Fletch fills the stall doorway.

THIRTY-THREE

ASTRID'S SEATED IN the armchair, legs crossed, when there's a tap on the door and Hank Senior comes into the room. "Hey, beautiful," he says, "Hello again."

Ever the cowboy wannabe, he's in well-fitted jeans and a wide, tooled belt, its silver buckle set with a turquoise stone. Gone is the flannel shirt and camo vest he wore earlier; now he's in a black and teal plaid western shirt. He's trim, with just a hint of a belly pressing against the snaps on his shirt front. His salt-and-pepper hair is still wet from the shower, combed back just enough to camouflage his small bald spot; he's freshly shaved and a hint of cologne surrounds him. He's got a bottle of wine and two glasses. He twists the top off the bottle and pours, then hands one of the glasses to Astrid, saying, "I know it's early, but it's five o'clock somewhere."

She takes a deep breath, blows it out through pursed lips, and accepts it.

"I got a few more things to take care of later, so I thought we'd have an early dinner. Max'll bring it up in about an hour. For now, a drink." He stands a few feet in front of her, lifts his glass and says, "To us. To the beginning of our life together."

She lifts her glass in response, looks up and meets his gaze for a moment before looking away, afraid he'd read malice in her eyes, and hopes he thinks she's being demure. He puts his glass on the end table and sits on the sofa next to it, takes her hand and gives it a gentle squeeze. "You are so beautiful," he says.

She resists the instinct to pull her hand away and manages to force a smile.

He releases her hand, then lifts a strand of her hair and tucks it behind her ear before picking up his glass again. "I've been busy since I left you, Lodge business, and a guest came in. I'm sorry I had to leave you alone for so long. I would rather have spent the afternoon with you. But I see you were busy. Got your clothes." He indicates the open boxes with clothes spilling out of them. "Did you think about what we talked about this morning?"

"Yes," she takes another deep breath.

"And?"

"And." She drinks half her glass of wine in a gulp, collecting her thoughts. "And I decided to accept your, umm, *proposal*."

"Well," Hank Senior smiles and some of the tension leaves his bearing. "That *is* good news!" He leans forward as if to pull her into his arms, but she stiffens away from him and takes another gulp of wine.

For the fiftieth time, she thinks, *Denver, please forgive me*, then rushes on. "Well, Denver and I were pretty much finished anyway, and you're an attractive man. When I said I liked you, I meant it." Her voice trails off; she gulps the rest of her wine, then continues: "No matter how I think about it, the main concern I have is, what happens when you get tired of me?"

"That won't happen, Astrid! I'm sixty-four years old. I'll die before I get tired of you."

"At the beginning, everyone thinks that."

"Okay." He sits up straight and cocks his head. "You have a solution?"

She squirms in her chair and leans toward him slightly. "For this to work, I need to make you happy," she says, forcing herself to look him in the eye. "You won't be fooled by me faking, umm, *enthusiasm*. For me to really be, umm, *genuine*, umm, that is, I can't be really genuine if I'm, you know, worried all the time, even though you're an attractive man." She manages to smile despite nearly gagging on her words. *Careful! He's wasn't born yesterday! Did I say he's attractive twice? Don't oversell it!*

"Okay." He frowns at her empty glass, then reaches the wine bottle and tops it up. "You have a solution in mind?"

"Well, first I thought you should marry me but to do that you'd have to get divorced first, it might be nasty, you would lose too much, you couldn't possibly agree so I wondered what's the next best thing?" She realizes she's rushing, and takes a sip of wine to slow her outpouring of words.

"A nice bank account, I imagine? You can forget that! I'm not going to liquidate assets to shunt a bunch of cash to a bank account you don't need anyway!" His eyes narrow.

"No, no! I know that's another thing you couldn't possibly agree to. But how about putting me in your will? That wouldn't be out of line for a second wife, would it? It costs you nothing and protects me if you die before I do. That's all." She drinks, surprised to find her glass nearly empty again, alarmed at the buzz she's already experiencing. This is no time for an alcohol-muddled brain!

He sits quietly for a few moments, the only sound his breath whistling in and out of his nose as he considers the idea. Somewhere outside, there's a loud *crack!* as if a tree branch has broken under the weight of the snow, and a car door slams.

Then he asks, "If I agree?"

"Then we're newlyweds." She forces a smile. She hears his sharp intake of breath as she shrugs her shoulders and leans forward holding her glass out for a refill, knowing he's looking down her shirt. She purposely wore the sloppy, over-sized T-shirt she uses to sleep in, and no bra, so that when she leaned forward, her breasts would be in full view.

He pours her wine, thinks for a moment, then says, "Done."

"Fifty percent?"

"Hell no! But I *will* leave you the ranch." He slides his hand into her shirt and takes her breast in strong but gentle fingers, his breath becoming husky. Low. "How's that?"

"Me and Bridey?"

"Just you."

"But Bridey…"

"Bridey's taken care of."

"Really? She doesn't want the ranch?"

"Shush!" he puts the wine down and slides forward in his seat, now grasping her crotch with his free hand. She grabs his wrist and tries to pull his hand away, but he resists; much stronger, he slides his hand to the waistband of her jeans, opening the fly.

She shrinks away, then pushes against her flight instinct, thinking, *careful, girl, remember the role you're playing! Your life depends on it.* "The eager bridegroom!" she says, forcing a chuckle and a smile onto her face. "The will first. Then I can relax, and we'll be eager together."

He sits back, studying her, then agrees. "Okay. The guy who checked in earlier is my lawyer. We can get it done this afternoon."

What? She focuses her attention on the wine in her glass, hoping her face doesn't betray her dismay. "It can be filed this afternoon?"

"Won't have to file it. Once it's signed at my end, it's legal. I'll just have him email it to your lawyer and it's a done deal."

"Oh! But … But I don't have a lawyer!"

"You can pick one. We'll set it up for you."

"Oh!" She shrinks back into the armchair.

A dark look clouds his face. She's reminded of her tenuous position, and wonders why he agreed to the will. He doesn't have to give her anything; she's his prisoner, he can rape her whenever he wants. He must want to do it. Why?

In a heartbeat, his friendly expression is back, and he says in a mild tone, "Enough about the fuckin' will, doll. Don't ruin the mood. I'll have some more wine. I should at least try and keep up with you! This is a celebration, after all."

"Yes. A celebration," she says quietly. She picks up the bottle and fills his glass.

"Here's to us, *wife*. Dinner won't be brought up for an hour or so. We have time for …" he nods his head toward the bed.

"Oh! Oh, well … You say there's a pool, and a hot tub. Why don't we spend tonight getting to know each other better, you know, in a different way? Dinner, a swim, some time in the hot tub? And then, you go home like it was a real first date, and then tomorrow…" She feels warmth spreading up her neck.

He shakes his head and cuts in, "No, Astrid, I'm *not* sleeping alone tonight."

"But a few hours won't make any difference!"

"Yeah, you're right, a few hours won't make any difference." The black look is back on his face as he drains his glass and stands. "I'll get the codicil to my will started and I'll book the pool room for our private session." And with that, he leaves.

Astrid stares at the closed door, stunned. Then she leans forward, elbows on her knees, and covers her face in her hands. *Oh, Denver! How I wish I'd told you I love you when I was in your arms! I was afraid to give my heart. I didn't realize I already had.*

She thought it would take weeks to get a will done, buying precious time for rescuers to find her. Then she reminds herself no one's looking for her now any more than when she was in the cabin, or in the bush. She won't be rescued. The best she can hope for is a chance to escape, which might not come for months. Whether she has sex with the monster tonight or tomorrow or three weeks from tomorrow makes no difference.

* * *

Hank Senior steps through the doorway to the billiard room and sees his lawyer at a table with Max. He has a nearly empty glass of beer and a heap of wing bones in front of him. "Ken," he says, "Can you come with me? I need a favour." Then he turns and goes through the great room to the back hall and his office. He's in the chair behind the desk when Ken comes in.

"Shut the door, wouldja, and have a seat."

The lawyer sits, and Hank Senior explains what he wants.

Ken starts shaking his head even before Hank Senior's finished. "I can't advise that, Hank!" he says. "That's the only real estate you've got that's free and clear. Bridey and Junior…"

"I'll leave Junior this place, as a joint tenant, with a right of survivorship."

"But the mill—it's on the ranch parcel. And it includes the timber berth and cut licences. How do you plan on separating that off, or do you? And what about Max?"

"He'll be fine. He's smarter than Junior. He can handle himself. He'll have no trouble with Junior." Hank Senior cuts him off. "I suppose at some point I'll should sub-divide off the five acres Fletch's trailer's on and assign it to him, but there might be no need. We'll see. He's off to Yemen in a couple months. That's a dangerous place for paramilitary.

"Come on, old friend, you know I've taken care of everyone. Bridey'll be at Nechako Manor permanently before long. And Junior! He's, well, you know him; he'd sell the ranch and piss the money away within a year, if he didn't wind up in jail first. I've been rethinking leaving it to him for a while now." He grins at the man across from him, swivels his chair around and pours two shot glasses of Glenlivet from the bottle on the credenza behind him. He slides one glass across the desk, holds his up and says, *"Prost!"*

They both shoot their scotch, and Hank asks, "So, how do we get this done?"

"Well, if you're determined to do this, and it looks like you are, I'll get it written up. I don't usually do wills, but I'm sure there's templates in the company system. I can log into it from my laptop. Or better, your computer here," with a lift of his chin, he indicates the monitor on the desk. "So you sign it, I notarize it, maybe there's someone else here who can witness it?"

"Max."

"Can't be anyone who's named in the will."

"Okay then, Bruce or Les. They'll be here soon."

"Okay. Of course, I need her full legal name, date of birth, her lawyer's name."

"Yeah, go meet with her. She doesn't have a lawyer, so you'll have to help her get one. With the offices all closed…"

"I'll phone a colleague. I'm sure I can reach someone tonight. Is it safe to have her talk to him? Is she likely to …"

"Gawdamighty, no! Don't even make the call with her in the room. This is a girl who busted out of the cabin that's been secure for decades and survived more'n a week in the bush. *Do not* underestimate her."

"Okay. I can ask him to watch for my email; he can respond to a read request, give his undertaking to file it as soon as the registry opens on Monday. I'll print it and give it to her. That should satisfy her. But then it's a done deal, you know. It has to be real, otherwise I might be disbarred, and I'm not going to ask a colleague to be part of a deception …"

"I know."

Ken shakes his head again. "I have to say it: this for a girl? Of all the girls there've been? Who is she? What the fuck has she got on you?"

"You're close to crossing a line, Ken."

"As your lawyer, it's my duty to give you my best advice. You don't have to follow it. But speaking as your friend, I hope you will."

"I see. You're thinking there's no fool like an old fool. But so you know where I'm coming from, this'll mean we're a *couple*, for as long as the 'honeymoon' lasts. Who knows how long that'll be? Otherwise she's not going to be, er, a *willing* partner. And y'know, I'm not a Red Pill guy, I'm not into rape, and unlike some of you young studs, I'm not in rut. I want all the niceties." He reaches for the Glenlivit bottle.

"You can get plenty of *niceties* from the ladies coming tomorrow."

"Yeah. Well, I won't pass on that, either, but you ever tried talking to any of them?"

"Talking?"

"Talking. All they care about is what happened on The Bachelor or some top model nonsense or who has what new trinket. Not Astrid. She likes to hear how it was when I came out here from Saskatchewan. How I got started in the logging business. How the logging operations work."

"Ahh! You're in love with her!"

"Pffft! Then I *would* be an old fool! I just don't like sharing my toys, and I'll take the course of least resistance when I can. You should've seen her face when I told her I could get this deal done today! I don't know what she's playing at. Maybe delay tactics? As if anyone's going to come to her rescue! But don't worry," he says as he refills their shot glasses and gives the lawyer a meaningful look, "it's a hollow gesture. There's *no way* I die before she does."

"Okay." Ken picks up his glass and raises it in salute. "Well then, congratulations!"

THIRTY-FOUR

DENVER STRAIGHTENS AND takes a step away from Rocky Duster, and lifts his hands, palms up, waist high. "Fletch! I was just—"

"I know where she is," Fletch cuts him short.

"Oh!" He drops his hands and breathes out. "You do? Where? I need to see her."

"That'll be difficult."

"Why's that?"

"Long story."

Denver blows a breath out through his teeth. "I'm in no mood, Fletch. Just tell me where she is and I'll go…"

"They won't let you see her."

"What? Who's *they*? Not the trucker?"

"Like I said, it's a long story."

"Well, get in the truck and you can tell me all about it on the way." He gives the horse one last scratch, leaves the stall, and goes to his truck, turning to Fletch to call out, "Coming?"

Fletch shrugs, then follows, climbing into the passenger seat.

The trip takes an hour on the highway, then another hour on a secondary road. After a series of turns he's not sure he would have managed without Fletch, Denver slows the truck, pulls up against the ridge of snow at the edge of the narrow roadway, and kills the lights. Fletch insisted they stop here, five hundred meters from the gate and out of sight of the buildings. The two men get out and make their way through ankle-deep snow and scrub brush until they come to the edge of the clearing. Fletch turns on his night vision binoculars and lifts them to his eyes, training them on the compound at the terminus of the road. After a moment, he passes them to Denver.

It's snowing and dark. Pink-orange light from the sodium vapour lamps every hundred meters or so illuminates the driveway and the formidable fence. Chain link and over two meters high, it's topped with razor wire and connects to river rock wings flanking the wrought-iron gate. Tall log columns at each side of the gate support a horizontal log.

Fletch says, "That's it. Spirit Bear Lodge."

At the far end of the driveway is a sprawling two-storey building with a prow-front central area and wings going off at an angle on each side.

"What a place! Looks like a hotel, a resort hotel," he whistles. "This belongs to Hazen?"

"Ay-yuh."

"Didn't expect a place like that out in the middle of the boonies."

"Started off with just the center part. It was a huntin' lodge then. Me 'n' Hank useta come here a lot. Now they call it a gentlemen's club. Maybe they still hunt, I dunno. Haven't been in there since I was workin' with the crew puttin' up that fence."

Denver studies the buildings and grounds, then trains the binoculars on the gate and fence again before passing the binoculars to Fletch. "There's a few vehicles by the big building. Recognize any of them?"

Fletch adjusts the binoculars and looks where Denver's pointing. "Yeah, Hank's Tahoe. Range Rover's out. They musta had a pick-up at the airport. And there's the Pastor's car."

"Pastor?"

"Ay-yuh. Pastor."

Denver shakes his head, studies his feet buried in snow. "What do we do, then? What if I go to that intercom at the gate and tell them I need to see Astrid and I know she's there?"

"You ain't gonna talk her out. You think they got all this to keep the deer outta the garden? You tell 'em yer here, you just tip 'em off 'n' they'll be ready for us when we go in."

"I wasn't expecting an invite, but I sure wasn't prepared to be stopped half a kilometer away." He sees the look Fletch gives him, clicks his tongue and says, "I know, you told me. But it's just ... well, just so unbelievable! I thought I knew these people." He bites his lower lip. "Anyway. I got side cutters, but if we're gonna sneak in, no use trying to cut the fence where they can see us."

"Ay-yuh, it's gonna hafta be a covert op."

Denver takes the binoculars Fletch is handing back to him and trains them on the fence again. "The lights go all the way around this place?"

"Just what you see, 'less they changed that, too. Fence is closer to the buildings at the side, there. It'll be dark out behind."

"So, we go around to the side. Behind the garage building over to the right there," he points to the overheight four-bay garage.

Fletch lifts his crooked right hand to indicate the small domes mounted on the poles under the overhead lights along the fence. "Have to stay in the bush where the cameras won't pick us up. Yer dually ain't gonna do it. 'Specially if it keeps on snowin'."

"Fuck." Denver throws up his hands, stomps around the bush a few steps, then says, "I'll hoof it."

Fletch shakes his head. "You really think you kin sneak in, find her, sneak out and walk back with her? Supposin' you manage that somehow, what if she can't walk?"

A bolus of cold dread explodes in Denver's gut. "Surely that's not possible!"

"The Pastor's here. It's possible."

It takes a few moments for that to sink in. Then Denver asks quietly, "What other option is there?"

"We go back. Git ordnance. And a vehicle that'll git us through the bush."

"There must be another way." He thinks about the RCMP. Would they bring a SWAT team? No, of course not, it's private property and they wouldn't have cause. Could they get a warrant if Fletch told them Astrid was being held there against her will? Fletch's word against that of the fine upstanding businessman Hank Senior? And Constable Villeneuve knows about that text from Astrid.

"There ain't."

"I know," Denver says, shoulders slumping. He blows out a big breath. "I've wasted time, insisting on coming out here like this. You've shown me where she is, and I thank you, but I can take it from here. If you can lend me that vehicle and ordnance you mentioned, I'd sure appreciate it, but I want you to know you don't have to do anything more."

"Ay-yuh," Fletch says, "I do."

*   *   *

Astrid is lying on her back in bed. Light from the propane fireplace flickers across the ceiling. Beside her, Hank Senior stirs in his sleep.

At dinner, he was charming, even funny, and the lasagne, salad and garlic bread were surprisingly good, although after more than a week of starvation shrinkage, her stomach couldn't accommodate more than half of it. Afterwards, he took her to the pool room. She had no swim suit, and couldn't avoid dropping her robe in front of him, but he just sat on a deck chair smoking a cigar and drinking brandy while he watched her swim. If she needed a reminder of how weak she was, her inability to swim more than a couple of laps brought it home. She bobbled aimlessly around until she was too cold to put off climbing out of the pool any longer.

Once she was in the hot tub, he dropped his robe and joined her. She expected him to climb all over her. He fondled her breasts, but that's where it stopped. Back in this room, he stood in front of her, untied her robe and slid it back off her shoulders. Her body involuntarily stiffened. She took a deep breath, clenched her teeth and tried to force her lips to curve up in a smile.

He was surprisingly gentle. Even so, she couldn't stop her body from trembling, and it was all she could do not to gag when he pushed his tongue into her mouth. When she felt his erect penis pushing at her, she was unable to banish the memory of Hank Junior, and she heard herself let out a sob.

Somehow, she got through it.

"I gotta say, Astrid, you talk a good game but looks like that's all it was, talk," he hissed when he finally flopped off her.

"I'm sorry," she said quietly.

"Sorry! Pfft!"

She can't stop her brain from replaying everything as if it's in a continuous loop, and with him sated and snoring beside her, she squeezes her eyes shut, and quietly cries.

*   *   *

"Can you really make the shot," Denver asks, "with no spotter?"

On the ride up in the Jeep, Fletch explained his rifle is a C-14 Timberwolf MRSWS, with night sights, muzzle brake/flash hider and sound suppression, the same as Canadian Armed Forces use.

"Were you in the Canadian Forces?" Denver had asked him.

"Wanted to be."

"But …?"

"Assholes didn't like this," he held up his crooked hand. "NGO's are okay with it, though. Spent some time in Columbia. Afghanistan. You learn stuff with them … Well. More like military police than just military, if you know what I mean."

Denver said he didn't.

Fletch explained, "MP's have to *take out* guys with military training." He snorted dismissively. "Hang on." Approaching the spot on the narrow roadway where they'd parked earlier, Fletch slowed the Jeep. There was no track, but he aimed the Jeep at a spot in the bushes next to the road and they ripped through it. Once into the tall trees where the undergrowth was scantier and the snow not as deep, the Jeep lurched along, parallel to the fence but lower and back far enough their lights couldn't be seen from the Lodge. They took a chance no one would be outside to hear the engine. At this time of night, and in a snowstorm, it was as unlikely as it ever could be.

Now, Fletch pilots the Jeep around an enormous Douglas fir and a rocky outcropping, then brakes a few meters from the cleared space next to the fence. After maneuvering the Jeep so it's facing back the way they came, readying for a quick exit, he turns it off. From what they can see of the Lodge from this angle, lights are on in the front, the main lounge area Fletch described, but the rest of the building is dark. There's a snow-covered car parked behind the garage.

Fletch points to it. "Astrid's," he says.

If Denver had any lingering doubts about Astrid being here, they evaporated. "D'you think we should wait for the lights to go out?" he asks.

"Nope. We should go to Operation Snowfire."

Denver sighs, and agrees.

They trot across the cleared area to the fence, cut a slash in the chain link, push through, and huddle behind the garage as Fletch prepares to climb onto the roof.

The first plan they'd discussed was Denver's. Dubbed Operation Sneakers, it was for the two of them to go in "dark", find Astrid and sneak her out while The Enemy, as Fletch calls them, slept. Fletch didn't like that plan, pointing out the obvious flaws: they don't know where she is, someone might still be awake or they might wake someone while looking for her, and she might not be alone. Denver bristled at that thought.

"Don't worry. I'll take out anyone who gits in the way." Fletch said.

Fletch favoured his plan, Operation Snowfire. He creates a diversion by shooting out as many of the overhead lights along the fence as he can, as well as doing as much damage as possible to the gate and the sign over it. They discussed disabling the transformer at the side of the parking lot, but discarded the idea as it wouldn't draw The Enemy out of the Lodge. Unless they've installed a back-up generator Fletch is unaware of, all the lights would go out. It will be difficult enough finding Astrid without fumbling around in the dark. In addition, the plan requires someone awake to notice the yard lights going out. They're banking on The Enemy thinking it's locals pit lamping deer and deciding it would be fun to shoot out the lights. Fletch is confident they'll get their rifles and hustle out to the berm to see if they can spot the perpetrators.

Denver expressed doubt they'd shoot, possibly at people, not seeing their targets. Fletch just snorted and said, "They call it gittin' off sound shots." He said they'd shoot at anything, real or imaginary, and wouldn't realize the shooter was on the inside. If they figured it out, noticed where the shrapnel flew or where bullets that missed went, and turned around, well, "They'll be sorry," Fletch said.

Fletch's comments were sobering. The working of his jaw left Denver no doubt he could and would do what he said. The realization chilled him right through his borrowed camo down vest and jacket. For a second, he thought about calling it off. Is shooting someone, possibly killing them, to get Astrid out justified? Maybe she doesn't want to come out.

"Trust me," Fletch told him, "She'll want to come out."

They may be bad people, but it isn't war. It would be murder. But if, as Fletch insists, they're armed and have no qualms about killing them—?

Of course, there's still the problem of finding Astrid, but with Operation Snowfire, at least some of The Enemy will be out of the building and the lights will be on, giving Denver a better chance to search.

In answer to Denver's latest question, whether he can make the shots, Fletch says, *"Hell*, yeah." When his rifle's assembled, he slings it across his back and pulls his ski mask over his face. They conduct one last radio check before Fletch steps up onto the bumper of Astrid's car, then onto its hood. He grips the gutter with both hands and vaults onto the roof.

"See you back at the Jeep," Denver says.

"Roger that," Fletch responds, then scurries crab-like up through the four inches of crusty snow to the peak.

Denver slinks along the shadows on the fence side of the garage. When he reaches the corner, he peers around to make sure he has a view of the driveway and what Fletch told him is the door leading into the back hallway. This is the door the Enemy is expected to come out of, and they'll leave it unlocked. Once they're away, that's the door he'll sprint for. He pulls back to wait out of sight of anyone coming out that way.

He concentrates on slowing his breathing, noting the frost from his breath accumulating on his ski mask. It seems to be getting colder, and snowflakes, while smaller now, are windblown. He wonders if it might be wishful thinking Fletch can make shots that seem impossible even in the best of conditions, and if a firefight is a real possibility. The weight of the Glock, borrowed from Fletch's arsenal and tucked into the back waistband of his jeans, is sobering.

When Fletch gave him the gun and its extra magazines, he said: "Double tap to the chest and one to the head." He must have read the dismay on Denver's face, as he asked if he'd ever shot a handgun. Denver told him he had, a Luger his grandfather got when he was overseas in World War II, but only to kill rattlers that came down from the ridge into the yard.

"But I'm guessin', never a person."

"No! Of course not!"

"Well, these bastards're meaner'n them snakes. Don't doubt it fer a second. If you hesitate, it'll be you goes down. You'll be okay with this li'l beauty. Not much recoil. Nine-millimeter Luger hollow point cartridges give you plenty of stopping power at short range." He'd stroked the Glock affectionately before handing it over.

Denver still can't connect the people Fletch talks about to the people he knows, or believe that tonight, he's calling them The Enemy and is neck deep in a plot that may require killing them. He hopes he doesn't find out if he can do it.

It seems an eternity before he hears the "zing" signifying Fletch got a shot away. There was no sound to indicate he hit anything, though. Then there's another zing and a clink. When he looks around the corner and toward the gate, he sees one of the lights is out.

Fletch shoots out three overhead lights before lights in the upstairs rooms go on. He holds off shooting more lights, concentrating his shots on the logs at the gate, until three men with rifles spill out the door and head for the berm as predicted.

In their thick camo clothes, Denver doesn't recognize any of them, and speaks quietly into his mouthpiece: "You know who they are?"

"Yeah. Hazens. And the asshole that owns all the restaurants."

The defenders sprint, zig-zagging back and forth, taking cover behind rocky outcroppings or depressions in the snowy ground—anything that provides cover—until they reach the berm, where they lie on their bellies to peer over the brow. They're aligning themselves against a threat from the gate area outside the fence, as hoped, unaware they're in plain view of the shooter on the garage roof. Fletch's low voice in his ear says, "I have the solution," and Denver imagines him training his sights on them.

"You been watching too many Flashpoint reruns," Denver chuckles humourlessly, then says, "Showtime." He pushes away from the garage wall and trots to the door.

THIRTY-FIVE

ASTRID JERKS AWAKE. Someone's pounding on the door.

"This better be fuckin' important!" Hank Senior grumbles, rolls onto his side, and sits up. He gets to his feet, fumbles for his jeans and pulls them on before going to the door. He opens it partway and has a terse exchange with someone in the hall. Then he closes the door, turns on the lights and hurriedly finishes dressing.

"What is it?" Astrid asks.

"Goddamn kids again! We'll get the fuckers this time," he tells her. On his way out, he flicks off the lights and says, "Nothing to worry about. Go back to sleep."

Astrid sits up, thinking, t*hey're discommoded about something.* Is this her chance to escape? But it's much sooner than expected and she needs more time to regain her strength; a decent swimmer, earlier tonight she'd had to rest between each length of the pool. It's only been a day since she laid down to die, after all. *I need more time*, she thinks, *more time! I'm still too weak! Besides. I'm safe here.*

She lies back down and pulls the covers up over her head.

The she sits bolt upright again. What if this is it? Her best and only chance? What if she doesn't get another chance like this for years?

But she needs more time. She huddles back down under the covers. Hank Senior has other businesses to run. He won't be here that much, so just a night or two once in a while. He didn't hurt her.

But he could! She sits up. When she tried to insist he wear a condom, for a heartbeat she thought he was going to hit her. It seemed to cost him an effort, but he controlled himself. He might not hold back next time.

But surely there will be other chances to escape once she earns his trust and has the run of the place. Maybe when the horses are here she can get through the fence in the treed area out of sight, follow the road out, but in the bush so their vehicles can't follow. Or make a break for it when they're travelling. *I just need more time,* she tells herself. If she tries to escape now, chances for success are slim given her weakened physical condition and the bad weather. She lies back down.

It's safer to stay here, for now. If she was caught trying to escape, there would be consequences and they might be nasty ones. She remembers the purses in the shed; his comment her life might be very short, and that he could hand her over for other men to use in unpleasant ways. And the flashes of malevolence she's seen cross his face! Like the condom issue: his low, menacing voice when he said condoms are to protect him from the clap, not to stop sluts from getting pregnant. Then in a lighter tone, he told her not to worry, he doesn't want her pregnant, either. They have morning after pills and will use those until she can start back on her regular pills again. And he was quite gentle.

Still, wasn't she one of those sluts? And he slips so easily into that other person, that *monster*, it's chilling. What if she can't overcome her revulsion at having him touch her, even, and he decides the second wife thing isn't going to work?

It suddenly strikes her maybe her insistence on the will was a mistake. If she's dead, she can't inherit. Did she sign her own death warrant?

Go with your gut, her mother would say. *You've seen the monster. Don't forget for an instant that it's there.* There may not be another opportunity for a long time. She can't pass it up.

Flinging the covers back, she turns on the table lamp, gets out of bed and goes to the dresser where she'd put away her clothes. She hurriedly dresses in jeans and a sweat shirt, and pulls her hair back into a ponytail.

"Shoes! Shoes!" she says, "they didn't bring me any shoes!" She settles on socks and slippers, then pulls out the rope she made that afternoon by tying clothes together. Tights worked well, but there weren't enough of them. She added in a sweater.

There was no jacket in the things they brought, but even dressed for the cold, she wouldn't survive another week in the bush. Her plan, hatched earlier today when she was preparing the "rope", is not to hike out through the bush, anyway. They moved her car so now it's parked behind the garage, where she can see it from her window. Did they put it there so it couldn't be seen from the road, or to taunt her, as if to say, "Here's your car. Let this be a reminder of your old life, the one you'll never have again"?

If the keys aren't in the ignition, they'll be under the floor mat or behind the visor, the two places Hazens always hide their vehicle keys. But it's never been good about starting in the cold, and in this weather? And the likelihood it would get stuck, having no snow tires?

A better idea would be to take one of their vehicles, Hank Senior's maybe? There's no way of knowing what vehicles are in the garage, or if there are more parked around the corner, out of view. Once she's out, she'll make for the garage and if she sees Hank Senior's Tahoe parked outside, she'll go for it. If not, she'll try the man door on the garage in hopes it's unlocked. If it's locked, as a last resort, her own car. It's a plan that requires luck and surprise to succeed. And she doesn't have a lot of time.

With extra socks stuffed into her pockets to be used as mitts, she ties one end of the rope around her waist, then gets two of the dining chairs and takes them to the window. A blast of cold air assaults her when she opens it, but the snow seems to be stopping and the moon has risen, so there's at least limited visibility. But that also means it'll be easier for them to see her.

And then—is that gunfire? What are they shooting at? She remembers Hank Senior saying something about kids. They wouldn't be shooting at kids, would they? But she can't convince herself they wouldn't. And if they see her, dangling from the window or running across the yard, she'll be an easy target. If they would shoot at kids, they'd shoot at her, too. She closes the window.

I have to go, she thinks, *but I can't go.*

But I have to go. She slides the window open again.

Standing on one chair and positioning the second so it's wedged across the opening, she ties the sweater sleeve to the chair leg, tugging on it to tighten the knot as much as possible. With a deep breath, she lifts one leg over the chair, and turning to face the building, holds the edges of the window and struggles to get her other leg over, wincing when the wound on the bottom of her foot presses against the frame. She adjusts her foot so she can put her weight on it without pain. Perched on the window ledge, she silently curses the slippers for being, well, *slippery*, and mutters, "Don't look down. Not that far, really."

Moving her hands to the chair, she takes one foot off the ledge and puts it against the building. Then the second foot. The chair pulls up tight against the window; her heart pounds when she wonders if the vinyl frame around the glass is strong enough to hold, or if the knots will slip apart when her weight's on the rope.

"Here goes nothing," she mutters. Legs quivering with nerves, she sucks in several deep breaths, takes the rope in her hands, and starts rappelling down.

* * *

Once Denver's inside, light from the hallway straight ahead is enough he can see he's in a large entry room lined with benches under rows of hooks festooned with jackets. No people in sight. Willing his boots to be silent on the hard floor, he crosses the room and cautiously enters the hall.

The first doorway is to the right, and there's enough ambient light from various digital read-outs on appliances and weak moonlight from a window to see it's a kitchen. No human activity.

A few steps further along, light pours from a wide doorway on the left. He holds up at the side of the doorway and slowly peers in. There's a staircase to his right, and a tall rock fireplace to his left. Looking through into the furthest reaches of the large room, he sees two men at wall-to-wall, ceiling-to-floor windows, attentively watching the goings-on out front. The taller one is fit looking; muscles bulge against his dark T-shirt, and a pistol protrudes from the back of his jeans. The other, in a shapeless sweatshirt, is running to paunchiness and is drunkenly unsteady on his feet. Denver marks the big man, and the thought comes unbidden that he's the first one to take out if things turn ugly.

He hears voices overhead. Someone is coming down the stairs. He flattens against the wall before cautiously peering around the corner again. There are two newcomers, both in fluffy white bathrobes, standing with the men at the window.

"What's going on?" one of the late arrivals, the obese man with crutches, asks.

"Someone's shooting up the place," sweatshirt answers.

"Yeah, them assholes."

"No, someone in the woods, shooting out the lights. Shooting at the gate, too."

"Who'd do that?" This time, it's a familiar woman's voice.

Trisha?

"Prob'ly the Indians," the obese man tells her. "They're still pissed we shot their fuckin' sacred Kermode bear. They came here again a few weeks ago, this time with a formal delegation, demanding to have it for their longhouse. Militant bastards! Said keeping it would be an act of war! We told them to fuck the hell off."

"Are we safe here? Can those Indians come in here?"

"Of course we're safe, honey. If they shoot the gate out and come through, our guys out there will take care of 'em."

"Can they shoot this far? The Indians, I mean. Can they, Max?"

"No, they can't." The fat man answers. Despite his crutches, he manages to push in between Trisha and the big man she'd called Max.

Trisha frowns and takes a couple of steps away from the fat man and says, "Oh, good! Well then, since we're all up now, let's party!" She circles the obese man and stands in front of Max before shrugging her robe off with a jiggle of her shoulders. Denver recognizes the short, filmy negligée she wore on Valentine's Day a lifetime ago. The sparkly stilettoes are new, though. She swings her hair and begins moving sensuously. "Ken, how about some drinks and some music? Max, would you like a lap dance now that my wet blanket boyfriend is otherwise occupied?"

"Max is busy," the fat man says, "but you can dance for me, honey! Max, turn on the stereo, and get the other two girls."

"Not Mr. Hazen's girl."

"Not your decision, Max!" the fat man barks. "*Mister* Hazen has no right to make her off limits to the rest of us."

"He's the boss."

"He's only one of the bosses, like I am, and I'm telling you, get the other *two* girls!"

He sees Max stiffen, but after a moment, the tension leaves his shoulders and he says, "You know where the stereo is, Pastor. Why don't you go and play what you want?"

Even at this distance, Denver can see the fat man's face and jowls turning red; he sputters, but Max turns and walks toward the hall, straight for him. He pulls quickly back and presses up against the wall, his hand reaching behind and closing around the butt of the Glock. But Max isn't coming to the hallway; instead, he trots up the stairs, and Denver quietly lets out his breath. As angry as the thought of Astrid being summoned to entertain the fat man makes him, it does solve the problem of how to find her.

He checks to make sure no one's looking toward the doorway before moving stealthily past it. There's a second doorway to the great room a couple of meters further along, just on the other side of the staircase. He peers around the corner and sees Trisha swivelling her hips as she turns her back to the man in the sweatshirt and says, "I've been practicing twerking, Ken. How am I doing?"

Ken, AKA Sweatshirt, watches her twitching buttocks, eyebrows rising. The obese man's crutches clatter to the floor as he thumps up behind Trisha, puts his hands on her hips and pushes his groin against her. She turns to him and says with a frown, "Hey! You know the rules. Don't touch the dancer!"

The Pastor grumbles but stands away, and as all three now have their backs to him, Denver crosses to the other side of the second doorway. When he's far enough into the dark hallway to be out of sight of anyone going to the kitchen, he holds up.

He hopes Fletch can stand the cold a while longer. Inside, Denver's too hot in his heavy winter clothing. He pulls his ski mask off and stuffs it in his pocket, then repositions his headset.

"Three male combatants inside," he whispers into the mouthpiece. *My god,* he thinks, *I called them combatants.*

"Roger that," comes Fletch's voice in his ear.

There's another volley of shots from outside, so Fletch is still shooting, drawing their fire. But how long before they get cold and decide they've had enough fun?

THE DARK RIVER SECRET

* * *

From the roof of the garage, Fletch sees the men on the berm getting to their feet; they huddle; there's pointing and arm waving, then they all turn toward the Lodge. He's sighting his rifle on the nearest one when his attention is drawn by a scuffling sound and an odd little squeak from behind the main building. He turns and sees someone in a heap on the roof of the mechanical room. He doesn't need night vision binoculars to make out a blonde ponytail. Astrid!

Seeing the window above and the clothes dangling from it, he deduces she climbed out and fell part of the way. "Good girl!" he mutters. "She's out," he says into his mouthpiece. "Target out. Enemy incoming. Retreat! Retreat!" He skitters down the roof, turns and slides his legs over the edge and with a kick against the wall, drops to the ground.

He trots to where Astrid is dangling off the roof, arriving in time to see her feet reach the nearest of the thousand-gallon propane tanks, but not in time to catch her; as she shifts her weight onto the snowy top of the rounded tank, her feet slip. "Agghhh!" She loses her grip on the parapet and makes a hard butt landing on the tank before sliding to the ground.

Fletch grabs her from behind and pulls her to her feet, covering her mouth with his hand. She's squirming and thrashing, trying to bite, but he holds strong and says into her ear, "It's okay. It's okay! It's me, Fletch. Denver's here too."

She stops fighting.

"I'm going to let you go. Don't yell, okay?"

She nods. Once released, she flips around to face him. "Fletch? What…?"

"No time! Behind the garage there's a hole in the fence. About a hundred meters into the bush, there's a Jeep. We'll meet you there. If we're not there in ten, drive away." Hands on her shoulders, he turns her in the direction of the garage and gives her a nudge. "Stay outta sight. Go!"

She looks back over her shoulder, hesitating for a heartbeat, then nods and hurries away. He notices she's limping and wonders if she got hurt when she fell or if the Pastor did something. She has no shoes and she can't get traction in the snow; she falls, but quickly gets up and pushes on.

He gives his head a slight shake. Was it a mistake, shooting the tires of the vehicles parked outside? But they never planned to escape down the driveway in an Enemy vehicle. And they hadn't conceived of Astrid getting out on her own, so there was no plan for that contingency, either. Definitely a failing on his part. Team Leader at New World Security would chew his ass out!

Will she be able to start the Jeep? If she's never had a vehicle with a choke and a glow plug, it's not likely she'll be able to figure it out.

If Denver doesn't get out, she's doomed.

* * *

The first girl Max brought down isn't Astrid, but since the Pastor said two girls, the other one must be.

Pale silvery light from the kitchen doorway is brightening Denver's place of concealment. The moon has risen, and if anyone comes into the hall, he'll be found. He's debating what to do when he gets Fletch's message and heaves a sigh of relief. He starts toward the back door, but heavy footfalls thunder down the staircase and he has to shrink back into the shadows.

"Party's over! Call 'em in!"

He recognizes the voice as belonging to Max. Does he have time to sneak out? *This could get ugly,* he thinks, and pulls out the Glock.

There's confused babble from the front room.

"Open the door that's right in front of you," Max growls, "and call them in! She's escaped!"

"Escaped?" Trisha asks. "Who escaped? What do you mean, escaped?"

"They're already coming in," one of the others says.

As if summoned, the back door opens and the three warriors crowd through. Despite being hauled out of their beds in the middle of the night in a snowstorm, they're in good spirits, laughing, bragging about what they hit, the unbelievable shots they made, how they showed those bastards they'd better not fuck with the big boys. They shuck their jackets and are working their boots off when Max joins them, crying out, "Astrid's gone!"

"What?" Hank Senior asks. "How?"

"Out the window."

"Well, she ain't gonna get far," Hank Junior says, reaching for his rifle.

"Aww, fuck," Denver mutters. He raises the Glock and steps into the light from the great room doorway, shouting, "Nobody move!"

The four spin to face him.

"The cowboy!" Hank Junior hisses. "What the fuck?"

Denver barks, "You all get out into the front room, there, and no one gets hurt!" He gestures at the doorway nearest them. They shuffle their feet but begin to comply when the Pastor, Trisha and the skinny young girl Max brought down first crowd the doorway, blocking it. Trisha's now wearing only thong panties and the sparkling spike heels, while the other girl is dressed in a school uniform.

Trisha looks at Denver and says, "Pfft! For fuck's sake, Denver! Put the gun down!" She takes a step toward him. He fires a shot into the floor in front of her, the sound of the blast reverberating through the closed space. She and the Pastor both scream; Trisha jumps back, breasts bouncing, and turns to collide into the arms of the nearest man, Max.

In the deafening silence following the concussion of the shot, the Pastor's sniveling is bizarrely loud; his robe has fallen open exposing his porcine torso. Urine patters the floor and puddles around his feet, the odour wafting up and mixing with the pungent chemical stench of the gunshot.

"Go on, all of you, get back!" Denver orders, and as he moves toward them, they back away. "Max, you can fondle my ex later. Right now, pull your gun out, very slowly."

Max seems to be considering options, then pushes Trisha behind him, takes his gun out of his back waistband, and holds it out.

"That's it," Denver says, "put it on the floor and kick it over to me."

Max bends over and lays the gun carefully on the floor. He kicks it toward Denver, but too hard; it skitters past him. He half turns, in time to see a man behind him picking it up. In a heartbeat, he realizes his mistake. In the urgency of the moment, he'd forgotten about Ken Sweatshirt.

"Ask yourself a queshun," Sweatshirt slurs, "Do you feel lucky?"

Denver raises his arms.

"Not such a fuckin' big man now, are you, asshole?" Hank Junior hisses. He strides forward and snatches the gun from Denver, then moves beside Sweatshirt, motioning with the gun, "On your knees! Face the wall!" When he's slow to respond, Hank Junior prods him with the Glock. "I said, on your knees!" He delivers another jab to the kidneys, this time hard, and Denver collapses to his knees. He feels the gun pressed against the back of his head.

"Junior," Hank Senior barks, "hold up!"

"I'm gonna take care of this fucker once and fer all!"

"You want to clean up the mess? Not here!"

"Not nowhere," comes a voice from the back entrance. They turn to see Fletch, rifle across his back and Beretta in his good hand, in the hall behind them. He points the pistol at each in turn, laser dots dancing across their chests, and nods in the direction of the closest doorway. "Git in the front room, like he said."

The three men, and Trisha clinging to Max, shuffle toward the doorway nearest them. The Pastor wails, wobbles unsteadily and grabs the young girl around the neck, pulling her up against him, choking her as he backs away.

"Don't go nowhere, you shitheads," Hank Junior calls out. "Drop your gun, Fletch, you stupid motherfucker, or I blast this asshole's head off right now!"

"I'd say you're the one who should drop your gun. Both of you, actually." He indicates Sweatshirt, who still holds the gun but has scuffled back into the far doorway.

'Yeah, see," Hank Junior sneers, "two to one. Can't get us both."

"Maybe not. But I'll make sure'n git you first."

"I'll blow this asshole's head off before I hit the ground."

"Doubtful."

"Just a reflex. Wanna take that chance?"

Fletch considers it for a moment, then lowers his Beretta. Some of the tension in Hank Junior's stance dissolves, and in that split second, Fletch points and shoots. The gun flies out of Hank Junior's hand. He screams and crumbles to the floor. Hot blood spray on the back of Denver's head starts rivulets down his neck.

Fletch now has the Beretta trained on Sweatshirt, who's holding out Max's gun ineffectually. The red laser dot from the aiming device is on his chest. He looks down at it and his eyes widen. That one Dirty Harry moment when he got the drop on Denver was all he had. He drops the gun, throws his arms up and shouts, "Okay! Okay!"

Denver jumps to his feet, heaves several deep breaths and tries to slow his pounding heart.

"I could've got you both. You should of known that," Fletch says to Junior. And then to Denver: "Hey, buddy, the guns?"

Denver nods, collects both guns and comes to stand beside Fletch, Glock raised.

Hank Junior is half sitting, crying and holding out his right arm with its hand dangling uselessly from the shattered wrist, looking at it in disbelief. Then he cradles it with his left hand, howling, "You asshole! Look what you done to my hand!" He rocks back and forth, wailing, "It hurts! God *damn* you, it really fuckin' hurts!"

"Maybe we can find you an aspirin," Fletch says. "Git up, you fuckin' whiney little bitch, and git in the front room. Or, I can put you outta yer misery right now."

"Agghh! Agghh!" Hank Junior groans, then lets out an agonized scream as he struggles to his feet. "Yer gonna pay fer this!"

"Already did," Fletch says, and turns to the group in the doorway. "Pastor, let go of the girl."

He shakes his head. "N…no!"

"She can't save you." The red dot dances on Pastor's forehead.

"Better do as he says, Bruce," Hank Senior advises. After a moment, the Pastor's death grip on the girl's neck relaxes. She wobbles, then slinks back behind Max to huddle next to Trisha.

"Any other girls here?" Fletch asks.

"No," Hank Senior says.

"Astrid's not here?"

"Nope. See for yourself."

"Yeah. I wondered what you'd say. You two," he motions to the girls, "come with us."

"Are you nuts?" Trisha shrieks. "I'm not going anywhere with you! Either of you! What the fuck's wrong with you, Denver? Bustin' in, shootin' people? Looking for your fuckin' girlfriend? She's in Dark River! I saw her there. You think I was unreasonable before? You'll be lucky to have the clothes on your back when I get done with you!" She lifts her chin defiantly.

"You, little girl," Fletch motions to the school girl, "you wanna come with us, git over here." She squeezes around the Pastor, skirting the urine pool, and crosses the hall.

"Are there any other girls?" Fletch asks her.

"I don't know," she responds in barely more than a whisper. "*She's* the first one I ever saw here."

Fletch turns and nods at Hank Senior. "Any other girls?"

Hank Senior shrugs and exhales loudly. "No."

"Pastor talked about two girls," Denver says.

Fletch appears satisfied, and nods. He tells the girl, "Go to the back door, there, get into a jacket. Boots, too."

"Wait outside," Denver tells her, "We'll be there in a minute."

Fletch half-turns his head to speak in low tones to Denver. "I sent Astrid to the Jeep. You go with that one. Once you 'n' the girls're away, I'm gonna take Senior's truck."

"Can you hold them here? There's a front door, isn't there?"

"Yeah, but unless they wanna go out in the blizzard in stocking feet without their coats, they gotta go past me."

Denver nods and follows the girl, quickly helps her into a jacket and herds her out the door.

* * *

Fletch backs along the hallway, Beretta trained on the crowd, until he gets to the doorway leading into the kitchen.

"You should go too, little lady," he lifts his chin in Trisha's direction, "you still got time."

"I'm not going anywhere with you … you monster! You seriously wounded him! What if he loses his hand? He might never be the same!" she shrieks and waves at Hank, who's moaning loudly.

Fletch shrugs. "Well, I hope he's never the same. But it's up to you, stay if you want. It's yer funeral." He backs into the kitchen, then turns, rounds the food prep island and crosses to the six-burner cooktop. He checks the knobs on the stove, then hops up to sit on the counter beside it, and wait.

THIRTY-SIX

Denver trots across the side yard and is around the corner of the garage before he notices the girl is falling behind. The snow is calf-deep, and his footsteps are too far apart for her to step into them. In his rush to get back to the Jeep, he didn't stop to think; she's not strong, and in boots several sizes too big, she's struggling. He goes back to her. "What's your name?" he asks.

"J-J-Jessica."

"Okay, Jessica, it's not much further. Up you go." He hoists her over his shoulder as easily as a bag of feed, and starts off again, only putting her down when they get to the opening in the chain link fencing. He pushes her through, bends to scurry through himself, and looks toward the Jeep parked just on the other side of the cleared area. He heaves a huge sigh of relief at seeing Astrid slide out.

He hurries to her, flooded with emotions: everything from rage that they'd taken her, to desire for revenge, relief she's alive and unhurt, and a powerful need to hold her, kiss her, love her. He urgently draws her into his arms. They hug tight, kiss, and then hug some more. "Oh my god, Astrid! My god! Thank god you're all right!" He kisses her again.

"I thought I'd never see you again!" Astrid sobs.

He kisses her cheek, her forehead, her mouth and her cheek again, squeezing her tight. Jessica lets out a quiet moan, reminding him their escape is still uncertain. "We have to go," he says, releasing Astrid and indicating the open door of the Jeep.

While he goes around the driver's side, Astrid and Jessica climb in the passenger side, with Jessica crawling through between the seat to squat in the back. He roots in his jacket pocket and pulls out his cellphone, unlocking it and passing it back to Jessica. "Here, call your folks," he tells her; then he attends to the ritual of starting the diesel engine with its glow plug and manual choke. When it starts, he coaxes the gearshift lever into second, and aims the Jeep back along the tracks made on the trip in.

"No heater in this old beast," Denver says, "sorry. It'll be a cold ride but at least once we're out of the bush, it won't be so rough."

What can be seen in the headlights can hardly be called a trail. Since he and Fletch drove in, it's snowed enough to obscure their tracks and make everything white. The best he can do is to look for two parallel grooves, aim the Jeep for them, and hope he's guessing right. Making matters worse, it's snowing harder again, blowing, too. Visibility is barely a couple of meters. If he gets the Jeep stuck—!

He looks at Astrid in the seat beside him, takes her hand again and squeezes it, reluctantly letting go when he needs both hands to wrestle the steering wheel. "No power steering on the old girl, either."

The Jeep lurches and in slow motion, the driver's side vaults two feet in the air. In the back where there are no seats, Jessica lets out a yelp as she's dumped against the passenger side window. Denver shifts into reverse, but the Jeep barely backs before the engine stalls. He starts it again and tries going forward and back. Once more, the engine dies. He gets out to look. When he gets back in his seat, he says, "The one wheel crawled up something, a rock, or maybe a stump. It's that articulated axle Fletch told me about. I think it's okay. Just hang on!"

What he doesn't tell them is that the front axel is only part of the problem. The back axle is nearly high-centered, its driver's side wheel wedged between rocks. He pushed one of the rocks out of the way as best he could, but he's not sure it will be enough. Worse, he saw the chain link fence, much closer than it would be if he was on the right track. So close, in fact, the Lodge is visible through the trees.

Not that long ago—was it even half an hour?—he witnessed their bullets shattering trees on the outside of the fence, so he knows they're in range. How long will Fletch hold them off? Is he on his way out now? How can he stop them from coming out, guns blazing?

When he felt the gun pressing against the back of his head and heard the excitement in Hank Junior's voice when he said he was going to kill him, any doubts he had about The Enemy's ruthlessness evaporated. He doesn't doubt they'll go to any lengths to protect their secret. All those purses! What ever they did to Astrid! And Jessica, who went missing so many months ago, her story yet untold. The truth of everything Fletch told him, things he hadn't been able to get his head around until that moment, hits home. If he has to use the winch to get them out, it'll take time. Too much time! They'll be sitting ducks.

Fletch is so much better at handling the Jeep. If they meet up at the road or even just near the road, the girls can be transferred into Senior's truck, and Fletch can take the Jeep back. Where is he? He should be out by now. Why isn't he responding on the radio?

* * *

Fletch hears muffled footsteps and hushed voices in the hall, then Hank Senior peers in. He looks at Fletch, reaches in to flick on the lights, and steps into the kitchen. Les comes in behind him. Both have pistols, and they hold up just inside the door.

"What're you doing, Fletch? Why're you doing this?" Hank Senior asks. "We don't want to hurt you!"

"You know the old saying, the hens come home to roost?" Fletch asks. "Mr. Hazen, they've came home."

"I don't know what you mean, son. You've known me all your life, you know you can trust me. Put down your weapons and we'll talk."

"Time fer talk was thirty years ago."

"We can work something out."

"Oh? Like what you worked out with that fine, upstanding Christian couple the Pastor found for you to foist me off on?"

"Well, that was a mistake, I realize it now. I'm sorry."

"You're *sorry*?" Fletch snorts. "*You're* sorry?"

"I get it, it wasn't good, I should've done something different, sooner, and you got a right to gripe. I can't change that. But the agreement, the deal

I had with them, sure, we can do something like that. What do you want? New house? How 'bout we move that trailer off. Build you something nice?"

"Or maybe I could just take the money and run, like they did? Or did they only take off after the money quit coming?"

"You don't know the whole story about that, son. Let's talk. Whatever you want, I'll take care of you, like I always have."

"That ain't true, is it? You only took care of me, to take care of *him*." He nods toward the door, where Hank Junior, supported by Trisha, has appeared. "The perfect son. The one Bridey wanted."

Hank Junior shoves Trisha aside and stumbles into the room, pushing between his father and Les. His damaged hand is inside his partly-open shirt, a dark stain blooming on it. He's pale and sweating, going into shock but vibrating with fury. "Shoot him! *Shoot him*, fer fuck's sake!"

"Now, now, Junior, we're not going to hurt Johnny. He's *family*, for chrissake. We're going to work something out. Like always."

"Give yer head a shake, you old fool! This ain't somethin' you can fix! He has to pay fer this! Look what he done to me! I gotta get to a hospital."

"Astrid's more important, Hank," Les says. "We gotta shut this down *now* and go get her."

"Shoot him, Les!" Hank Junior screeches.

"No one moves." Fletch says. The red dot moves from Hank Senior's forehead to Les's chest, but remains steady as he pulls a Bic lighter out of his jacket.

"There's two of you!" Hank Junior screams. "Shoot him!"

"Sti-i-i-ll don't mind the odds," Fletch drawls.

"Do I smell…" The colour drains from Les's face. "Jesus! I smell propane!"

"I guess I should'n'a turned all these knobs past the clicking sound before the gas ignited."

"You think you'll gas us?" Hank Junior smirks. "You really are a stupid motherfucker besides being a deformed freak! I should've hit you over the head with a rock years ago!"

"What's he doing?" Trisha asks. "He can't gas us, can he? We can't be gassed…?"

"You know propane's heavier than air, right?" Fletch asks. "I've had all six burners pumpin' on high since I first came inside, while you were busy with my partner. That'd be what, ten minutes? I wonder how much propane is pooled on the floor. I can't figure it out. I'm dumber'n a bag of hammers. So. Anyone else wanna take a shot at calculatin' it?"

"Johnny," Hank Senior's face is creased with concern, "turn the gas off!"

"Oh, I know, some of it's run out the door, so it's most likely impossible to figure how much is in here. And you've stirred it up, millin' around like you done. I don't know—mixed with oxygen all nice like that—would a muzzle flash be enough to ignite it now?"

"Let's talk! Look, gun down," he puts his gun on the island and stands away from it, hands open. "We're all friends here! Family! Name your price! You want a membership here to go along with that new house? More money every month? Anything you want! Just name it!"

"Too late, *Dad*." He lights the Bic in his crooked hand.

"*For god's sake, Johnny*," Hank Senior cries, "put that out!" The colour drains from his face; he scurries around the end of the island and starts toward Fletch.

Fletch smiles and says, "This is for Heather," as he lowers the Bic to the stove top.

* * *

Denver depresses the clutch, pulls out the choke, and when the glow plug's red, turns the key. With a gewer-gewer-gewer, the engine turns over but doesn't start. Again and again, it coughs and almost starts. It started more easily before; what's wrong now? How long before the battery's dead? Is it flooded? No time to bleed it off! There's a can of ether in the dash compartment. Will he have to use that? In desperation, he pushes the gas pedal to the floor and turns the key.

The engine roars to life. He carefully presses the choke back in, and breathes a sigh of relief when it keeps running. He works the gearshift into low, turns the wheel to the right, and sends a silent prayer to a god he doesn't believe in before carefully accelerating. The Jeep crawls forward. Its angle steepens; he hears Jessica in the back, sobbing, "No one's answering!"

Astrid takes a few deep breaths as if to calm herself, then reaches back between the seats, clasps the girl's hand and says calmly, "It's okay! Denver's a really good driver! We're going to be okay. *You're* going to be okay."

For a heartbeat, Denver's not sure about that. Has he made things worse? Then the wheels turn; the Jeep clears the impediment, thumping down so it's level again, and crawls steadily forward as if nothing happened.

Releasing a breath he didn't know he was holding, Denver wonders if they're close to the road. How long had it taken Fletch to drive in? Twenty minutes? And they've only been outbound ten. Maybe less. Hasn't Fletch made it out yet? Shouldn't he see a vehicle coming out from the Lodge? Does radio silence mean Fletch has been taken out? If so, will they be intercepted at the road?

An ear-shattering *ka-boom!* shakes the Jeep, the trees and the very ground. Snow and dead branches rain down around them and thump the roof, followed by other odd debris. A boot. Something with dark fur on it. A large soup pot hits the snow just in front of them.

Through the trees, they can see the middle of the Lodge is a tumbled pile of debris that looks as if a child smashed a Lincoln Logs house; then flames leap skyward and begin to lick greedily along both wings. More, smaller, explosions are heard, and then another major blast levels what's left. For a moment, it seems the fire's been blown out; but soon, small tongues of flame appear and grow tall again as they spread along the entire length of what only minutes earlier had been a sprawling, two-storey log building.

"Oh my god," Denver says.

"Mom?" Jessica starts crying loudly.

THIRTY-SEVEN

"You know it's impossible for two blue-eyed parents to have a brown-eyed kid, right?" Dallas says.

"Of course I know. Everyone knows. I know what you're getting at and I don't like it." Denver forces a smile for Astrid's benefit; he waves good-bye as she drives away. Once she's far enough off not to see it, he allows an angry frown to slide onto his face. "Why do you give a shit?"

"Don't tell me yer okay with yer girlfriend havin' another man's baby!"

"She was raped. What don't you get about that?"

"She didn't have to keep it."

"None of your business."

"That's right, unless you marry her 'n' that monster's spawn is the next generation of Danielsons on the Triple R yer always so worried about! We need to hang onto this place for *that*?"

"Yeah, that's a convenient fuckin' *stupid* excuse to get your way, isn't it!?" Denver scowls as he gives Dallas a dark look, then turns and trots up the stairs and back into the house. *Goddamn you, Dallas*, he thinks, *we butt heads more and more often these days. It's bad enough we argue about ranch stuff, but do you have to keep picking on Astrid?*

He pours the last of the coffee from Wilson's old percolator on the back of the stove into his mug, takes it into the living room and slides into the recliner. For months, he's been pondering what to do. His relationship with his brother, testy for years, has become downright toxic. Dallas wants the money for his share of the ranch, so he can go south. Compounding the problem, there's Abilene, who wants her share, too. Denver could possibly finance a buy-out, but the loan would be so huge he'd be a slave to the payments, if he could qualify for a loan that size at all.

No two ways around it.

It's time to put the ranch up for sale.

* * *

Astrid touches the screen to bring up the nav system, not because she needs directions, but to confirm her ETA back home. If that six-thousand square foot log house on all that land can be called home.

She marvels again at how her life changed when she made that one insignificant decision to run an unfamiliar trail. She clicks her tongue and shakes her head to think she'd stupidly congratulated herself on giving Fletch the slip!

She adjusts the rear-view mirror to glance at Elise, in the child seat behind her. Her cheeks are rosy. She's teething and has been feverish, waking up several times during the night despite having been sleeping right through for months. Being in the car has worked its magic. She's finally asleep.

Denver was understanding. The crib he and Wilson hauled up from the basement was set up beside their bed, so when Elise was fussing, it disturbed his sleep, too. He even got up and walked the floor, talking in low tones to soothe the baby who looked so tiny in his arms, to let Astrid sleep for an extra hour. When she came into the kitchen about six that morning, he was at the table with Elise on his lap. He'd given her a bottle and Wilson was feeding her Pablum, making funny faces, cooing at her. They'd even changed her diapers and put her in a clean onesie. She thought it may have been better to change the onesie after feeding, but the scene was so beautiful, she couldn't bring herself to say so.

Shane and Barney came in looking for breakfast and had to content themselves with coffee until Wilson was done with Elise. He'd told them in his gravel-truck voice if they didn't want to wait for him to make breakfast, they could go right ahead and make it themselves because he had more important things to do at that moment. When Astrid wanted to pitch in, Wilson told her to sit down and enjoy her coffee. Dallas came, surveyed the room, and left, slamming the door behind him.

Wilson is absolutely gaga over Elise, and Den assures her he doesn't care he's not her biological father and wants to be her daddy. They'd be a great support system; Doctor Malone stresses that's important. But there's Dallas. He's an enigma. She doesn't want to come between Denver and his brother, but Doctor Malone says all she can do is make sure she's not doing anything to inflame tensions. She touts the Serenity Prayer: "have the courage to change the things you can change, the serenity to accept the things you can't, and the wisdom to know the difference". Dallas is something she can't change.

And the house with its constant reminders of the Hazens! Double H: Hazens Horribilus! She chuckles. Better to laugh about it than to cry. Trying to make it hers hasn't worked. It's still the Hazen's house. Why doesn't she jump at the chance to leave it? Why doesn't she tell Denver she'll marry him, at least live with him? How many times does he have to ask? What's holding her back?

Doctor Malone keeps bringing it up. Maybe it's time I stopped changing the conversation.

THIRTY-EIGHT

There's a new decoration just above The Serenity Prayer in Doctor Malone's office with the words: "LOYALTY is hard to find TRUST is easy to lose ACTIONS speak louder than words" in loopy white lettering hovering over a background of misty gray trees and rocks. Astrid wonders when clichés stencilled on irregular slabs of barn board came into vogue.

"Thoughts on my new piece?" Doctor Malone interrupts her reverie, breaking the silence.

"It's … interesting." Astrid glances at Elise, who's standing holding onto the shelf in the corner play area, choosing the next toy to fling to the floor. She reaches for something, loses her balance and lands on her backside. Undeterred, she pulls herself back up, selects a pink giraffe, thumps down on her bum and shoves it in her mouth.

"Before I forget, I've set up that meeting you requested, just figuring out a date that works for everyone. Some of my colleagues suggested including medical doctors, and one has already got a corporate sponsor pretty well buttoned down!"

"Already? That's amazing!"

"Yes, everyone's excited about Heather's House, nothing but positive feedback. It's preliminary at this point, of course; you'll need to get your lawyers working on details; get the government stuff rolling. Are you living in the trailer yet?"

"No, but we have started moving a few things. There's a bit of work to be done before we can live there."

"It's a big change. How are you feeling about that?"

"You know, as crazy as it sounds, the thought of moving out of that huge beautiful house feels like a weight lifting off my shoulders. I'm actually looking forward to living in that little trailer, and I'm enjoying getting the clean-up of the yard, clearing, putting in the new driveway, painting, building the new porch and so on, done. I'm doing a lot of it myself. Plus, I think I told you I've been working with the local feral cat rescue, trapping cats to get them spayed and neutered. The ones that're tame enough are being adopted, the wild ones will just live out their lives where they are. That's a big job in itself! But being busy helps me, I guess. The guys that're doing the stuff I can't do are glad to have the work, since I had to cut their hours with the mill slow-down, so it's positive all around. And it's not permanent, just a place to stay while I decide whether to sell or build. Whatever happens, Heather's House will go ahead."

"Good." Doctor Malone nods. After several minutes of quiet, she prods, "How is Denver with all this?"

"Good. Really good, actually. When he was here last week, he was a big help. He's amazingly capable, knows how to do so much, you know, the physical work and the legal stuff. He's also really good with the guys. The only thing is, he keeps asking me to marry him. Says he'll change his name to Ingebritson, if it'll help me make up my mind." She chuckles, but even in her own ears, it sounds forced. "We both have Scandinavian roots, after all."

"That's a Norwegian thing?"

"More Swedish, maybe, if there was no male heir for the farm. He was teasing. He knows I'd never curse anyone with *that* surname! Bad enough Elise and I have it!"

"I admit when I first heard it, I thought it was awkward, but now that I've gotten used to it, I rather like it. It's sort of musical. And it is who you are, after all."

"Hmm. But my father, you know, umm, it's just ... Just."

"But you're not him, Astrid. Does anyone really think less of you because of him? How many people even remember that whole tragedy? Do you think maybe your negative feelings about the name are self-imposed?"

"I …" Astrid cocks her head, her brow furrowed. After a bit, she says, "But I can't marry him, not yet. I know I'm not being fair to him. But I'm just … well, I guess I'm afraid to let him go. Afraid to keep him and afraid to let him go. I should let him get on with his life."

"It's his decision, Astrid; he'd move on if he wanted to. But tell me one thing. If he had asked you to marry him before you were abducted, what would your answer have been?"

"I would have said yes." Astrid shrugs and looks away. "Things are different now."

"From what you've told me, he's a man who loves you, and believed you loved him, enough to put himself in harm's way to find you, rescue you. Now, nearly two years later, he still wants you. You said you would've married him if he'd proposed before you were abducted. You barely knew him then; if anything, it should be an easier decision now."

"But—Elise."

"Yes. You say he understands why you didn't have an abortion when the morning after pill didn't work. He didn't pressure you to do it, he understood how your previous abortion haunted you and left the decision to you."

"Yes. She's *my* baby."

"And you say he's good with Elise. So now you have a baby, and he wants both of you. Unless I'm missing something, Elise is not a deal breaker."

Astrid gazes out the window.

Finally, Doctor Malone says, "Last time you were here, we talked about how it's common for rape victims to blame themselves. Have you thought about that?"

"We talk about it every time, in every session."

"How are you feeling about it now?"

"Well, it *was* my fault."

"Okay, let's go over it again. *Why* do you think that?"

Astrid squirms in her chair, looks at Elise again, then folds her hands in her lap and studies them. "You know I didn't have to go into that shed," she says quietly. "If only I hadn't! My mother always got after me for being too nosey, too snoopy. 'Curiosity killed the cat', she'd say. I'd ask, how? *How* does curiosity kill a cat? She'd just shake her head. But I get it now. Except if I'm the cat, I'm not the one that was killed. It was all the others." Her lower lip quivers. She catches it in her teeth to keep it still.

Doctor Malone says nothing, waiting for Astrid to continue. When she doesn't, she says, "Don't forget, but for your curiosity, that other girl would have ended up like all the other victims. You saved her life! Hold onto that! And the neighbour …" she looks down at the notebook on her lap.

"Fletch."

"Yes, Fletch. Let's talk about him again. You thought he was stalking you."

Astrid nods.

"He was following you. Watching you."

"Yes."

"Why?"

"You know why."

"I do. But I want you to tell me again."

"He wasn't stalking me," Astrid says with a sigh. They've talked about this so many times! Doctor Malone keeps wanting her to tell her the same things again and again. She sighs again, and continues, "He was guarding me. Because Hank Junior said he was going to get me."

"So, it was only a matter of time before Hank Junior took you. Just like the others. It didn't matter whether you discovered his secret or not. He was only waiting for the opportunity. Isn't that right?"

"I guess so."

"You *know* it, Astrid. You know it here," she taps her temple, "but you just don't quite know it here." Now she puts her hand on her heart. "Not yet, anyway. I sense you're getting frustrated, but we'll keep talking about it until you do know it *here*."

They fall silent for a space of several more minutes, before Doctor Malone says, "You also know Fletch's reasons for being involved in that dangerous rescue."

"Yes. He told Denver he'd screwed up, that Hank got me on his watch. Like it was his job, being my bodyguard. He died because of me."

"Ahh."

"They all died because of me. And I ended up with a huge property and a pretty decent business as a result."

"But Fletch planned his suicide, and Fletch orchestrated the attack on the Lodge, planned the explosion. Why isn't Fletch to blame for their deaths?"

Astrid's chin drops, and she brings her shoulders up in a shrug.

"Okay. We'll get back to that." Doctor Malone turns a page in her notebook, reads for a moment, then asks, "Why is it you don't think you deserve your inheritance?"

"Well, I'm not related, of course…"

"Are there other relatives?"

"Just his sister, and Bridey, I suppose."

"Bridey's taken care of, you said. For the rest of her life, even she is someday well enough to leave Nechako Manor. And you said the courts ruled the will was valid and dismissed the sister's challenge."

"Yes."

"So, why would Bridey, or the sister, be more deserving? Do they have more need?"

"No. But I…"

"Is it your feeling of unworthiness, Astrid? Are you still punishing yourself for what your father did?"

"No." Astrid looks at Elise again, watching as she gets up and toddles from the shelves to the toy bin. After a few moments, she continues quietly, "Maybe. I … maybe I worry I'm like him. I manipulated Hank Senior into putting me in his will, after all."

"Couldn't he have raped you without giving you anything?"

"He didn't rape me, though."

"Astrid, the man had absolute power over you. You did what you had to do to stay alive. Whether he had to physically restrain you or not, that makes it rape."

Astrid is holding one fist in the other, massaging her hands, staring at the floor. She takes several deep breaths, squirms, and finally says in barely more than a whisper, "But I think I … I mean, I did. I went along with it."

"Ahhh, I see," Doctor Malone interjects quietly. She looks at the clock and shakes her head. "I want to address that small detail, and we'll also get back to your firmly-held belief your seventeen-year-old self should have somehow saved your mother, but our time's up for today. Think about it, and we'll start there next week." Doctor Malone clicks her pen and sets it and her notebook aside, then gives Astrid a warm smile.

"For now, remember you are strong. You can do anything you put your mind to. Look what you're doing with Heather's House! And it took real strength, mental as well as physical, to escape, and survive, when so many others before you perished. I wish I could snap my fingers and stop you from believing you've done something shameful. For now, at least try to forgive yourself. Can you do that?"

"I will." Astrid gets to her feet and stands chewing her lower lip, deep in thought, then goes to the play corner and gathers up her baby.

Doctor Malone escorts her to the door. "And also, Astrid," Doctor Malone says, "I'd like you to consider having Denver come to a session."

After a moment, Astrid says, "I think it would be okay now."